# THE CITY OF EVIL

Book One of *AMRA'S JOURNEY*

## ALAN GOLD

HarperCollins*Publishers*

*This book is dedicated in gratitude to my wife, Eva,*
*and to the memory of her mother and father, Yosi and Bella Weiss,*
*and in memory of my father, Alex*

This novel is entirely a work of fiction.
The names, characters and incidents portrayed in it are the work
of the author's imagination. Any resemblance to actual persons,
living or dead, events or localities is entirely coincidental.

HarperCollins*Publishers*
77–85 Fulham Palace Road,
Hammersmith, London W6 8JB

This paperback edition 1999
1 3 5 7 9 8 6 4 2

First published in Australia by
HarperCollins*Publishers*

Copyright © Alan Gold 1998

The Author asserts the moral right to
be identified as the author of this work

ISBN 0 00 651270 4

Set in Bembo

Printed and bound in Great Britain by
Caledonian International Book Manufacturing Ltd, Glasgow

# ACKNOWLEDGEMENTS

This book had its genesis in a trip which my wife and I took to Slovakia and the Ukraine in order to trace her roots. Having left the east of Europe as a two year old, she had no sense of completion of her childhood, no visual memory of where her parents had lived and suffered, no feeling of closure to their lives. What we found when we returned surprised us.

Almost nothing had changed in the half century since her mother and father were brutalised, first by the Hungarian occupation, then by the Nazis and then by the Russians. The houses, the neighbours, the districts were all intact, as though no influence of the outside world was capable of having any effect. Everything was the same ... everything except the absence of the Jews who had lived in the areas and contributed to the culture for centuries.

Of the many people who helped me with this book, none has been more generous and understanding than my wife, **Eva**. Her constant challenges of my assumptions, and honing of my ideas, made the writing process a shared joy.

My daughter and researcher **Georgina** was a wellspring of knowledge, with an assured ability to tease out the most reluctant facts and connections for my use. My sons **Jonathan** and **Raffe** were generous in their patience and forbearance.

I am also indebted to all the wonderful people at **HarperCollins** for their support, especially **Barrie Hitchon, Angelo Loukakis, Laura Harris, Nicola O'Shea, Darian Causby, Richard Parslow, Kaye Wright** and **Jim Demetriou**.

To **Jennie Roberts**, friend, critic and soulmate, and to **Susie Rourke** my editor for her valuable insights, my sincerest thanks. I am also deeply grateful to **Jill Hickson, Sophie Lance** and **Gaby Naher** of **Hickson Associates,** my literary agents, for standing firm on my side of the table.

Many experts in different fields were invaluable in providing me with information and forcing me to correct my assumptions. They also gave me generous additional information when I didn't realise I needed it. However, the entire content of this book is mine alone, and any failings must not be laid at the feet of these people: **Dr Ruth Wajnryb**, linguist, scholar and friend, for allowing me insights into her research concerning the difficulties of the language of Holocaust transmission; **Professor Martin Krygier** of the Faculty of Law at the University of New South Wales; **Professor Konrad Kwiet** of the Faculty of German at Macquarie University; **Professor Colin Tatz** of the Department of Political Science and Director of the Centre for Comparative Genocide Studies at Macquarie University; **Dr Vera Ranki** for her assistance with aspects of European law and property rights; **Catherine Hewgill**, principal cellist with the Sydney Symphony Orchestra, for her insights into the performance of music.

This book could not have been written without the extraordinary friendship, help and dedication of a group of scholars who offered us assistance in Slovakia and the Ukraine: **Dr Martin Witten** of the University of Wuppertal; **Dr Laco Olexa**, Director of Archaeological Studies in Kosice and pre-eminent expert on early human society in Eastern Europe; and his colleague **Viktor Musil**.

My friends and colleagues in **Writers' Bloc** were, as always, stalwarts when the going got tough.

Alan Gold can be contacted via his web site at http://www.cg.com.au

# PROLOGUE

## Ruthenia, 1903

Nussan the farmer felt surrounded by enemies. No matter what the season, Almighty God sent enemies to plague him. Year in, year out. Without respite. He had been working for nine hours since the early morning with only the satisfaction of a drink of beer and a midday *schlug* of schnapps to relieve the aching tiredness deep in his bones, but he was nowhere near finishing what had to be done.

He straightened his back and wiped his eyes, his neck knotted from the strain of the plough. It came as something of a surprise, but he realised that, despite his aches and pains, he was smiling. He usually managed to smile, even in the worst of adversity, when he was so tired he couldn't even lead his horse back to the stables. Smiling was his way of fighting back, his personal, inner message which said, *'No matter what God does to you, Nussan, you've got your health, a good wife, two beautiful children and a wonderful new daughter and usually enough food on the table to satisfy a ravenous hunger.'* That was reason enough to smile in adversity.

And who knew more about adversity than Nussan? Sometimes he felt like one of the ancient people he read about in the *Torah* every *shabbos*. Like one of the patriarchs. Every time those poor bastards looked up to heaven with their sweat-blinded eyes, there always seemed to be a plague sent by a merciless God to torment them. Nussan felt that he was being tormented just as God had tormented Job. Now why would a merciful God – so the Rabbis called him – do the sort of things He did to Job? Of course, things were different these days. The plagues which Abraham, Isaac and Jacob suffered were dust storms, insects, plunderers, idol-worshippers and marauders. Today's plagues were vicious landlords, taxes, debts, anti-Semites, pogroms, massacres and drunken madmen from the Christian village who came just to torment his people. But when you boiled it all down, nothing much had changed in three thousand years. God was still as uncaring about his Chosen People as He'd ever been. Still testing them, ensuring they were worthy. Ha! Worthy of what? Of plagues, that's what!

Nussan the farmer was a man whose life was lived in competition with everything the Almighty could throw at him. But he didn't take it on the chin like the Rabbis told him he must. He didn't pray and fawn and thump his heart in prayer and beg. Like Hell! Life was alright for the Rabbis and the other town dwellers. They could haggle and bargain and earn a salary. They could control their livelihoods. Mendel the tailor could work a few hours more a day if he was short of money. So could Yossele the shoemaker and Shmuel the coalman. It was a simple formula. Money is tight, work more. But life wasn't that simple for Nussan the farmer. And God Almighty, safe and protected by the clouds which always seemed to hang low over this godforsaken part of Ruthenia, was untouchable.

Only the other day, Nussan's horse had been pulling the plough when his foot slipped into a rabbit hole and he went lame. No bones broken, thank God, but Nussan didn't know that. All he knew was that his horse was lying on the ground, whinnying in pain and fear. So Nussan lost his temper with God. He picked up a branch and stormed over to a corner of the field (his only field, the one the landlord allowed him to plough) and he shook the branch at God and threatened him.

'Look you! You listen to me, I've had enough,' he yelled at the sky. 'You think you've broken me, don't you? You think you've broken my spirit. Well, you haven't. But I'm not going to take this any more. Now just leave me alone and find some other poor bastard to pick on.' And Nussan had waited, breathing heavily, sweat pouring from his brow, his anger still fermenting, listening to the agonising, contemptuous sound of the Almighty's indifference and silence. He screamed in agony and frustration and threw the stick at the cloud. But the stick just fell ignominiously to earth and Nussan trudged back across the field feeling foolish. He stroked his horse's head and massaged its limb until the animal was able to limp home, leaving the field still unploughed and dangerously close to the time when Nussan would have to plant the corn in order for his family to survive.

The horse recovered. Nussan apologised to God, and together – God, the horse and Nussan – they continued to plough the field as they had done year after year, and as Nussan's father had done for years before that.

Today Nussan was ploughing an area in the upper corner of the field that, in all the time that he had been farming he had never known to be touched. Frankly, that's why the landlord had allowed Nussan's family to farm the field, because at least one-third of it was unusable. Yet the *goyishe* bastard still charged him the same rent as for a whole field. Nussan and a friend had spent a week at the end of the growing season the previous autumn clearing rocks. Their reward for the backbreaking work was that a large patch of land, which had never been ploughed, was now available for use. Of course the soil had never been turned and so it would be difficult, but he had to make a start somewhere. It had been a terrible job, digging up the rocks, breaking them into manageable pieces and dumping them close to the river. At one stage, Nussan had thought his heart would give out, but between them they had managed to clear a large enough portion of the hill to grow at least another twenty per cent of crops. When they'd finished, the landlord rode out and congratulated Nussan on the work. Arrogant pig. His son had been with him, dressed in velvets and wearing a silk cravat, sneering at Nussan because he was wearing a filthy, torn shirt and patched trousers. What did the young landlord know about work, with his soft, girlish hands?

The old horse, used to turning a sharp corner when he got to the foot of the hill, refused at first to go forward into the unfamiliar territory, but Nussan smacked him on the flanks and eventually the plough bit into sod it had never before encountered. Of course there were stones and tough clumps of roots and other vegetable matter to be tossed aside, but the earth was rich and well-drained, and Nussan knew that the hard work would in time reward him and his family.

By the middle of the afternoon, Nussan had managed to uncover and expose most of the new area for the first time. He gave his horse a few minutes rest as he mopped his brow with his neckerchief, swatted away the insistent flies and took a flask of water from the pack he had dumped at the foot of the hill. He sat down in the shade of a tree and viewed his handiwork. The rows weren't parallel but at least he had made a solid start on the hill. There was only about one third to go, then the climb for the horse would become too precarious. Nussan bit into the food that his wife had made him, a huge chunk of corn bread, pickles and a wedge of goat's cheese. Although he had eaten this or similar food every day for heaven knows how long, today it tasted like manna from Heaven and he mumbled a small prayer of acknowledgment to God. *'Blessed are you, Oh Lord our God, King of the Universe, who brought forth bread from the earth.'* Then he added, *'And thanks also for the pickles and the cheese, God.'* He liked being irreligious. It was one of the few moments of power in his otherwise impotent existence. His back was hurting from the hard work of ploughing the new land, but it was a good hurt, a pleasant hurt. His wife Serel could massage his back for him. He would enjoy that. He smiled. She was a good woman, Serel. Intelligent, good-natured, laughed a lot and good in bed. Not like some of the wives his friends complained of.

A horsefly settled on his cheek and brought Nussan back to reality. The sun was already approaching the far hills and he had at least another two hours work to do before he could rest. He ensured that his horse had eaten enough hay, kissed it on the forehead and whispered into its ear, 'Come on, old boy. A bit more work before you can stop'. The two of them struggled back up the hill where Nussan reattached the plough and they marched slowly forward as soldiers-in-arms against God and His malice.

When he was almost at the top of the hill, at the point where the horse was unsure of its footing on the steep incline, Nussan's plough hit a large hidden rock. He sighed. He was only a quarter of the way along the new furrow, but that was typical of his life. One step forward, two back. He looked down and saw what he had already completed that day. He had added considerably to the quality of his holding – it had been a good day's work. He felt satisfied. He looked at the rest of the unploughed ground and was in two minds about giving it away. It would be a hell of a job digging up this hidden rock. After all, it was the last furrow, and he was hot and wanted to get home. But something stopped him from giving in. *'Don't leave things half done, Nussan,'* he muttered to himself, remembering his father's words, *'Always finish the job you're doing, Nussan, because if not, it'll only be there in the morning.'*

So he got a pick from where he had left his other tools and started to dig out the earth around the stone. It was bigger than he'd thought and he was tempted to leave it, but, eventually, after struggling this way and that, he managed to pry it free of the grasping fingers of the earth. It began a slow roll down the decline, much to Nussan's annoyance. Now he would have to break it up and get rid of it near the river. Looking into the hole, Nussan was surprised to see that it held another stone. But this one looked strange. It was almost flat, as though it had been placed there. He knelt down and further loosened the soil until he had exposed some more of the flat stone. It looked frighteningly like a gravestone, though there were no markings on it.

Nussan said a small prayer for protection and spat over his left shoulder to ward off the evil eye. He worked further into the earth to find the corners of the stone. The hole was now waist deep and sweat was pouring from him. He tapped his pick on the centre of the stone – it sounded as though there was a space underneath. Now he was truly frightened. Shadows were already lengthening and the light in the field was disappearing. There was something other-worldly about this. He could feel his heart beating against his chest and it wasn't just from the hard work. He tried to remember the prayers he had learned in *cheder* about evil spirits and God's protection from the demons and the evil eye. '*Make this safe, God,*' he mumbled. If only he had been a better Jew, and paid more attention in *shul*, he'd know what prayers to say, what to do.

Exposing the corner of the stone he worked his pick underneath and, using all his strength, raised the huge slab a fraction, letting light enter a cavity that had been closed to the sun for millennia. Earth ran down from the wall he had dug into the space below as he levered the slab higher and higher until it was almost vertical. Propping it against the wall, Nussan looked down into the cavity and screamed in horror. The dry, broken fingers of a skeletal hand pointed at him, reaching out from deep within the earth.

Panic rose in his chest, and he sprang back from the hideous sight, pressing himself against the earthen wall. He spat over his shoulder three times for protection and mumbled whichever bits of prayers came to his mind. After a few moments the panic began to subside and reason took over from fear. Taking deep breaths, he tentatively bent down and touched the skeleton. It was definitely a human hand, no question about that. But how old was it? Nussan wasn't good at guessing the age of people who were alive, let alone dry bones in the earth. Once, many years ago, he had helped the gravedigger move some ancient graves and had seen the skeleton of an old rabbi who had died a hundred years earlier. But that didn't seem to be anything compared to this. If he had to guess, Nussan thought that it had probably been here far longer than the Jews who had come to the area in the eleventh century. It could even be prehistoric.

And now Nussan began to wonder whether this skeleton could be of value. Maybe to a museum? He'd heard about museums in Prague and London that were interested in these sorts of things. The skeleton wasn't on his land, he was only the farmer, but maybe he could share his find with the owner. Suddenly the skeleton began to take on an entirely different significance.

Slowly he worked the earth to reveal more of the bones. A limb here. Further over, a thigh. Then a skull. And all the while Nussan mumbled half-remembered prayers from the days of his childhood. It was when he was clearing the earth around the ribcage that his eyes lit upon the most exciting thing he had ever seen in his entire life. For there, buried deep in the cavity of the skeleton, was the most beautiful necklace ever made, a work of such beauty that, initially, he forbore touching it out of reverence. It was as beautiful as the gold ornaments he had seen around the necks of rich women in picture books, the heavy necklaces and chains worn by Tsarinas and princesses. Nobody in his *stetl*, nobody in the main town, wore anything comparable to this. This was huge, large and weighty, and looked wonderfully expensive.

When he finally removed it, it was about the size of a large coin, but thicker and heavier than any coin he had ever held in his pocket. Nussan poured water over it from his flask and even more beauty was revealed. The markings on it were incredibly lovely, carefully carved to form the most intricate of patterns, circles leading into deeper circles until they seemed to disappear into the very centre of the amulet. His hand was shaking. He looked at the amulet carefully. On one side was some sort of symbol, a horse. But then he looked closer and saw horns – it was a bull. He turned it over. On the other side was a fat bird, perhaps an owl. The amulet itself was on a chain of gold which was as heavy as the charm it carried. Nussan spat twice into the ground and mumbled a prayer of thanks to God. But then he recited another half-remembered prayer to protect him from the evil eye because, even at first glance, he could see that there was nothing Jewish about the amulet, nor was there anything Christian. It held none of the crosses or religious symbols he'd seen outside the churches in the main street of the town. Could it have been made before the Christians? Could it be that old?

If it was, it must be worth a fortune. He was a rich man. He looked up and shouted to the sky, 'God bless you! God bless you for this, dear Lord. You've made me a happy man, a rich man. God bless you for this. God bless you!'

Nussan's wife stared at her beaming husband as he stood there, still covered in sweat and dirt but grinning like a *shickerer* who had just come home from the inn. Normally when he came in after a day in the fields he was grumpy and ill-tempered until he had washed and eaten. Today he had rushed through the door, screaming her name and telling the entire household that they were rich, rich beyond their wildest dreams.

Serel's eyes glazed in amazement as Nussan proffered the amulet towards her, like a doctor handing over a newborn baby. But suddenly he changed his mind and slipped the necklace and amulet over her head, brushing her chestnut curls with his hands.

Serel had never owned a necklace and had no idea what one should weigh. But this one was so heavy it felt as if it was bending her neck. She held her hand to her chest and fingered the amulet. A lightness came over her spirit, a sudden heady moment of excitement, like a first kiss or unexpectedly seeing a man swimming naked in the river.

But then the sun went behind a cloud. 'What do you mean, you found it? Just like that. *Punkt!* In a field. What am I, a fool? You stole it, didn't you! You found it on the road and picked it up and stole it. Didn't you? Some rich woman dropped it. You're mad. We'll be arrested. We'll all be hanged for theft,' she shouted, her voice rising in anger and panic.

Nussan put his finger to her lips. 'Hush,' he said. 'Look at it. Feel it. This isn't the jewellery of a rich city woman. This isn't what ladies in Prague and Kiev have made specially for them by jewellers in Paris and London. I found it in the ground. See, there's still dirt on it. This is old, Serel. This is really old. This comes from times long past. Maybe a thousand, maybe two thousand years ago, I don't know.'

But Serel shook her head more violently still. Fear began to consume her. She snatched the necklace and amulet from around her neck and held it away from her, as though it carried some kind of disease.

'I don't want to keep this, Nussan. There's danger here. If the town gets to hear about it, we could be in trouble.

Oh God, what have you done? Please God protect us from your stupidity. Nussan, you have to turn this in to the constable or give it to the landlord. It's his by rights.' She shook her head again, 'I don't want it.' She waved the necklace at him, willing him to take it from her so that she wouldn't be tainted by its danger.

Nussan suddenly became very angry. 'Do you know how hard I work in the field every day?' he shouted. 'I break my back just to grow a few vegetables and then when I've got just enough to feed the family and pay for some meat, the landlord takes half of it just for the privilege of letting me work his land. And now! Now when I have a bit of luck, the first luck I've ever had in all my life, you want me to give it away. Is that it?'

He was shaking with rage. Serel's reaction was so different from what he'd expected. He thought that they'd be celebrating tonight with special *shabbos* food and maybe some wine and, maybe, when the children were asleep, some loving comfort. But it was all going wrong, as every damn thing went wrong in his life.

Still furious, he shouted at her, 'I'm going to hide it in the barn under the horse shit where the authorities, with their soft, white hands, won't bother to look. And then we're going to find somebody who'll buy it from us so we'll have money to leave this godforsaken hole of a town and go to America.'

Serel was on the verge of tears as Nussan snatched the necklace from her outstretched hands. She loved and respected her husband even when he was wrong. She'd caused him pain and anger, but he was so misguided, so unrealistic. They were *stetl* Jews. That was all. Not rich and important people. Didn't he understand? Poor people weren't entitled to these sorts of things. He talked about luck. Other people were lucky, not him, not her. Nussan wheeled around and walked out of their tiny house, slamming the door. The sudden noise started baby Eva crying in her crib.

Nussan didn't go back into the house after burying the amulet. Instead he washed himself with what water remained in the horse's pail, dried himself on a rag and stormed up the hill towards the inn where he would get *shicker* whether there was anybody else there or not.

Two hours later he was still sitting in a corner in the smoke-filled room. There was little air, and it was fiercely hot, despite the windows being open. But the schnapps still tasted good and was anaesthetising his anger. Around him had gathered Reb Abram the beggar, Reb Shmuel the coalman and Reb Pinkus the baker, all of whom had ceased their labours in the mid-afternoon. Nussan was by far the most drunk. Even so, he kept his mouth closed about his momentous find. He wanted to whisper conspiratorially to Reb Shmuel, but knew he couldn't risk it. Shmuel, realising something was going on, but too drunk to care, put his arms around Reb Nussan and kissed him on the forehead. It was then that Nussan decided he could trust his oldest of friends. When he heard the news of the discovery, Reb Shmuel kissed him again and promised to remain silent into his grave. He spat over his left shoulder to ward off the evil eye in case he inadvertently broke his promise.

An hour later, more men wandered into the inn, along with local townspeople who had come to wash the dust from their throats before wending their way home to wives and children. The table where Reb Nussan had been drinking alone that afternoon was now crowded with men whom he had known since childhood. Some he liked, some he could take or leave, and others were his enemies, but in his current state each and every one was his best friend, as close to him as a wedding guest. And each and every one in turn promised, before God in Heaven and with a full understanding of the danger of the evil eye, that he wouldn't breathe a word of Reb Nussan's unbelievable fortune.

Just who it was that told the local constable, Nussan would never know, but the following day the constable told the town's burgher that a valuable find had been made in the field which the Jew, Nussan, farmed. The town's burgher informed certain members of the town's council, who in turn told the local Russian Orthodox priest, who in his turn whispered the news to the head of the local group of the Black 100, and so the identity of the informant was lost to history. As soon as Mikhael Ostrovski, a forty-five year old factory superintendent who hated the Jews of the town with a biting vengeance, heard about Nussan the farmer's find, he decided to get the boys together to teach the Jews a lesson or two. Word had come down from Kiev that the authorities would turn a blind eye to a bit of trouble, and that was all the encouragement Ostrovski needed. It took him no more than a day to raise the twenty-three local members of the Black 100.

They prepared to mount their horses three nights after the evening that Reb Nussan the farmer had divulged his secret. The twenty-three men rode cautiously from the Christian part of the town along the single road which led to the Jewish *stetl* down at the bottom of the hill. As they got closer, the mood of caution left them, they were suddenly charged with excitement. They spurred on their horses until the vibrations from the animals' hooves roused sluggish men and women from their deep slumber to wonder what was happening. As the horses galloped closer to the *stetl*, the Black 100s began to shout and yell like Cossacks. Their torches joined together as one flaming brand to pierce the dark.

Jewish men, who realised instinctively that they were listening to the start of a pogrom, jumped out of bed and looked through bedroom windows at the advancing spectre. They knew from years of bitter and deadly experience what was happening. They barked orders to their wives, '*Grab the children! Follow me downstairs into the cellar quickly.*'

Mothers and fathers ran into their children's rooms, dragged terrified infants from their beds and pushed their hysterical families down stairs and into basements, where heavy iron-banded doors could be shut firmly against the evil eyes of the horsemen of the pogrom. Silent prayers were raised to God in Heaven from the depths of the forty cellars in the town as the horses and riders of the Black 100 thundered around the mud streets of the *stetl*, terrorising the inhabitants still above ground. The wails of men and the sobbing of women and children were drowned out by the thudding of hooves and the whooping and yelling of the hunters. The men threw their flaming torches up on to straw roofs, or into wooden buildings, which soon exploded with a roar of flames.

The riders drew their swords, waiting to strike down any Jews stupid enough to flee from their houses in fear of the flames. Two people did – an old man and an old woman who were too poor to afford a cellar. The riders wheeled their horses towards the elderly fleeing couple. Ostrovski, the leader, raised his sword high into the air and lunged at the stumbling old woman, who was desperately trying not to plunge headlong as she gathered up the skirt of her old torn nightdress to help her thin legs run faster. He struck her across her back. She pitched forward, the sword severing her spinal cord, and was dead as she tumbled into the gutter. Another rider cantered towards the old man who was trying to escape into a field. He aimed the point of his sword at the centre of the old man's shoulders and drove it easily through his rib cage and into his heart until it pierced all the way through his body.

The horses were wide-eyed with panic at the crackling and roaring of the flames. Pulling his horse to a halt, Ostrovski shouted out, 'Let's find the Jew, Nussan. He lives down here.' He pointed his sword towards a darkened house, whose outlines were barely illuminated by the fires of the town.

Nussan heard the men coming. He had been drinking late at the inn again, celebrating his new riches, and had just arrived back at his house. He took refuge in the bushes. While the riders circled the *stetl* and burned down the houses of his friends, Nussan could only crouch helplessly and watch them wheeling around like demons from a nightmare. He prayed to God that they wouldn't come this far out of the village. Not to his house! Not to attack his wife and children. Please God, no!

But like the avenging angels of death, the twenty-three men rode swiftly towards him. He should have stayed hidden behind the bushes but in the panic of his drunken state, he ran for the house. Terrified as he was, he had to save his wife and children, but halfway towards the front door, the men arrived, their horses' hooves trampling Serel's vegetable garden.

'Jew! Stand still. Are you Nussan the farmer?' Ostrovski shouted.

Nussan crouched in terror and felt himself pissing in his pants. 'Jew. I asked you a question!' Ostrovski repeated. 'When a Christian asks you a question, you answer. Now, are you Nussan the farmer? Answer me or I'll cut your balls off.'

Nussan nodded.

'This gold that you've found. Where is it? It doesn't belong to you. I want it.'

The other men on horseback roared with laughter.

Nussan shook his head and tried to stand, but he fell into a dead faint. He was awakened moments later, his body soaking. The men had thrown a pail of water over him. He was pinned to a wall by the rough and vicious hands of three of the men, supporting him so that his feet barely touched the ground. The point of a sword was pressing into his throat. Mikhael Ostrovski's face was so close that Nussan could smell his sweat and his foul vodka breath. Mikhael spat in fury, 'Listen, you filthy Jew scum. I want to know where that gold is. I'll give you ten seconds to tell me or we'll tear your place apart, bit by bit.'

He spat in the Jew's face, the spittle hitting him on the cheek.

Nussan shook his head. He was still drunk, trembling with fear. He couldn't focus his mind, couldn't remember where he'd hidden the amulet. Until he heard the words, 'Just kill the bastard and we'll rip the place to pieces.' Then he suddenly remembered. He'd tell them, just to get them to leave him alone, to save his family.

Nussan opened his mouth, but Mikhael laughed cruelly and drove his sword through Nussan's heart with the force of true hatred, pinning him to the wood of his horse's stable. The animal reared up and whinnied in terror. Mikhael tugged and withdrew the sword from the wooden door. Nussan's dead body slumped to the ground.

What the Black 100s didn't see while they were killing her husband was Nussan's wife, Serel, racing across the fields at the back of the house until she reached the river. There she lay with her three children as the madmen killed her family and friends in another of their murderous pogroms, ransacked the house, threw their clothes out of the windows and destroyed their precious furniture – all in their search for the gold amulet. Serel hadn't heard one word of the conversation between Nussan and the murderers, but she knew with every instinct in her body that it was all because of that cursed amulet.

The men continued to ravage the house, drinking bottles of wine and schnapps, until their drunken debauchery became even more violent. When they had pitched everything out of the windows, but still hadn't found the gold amulet, they set fire to the house in retribution. They watched the flames attack the curtains, the wooden beams, the innards of the broken furniture, and roared with laughter when the fire entered the roof and sent up a plume of flames high into the dark night air. Then they mounted their horses and rode away.

But Serel wasn't laughing. She was clasping her terrified children to her body, trying not to increase their fears by wailing to Almighty God.

Only at dawn, when smoke from the village hung like a doomcloud over the valley, did Serel rise up from the riverbank and look at the scene of devastation from the pogrom. Only then did she walk, with her three children, back to her house, knowing in her heavy heart that her stupid and greedy husband had brought this ruin and destruction upon her house, her family and upon all their neighbours and friends. Nussan's lifeless body lay in the horse shit and filth outside the stables. The children screamed in horror, and Serel hustled them away, instructing them to find the *Rebbe* and tell him what had happened. She would do her crying later.

She knelt, kissed her husband's cold, white forehead, then looked at the remains of her house, still smouldering, wisps of grey smoke rising into the dark morning clouds. She searched the filthy ground in front of what was once her safe and warm home, finding a dress, some clothes for the children, and a pot which she might be able to use along the way if she could gather some vegetables and herbs. She also found a large cloth, a sheet, into which she placed what little remained to her. It made a pathetic bundle.

Serel stood and walked to the gate. She looked up the road to the village to try and find her children. Men and women were wandering around in a daze, shaking their heads and crying. The old *Rebbe* was trying to comfort the broken souls. Her children waited dutifully to speak to him. Some men were already saying prayers in the blackened carcass of the *shul,* while others were picking through the burnt scraps of the holy *Torahs* to see what, if anything, remained of God.

She walked down the road and gathered up her children before the *Rebbe* had time to talk to them. Then she returned to her house, biting back tears of anger and fear. Holding her youngest, little Eva, in her arms, the two others following meekly, Serel looked into the carcass of their home. She stopped. Her husband had died for it, the village had been destroyed for it, but much as she hated it, it was her only means of survival. Serel told the children to stay where they were, not to re-enter the house, and walked into the barn.

The horse was quiet now that the noise and fire had died down. It snorted and whinnied when it saw her. It needed to be fed but Serel had more important things to do. Should she take it with her? It was valuable and it would make the journey much easier, but it would also make her prey to robbers along the way. Horses were worth much more than people. Serel looked around the barn and saw the pile of dung where her husband had hidden the treasure. She took a spade and shifted it, uncovering the amulet. She spat on it in disgust, but dropped it into the pail to wash it clean of the dried horse shit.

Outside in the damp early-morning air, Serel stroked her children's hair, whispering to them that everything would be alright. She picked up her baby again and comforted her, as she did her other children, smoothing their hair and tidying their clothes before they began their journey. They all stared at the lifeless eyes, the dead body of their father, her husband. Serel had neither the time nor the strength to bury him. She put the gold amulet inside her bodice and started to walk to America.

# CHAPTER ONE

The silence in the courtroom was oppressive, enveloping everything and everybody. Its leaden weight distracted Sarah Kaplan's focus for just a moment, at a time when she needed to summon up all her reserves of concentration. This was a pivotal time, a critical moment in the performance, one upon which so much could turn. That's how court cases were. That's why American justice so often lost out to performance.

The only sound Sarah could hear was her own heart pounding. Then the nervous coughs and guttural clearing of throats imposed themselves upon her. She sat rigid, composing her thoughts, rehearsing her opening words. It was a moment of pure theatricality designed to draw the two or three hundred people in the room to focus their attention solely on her.

She could feel the eyes boring into her back, some willing her to stumble, to stutter and fail; a handful of others, ugly and hateful people, praying silently that she would succeed. But Sarah had been ignoring the demands of her client and his compatriots for the entire time that she'd been involved. All she was thinking about was the American Constitution, how it was imperative that she speak clearly and convincingly, that it was her duty to safeguard the sacred rights endowed by the Founding

Fathers upon every man, woman and child in the country, even the rights of her execrable client, no matter what hurt would undoubtedly ensue.

The judge, swathed in authoritarian black robes, sitting half hidden behind his high judicial bench was perfectly used to the theatre of the courtroom. He allowed the young advocate another few moments of composure before coughing gently, a soft though eloquent statement which said, 'That's enough, Miss Kaplan. Everyone's primed. Now's the time to get on your feet and defend your client'.

Sarah stood. Again she paused, allowed herself the mandatory couple of seconds, before pushing back her chair and walking over to the jury box. Every movement was studied, every word she was about to utter had been rehearsed in her partner's office the previous day. She breathed deeply and exhaled, clearing whatever rotten air had gathered inside her by her proximity to her client. She scanned the jury box. For the last quarter of an hour the jury had been listening to the gentle and scholarly Professor Jacob Klein, representing an elderly woman who, a damaged lifetime ago, had lived through five years of the ultimate nightmare of Buchenwald Concentration Camp. But everyone knew that the case was really being run for and on behalf of the Jewish Anti-Defamation League. Professor Klein had opened his case eloquently and gently, reliving the reality of the Holocaust through the experiences of the woman who sat, bowed and broken, in the plaintiff's chair, quietly sobbing every now and again as her lawyer painted his word-pictures of a life destroyed.

In the centre of the back row of the jury box sat a middle-aged woman who attracted Sarah's attention. Every jury had its own dynamics – there was always one individual around whom the jury would slowly coalesce, one juror in whom the others would place their trust to act as their collective spokesperson, their universal conscience.

Sarah looked for someone who exuded feelings of stability and confidence in an environment which, to most people, was hostile and foreign. She settled on this woman, who looked like everybody's idea of an aunt, smart and sharp, but comfortable.

'Ladies and gentlemen of the jury,' she began, smiling at the older woman, who involuntarily found herself smiling back. Sarah's approach was totally different from that of Professor Klein, who stood formally behind his desk as if it was a lecture podium, never once venturing out into the theatre of the court. Again she waited a couple of moments for the jury to focus its attention. 'During the next few days you're going to be subjected to a re-telling of the hideous details of the Holocaust. Professor Klein, a distinguished academic and intellectual, is an advocate who is also a deeply passionate man, involved in the cause of human rights and justice. He is going to present you with thirty witnesses, all of whom have tragic direct experience of the Nazi death camps, the brutality of the SS, the work of the monstrous *Sonderkommandos* and the whole litany of the genocide by the Nazis against Jews, gipsies, Communists and the physically and mentally handicapped – human beings that Adolf Hitler classified in his insanity as "subhumans". Professor Klein, I'm sure, will expect me to attack these witnesses, to claim that they are suffering from delusions or maybe even that they are outright liars. That's the job of a defence lawyer, isn't it, ladies and gentlemen? To attack the prosecution's case and to refute the details so that my client, Frank Darman, walks away scot-free with his reputation intact.

'Well, I won't be doing that, despite my client's instructions. Over the last two months I have been briefed by him in the entire panoply of Holocaust denial. He's told me that the attempt to annihilate the Jewish people didn't really happen, that the Jews died from typhus and typhoid, that the Germans weren't guilty at all of aggression and atrocities, that the real crimes were committed by the Americans, the Russians, the British, the French, all egged on and supported by a covert Jewish financial cartel. He's told me that the gas chambers couldn't possibly have dealt with the millions of people that the Jews claim were killed. In his perverted and distorted mind he really believes that the entire Holocaust was a charade, concocted by the Jews to extort hundreds of billions of Deutschmarks from the Germans and dollars from America so they could build the infrastructure for Israel and gain universal support for the Israeli cause.'

Sarah turned and looked at her client, who was sitting staring dumbfounded at her. For eight weeks she had listened to his mind-numbing self-justifications, resisting her desire to howl in agony, resisting the urge to utter just one word in refutation of his loathsome claims. He had insulted her intelligence by assuming that her silence was tacit approval of his argument. Daily she had threatened her partners with withdrawal from this case, which nauseated her to the point of illness. But all agreed that a far greater principle was at stake than the fortunes of one revisionist historian and his obscene delusions.

Sarah had stuck it to the bitter end and now, after eight debilitating weeks, she was enjoying her moment of revenge. Her client was frowning, poised to stand and deliver a broadside against her in the open court. This wasn't how he had instructed her to run the case. Well, to hell with him. She was going to get him off, but for all the wrong reasons and in a way which would damage him irreparably.

Sarah turned back to the jury, 'Those, ladies and gentlemen, are the views of the man whom I have the dubious honour to defend. He is sitting there right now thinking that I'm going to put the Holocaust on trial. Well, I'm not. I wouldn't insult your intelligence, nor do any further damage to those witnesses whom Professor

Klein will call to reiterate what is one of the indisputable facts of the twentieth century — that the Holocaust really did happen and that six million Jews, and countless millions of others whom Hitler detested, were killed as a result of his insanity.'

Darman sprang to his feet and shouted across the courtroom, 'I want to talk to you and I want to talk right now, missie.' He looked at the judge and barked, 'Your honour, I need a recess immediately. My counsel is damaging my case. She's going directly against my instructions and screwing me up big time.'

The judge looked sternly at him. 'You chose your counsel, Mr Darman, not me. You briefed her to defend you. How she does it is between the two of you, it is not the business of this court. If Miss Kaplan breaches your trust and runs your case improperly, there are tribunals for your relief. But my courtroom is no such place. You've had months to work out a strategy.'

Darman interrupted furiously, 'But she's not using the tactics I wanted . . .'

The judge continued, 'Miss Kaplan is an experienced trial lawyer, Mr Darman. She's chosen to defend you in a way which you may disagree with. Of course, you have the right to dismiss her and appoint other counsel, but I must warn you that if you do so it will greatly inconvenience many elderly and frail witnesses who are already under enormous emotional and physical strain just being here. I don't know in which direction your attorney is running your case, but that's between you and her. If you do decide to waste this court's time, after eight weeks of preparation, I will show you no tolerance whatsoever. You'll not get a deferment out of me, Mr Darman. If you and your counsel couldn't agree on tactics before the matter came to court, then it's too late now.'

'But your honour,' shouted Darman, 'I didn't know she was going to say these things.'

'That's not my problem, Mr Darman, it's yours. Do you wish to dismiss Miss Kaplan? If so you must do it immediately, but I'm only going to give you a twenty-four hour adjournment to brief a new lawyer. Not a minute more. I would point out that she's duty-bound to do her best to get you an acquittal. Perhaps I could suggest that you question her tactics at the end of the day, rather than at the beginning.'

Darman was breathing heavily, his face flushed with anger. He could feel his blue suit and conservative white shirt sticking to his body. He combed his fingers through his thinning grey hair. He sat down slowly, looking menacingly at his advocate. With a wry smile, Sarah turned back to the jury and continued.

'There is no question, ladies and gentlemen, about the reality of the Holocaust, despite my client's protests. The death of millions and millions of people isn't on trial here. What is on trial is the right of men like Darman and the other Holocaust deniers to make these hurtful statements. What is on trial here is an issue which our forefathers were all too aware of when they wrote the Constitution, when they realised the need to enshrine one of the most contentious and important of the rights, freedoms and privileges that we as a people enjoy. That's the right granted to us under the First Amendment concerning freedom of the press and freedom of speech. Contentious? Yes. Because Frank Darman has as much right to the protection of the Constitution to state his view as do you and I. The hidden agenda here, ladies and gentlemen, is that of the Jewish Anti-Defamation League, which hopes to create pressure on the Supreme Court to introduce the same laws which apply in Germany and Israel, and a small number of other countries, where Holocaust denial will soon be deemed a criminal act. Sounds reasonable, doesn't it, ladies and gentlemen? But prevent people like Frank Darman from speaking,' she turned and pointed an accusing finger at him, 'and soon other laws could be enacted to curtail our freedoms further. Stop him from denying the Holocaust and the groundwork has been laid for the introduction of some other law, which may be used to stop me talking about my religion.' She shook her head in concern.

For the next twenty-five minutes Sarah Kaplan explained to the jury why she was presenting the case in the way she had decided, why she had rejected her client's instructions to fight the details of the Holocaust. 'Just because Darman is spouting obscene nonsense,' she told them, 'it doesn't diminish his right to say it. Not in America, it doesn't. Don't misunderstand my role in this, ladies and gentlemen. I have no intention ever of agreeing or empathising with a man whom I personally detest, a man whom I'm sure every right-thinking person in this country should detest, a man whose personal views are obnoxious to me, my colleagues, my family and my friends. A man who can look with equanimity at pictures of the Holocaust, at the mountains of skeletal bodies or empty shoes or spectacle frames or false teeth, the sole remains of millions of human lives, of entire communities and towns and villages with a thousand years of history in Europe. A man who can look at the overwhelming common experiences of survivors throughout the world who all tell the same story, and yet can devise an obscene conspiracy theory to hide his virulent anti-Semitism.'

Again she turned to him, accusing him with her eyes. 'And don't think that I am so naive, ladies and gentlemen of the jury, that I can't see why Frank Darman and his backers approached my law firm to fight this case for them. It is precisely because we're Jewish. He wants you to believe that he's not an anti-Semite, just a dedicated historical researcher, fearlessly seeking to expose unpalatable facts.

'So, if I have such a strong and violent detestation of such a man, why am I here defending him, opposing

Professor Klein and the Jewish Anti-Defamation League who want to stop the rubbish this man and others like him are spouting?

'Why am I here? I'm here to defend our basic American freedoms. I'm here to show that the Constitution is more important than Frank Darman, all the other Holocaust deniers, and all the racists, bigots, misfits and conspirators put together. That, ladies and gentlemen, is why, for the next few days, I shall put my disgust to one side and defend America by defending Frank Darman.'

She crossed the floor slowly and sat down again beside her client, who turned and looked at her with cold, barely restrained fury. 'You fucking bitch,' he hissed. 'Win or lose, I'll get you for this. That I swear.'

Sarah put her fingers to her chest, as she so often did, and felt the edge of her ancient family heirloom, hanging around her neck. It was something she did unconsciously, now more than ever before. Whenever she felt uncomfortable or under pressure she would reach up and touch the smooth, refined outline of the amulet. She turned to Darman and replied, 'Just make sure you settle our account first.'

# CHAPTER TWO

'David,' she called, 'shall I pour your coffee? You're going to be late for rehearsal.'

Sarah looked at the kitchen clock for confirmation. She felt remarkably fresh, considering the events of the previous day. She had slept long and deeply, yet she could imagine her colleagues from the office rising sluggishly from their beds, regretting the revelry of the previous night. Sarah had left the office party early, being in no mood to celebrate with her colleagues and the partners. For all she knew, they were *still* knocking back the Veuve Clicquot in honour of her victory. Arriving home by nine, she'd spent twenty minutes under a jet of hot water, trying to wash away the filth that still clung to her from her association with the odiously self-righteous Frank Darman.

Darman's continual condemnation of her courtroom tactics rang gloriously in her ears, especially when the senior partner had told him curtly that it wasn't just Sarah's decision to run the case the way she had, but that her decisions were backed by the entire firm. He'd added the codicil that if he had taken the case, he would have used precisely the same tactics. And Sarah had found it hard to bite back a smile when Darman stormed out of the office, screaming at her that he'd spend his last dollar destroying her, just like she'd destroyed his reputation in public.

In bed that night, David had asked her how the case went. 'Score one for the American Constitution, zero for common sense and decency,' she'd replied tersely, rolling away from him. The last thing she had wanted was for anybody to touch or caress her. She felt no cause for congratulations. She had done the right thing for the right reasons, but the results were horrible. She recalled the look of despair, of incomprehension, in Professor Klein's eyes as the foreperson read the verdict. Sarah had glanced at the plaintiff's desk. The people of the Anti–Defamation League were staring at her in disgust and anger, but it was the look in the plaintiff's eyes which would haunt her, the old woman who had spent half a day sitting in the witness box, telling how she had been repeatedly raped by guards and experimented on by men who called themselves doctors, how the illnesses caused by the experiments had stayed with her for the rest of her life, and how she'd been unable to sleep through a single night in fifty years without waking up in the middle of a nightmare. There was a look of immense sadness in her eyes, as though she had been betrayed. Sarah hadn't dared to look at Professor Klein again. She knew he would be feeling utter contempt for her. At least, last night, David had tried to be supportive.

'You don't look as if congratulations are in order,' he'd said when she'd finished her marathon session in the shower.

Sarah hadn't replied.

'Sarah, you knew you'd feel this way. It was your choice to take the case.'

'There were important principles at issue.'

David had said nothing more. Anything he'd said would have sounded trite, and Sarah knew all the arguments anyway. He had stroked her shoulder with gentle lineal motions, as though he was playing his cello, and she had fallen into a deep and satisfying sleep.

David had wanted to get up early this morning as he had a rehearsal of the Dvorak cello concerto under a conductor new to him, and was keen not to be late. The *New York Times* lay folded on the table. Sarah was too frightened to open it, to look at the way in which the case had been reported. Under normal circumstances, she would have opened the paper and cursed at the minuscule amount of space awarded to her by the paper's editors. This time she knew she would be front page news and, God knows, she didn't want to see. Even more, she didn't want her parents to see. They had been phoning her daily since the start of the case, questioning her involvement. What did they care about the principles of the Constitution and the defence of the First Amendment? All they cared about was that their daughter was trying to help their enemy. For them, the issue was much simpler than it was for her.

Sarah stood and walked over to the stove to pour herself another cup of coffee. Cars streamed down below, along the narrow avenues, threads in the fabric of New York. Her eyes focused on her reflection in the window. She felt refreshed, but looked haggard. The last ten days, and the eight weeks before that of pre-trial meetings, had drained her. Her skin looked sallow, there were hollow circles under her eyes and her body had lost the tone it usually enjoyed from an hour's workout each day. Much of the problem had been having to deal with Darman and his cohorts from the Institute for Historical Research and Review – people who were claimants to the title of historian, researcher or academic. The Institute, which housed social malcontents and rabid anti-Semites like Frank Darman, had no standing at all in the wider academic community. A cursory glance showed that it was funded by extreme right-wing groups and individuals who held wealth and power in their communities, people who were proud of their hatred for Jews, Asians and Blacks.

Sarah sat down to nurse her third cup of coffee. She looked at the toast she'd made for David. She knew she should eat or the lack of food would make her feel sick by the middle of the morning.

David came into the kitchen and kissed her on the forehead. He was freshly shaved and his long black ringlets were still wet from the shower. Tall, thin, studious, he could have been the type of academic whom infatuated students followed along the corridors of a university. He had a patient acceptance of life, an innate understanding of those forces which seem to control the existence of people and events. But David had left the academic life at the Conservatorium, for his chosen career was as a musician. Music had proved to be a sublime outlet for his inner passions. Sarah had never in her life met a man more intense, more passionate, or more decent and perceptive than David Rose.

He sat at the kitchen table and immediately noticed that the *New York Times* was still folded shut. It was the first time in their two years together that the paper was not spread over three-quarters of the table as Sarah devoured every word with her breakfast.

He picked it up and placed it purposefully on the seat beside him. 'Depending on what time the rehearsal finishes, do you want me to pick you up for lunch?'

She shook her head and reached over to hold his hand, 'No, honey, I don't know how my day is going to pan out. Could be just the usual, or there could be mob scenes in the office.'

'Mob scenes?' he asked.

'The press. I managed to avoid them immediately after the trial, and last night I deflected all the phone calls to the partners, but I can't see them waving goodbye to millions of dollars worth of free publicity for much longer. Knowing them, they'll want me to be on every talk show in the country.'

David shook his head. 'Free publicity is one thing, Sarah, but once you get onto the talk show circuit, they're going to be hammering the shit out of you. "*How could somebody like you represent somebody like him, Miss Kaplan?*" I'm not sure it's good for the firm's image and I certainly don't think it's good for yours.'

Sarah snapped, 'I'm not walking away from what I've done, David. I'd defend that son of a bitch again under the same circumstances.'

'You don't have to justify yourself with me, Sarah,' he said calmly and drank his coffee. If she was already snappy with him, how was she going to cope with the rest of the day?

The face staring at Joshua Krantz from the front page of the *New York Times* was attractive in an intense, anxious Semitic way. The coal-black eyes, the determined mouth, the glistening hair which framed her face in a stylish, typically New York, young-Jewish-professional-woman cut, were not exactly straight out of Central Casting but certainly attractive enough to suggest an actress or bit player. No, this face didn't belong to a smouldering movie goddess, but there was an honesty about her which appealed to him. This was somebody who was much more in-your-face than any of the fawning sycophants of Hollywood.

So how could a woman who looked like this, with those brains and Jewish to boot, how could a woman like this defend a Nazi prick like Frank Darman? A man who sent his screwed-up bullshit denial material to half the Yids in Hollywood, who'd been targeting the presidents of Californian banks and Los Angeles law firms and studio execs for the last couple of years with his offensive crap. And just when the Jewish Anti-Defamation League had finally had enough of him and his associates and decided to throw the book at him, this — what was her name? Josh read the caption — this Sarah Kaplan had got him off. He read the caption again, '*Lawyer Sarah Kaplan pictured after successfully defending Holocaust denier and revisionist Frank Darman. Miss Kaplan writes an OpEd piece on page 78.'*

Josh opened the paper to the OpEd section and searched the slabs of grey print, unrelieved by any image or photograph, for the piece written by the young lawyer. He folded the page open, but decided to wait until he had been served with his breakfast before he read it.

His Filipino maid, hovering in the background, asked, 'Would you like your muesli now, sir?'

He nodded. No matter how many times he told her to call him Josh, it was always 'sir'. Something cultural, perhaps, a hangover from the days of the awful Ferdinand and Imelda Marcos.

The muesli was precisely as he liked it, lightly toasted in honey with not too many nuts and lots of dried fruits. He poured skim milk over it and slowly munched the paste. Breakfast was the one time he insisted on being alone with his thoughts. Josh Krantz had breakfasted on this terrace almost every morning at the same time for the past eight years. The only exceptions were when he was in another part of the country or overseas on location. Then his Filipino servants usually travelled with him and tried to replicate the security of his home in every hotel room.

The terrace was bathed in the early morning sunshine of a Bel Air day. He was sufficiently high above the town to escape the noise, but nowhere in Los Angeles was high enough or far away enough to escape its pollution. The thick smog which clothed the city was less dense at this height, but still managed to obstruct his view of the ocean and the surrounding countryside. It was getting worse every year. He was within a year or two of making the decision to sell up and move up the coast to somewhere like Nepenthe, only a helicopter ride from Los Angeles but still clean enough to be the lungs of the Big Sur.

Josh turned to the trade papers. His studio shares, he noticed, were still high, indicating Hollywood's – and indeed New York's – continuing approval of his money-making endeavours. His last three films had been extraordinarily successful. Even with his lifestyle and supporting two expensive ex-wives, he had more money now than he would ever be able to use for the rest of his life. His two self-indulgent movie-making disasters half a dozen years ago had by now been forgotten by New York bankers. His films had redeemed themselves financially and so everybody was living off his back again.

It was a good life. He finished his muesli, wiped his mouth with a cloth serviette and sipped the black coffee. Yes! It was a good life. Imelda removed his empty plate. Jesus, what was her mother thinking of? Naming her daughter after a woman with the world's greatest shoe fetish. Shortly she would return with flapjacks, syrup and low-calorie ice-cream. It was an indulgence that would cause him to spend an extra half an hour in the gym at lunch time. If, that is, he was honest with his personal trainer.

Josh picked up the lawyer's article, but as he read the heading he realised with a degree of shame that his intensity and focus just weren't quite there. He was still thinking about last night and the way Adrianne had come on to him. Legs up to her throat, swathed in sheer black nylon, breasts so pert he could have balanced a coffee cup on them. A stomach firm and taut from devoting her life to celery sticks and carrots just so she could have the privilege of screwing the ass off Hollywood's best director. He shook his head and smiled. Amazing! These kids, models, wannabe actresses, were desperate for a chance to get into a movie. In the old days he could have walked down any street in Hollywood, snapped his fingers and taken home any one of the numerous girls in the immediate vicinity, all hanging out waiting to be seen. These days he just didn't have the interest. Over the past five years the desires which had initiated the destruction of his first two marriages had evaporated. Now he was looking for a relationship.

He had forced himself to live a more normal life – as normal as any life in Hollywood could be. Even when dealing in images and making fantasies, he clung on to reality by creating an order which he forced his life to follow. Breakfast at the same time, regular exercise, light recreational drugs only – never coke or heroin. And limiting sex to people whom his mind, as well as his body, desired. Under normal circumstances he had learned to control the compulsion, but last night had almost been an exception, one which weighed on his mind as he ate his breakfast.

He had just arrived at a studio party to celebrate some totally artificial occasion, when one of his publicists had walked up and commandeered him in a proprietary, even arrogant, manner.

'Hey Josh,' he said. Joshua barely knew the man, some pint-sized prick from marketing. They weren't called press agents or PR men or publicists any more. Now they were all involved in 'marketing' – worse results for twice the money. 'Hey Josh,' the little PR man repeated. He was in his mid-forties, as high as he would ever go in the Hollywood establishment. Born a nothing, would always be a nothing. But a nothing with pretensions. The only excitement in his life was rubbing shoulders with giants like Sharon Stone, Paul Newman, Dustin Hoffman or Kevin Costner. He was all ego-by-association, telling his suburban wife and kids that today Daddy had a meeting with Robert Redford or Glenn Close, not having the balls to tell them that all he did was facilitate the fusing of bottom-feeders hungry for news with sharks hungry for exposure.

'Hey Josh,' the guy persisted as Josh turned away to ignore him. He had started the evening by drinking a couple of tequilas and was already feeling heady. His reactions weren't quick enough to avoid the PR guy, and there were too many people around for him to bawl him out.

'There's a girl I want you to meet,' the man exuded as he stood beside Josh. 'Her name's Adrianne. French father, Spanish mother. Drop dead gorgeous. Figure to die for. She's been on stage in New York and she's in town wanting a break. Thought you might like to talk to her.'

Josh eyed the little man contemptuously. He knew he worked for him, but had no idea of his name. But he shrugged his shoulders, meaning, 'I'll give her ten seconds'. Excitedly the little man hurried off. Had he promised her introductions so he could screw her? Was Josh the pay-off? What the hell. He was alone and there were the usual satellites orbiting him, trying to catch his eye with an ingratiating smile. He wanted out, but it was still too early to go home to an empty house. He had a house full of servants, but nobody who spoke his language.

'Josh, this is Adrianne. What did I tell you, honey? I said I'd get you a meet with the big man.'

Adrianne was a head taller than the little PR guy. For once, the public relations industry was telling the truth. She was an extraordinary beauty. Olive skin, luminous black hair, bottle-green eyes and she was wearing a black cocktail dress that just invited unzipping and removal.

'Hello Josh. I'm honoured to meet you. I've been hoping we'd meet. I'm a great admirer of your work.'

She was gushing. It turned him off. Why did people have to gush in his presence, for God's sake. He wasn't fucking royalty. He wasn't the Pope. He was a movie-maker. Big deal! No better or worse than a writer or a painter. Just a guy who created images on celluloid.

'Nice to meet you, Adrianne,' he said. 'So, are you with a studio?'

She shook her head. Before she could answer the little PR guy intervened: 'Adrianne is looking for an agent. She doesn't want the usual hustlers and crap artists. But what she's mainly looking for is a break. She'll take anything. Do anything.'

Josh looked contemptuously down at the PR man. 'That's good,' he said. 'Look, I hope you'll excuse me. I've had a big day. I need to get some sleep. Good luck in your future here, Adrianne.'

Josh turned and walked away without acknowledging the presence of the PR man. As he reached the outer reception area, the noise of the party receded. Walking down the corridor to his own office, he picked up the phone, dialled the number for the garage and instructed them to bring his car to the front of the building. As he turned back to the office door, Adrianne appeared. The light of the corridor was behind her, it encased her body in a halo of sensuality. She was extraordinarily beautiful.

'I know you're going to think I'm really pushy but I guess I'll only ever have one opportunity of meeting you for the first time. Next time it's going to be the second time and it won't be as exciting.'

Josh smiled.

'Do you always walk out on people the minute you meet them?' she asked.

'I found the guy you were with irritating.'

'He was just trying to help.'

Josh shook his head. 'Don't believe it. He's a drop of used oil in the machine called Hollywood. What's he promised you?'

'Aren't you more interested in what I promised him?'

She was good. She had a quick wit and wasn't the standard model issue, fluttering eyelashes, capped teeth and silicon tits. 'Have you offered him anything?' he asked.

'Don't be ridiculous,' she said.

He didn't know whether her confidence was real or artificial. Either way he found it appealing.

'He didn't have the guts to ask me for anything. Just sniffing around. That surprised me. I could feel him wanting to. That was the subtext from the very beginning. *"Sleep with me and I'll introduce you to the biggest names in Hollywood."* But it never came.'

'Then neither did he,' said Josh.

Adrianne burst out laughing. 'And is this the end of our first meeting?' she asked.

'Adrianne, I'm tired. It's been a long day and I'm way beyond infatuation with pretty girls.'

'I know you are,' she said. 'You're twice married. You live alone in a mansion in Bel Air with four Filipino maids. You have a condo in Florida, a castle in the south of France and you own part of a winery in the Napa Valley.'

Josh eyed her closely for a moment, then shrugged. 'You could have read that in any gossip column.'

She smiled, 'I did.'

'So you've done your research, congratulations. What do you want to do?'

'Get to know you, to prove I'm smart and I've got talent. And a Masters degree in theatre,' she said.

'Great. But why me? And why like this? So I can give you a part? You're a pretty girl. You've got a great body, sexy voice. You're bright and clever. You'll find an agent in no time flat. In time, you'd get to know me professionally without having to screw me. Why this?'

'You could be talking about any actress, Josh. I'm not any actress, believe me. I've had screen tests and I melt the camera.'

Josh shook his head. 'Hollywood's gone way beyond sirens and smouldering lips. We're not into that any more. We're into brilliant acting, great stories of social importance. You're ten years too late, honey.'

'I'm a good actor, Josh. I've got a real screen presence. All I need is you sitting in the director's chair telling me what to do.'

He was tempted. Very tempted. But he already knew the ending. They'd go to bed, he'd make promises he would regret later, one or both of them would get hurt. That was Josh five years back. Not now. Not these days.

He moved closer to Adrianne and gave her a tender kiss on the cheek. 'Leave your address and telephone number with the night receptionist. I'll organise a real screen test. When I've seen it I'll give you an honest appraisal. It may hurt, but at least you can go on from there. No bullshit. That's a promise. And one other promise – there'll be no strings attached. None.'

Adrianne gave him a crestfallen look. 'Are you sure that's all you want me to leave you with? Just my address and telephone number.'

'I'm sure,' he told her gently.

Adrianne's soft voice and perfume were still in his mind as he drove slowly west down Santa Monica Boulevard towards Beverly Hills and then on to his home in Bel Air. When he had first come to Hollywood from San Francisco all those years ago, the suburb had been predominantly white and rich. Now it was grubby, shabby, and had been taken over by street gangs, drug kids and hookers. Even the houses and apartments looked diseased.

Further out, away from the neon lights and artificial sunsets, the housing was still rundown, largely occupied by Blacks and Latinos and increasing numbers of Chinese, but it was somehow safer, more domestic. Yet just up the road in Beverly Hills were huge palm trees, wide avenues, cosmetic gardens tended by Japanese gardeners, and houses which cost multi-millions of dollars.

He couldn't help smiling at the obscene disparity of it all, the way in which America had turned history upside down. Today Hollywood was a *stetl* housing the immigrants, the poor, people despised by the rich. Up the hill were the wealthy, the powerful. In the old country, the Jews had been down the bottom of the hill; now they were at the top.

He drained his second cup of coffee of the morning, enough for breakfast, and watched a plane descending into the smog that hid LA. He picked up the article written by the lawyer and started to read:

*Yesterday, in a Federal court, the American Constitution won a resounding victory. Unfortunately the victory it won was at the expense of people who had been brutalised in the bloodiest and most heinous immorality ever committed in human history . . .*

# CHAPTER THREE

It had been three weeks since the end of the Darman case,
but Sarah was still suffering flak from the Jewish
community in New York, Chicago and the West Coast –
in fact, almost everywhere in America. She had been the
subject of abuse, ridicule and contempt, as well as hurtful
and hateful letters in the Jewish press. Some had been
couched in didactic terms; in others the writer acted as
mentor, citing her youth and lack of world-view as the
reasons for her terrible error of judgement in taking on
such a case. But the most hurtful were from other lawyers
who strutted the pages like peacocks, pontificating about
how they wouldn't have touched the case for all the
money on earth. The partners of Friedlander, Abrahams,
Stein & Goldfarb had defended her to the hilt, but, in the
end, people still wanted to abuse her personally for daring
to defend a neo-Nazi. David had supported her as best he
could, but between eight in the morning and eight at
night, she was on her own.

Which was why, at the end of a particularly harrowing
morning of snide interviews with insistent reporters, she
had sought refuge with a woman she could trust,
somebody who was fiercely objective, yet warm and
human. The Dean of the Faculty of Linguistics, Professor
Miriam Neisser, was one of the few women in whom

Sarah felt she could confide her innermost thoughts and fears, and in return receive insight and wisdom into ways of coping with the current crisis. Thrice married, thrice divorced, Miriam Neisser was tall, stately and had a bearing which her friends described as regal, her critics as fearsome, and her enemies as pompous. Those few enemies, who denigrated her in academic circles, were the lesser lights of linguistics who had fallen foul of her insatiable demand for intellectual integrity, people satisfied with compromise and with easy solutions to imponderable problems. But her friends, those who had supported her as she rose from research assistant to Noam Chomsky to fully-fledged dean of a major undergraduate university, believed her to be a torchbearer, a woman who led the fight in academia against the dilution of standards at the behest of commerce and the infectious disease of corporatism.

'What did you really expect, Sarah?' Miriam Neisser asked her ex-student, one of the many who had kept in touch with the dean years after they had left her umbra. 'You played with fire, you're getting burnt. It's part of the problem of fame. They love you when you reflect their image of a good guy, but they can't wait to cut you off at the knees when they see you supping with the enemy.'

'But I was right to defend him, wasn't I, Miriam? There were bigger issues at stake than getting him off. There's the whole question of our rights to state our opinion.'

'You're asking me for affirmation. It's something I can't give, Sarah. Only you know whether your actions in defending this man were right or wrong. As to the First Amendment – yes, I think on balance you're probably right to have taken on the case. But when you agreed, did you weigh the cost? Sometimes big issues have a devastating effect on little people, which in time outweigh the size and importance of the issue. Look, if you're asking me for support, I'll support you as a friend. But I won't support you professionally if you've done something at the expense of the wider community to support your narrow interests.'

'I did it because it was right.'

'If that's what you believe, then why are you here?'

'Because there's so much shit being thrown at me. Personal stuff. I acted in a professional capacity, and people are attacking me personally. It's just not fair. I'm getting it in the media, people phoning up pretending to want to talk but actually wanting to abuse me. Even when friends come around to support me, I know in my heart they're more curious than anything, wanting to get the inside running on Sarah Kaplan, just because I'm in the news at the moment.'

Miriam Neisser nodded and stood up from her desk. Her window looked out on to the East River. It was a place of meditation in a frenetic life, offering moments of introspection, watching ships gently plying their trade in an eternal yet ever-changing artery. It was the window she'd looked out from when Sarah had first come into her office all those years ago, to interview her for the student newspaper. Miriam hadn't had the time, but she'd allowed half an hour. Yet the interview had lasted two hours, during which time Miriam had become increasingly attracted to the young student's mind, her passion, her perception. It hadn't been an interview, it had been an exchange of ideas. And since then, Miriam had monitored Sarah's progress through school, graduate college, and then as an up-and-coming lawyer. She'd blossomed into a fine, confident and valuable young woman, one in whom Miriam had invested care and attention. Miriam was saddened to see how the pressure of the past few months had taken its toll on Sarah's normally robust spirit.

'You remember that I used to work for Noam Chomsky, up at MIT? Well, in the early days when he was still a linguist and not a media plaything, he was an intellect the like of which I've never experienced before or since.

He had a mind which was so deep, it was almost unfathomable. The researchers and students would sit for hours talking about ideas and philosophies on the nature of linguistics, and while we'd be tinkering around the edges, he'd suddenly have this extraordinary insight and change the course of the science.

'But then fame got to him. The media and the talk shows got to hear about him and they soon cottoned on to the fact that here was good value. He was passionate about left wing causes, about the damage the media is doing to this country, about conspiracy theories, and so every time he said something it made headlines. In the end it changed him. He became a performer. The tragedy isn't that a great man is now constantly embroiled in controversy, the real tragedy of Noam Chomsky is that his mind, his real genius, is wasted fighting media fires.'

Miriam turned from the window and looked at Sarah. 'I realise you're not a Noam Chomsky. Neither am I. But you're starting to sound like a character from *King Lear*. Be careful that you remember who you are, and what you're there for, and that you don't become an invention of the media.'

Sarah was horrified. 'Do you think I sought this attention? Do you think that I wanted the abuse, the vilification?'

'Didn't you know it would happen?' asked Miriam.

Sarah remained quiet.

'If you knew it would happen, Sarah, why did you accept the case?'

'Because there were important legal principles involved. Because we were fighting for . . .'

'Sarah,' Miriam interrupted, 'you fought the case because it would improve your career. You know it, I know it. The people that fight these sorts of cases for the principle, people who have the stature to close their eyes to the fact that they're representing men like Frank Darman, are retired law professors, or Alan Dershowitz from Harvard, not Sarah Kaplan, an associate partner in a middle-ranking law firm. Darman came to you because you were a young Jewish woman. He wanted to make the point that he wasn't anti-Semitic, he even said so in court. He was using you. If you didn't realise that, you're naive. If you did realise that, you're implicated, and what you're saying now is hypocritical. You can't have it both ways, Sarah. You of all people should know that.'

Sarah retreated from Miriam's searing gaze. She had come for approbation, but instead had received an uncomfortable revelation, one that she'd been denying since she'd first seen Darman's condescending face in her office. While Miriam was speaking, quietly but insistently, Sarah questioned whether it was what she really deserved. And it was. She nodded slowly.

'I just feel so low, Miriam. Of course I anticipated some of this would happen, but not to this level.'

Miriam Neisser walked around the desk and sat in a chair opposite Sarah. She reached over and held her hand, a mothering gesture. 'Sarah, we all miscalculate. This circus isn't going to last long. The media has an attention span of twenty-four hours. They'll lose interest in you as soon as there's a massacre of hapless civilians somewhere, or an act of genocide in some unpronounceable African country which will consume the media for a couple of days, or some crazy gunman will walk into a restaurant and shoot twenty people, or who knows – maybe Saddam Hussein will get caught dropping chemical weapons on the Kurds. Something's going to happen to knock your name off the media's menu. They'll find some other tasty morsel for their feeding frenzy.'

'Or mortal,' quipped Sarah.

'I'm sorry if you wanted me to throw my arms around you and protect you, but you're not in school any more. You can't be protected from being molested by the real world.

You've just got to stand up to it, grow a thick skin, smile and say, "*Fuck you*". I could help you when you were my best and brightest student, but today. . .' Miriam shrugged in sympathy and looked at her watch. 'Hey, it's getting on for lunch. Why don't I take you down to the canteen?'

Sarah smiled. 'I'm a lawyer, I'm rich. I'm not an academic like you. I can afford a restaurant.'

'You're on,' said Miriam. 'There's a cheap Italian just opened around the corner.'

'Sounds good,' said Sarah, standing and grabbing her purse.

The two women walked to the restaurant and ordered their meals. Within minutes huge steaming bowls of spaghetti and linguini lay between them. They helped themselves to equal amounts from both bowls. A crisp white wine and Italian salad made the meal complete.

'How's your research coming along? Last time we spoke, you were just finishing the interviews with the children of Holocaust survivors,' said Sarah.

Miriam wiped a stray piece of pasta from the corner of her mouth, and said, 'Talking to the children is sometimes harder than talking to the parents. Not that there's much point in talking to the parents. Every time I've tried it, they can't seem to comprehend what my research is all about. Anyhow, now they're old, their memories have been compartmentalised, closed up, locked away. But for the children, there's this overwhelming feeling of frustration. They want to know things, but they feel that, even though they're adults, they're being denied their history. Of course, much of the message of what their parents suffered still gets through, via a myriad of indirect paths that probably make the transmitted trauma worse than a direct telling would have done in the first place. But then that's another of life's little ironies, I suppose.

'For me, it's particularly difficult research, especially when I go back to the parents for confirmation of the language. I'm dealing with suppurating emotions which haven't healed in over fifty years. They've just put a lid on them and let them fester. Yet somehow I have to remain distant and academic while listening to stories which defy belief let alone comprehension.'

'Are you coming to any conclusions?' Sarah asked.

Miriam smiled. 'Conclusions? Isn't that a lawyer's word? If there's an argument, let's test it out in court and see who's right and wrong. Linguistics isn't about conclusions, Sarah. It's about understanding the way our minds work through our language. It's about finding out why things are said and done. But, mainly, it's about how language shapes and constrains and constructs our various realities. This research that I'm doing into the language of the Holocaust is opening my eyes to a lot more than linguistics. I'm actually beginning to come to terms with understanding aspects of the human mind. You know, one of the overwhelming commonalities amongst Holocaust survivors has been their inability to relate their experiences to their children, to tell them of the suffering they endured, the brutalities and the deprivations. You'd expect that, wouldn't you? You wouldn't want to hurt your own children by telling them what you've been through. But the staggering thing that I'm finding is that these self-same victims are quite prepared to describe what happened to their grandchildren.'

Sarah looked up in shock.

'That's right, Sarah. I've spoken to fifteen, twenty year old grandchildren who know much more about what happened to their grandparents in Auschwitz, Buchenwald and Treblinka than their parents know.'

Sarah reflected for a moment on her relationship with her own grandmother. 'Is that because grandparents and grandchildren don't have a generational problem? I know I found it easier to talk to my grandma than I find talking to Mum and Dad.'

'Maybe,' said Miriam. 'One of the obvious reasons is that, because it's a new generation, more time has passed since the events of the trauma. The grandparents still want to protect the kids, of course, but now they've become more adept and experienced at packaging the message. And the kids are less sensitive to the, by now, less palpable pain of their grandparents, which means that the communication is more direct, less sanitised. We're working on this research right at the moment. But what we're finding really interesting is the language of communication, the way the Holocaust survivors find to describe their experiences. The words they use. The way in which they desensitise the horror, make it somehow clinical, abstract, almost scientific.'

'Like the inscrutable way the Chinese deal with things?'

'Not in the same way,' said Miriam. 'Holocaust survivors, or people that have been a part of genocide, or even those that have survived some other urban horror, tend to fall back on clinical language. With the Chinese it's very different. They have a public persona which is all to do with honour, and believe that the showing of emotion in public is a slight against the honour system.'

'So where is this all leading?' asked Sarah.

'I hope it's leading to a better understanding of how to help people who have suffered. Many of the survivors have enjoyed no relief by allowing their emotions to seep out. Often horrible psychiatric problems develop in later life. Perhaps if we can find a key to enabling sufferers to open the locked cupboards in their minds earlier, much sooner after the brutalising experience, we'll be able to offer them some form of relief. Right now, we really don't know the language to use when somebody's been through the sort of experiences that these people have suffered.'

Sarah sipped her white wine. The glass was frosted and there was a lipstick smear on its rim, a reminder that she'd need to do a repair job before she returned to her office. Partners could get away with a four-hour lunch, associates couldn't.

Miriam looked at her sympathetically. Her whole manner since she'd entered Miriam's office had been that of the propitiant, offering friendship and a meal in return for Miriam's favours. Yet throughout the meeting, Miriam had been severe, unbending and occasionally prolix in explaining that Sarah was now on her own, responsible for her own actions. She held out her hands now and grasped Sarah's, as though the two of them needed to combine their strength to hold Sarah's wine glass.

'I've been a pain in the butt, haven't I?'

Sarah looked at the older woman in surprise. 'Years of fighting academic and political battles have made me war-weary, battle-scarred. You came to me for comfort, I gave you none. I'm sorry.'

Sarah smiled. 'You gave me what I needed. An objective voice.'

'No,' said Miriam. 'You have one in David. What you needed was support. I feel I've let you down.'

Sarah shrugged. She noticed that Miriam looked much older than the last time they'd met. More lined, more careworn. 'Your research is taking its toll of you, isn't it?'

Miriam nodded.

'What did you think of my OpEd piece in the *Times*?' she asked. She'd been careful till now to avoid mentioning it. She knew Miriam would have disagreed with every word.

'I thought it was very well argued and cleverly considered,' she responded, too quickly.

Sarah laughed. 'Do I have to ask again?' she said.

This time Miriam smiled and nodded. 'You know I disagree with you, Sarah. But it *was* well argued and well considered. Trouble is, Sarah, that you're talking like an armchair theorist. I'm wondering about the reactions of people of your parents' and grandparents' age. How are they going to feel about a young woman of very limited experience telling them that their hopes and aspirations, their yearnings and desires, are all built on a morass, that the only solid ground to stand on is right here in America? Rather makes me wonder about our religion in general.'

'Miriam,' said Sarah, 'we've come through a millennium of torture, pogroms, rape, forced conversions and genocide. And our parents and grandparents still look back to their ghettos and stinking villages, where people hated them, as if it was home. "Ah! The old country!" For God's sake!'

But Miriam didn't want to get into an argument. She was curious about one thing. 'Was the OpEd piece written by Sarah the lawyer, Sarah the young American Jew, Sarah the rebellious daughter . . .' she hesitated, judging the young woman's mood '. . . or Sarah the deracinated, wandering Jew?'

Sarah looked questioningly at her mentor.

'Sarah, the article sounded a bit like you were standing on top of a mound shouting to everybody, "Hey look at me! I'm taller than everybody!" I read it and thought of Shakespeare. Doesn't it say in Hamlet, *"The lady doth protest too much"*? I read your OpEd piece several times, looking below the surface of the words, deconstructing the meaning. And each time, I saw an insecure woman desperately clinging to the present. My fear for you, Sarah, is that you're closing your eyes to the past because of your inability to see yourself clearly in the future.'

Sarah was silent. She went to sip her wine then realised it was warm. She picked up her fork and played with the few scraps which remained on her plate. Miriam knew that it was a pivotal moment, one in which the perceptive and intelligent young woman was hearing an inner voice. Miriam stood, kissed Sarah on the forehead and stroked her hair.

'Why don't you stay and finish the wine. I'll just wander back.'

She started to move away, but Sarah reached up and clasped her hand. They looked at each other, their conversation was unspoken. Miriam smiled gently and squeezed Sarah's hand, then walked out of the restaurant and was swallowed by the river of people in the street.

Sarah sipped her wine. She didn't notice any longer that it was warm. The waiter, seeing one of his customers disappear, moved forward to clear the plates, but then stopped. The look on Sarah's face, as she stared into infinity, told him to wait a few extra moments.

By the time Sarah returned to the office, she was feeling more able to face the barrage she knew awaited her. Perhaps it was time to really put that piece of Nazi slime behind her. Darman was still using every avenue in the media open to him to attack Sarah and her firm for the character assassination that she had performed, but she would have to deal with that later. Right now, she had a job to do, something she wasn't looking forward to. The office junior had been with the firm for three months since leaving school in grade ten. The daughter of a friend of one of the paralegals, the firm's human resources director had agreed to give the kid a start in life by putting her on Sarah's team as the most junior of assistants, but her work was so far below even the lowest standards acceptable to the firm that not even Sarah could do anything with her. She had to go. Human resources had offered to fire her, but Sarah wanted to do it personally as the girl looked up to her as a mentor. She planned to do it gently, supportively.

Sarah steeled herself for the coming interview but no matter how she couched it, the dismissal would devastate the kid. She was so eager, but incompetent. There was nothing else Sarah could do.

'Donna, could you ask Natalie to come in here?' she said over the telephone.

'Certainly, Sarah.'

'Oh, and Donna, no visitors, please.' She put her phone on divert so that her secretary would also answer all incoming calls.

Sarah straightened the papers on her desk. She had rehearsed what she was going to say. She would be direct in firing her, but solicitous. She would point out the opportunities in the world outside of office work. But when she started to imagine Natalie approaching her office door with a sense of trepidation, knowing that she'd been warned in writing three times, Sarah's carefully rehearsed words evaporated. It was odd: she was able to stand and deliver a twenty-minute speech in court without once referring to her notes, yet she couldn't tell a sixteen year old girl that she was being fired because her work wasn't good enough. Sarah shuffled the already geometrically precise sheaf of papers again, took out a yellow legal pad and began to write, 'The rain in Spain stays mainly . . .'

The knock on her door made her jump. 'Come in,' she said, but the face that appeared was Donna's.

'Sarah, I'm sorry to disturb you but you have to put the Natalie thing on hold. Before I could phone her, I got a call from Mr Friedlander – he wants to see you immediately.'

'Now?'

'Now.'

'What's it about?'

'He didn't discuss it with me, Sarah.'

'No. No, of course.'

Sarah stood and walked towards the door. Her secretary gripped her arm as she passed, 'Sarah, do you want me to fire Natalie?'

Sarah smiled. 'Thanks Donna, but it's my responsibility. I just wish she wasn't so damn nice. If she was a bitch, I'd hand it over to HR.'

Donna shrugged. Sarah crossed the office floor to the bank of elevators and rode the eight floors upwards to the hushed atmosphere of the senior partner's suite. She rarely ascended to this level. As an associate partner she was important to the firm, but not yet sufficiently pivotal to its income or reputation to deserve being elevated beyond the floor where the graft and details were done. Up here, in the rarefied hush of middle-aged secretaries tapping at silent keyboards and grey-haired men and women of venerable status walking down thickly carpeted corridors, was where the really big money came into the firm. This was the floor where presidents of giant corporations picked up their telephones and got straight through to the private lines of the partners, some of whom were amongst the most senior men in New York legal circles. This was the floor where politicians and Supreme Court judges phoned their old friends for a quiet word, and where the older partners were rewarded with elevation to the judicial benches before retirement.

It was a world that was waiting for Sarah if she stayed the course and made the grade. The early signs were already there – gifts of perfume from partners when she won significant cases, bonus cheques that seemed to arrive with increasing frequency, notes about her performance on the front page of the staff newsletter. Everybody knew she was being groomed for full partnership. But if she got there, it would be by her ability alone. The partners' floor was no sinecure. Influence couldn't get you elevated, just your performance and the income you earned for the firm. Influence only worked when you were already up there.

She felt the effect of the elevator on her stomach as it ascended, and began to wonder why Morrie Friedlander of all people would demand to see her. What was it Donna had said – "*immediately*"? What the hell could it mean? Trouble – that was certain. A knot of fear began to grow in Sarah's stomach. The firm had recently retrenched a dozen or so paralegal staff as well as one lawyer. Admittedly he was somebody at a lower level than Sarah, indeed someone known for his inefficiency and extraordinary ability to look busy and delegate his work to assistants, but nonetheless he was a man with a family. The dismissal of the junior staff had caused shock waves to resonate through the secretarial and administration levels of the firm. Tightly huddled meetings took place in the dark ends of corridors, long low-level phone conversations were held, people whispered out the sides of their mouths.

The firm's employed lawyers and associate partners at first looked on at the paralegal staff in sympathy, and tried to give them reassurance. But when their immediate colleague, the lawyer, was suddenly fired at the end of the working week it was as if an evil-smelling vapour had spread through the entire building. Junior lawyers sought urgent meetings with their seniors for assurances about their futures, associates demanded consultations with partners. Men and women who carried the legal responsibilities of the firm began to stay back late into the night, scrutinising their time sheets to ensure they were extracting the maximum billing hours without contravening legislation. Invoices were revisited to see if they could be bumped up by additional work or disbursements. Clients to whom lawyers hadn't spoken in months, even years, were suddenly telephoned and their health was inquired after, as well as the current status of their business. All and any help was willingly offered. But more than all her colleagues, Sarah remained distant from the self-generated hysteria. She had felt safe and secure in her professional life – until now.

While others were panicking about their futures, she had been in the middle of a different maelstrom. Her job was invulnerable while Darman was pleading his innocence before America. Naively she had expected that her stunning success and the media controversy it engendered would make her inviolable, even after the case was finished. But nothing was secure, except the inevitability of insecurity. Stories abounded in the newspapers of middle- and senior-ranking executives being called to meetings with their bosses to be told that the firm was downsizing and their services were no longer required. The stories usually went on to describe the devastation of the former executives' egos, their loss of health, appetite and will to continue. Some even found relief in suicide. Divorce was commonplace. Was this what the meeting with Morrie was all about?

Her mind raced urgently over her present and past workloads. She was certainly contributing more than her fair share of billing hours. She knew that her time sheets were at least twenty to thirty per cent fuller than other lawyers on her floor, but maybe that wasn't enough. Maybe now the Darman case was over, she would become the sacrificial lamb to appease the firm's critics. Maybe the firm had finally had enough of the broadsides from the Jewish community and were about to use her for their own target practice.

She walked out of the elevator and was greeted by the secretary at the reception desk. The view, which here overlooked the apex of Manhattan Island and the Statue of Liberty, never failed to delight Sarah on the infrequent occasions she visited this floor. Now it looked oddly comforting. For generations of exiles the Statue of Liberty had been a symbol of welcome and security. And in the space of a few moments, having moved from complete confidence in her own environment to insecurity in these upper echelons, she suddenly felt as adrift as those millions of boat people who had sailed through the harbour at the beginning of the century.

'Sarah, could you take a seat. Mr Friedlander's on a call.' The secretary's voice interrupted her reverie.

Sarah sat down in the deep burgundy armchair. She picked up the latest edition of the *American Law Journal* and flipped through it. Her mind was still roaming over what could result from the forthcoming interview. Why the hell would the firm's most senior partner want to see her? She sank further into the deep armchair, her legs feeling like jelly. She knew Morrie Friedlander to talk to, but only at the firm's social gatherings, or on the occasions that she was invited to a debriefing at a meeting of partners about a case she was currently handling. If he wasn't calling on her to take the rap for the Darman publicity, then she must have done something unbelievably wrong for it to have come to this. Partners sacked their lawyers and associates, not the guy at the top. God Almighty, what had she done?

'Sarah, Mr Friedlander will see you now. You know where his office is.' The receptionist pointed down a corridor, lit subtly by the pin spotlights on the works of art adorning the walls. Sarah knocked on Friedlander's door. She could hardly walk, her legs felt powerless. Her heart was thumping so loudly she could hear it.

She waited, holding her breath, and telling herself she was overreacting. There seemed to be no response from inside. Instead, after a moment, the door opened and Morrie Friedlander greeted her with a beaming smile. Old enough to be her father, or maybe even a young grandfather, he gently shook her clammy hand. He was a cultivated, cultured man who smelled of aftershave, a scion of his local synagogue, B'nai B'rith and the United Israel Appeal. His face often adorned the front pages of the Jewish press.

'Sarah, thank you for sparing the time.'

She smiled weakly, her throat dry as he escorted her to one of his armchairs. His office was designed to expose the breathtaking views beyond his windows, yet still retain the formality of an office of law to enable him to focus his mind as he worked. There were the mandatory ranks of books filling the wall opposite his desk, and the discreetly camouflaged doors leading into his private bathroom, dining room and partners' boardroom.

This was power. This was what worried Sarah — she could have been a part of it, one day. Which was why being fired was so unfair. She'd worked her butt off. She deserved reward, not censure. And she'd tell him so. She formulated the words in her head as he led her across the office floor: '*Look Morrie, I've worked damned hard for you.*'

'Sarah,' he said, his voice avuncular, warm and comforting, 'I'll come straight to the point. As a result of all the publicity you've been getting, we've had a call from a very influential man. Somebody from the West Coast. He wants to retain your services.'

Sarah felt such relief sweeping through her body that she almost burst into tears. A warmth, a glow, suffused her. She almost leapt out of the chair and threw her arms around Morrie Friedlander. She could barely contain the broad smile of joy that covered her face. Morrie appeared not to notice.

'The call was from Joshua Krantz, the film director.'

Sarah's smile disappeared just as quickly as it had arrived. 'Excuse me?'

'Joshua Krantz wants you to work for him.'

She nodded. 'Right,' she said. 'Great.' Her mind was swimming. Joshua Krantz. '*The* Joshua Krantz?'

Friedlander nodded, 'In one! He phoned me this morning. Told me he'd read your OpEd piece in the *Times* and disagreed profoundly. That's why he wants to use you. He wants you to be devil's advocate for what he wants to do.'

'Joshua Krantz wants me to represent him?' She felt like an ingenuous fool. She knew she was repeating herself. It was a mixture of relief and surprise.

Now Friedlander was amused. 'He wants you to get his grandparents' house back.'

'Who's taken it?' she asked. She laughed at her own mistake. So did Morrie. 'I mean, what's happened? Who's got it? Why me? This is crazy, Morrie. I'm only . . .'

Morrie interrupted her, 'I tried to tell him I'd be delighted to handle his matter personally but he was very direct and told me he's got plenty of high-powered lawyers already. What he wants is you. That OpEd piece you wrote really affected him. I also assume that he's been reading a lot of the publicity that's been raging around you. I assume that he wants somebody who's in the public eye. He wants to make a bit of a song and dance about getting his grandfather's house back.'

Sarah nodded. There were a thousand questions racing around her mind, but she was so surprised by the turn of events that none of the questions really made much sense. Except one: 'Where is the house?'

'It's in Slovakia, about fifty kilometres from where your grandparents came from.'

Sarah felt a cold shock sweep through her. Representing someone like Joshua Krantz was the big break that every young lawyer in America prayed for. He was drop-dead gorgeous, fabulously wealthy and lived a Hollywood lifestyle which had enormous appeal. But what did this have to do with her personal history? Just because her grandparents had come from the same area! Her surge of enthusiasm became tempered with a feeling of caution, a concern about becoming over-exposed.

'Morrie, is there a subtext? What have my grandparents got to do with this?'

Morrie looked at her in surprise. 'Absolutely nothing. He wants you because you have an unusually high profile at the moment. You've caused a lot of controversy. And that's exactly what Joshua Krantz wants. You see, now that Eastern Europe is opening up, Joshua feels that more and more people are going to be looking back to their ancestry, what happened to their parents and grandparents, and they're going to be seeking reparation, restitution. Very little has happened yet, and what *has* happened is all under-the-counter stuff. Krantz has got a lot of money and he's willing to make a noise, a big noise in fact. He's willing to spend millions bringing this issue out into the open.'

'What issue?' asked Sarah.

'The issue of Jews – no, not Jews, refugees – being forced out of their homes and having their property stolen and sequestered. Now their children and grandchildren want to return to demand the family property back. It's not just the money side. His place is worth *bupkess*, but he's willing to spend his money on the principle.'

Sarah stood up. Her body felt as if it was full of electricity. 'Then why the hell is he coming to me? This whole thing is crazy. That OpEd piece I wrote, that was the diametric opposite of what he's after. I said that people should close their eyes on the past, turn their backs on it. That Europe, especially from Germany to Russia, was a land filled with such hatreds, such dangers, that looking back can only harm us. Look at the growth of neo-Nazism. Look at . . .'

Morrie put up his hand to stop her. 'Sarah, I read and approved your article before it went into the paper. I told you then that I don't agree with you, but now isn't the time for us to have an intellectual discussion. We've got the potential to land one of the biggest private clients in the country, certainly one of the biggest names in the entertainment industry. And the entertainment business is bigger than most of the corporations we deal with. If we can persuade him to bring in his corporate work from his studios and his television interests, it could be a bonanza worth tens of millions.

'Sarah, this could be big for us, and very big for you. If Joshua Krantz gets on well with you, you could end up handling all the work of his studio. I know you're on the way to becoming a damn good trial lawyer, probably one of the best we've had. But corporate law is where you should end up and this could be a fantastic opportunity for you. Corporate law is where the money is, Sarah, especially in a firm like this. And when you're dealing with Hollywood, you're dealing with multi-million-dollar deals.'

Sarah was stunned, her mind split in two. Morrie thought she was pondering the future; Sarah was actually thinking back to her lunchtime conversation with Miriam Neisser.

'He wants you, young lady,' Morrie said with a look of pleasure on his face. 'He doesn't want me or Jack or any of the other partners. He's got a bevy of top LA lawyers working for him. He wants you. And the one thing you're not going to do, my dear, is jeopardise a bucketload of manna from heaven. Do I make myself absolutely plain?'

His smile was still broad, but the icy determination which Morrie Friedlander had exhibited over the past forty years hung between them. A determination which had enabled him to expand the size of the firm from a two-man partnership in suburban New York to its current status.

Sarah nodded and sank back into her chair. Friedlander smiled and stood to pour her a cup of coffee. She thought for a few moments. For the past three weeks she had been abused by the entire community for supporting a piece of Nazi filth like Frank Darman. Helping Joshua Krantz get his grandfather's house back and righting the wrongs done to one Jewish family could also help redress the damage done to her reputation. Maybe, just maybe, this would benefit her as much as it would the firm. Maybe she should call Miriam for another chat.

She wondered where her conscience sat in all of this.

Sarah's meeting with Morrie Friedlander continued for another hour and a half. They discussed what research needed to be undertaken before Joshua Krantz visited the firm the following week to begin their assignment. They discussed Sarah's lack of international experience, her ignorance of Slovakian and Czech laws, international and local treaties and how they related to the return of sequestered properties, and how these could be overcome by procuring the assistance of the experts in the various fields, acting as consultants to the firm for the duration of the matter. They discussed how she would approach the Ministries in both the Czech Republic and Slovakia, how the new laws relating to lustration – the opening of old files kept by the former Communist secret service organisations – could affect her claims.

She would be so swamped with behind-the-scenes backup, Morrie assured her, that she would merely be acting as a figurehead, someone to liaise with Joshua in order to keep him happy. She would be the swan, graceful and untroubled on the surface of the water, but there would be other unseen legs paddling furiously beneath her, doing all the swimming. It was a statement which, under any other circumstances, would have outraged her. She would have found it demeaning and patronising. But she was the first to admit that, in areas where she was almost totally unskilled, it made her feel much more comfortable to know that she wouldn't be handling this alone.

It was quarter to seven by the time Sarah left the building in Wall Street. Clutching her briefcase, she ran to the edge of the sidewalk, pushing through the mass of pedestrians so she could stand in the road and yell 'Taxi!' at the top of her voice. She swore under her breath repeatedly as each successive Yellow Top flashed by, the drivers studiously ignoring her. Eventually, an empty one spotted her and swerved through three lanes to screech to a halt in front of her.

New York was suffering the tail end of its rush hour, and she had to travel all the way up to midtown, to Carnegie Hall. She told the driver to hurry, but her sense of urgency didn't impress him one iota. Sarah looked at her watch for the fifth time since leaving the building. She had sworn to David that she wouldn't be late and would meet him in the dressing room before his appearance. He was counting on her.

As the taxi weaved its way through the traffic on East Broadway and then north on to FDR Drive, she opened her briefcase and searched for her make-up. The powder compact had secreted itself inside a legal journal, her lipstick was buried in the morning's newspaper, and her eyeshadow in a couple of briefs she was handling for a colleague who was on holiday. It took every inch of concentration to make up her face. When she arrived at the Hall, she would have to rush straight into the auditorium if she was to have any hope of being there on time.

By the time the cab turned off FDR just before the Queensboro Bridge exit, she was already on to her hair. Fortunately the driver was one of those aggressively silent characters, whose only communication was an occasional grunt at other drivers. The last thing she needed was a driver who insisted on telling her the story of his life.

Sarah paid the cab off at the corner of 7th and W57th and ran to one of the doors of Carnegie Hall. How was it that the other ticket holders, still milling around in their hundreds, didn't feel the same sense of urgency? How were they able to arrive without a care, without sweating and swearing, casually walking from the subway or from parking lots as though they'd been preparing for this moment the entire day? Was she the only person who worked a crushingly long day, and then had to support her lover's career at night?

She joined the queue entering the assembly area. It was a warm summer night, the best that New York had to offer. Even the evil fumes of the traffic were subsumed by the strength of July's perfume. The trees were in blossom, and birds were twittering in the branches. Her mood became elevated, almost elated, until she thought of David, waiting anxiously for her, pacing the floor, needing her.

She found her way to her seat, sat and breathed deeply. She said a small prayer on David's behalf, closed her eyes and concentrated all of her memory on the way his face had looked in bed this morning, while he was still asleep. She hoped that by some paranormal phenomenon, he would feel her thinking about him, loving him.

By the time she opened her eyes, the lights were already dimming, the audience was falling into silence, and the conductor, a gaunt, studious man in white tie and black tails, was manoeuvring his path through the string sections to a rising level of applause. Behind him, nursing his Guarnieri cello as though it was a newborn baby, walked David Rose. Sarah applauded wildly and studied his face carefully. Was his frown one of nervousness, or just because the stage lights were still too high? Was he nervous? Should she cough to let him know she was there?

It was only his second appearance as a soloist at Carnegie Hall and, despite an afternoon spent in meditation, David walked into the auditorium in a state of anxiety. For the past hour he had been limbering the muscles of his arms and fingers, playing scales and practising the opening pages of the concerto. He'd been called fifteen minutes earlier, and had waited in the wings for the appearance of the Maestro, who squeezed him on the shoulders and quipped, 'The first thirty years are the worst'.

And then the walk-on. Sarah should have been there. He realised she'd been held up, and he understood, but it would have been nice for her to be in the wings to kiss him just before the walk-on. Or maybe not. Maybe on this night of nights, she wouldn't have been good for him. His body had taken over from his mind and was electrified, every fibre ignited by an almost uncontrollable urge to move or perform or sing or scream or . . . or make love. He'd often felt sexually aroused just before the walk-on, more alive than at any other time in his life. And the height of his arousal was his need to release the tensions in his body, tensions which he knew would disappear if he were to make love with Sarah. His sexuality would be the most potent, the most all-consuming of his life, but it was the strength of desire, the unconsummated urge, which gave passion to his music.

He could hear his and the conductor's feet treading noisily on the wooden floorboards, the only sound in the silence until the eruption of applause, for him as soloist, but mainly for the internationally acclaimed Maestro.

As they neared the podium, the orchestra members showed their appreciation also. The violinists and violists tapped their bows on the music stands; the brass, percussion and tympani players showed him similar respect and appreciation. At the front of the stage, the conductor shook hands with David, then they both bowed. The Maestro mounted the podium and bowed again, curtly, in recognition and appreciation of those who had travelled into the centre of the city to listen.

David also bowed, but rather more diffidently. His conductor, Carlo Felice Braganza, was an old hand at the music scene and had conducted most of the world's truly great orchestras. His appearance as guest conductor with the New York State Orchestra had drawn the huge crowd to Carnegie Hall, and for David Rose, a relatively young and still obscure cello virtuoso, to have been selected to play the Dvorak was a mark of singular honour. He had only been playing as a soloist for three years and had only twice been invited overseas. He bowed a second time, following the lead of the Maestro, who now turned to face his orchestra and gave David a nod, telling him to sit down and prepare to play.

David bowed to the audience one last time in nervousness, and took his cello over to his chair. He looked at the floor for an existing spike hole and drove his cello downwards so that it wouldn't slip during his performance. He held its finger board, its throat, close to his cheek, silently whispering to it for help to play perfectly in front of this large and important audience.

The Maestro held his baton high in the air and the coughs and shuffling of the audience came to a climax and then dropped suddenly to an absolute and oppressive silence. David searched the front three rows for Sarah. She looked flushed with pride. Then he looked upwards, to a dim and distant point in the far dark reaches of the hall, and concentrated on eternity. The last thing he wanted was to acknowledge the existence of the audience, and especially of Sarah within the audience. At this moment he didn't need any distractions.

He gripped the bow firmly, then relaxed his grip, like a golfer practising a swing before he addresses the ball. The conductor nodded to the oboeist, who played an 'A'. David fine-tuned his cello. Once he was satisfied, the Maestro nodded to his orchestra.

Silently, David muttered to himself, 'God help me, Antonin.'

In the sudden, nerve-numbing silence, David prayed that the phrases which he had heard so clearly in his mind earlier in the dressing room would still be as fresh and vital when the conductor raised his baton, and that the music would sound as sweet to the hundreds of people in the audience, hushed by the occasion, waiting for the opening strains of the cello concerto.

The Maestro's baton hand suddenly descended and the electrifying opening chords of Dvorak's great concerto for cello in B minor, his Opus 104, filled the hallowed auditorium of Carnegie Hall.

When the Czech composer wrote his concerto in America in 1894, he overcame many of the difficulties experienced by previous musicians. It was a stunning piece, an immediate success. Even Brahms had been heard to say, 'If I had known it was possible to write a cello concerto like this I would have done it myself long ago'. Dvorak, ever the genius, had given his soloist nearly four minutes of orchestral introduction to set the scene. Four precious minutes in which David could sit in front of the audience and caress his Guarnieri, seducing it, whispering into its ancient varnishes, begging it to be resonant, to help him amplify the genius of each note, each scale, each phrase of the towering work. Four blissful minutes to control his breathing, his heart rate, loosen the muscles that were tautening again under the tension of the spotlight. And then the trance began. He continued to stare at the point of eternity high up in the gods of the hall, and felt himself transpose from reality. He was removed from Carnegie Hall into a place of quiet and calm, where his mind and long-practised mantras took control of his body as he waited for the conductor to look towards him for his introduction.

His tensions abated. He felt at peace, listening to the phrases of the orchestra that he would be playing in his turn. David returned from his meditative state and began to listen carefully to the chords of the orchestra. He still had two more minutes in which to relive in his imagination the music which came from those first few opening strokes of the bow. In his mind, he saw his hand firmly executing the composer's instructions. He saw his left hand caressing the cello's throat, each finger pulsating to create just the right amount of vibrato. The music in his head began to resonate with the tones his imagination could hear coming from the instrument, until they were as one.

Now he was ready. Now he knew what would happen when the conductor and orchestra finished their glorious introduction and the imperious head of the Maestro turned towards him in expectation. Now, only now, were he and his instrument ready to respond fully with the dark sexual melody.

David looked at the conductor whose stern face had suddenly transmuted into that of a man enraptured. The score was open on the lectern in front of him, but he wasn't looking at it. Instead he joyously led the orchestra through the swelling bars, the first crescendo, then opened his eyes, looked towards David, smiled in encouragement and gave a tiny nod.

Only at that moment did David truly believe that he could play the piece. Only then did he and his instrument truly become one. Only then did his passion take over from his mind and the sexual tension became pure, unbridled bodily pleasure as the music, which was swelling in his heart, burst out to the audience in the opening allegro, a movement which made them strain forward in shock and pleasure, seeming to beg for more.

The moment Sarah heard his strong and confident introduction, her anxiety that David would play as perfectly and flawlessly as he had played every morning, afternoon and evening for the last four weeks disappeared. She offered a prayer of thanks to whoever in heaven was listening: 'Thank you God. Thank you angels, thank you everybody for making my beautiful and wonderful David play so brilliantly.'

She settled back in her seat and listened. His rendition was stern, authoritative, and yet at times had more than a tinge of impishness. Somehow David had found the subtle blend of the pomp and majesty of the Czechoslovakia of Dvorak and the gutsy, brash New World charm of the America for which the composer had written his classic piece.

Five or six minutes into David's solo the entire audience was with him; any nagging doubts about his youth or inexperience were put aside. Sarah sensed the mood in the auditorium and felt immense relief.

The phrases of the allegro opening movement rose and fell as David seduced his instrument to greater and greater heights. Sarah looked around the audience. Slowly it dawned on her that the rapt attention might be more than a love of music. Somehow she sensed an element of seduction going on here, as if David were making a move on another woman right in front of her. What the hell was happening? She looked back at her lover and listened even more attentively, watching his face closely. It was as though he was no longer there, as though his body was on the podium but his mind was floating on a plateau of ecstasy. His face seemed to glow in the warm lights of the stage, his hooded eyes those of a man enraptured. More than any other performance of his that she had witnessed, David appeared to be a part of his instrument and was commandeering the emotions of the audience. His music was of such passion, such intensity, that it seemed as if he was reaching out and caressing every man and woman in the auditorium, like Mephistopheles, seducing them to join him on his journey in search of . . . in search of . . . she didn't know.

She was surprised by the way in which his manner was changing minute by minute. There was an intensity, a fervent pulsation to his movements. His eyes were closed, his legs open to receive the body of the cello, his hands stroking her delicate throat. And the music which his lover made was the celestial harmony of the music of the spheres.

Sarah felt a flush of embarrassment at the unworthiness of her thoughts. More than unworthy, silly, childish, jealous. He was a cellist, for God's sake. He was doing his job.

But then she glanced at the woman beside her. Her mouth was slightly open, her lips moist, as she listened with such joy to David's playing. The look in her eyes was more than that of somebody concentrating on a fine performance. This woman, this stranger, had joined David in his sexual encounter with the music. And Sarah was jealous.

She berated herself for being stupid. It was a public performance of the Dvorak cello concerto, that was all.

Sarah turned and looked at another woman close by, whose eyes were glazed as she listened with the same rapt attention. As did a woman sitting two seats from her, and another and another. The men too were held by the music, but not with the same concentration, not with the same depth of feeling. It was the women who were experiencing the sexual union between her David and his cello. But he was her lover, not theirs!

Her lover in private, Sarah amended. When they were alone together, she shared with him the washing up, the shopping, the housekeeping, the bills and their bed. She bathed with him, nursed him when he was sick, and he was a considerate, decent and passionate lover with her.

She closed her eyes, trying to regain the confidence she had enjoyed yesterday and the day before. The music had all but disappeared from her mind. All she could think about was the unworthiness of her thoughts, of how David would feel if she ever expressed them. She thought of when they were in bed together, last night. They had made love, and he had stroked her body, touching her in all the places where she loved so much to be touched, opening her legs, kissing her, warming her, seducing her to greater heights. Just as he was seducing his cello now. In public. In front of all these people. Gently drawing out from its hidden and most private recesses its symphony, its song, its voice.

She bit her lip. She was being ridiculous. Why the hell was she jealous of a man who loved her so much? A man who was performing a piece which made every man and woman in the audience fall in love with him!

Sarah's eyes snapped open. God Almighty, could she ever attend another of his concerts?

# CHAPTER FOUR

Their needs were opposite. Tonight he needed noise and bustle, friends throwing their arms around his neck and kissing him, people coming up to him and reaffirming his talents, to enable him to descend from the heights to which he had been elevated by Dvorak. She needed to spend time alone with him, to be his guide, nurse and comforter, to be part of him rather than the umbra of his reflected glory.

'You know Sarah, don't you?'

'Hello, this is my friend, Sarah.'

'I couldn't have done it without Sarah pushing me every day.'

And she sat on the periphery, nodding, smiling and deprecating at his attempts to include her in his moment of triumph. Their social lives invariably intertwined but their professional lives were usually separate. David never usually enjoyed post-concert parties or revelries. He always played his best wherever he was, then preferred to retire to their home and to unwind in a warm bath or her loving embrace. But this was different. His spectacular success at Carnegie Hall was being lauded by others. The crown had passed down to him, and now all the acolytes were performing their obeisance. They had dragged him away to a nearby restaurant where they celebrated his status. It was even rumoured that Maestro Braganza might show up for dessert.

Sarah, who knew many of the musicians and publicity people from Carnegie Hall through her association with David, was invited along as an afterthought. She sat next to him through the dinner, smiling and nodding, kissing and accepting congratulations for being his girlfriend.

'Yes, he was brilliant.'

'We've been together for two years.'

'Of course I'm proud of him, deeply proud.'

She loved him so intensely that she was thrilled that at last he was being recognised for his brilliance, not only by audiences but also by his peers. But as the evening wore on, her mind kept drifting to her own dilemma, and she felt guilty for stepping out of his limelight. How could she be thinking of Joshua Krantz and the meeting tomorrow when she should be devoting every moment of her attention to David and celebrating his long-awaited recognition?

In the middle of the hubbub, Sarah realised that she was nervous. It was absurd. She was used to dealing with prominent people. Through her work, she had got to know judges, politicians, academics, people whose faces appeared regularly in the nation's newspapers, who performed on television panels and pontificated about society's ills on talk shows. New York's scintillating power community had blinded her at first, but she quickly got used to it and, from a close-up perspective, quickly perceived the flaws that most New Yorkers never got close enough to see. At thirty-one, she was no longer giddy around celebrities, so her nervousness at meeting Joshua Krantz for the first time was puzzling.

The following day, Sarah realised that her manner was strained, that she'd made more visits than usual to the coffee machine and that her instructions to her secretary were a little unfocused.

Joshua was going to have lunch in the boardroom of Friedlander, Abrahams, Stein & Goldfarb, after which he would have a conference with the senior partners and Sarah. By eleven in the morning, Sarah realised that she'd done so little that the pile in her in-tray had barely diminished. She had promised the advice she was working on to her partner, Jack Abrahams, by lunchtime at the latest. And there were trials in which she was about to appear that needed urgent attention. There was so much to be done that she'd have to work late into the night if tomorrow wasn't going to be a disaster.

Donna walked into her office, 'Coffee and valium?'

Sarah looked up in surprise, 'That obvious?'

Donna nodded. 'Same with the rest of the girls. Hey, we're talking Joshua Krantz! Current marital status, single. Looks gorgeous, and so sexy he rattles when he walks. Wealth in the billions, Hollywood lifestyle. Get my drift, girl? Who wouldn't be drooling? Marry him and you'll never have to queue for theatre tickets again.'

'You don't surely think that I'm . . .'

'If not, you're crazy. *MS* magazine called him the world's most eligible bachelor even when he was married to Angie Carr.'

'Which means he screws around,' said Sarah, more disdainfully than she intended.

'Which means he's a lifestyle all of his own.'

'Donna, I'm representing a client. Not looking for a husband.'

'Bullshit, girl! You can't tell me that you'll stay all cool and collected when Josh Krantz struts his stuff upstairs. I've seen him on the front cover of *Esquire* magazine. I'd lie down in the gutter if he'd walk over me.'

Sarah looked at her secretary's ebony face. It was impassive, impossible to determine if she really meant what she'd said. And it stayed that way, until Donna burst out laughing, her mirth filling the entire office.

'Hey, lighten up Sarah. Go with the flow. Sure he's a client, but he's your way in to meeting people like Harrison Ford and Michael Douglas. And when you do, you be sure to invite me to *that* dinner party.'

'Get out of here, will you. I've got serious work to do.'

An hour and a half later, Sarah received the call she'd been anticipating all day. Morrie's secretary invited her up to level 118 for lunch in the partners' dining room. As she headed for the elevators, secretaries and paralegals ribbed her goodnaturedly. Sarah escaped to the privacy of the elevator and realised that her heart was pounding. Surely it wouldn't be like this all the way through lunch?

The staff on the lower floor had to wait another hour and a half before the receptionist on level 118 phoned down to warn her counterpart on Sarah's level eight floors below that Sarah and Josh were stepping into the lift. The receptionist on the lower floor made a few pertinent telephone calls. Secretaries and some paralegals looked up in curiosity.

The doors of the elevator slid silently open and Sarah emerged, deep in conversation with a tall, thin, bearded, slightly but fashionably unkempt, character dressed in jeans, loafers and a polo shirt. He could have been a graduate student rather than one of the world's richest and most famous movie directors.

Sarah walked through the office, concentrating her focus on her own office door, talking about the issues they'd discussed over lunch. When they finally reached her office, she introduced Josh to Donna who asked, 'Can I get you a cup of coffee?' Her accent had become mid-Atlantic, rather than the deep Southern she was born with.

'I suppose mineral water would be out of the question?'

'Not at all,' said Donna brightly. 'Ice and a twist?'

Joshua beamed. 'That will do fine.'

They walked into her office and Sarah closed the door purposefully. She hadn't wanted to bring Joshua Krantz down to her office. Not that it wasn't attractive, and it had an interesting view of uptown New York, but it was modest in comparison to those of the partners. Morrie Friedlander had offered them the use of the boardroom but Josh had declined.

'I'd feel a lot more comfortable if I was working downstairs with Sarah,' he had told the managing partner. 'We need to roll up our sleeves and get down to some serious business.'

Morrie had demurred gracefully, but Josh was sharp enough to understand the subtext. He hadn't been into an associate partner's office for years, but he could still remember what one looked like, and that was where he wanted to be.

Josh sat in the utilitarian, tubular aluminium armchair and Sarah sat opposite him, the coffee table between them covered with briefs and law journals.

It was time for her to face reality, despite the instructions she'd been given by Morrie.

'I hope you enjoyed lunch.'

Josh smiled. 'You've got really nice colleagues. Different breed from LA lawyers. Here they're more genteel. All that Boston upbringing.'

She smiled, and hesitated. She was using the tactics of the courtroom – momentary delays, the potency of silence, in order to get the jury to concentrate on what she was going to say.

'I think there's a couple of things I'd like to bring out into the open, now that we're alone and I don't have my employers breathing down my neck.'

He smiled. He had a wonderful smile, gentle but masculine. Just the kind she loved to look at. Her first lover at college used to smile like that. Sarah looked at Josh's hands. They were long and thin. Sensuous hands, like David's.

She collected herself and forced her mind on to the issue she needed to raise before getting down to business. But before she could begin, he interrupted her.

'Sarah, I'd also like to lay something of a personal nature on the table, if we're going to work together successfully. I'm well aware of your philosophy, and I assume that you've argued with the guys upstairs that you'd find it difficult representing me. I know all about your feelings about going back to Europe. You made it very clear in your article. I also assume that your objections were overruled. But we're not adversaries, Sarah. I could buy all the yes men in America if I wanted to, but that wouldn't do me any good. My reading of you is that you tell it like it is, if you think I'm wrong, you'll tell me. Am I right?'

She nodded, surprised. That *was* going to be her approach. But there was something else.

'Yes, you're right. But it goes beyond that. There's something that I need you to understand clearly before we travel too much further down the road. I'm a trial lawyer. My speciality is getting people out of trouble. I stand up in courts of law, marshal facts and present them with force. I'm good at what I do, Josh, but I work in a very small arena. Despite your enthusiasm, I'm really not sure I'm the one you should be talking to. Morrie would kill me if he heard me say this, but you need an international lawyer, or somebody who's into property or corporate. Not me.'

He nodded and reached over to touch her shoulder.

'That's a good first step. Getting it out into the open,' he said. 'You think I don't know you're a trial lawyer? I deal with corporate lawyers all the time, Sarah. I know their strengths and, believe me, I know their weaknesses. What I need is an advocate. Somebody who isn't scared of in-your-face criticism. Okay?'

Sarah nodded. She had gone as far as she was willing to go, with statements that neatly blended her conscience with her career aspirations.

'Good,' he said. 'You know, in my own way, I suffer from much the same problems as you do. When I begin to read a script for a new movie, the first thing I do is give it to other people in the office, get lots of opinions. But there's always somebody who hates the script, who doesn't think it's a good subject or won't make money. That's the man or woman I argue with – not the ones who agree with me. We might spend hours discussing his or her objections, shouting and screaming at each other. And you know what? In the end, I come out understanding the movie a lot better. It sharpens my focus, makes me consider things I'd not realised.

'That's why I want you to represent me. Because you'll hone my ideas, sharpen my mind. I know I'm doing the right thing, Sarah, but you'll make me think laterally, question the obvious, make me re-evaluate my motivations. Your OpEd article made it clear where you stand. I disagree. You think the old world is dead and buried for Jews and that we shouldn't look back to it as our home, that it should be expunged from our racial memory.'

She interrupted, 'Not quite. What I argued was that it has a valid place as history, but that we Jews shouldn't look back on it as some sort of place where we were somehow more real or better Jews just because our parents and grandparents came from there. America's just fine for me. I think that after a thousand years of anti-Semitism it's time to accept the reality and pull down the shutters on Europe. My point is this: when the Jews were expelled from Judea by the Romans they settled comfortably in Arabia and in other parts of the Middle East. It was only when they went to Spain and then moved across Europe that they came head to head against the Catholic Church and all the anti-Semitism which that engendered.

'A thousand years, Josh. That's enough. It's time to accept that the Europeans, in general, can't stand Jews and don't want us around. And it's time for us to accept that Europe never was home. Not like America and Israel have become our homes. Why yearn to go back and look at the

Old Country when all the Old Country wants is to see us dead and buried?'

'You can't turn your back on a thousand years of Jewish history, Sarah.'

Sarah wanted to argue further, but her professionalism won out. 'We're getting into territory which we can talk about at another stage, Josh. Meantime I'm costing you two hundred dollars an hour and I'm here to do a job. We need to talk about your grandparents' house and how precisely we're going to get it back.'

Josh suddenly felt gratified in his choice of Sarah. She wasn't just lovely to look at and talk to, with captivating eyes and sensuous lips, but there was an honesty, a decency about her. Lawyers in LA were quite happy to discuss the weather as long as he was paying them double, often treble, Sarah's fee. Having a lawyer try to save him money was a unique experience.

He slumped back into the chair. She thought he might put his feet up on her coffee table.

'How can I put it? This thing of mine, this need to get my grandparents' property back, it's something I've been thinking of ever since I was at college, whenever I asked my Mum and Dad about our family history. Mum left Slovakia with some money. Her family sold their house and belongings and moved to the States. But Dad's family, theirs was a different story. Dad told me that his parents came from Eastern Slovakia, from a tiny little hick village thirty kilometres from the second biggest town in the country, a place called Kosice. South-west of Michalovce, and north-west of Trebisov. To put it into a geographical perspective, it's a stone's throw from the Ukrainian border and just north of the Hungarian border.'

Sarah picked up a pad and began writing notes.

'Don't bother taking this down, Sarah,' he said. 'I've had my people in LA write the whole scenario out for you, with maps and everything.'

She put her pen down and settled back. There was a knock at the door and Donna came in carrying a tray of coffee and mineral water and a plate of biscuits. The coffee was served in a porcelain cup and saucer borrowed from the partners' kitchen. My God, Sarah thought, they were really setting out to impress.

When Donna had left, Josh continued, 'Dad and his parents came from a town which today is called Novosad. It means New Town, but when he lived there, it used to be called Ujlak. Not far from where your family came from. See, I remember everything you wrote in the *Times*.'

Sarah failed to respond. She didn't want this to get onto a personal level. 'So all you want me to do is to bring proceedings against the current owners and occupiers to repossess the house for you? Take it back from its occupants. Not demand compensation or reparations or anything from the Slovakian government?'

'Yep.'

'And if there have been improvements to the property since your father and grandparents lived there, are you willing to compensate the new owner for the work he's done?'

Josh nodded.

'You're aware, of course, that this whole question of repossession of property is fraught with difficulties; that some European countries permit it, while others don't. It's a very grey area, especially when we're dealing with the former Czechoslovakia. They're very touchy about the subject, and they've received a lot of criticism because of it, especially from Germany. They've been accused of being racist.'

Josh looked at her in surprise. It was gratifying. She was on comfortable ground at last, acting the role of the lawyer.

'You see,' she continued, 'the Czech government was quite willing to negotiate for the return of stolen property to Czechs or Jews or others, but it refused to return property to the Sudetenland Germans, whom they booted out just after the end of the Second World War. You'll remember them from your schoolboy history. They were the people who lived in Czechoslovakia, but who threw flowers at the German tanks which rolled over the border at the beginning of the Second World War. The Czechs have never forgiven them.'

She looked closely at Josh, and decided that now was the best time to broach the question.

'Josh, Morrie Friedlander forbade me to ask you this, but I'm going to anyway. He said that I should be satisfied that you were doing this on principle. But I still have to know why. Why are you starting this whole thing? Sure, we can do it for you. Start a great big international legal challenge, make lots of noise. But you know as well as I do that, at the end of the day, the Slovakian government isn't going to let you walk in there and take back a house from one of its citizens. They'll tie you up in court for years and cost you millions. Even if you win, and I stress the word "if", what's the house going to be worth? A house that you would never even want to live in once you owned it. That's worth nothing. Surely there are other matters of principle that you could fight without going to the expense of all this, Josh.'

'You don't think we'll win?' he asked.

'I don't know. I'm not an international lawyer. Everything I've just told you came out of an afternoon's research in law journals in our library. I'm out of my depth. I don't know why you want me. We've got good people here that could help you. Why me? Just because I wrote some article in the paper?'

He sipped his water and smiled. 'I want you precisely because of that article in the paper, precisely because you've got such a high profile right now . . . and mainly because you've got the balls to sit here, against

Friedlander's instructions, trying to fire me as a client. That's why I want *you*, Sarah. Not the guys in suits upstairs.'

Sarah looked disbelievingly at him.

'It's you I want, Sarah! Your passion, your zeal. Of course I could use my own lawyers in Los Angeles, but they're just going to tell me what I want to hear. I've had a gut full of lawyers. Ever since I began making movies I've been embroiled in lawsuits. The more successful you are, the more lawsuits people throw at you. I've been accused of plagiarism, breach of copyright, breach of contract, paternity, every damn thing they can think of to try to extort money. I've had it up to my eyeballs with lawyers. But I saw the way you defended that bastard Darman, and what you wrote in the OpEd piece. There's a searing honesty about you which I find incredibly refreshing. I know you know nothing about international law, but if you want an opinion, you just flick your fingers and I'll have twenty of the country's best legal minds to advise you. You want to know about Slovak law, I'll have a team from Bratislava University support you. You want to know anything, I'll raise my eyebrow and it'll be there for you.'

Sarah eyed him suspiciously. Then she grinned and said, 'Remember what Henry Ford said? Somebody asked how he could run a large car company without a university education. He told them: "Who said I haven't got a degree. I've got ten PhDs and when I press the button on my desk, they all come running."'

Josh shrugged his shoulders. 'Henry Ford was a vicious anti-Semite.'

'So you want me. Fine! I'm not going to pretend I'm not flattered. And thrilled. And you want me to get back a valueless house your grandparents used to own. Fine. Just so long as we both admit that we know what's going on. The subtext is that you want to expose the Slovakian government, and the Hungarian, Russian, German and all the other European governments, for what they've done to the Jews during this century.'

He nodded sheepishly. It was endearing, but hardly appropriate. They were dealing with months of hard work, millions of dollars, and he was acting like a kid caught out by a school teacher.

'But it's still crazy, Josh. It's still pie in the sky. If the Slovak government lets you win this case, then there's a million American Jews, six million, I don't know, who are going to take lawsuits against the governments of Austria, Germany and all of the rest of those sons of bitches. They're going to want to get their family properties back. It's going to create a precedent which will cause the biggest property turmoil in the history of the world. How far are we going to go back? Will the Kurds get back Armenia? Will the Aborigines get back Australia? Will Inuits claim Canada, or Redskins demand back California? See what I mean? No government's going to allow that to happen.'

He eyed her sympathetically.

'Sarah, the Aborigines have got back parts of Australia, as have the Inuits their land, and the American Indians. Anything's possible. But the truth is that I don't even want the house back. I just want to make front page news.'

'But you are front page news,' she said.

'Yeah, but the front page is always about me. This piece of front page news is going to be about what the Slovaks and the people of the village did to my grandparents. How they kicked them out of their home they'd lived in for ten generations, how they stole from my family, how they turned their backs on them when the authorities came for them, how someone in their village sold them to the Stalinists for the crime of being Cosmopolitans and Jews. How they forced them to leave home in the black of night with only the clothes on their backs, how my grandmother stood on the roadside weeping, and my grandfather tried to protect my father who was little more than a kid. And all this, Sarah, just a couple of years after they'd struggled to build a life after somehow surviving concentration camps.

'Well, it's time for a bit of good old-fashioned, American-style retribution. I'm sending in the Marines. Because I'll tell you what's going to be on the front page of papers all around the world – people are going to be reading all about the grandson's revenge. About how the grandson of Moishe and Vilma Krantz stormed back into town and threatened every motherfucker in the place. Exposed them and their sins for what they did to my family and the families of millions of other Jews. I'm going to turn on one of my arc lights so that the whole world can see their shame and their guilt.'

Sarah felt the passion in him, saw that his eyes were focused on a distant point outside her window. She realised she had been holding her breath while listening to him, just as she had done when David had begun to play the Dvorak cello concerto.

# CHAPTER FIVE

Sarah's breakfast on a workday morning usually took less than ten minutes. But, as she skimmed the pages of the *New York Times* and came to the article, all thought of food left her mind. She held her coffee cup motionless at chest height until she had read to the story's end. Her coffee cup maintained its altitude until she had finished the entire story a second time, just to be certain she wasn't hallucinating. A flush of anger, then frustration, came over her. Two weeks work down the drain!

Sarah heard David leave the bathroom, and called to him, 'Come here. I think I'm going crazy.'

Naked, and smelling pleasantly of soap, he padded into the kitchen and looked at the article.

'Oh, shit,' he said quietly.

'My thoughts precisely. This blows any advantage we may have had.'

Sarah finished her breakfast, though her appetite was seriously diminished, and got a cab to the office. There was a message from Morrie Friedlander asking her to see him the moment she arrived.

She was shown into his office without any of the usual formalities. As she walked in, he slapped the paper down on his coffee table.

His voice was measured and stern. 'I can only assume that you had nothing to do with this?'

'Of course not. He got his PR agency or whatever to do it. He's crapped on us from a considerable height. Now everybody knows. Including the Slovakian government.'

'I've been trying to get hold of him, but it's only five in the morning over there. His phone's on divert. Jesus! What a disaster. We'll have to call a partners' meeting first thing. I want you to bring everybody up to date and stay for the discussion. Between us we'll come up with something.'

Sarah nodded.

Over the next half hour, each and every partner of the firm was told to cancel all appointments, no matter how pressing. Within an hour, Sarah was standing at the head of the table, presenting most of her work during the past two weeks: Slovakian law, international treaties and a myriad of other details necessary to prepare the case properly.

Half a dozen open copies of the *Times* lay on the boardroom table, each turned to the same page. The headline, **TOP MOVIE DIRECTOR IN QUEST FOR RETURN OF GRANDPARENTS' SLOVAK HOME**, ran across two pages. The meeting had a certain surreal feeling, as though they were media critics discussing the treatment of a fast-breaking story, instead of lawyers wondering how to rescue their firm's reputation and their client's case.

'There are two areas we shall not be exploring this morning,' said Morrie Fridlander, when Sarah completed her report. 'One is firing the client. The second is responding in the media. If a newspaper calls, I'll give them a "no comment" and the matter should die in the next forty-eight hours ... in America. What the hell damage he's done to us in Slovakia is anybody's guess. Now, any observations? Or better, any brilliant suggestions for how to tell our megastar client that this is one project he's not directing?'

Jack Abrahams was the first to respond. Sarah was his direct responsibility, and he was closer to the action than any of the other partners, so was at less of a loss than them.

'I think Morrie may be a lot closer to the truth than any of us believe. Since the moment he walked in here, it's been as if Josh Krantz is on some movie set. Lately I've been getting the feeling that we're all bit players in his grand scheme. This –' Jack pointed to his copy of the *Times* '– seems to prove it. He's running his own agenda, calling his own shots. And this firm is his cast of extras. God knows, it's great publicity, but the PR campaign wasn't meant to start until Sarah had set things in motion in Slovakia. Going public so soon could have horrendous repercussions.'

'Catastrophic,' Morrie responded. 'The Slovakian government could refuse to issue visas. They could refuse permission to anybody from our firm to perform work in the country. If they don't, they could easily refuse Sarah, or the law firm we employ over there, access to government records. This could tie us up in knots, even make the case unfightable. Damn!' he hissed. 'This publicity shouldn't have happened for weeks. It could have been a gold mine for us, put us on the front page of every damned newspaper if we'd handled it properly. But right now it could jeopardise everything.'

The partners remained silent, wondering what course of action to take. Jack looked at Sarah.

'I think you'd better go to Bratislava immediately. Today if possible, tomorrow at the latest. Get in before the Slovak government has a chance to react. If they're like the Russians or the Poles, it'll take them weeks before they realise what's going to hit them.'

Sarah blanched in surprise. 'Now? I can't go now, Jack. I have commitments.'

But Morrie nodded in agreement with his partner, 'Jack's right. Pack your bags and leave immediately. Get our travel department to organise everything you need. Top priority.'

Sarah thought about her responsibilities, especially towards David. The interviews that he wanted her to practise with him, the performances he was due to give, the dinner parties, the social arrangements. Then she looked at the partners and realised that her private life meant nothing to them.

She returned to her office, and checked the time in LA. It was still early morning over there, but by now she was sure that Josh would be conscious. She dialled his number. It was answered by one of his Filipino maids. Within a moment, she was talking to her client.

'Hope I haven't disturbed you,' she asked.

'You're phoning because you're pissed with me. Right?'

'I don't understand,' she said, trying to sound ingenuous. She'd been told how to handle it by Morrie, but, as usual, Josh seemed to have a sixth sense about these things.

'Sure you do. The story in the *Times*. Are your partners apoplectic? Is Morrie purple in the face and clutching his heart?'

Sarah tried not to smile. David had once told her that her facial expression was so often reflected in her voice.

'He and the other partners are a bit concerned about your sidebar campaigns. Naturally they'd prefer you to leave the strategy to us. But that's really your business, Josh. I'm only here to do the law thing.'

'You are pissed with me. Morrie I don't care about. You, I care.'

'Josh, I'm not pissed with you. But you're making my job a lot harder. This isn't some movie we're doing with preproduction hype. There are some very serious implications here. If we make it to a court, especially an international body of justice, the judges aren't going to be too impressed with reading all about it in the *Hollywood Reporter*.'

'I'm doing it for very good reasons, Sarah. I'll tell you about them next time we meet. I'm fighting those mothers on several battlegrounds. Yours is only one of them.

Publicity and political pressure on our State Department are a couple of others. I've thought this through very carefully, Sarah. I know what I'm doing.'

'Josh, I think I ought to let you know that I'm going to Slovakia immediately. I did tell you right at the beginning that part of your costs would have to include my travelling to . . .'

'Can you make it next week?'

'No. Next week will be too late. This publicity of yours could force the hand of the Slovakian government. They may refuse us a visa.'

'Not a hope in hell. I've checked it out. It would be against their interests to do that and could put them in jeopardy of international treaties. They're keen to deal with the United States, and they're lobbying for most favoured nation status right now. That's why I've put my toe in the publicity sea. I've put them on notice. We've got them cornered.'

Sarah didn't know about any of this. She felt like a pawn in a chess game. She felt for her amulet, and began to trace its outline with her fingers. But she was puzzled about what he'd just said. 'Why next week?'

'Because this week I'm in a series of meetings which I don't want to cancel. Anyway, the cameraman I want to use is in Canada right now.'

'Cameraman? What are you talking about?'

He ignored her. 'If we all go over to Slovakia together, it'll be a whole heap more convenient. I'll make the travel arrangements. My studio owns a travel agency.'

'You? What are you talking about? Josh, I'm going alone. There are some delicate negotiations to conduct, lawyer to lawyer. You can't come with me! I have to go there alone. You can go over another time, separately.'

'Wanna bet!'

'Joshua, I'm serious. This isn't a game . . .'

'And I'm serious, Sarah. See you at the airport.'

He hung up the phone, and wondered what colour Morrie's face would be when Sarah told him the latest bit of news.

For Sarah, just being in Prague was a surreal experience, as though she was a part of, and yet distinct from, the mass of humanity which flowed around her. A rock holding firm against the onrushing torrent of a flooding river. She stood on the Charles Bridge, looking up towards the imperious outline of Prague's Hradcany Castle, its walls shimmering in the warm evening air, dominating the city.

Yet as Sarah gazed up at it, what struck her most forcibly was not the gothic heaviness of the fortifications, but the exquisite lightness of the entire structure. She'd seen castles in Britain, monumental structures which dated back to medieval and Elizabethan times. While they, too, could only be classified as overpowering, they seemed to lack a human dimension. But not so Hradcany. Even from far below, standing just above the waters of Smetana's musical river, she sensed the grace of the burdened walls and the buildings which were encompassed by them. And her feeling of lightness, of being a witness to the glories of the castle, was enhanced by the thousands upon thousands of tourists streaming past her.

But, while she appreciated the beauty of the castle, Sarah was in no mood for fun. Even before she had landed in Prague, tension had begun to suffuse her body. As she left the plane, the first thought which struck her was that this was 'old Europe'. A Europe which was artistically and culturally peerless, with magnificent buildings and wondrous creativity, the zenith of humanity's intellectual and social achievements for two millennia. But Sarah was determined not to be a fawning sycophant to the genius of the old. She looked beyond the literature, the architecture, the paintings, the triumphal music and saw the hidden, black heart within that arrogant, powerful body. Ever since hearing the stories of the brutalisation of her family, told by her mother and grandmother, Sarah had viewed Europe as a hostile environment, an alien place in which she would never willingly set foot. It was a place in which her people had been tortured and exterminated; a place which had perpetrated the most heinous crime in all of history against her people.

Yet at the behest of commerce and the insistence of her employers, here she was in Prague, standing on the ancient Charles Bridge with its facing rows of statues.

Sarah and Josh had begun the legal process in Slovakia, by initiating their matter with one of Bratislava's largest and most prestigious law firms, who promised to report back on the feasibility of the project within a week. Rather than wait around for results from a punctilious European law firm, Sarah had decided they should fly to Prague where she could determine the Czech government's legal liability. When the house was sequestered, it had been in Czechoslovakian territory. Even the Bratislava law firm thought her visit was a good idea.

But, to everybody's surprise, Sarah's particularly, Joshua suddenly announced that he wouldn't be spending time in Prague; he was going off alone on a pilgrimage to find his family's former home in Novosad, the new Slovakian name for the town of Ujlak.

Now, alone in Prague and with time to herself to think, something occurred to Sarah. It was odd how the shifts in hegemony changed the name of a place, yet the culture of the people continued as if nothing had happened. She was sure that shifts in borders or changes in place-names meant little, if anything, for the people who lived there. But not so with the Jews. They had to change with changing circumstances, had to uproot themselves and move on at the whim of a king, or Pope, or overlord. And, in whatever new land accepted them, they changed their dress, their culture and their ways in an effort to blend in with the surrounding dominant society, asking only to be left alone to pray to their God in their own way with dignity and in peace.

When Sarah had questioned Josh about why he was going to Novosad alone, he'd told her that, now they were in the second stage of their mission, he was quite happy to leave her and his film crew in Prague. What he craved, he told her, was solitude and isolation. He needed to be alone in the country which had been so hostile to his father and his grandparents. He needed to go back alone to the home in which his family had once lived before being so mercilessly expelled and fleeing to America.

Sarah had expressed her misgivings about being left alone to lead the assault on the government, but Josh had reassured her. 'Sarah, you're heading up a formidable team of lawyers. You're doing a fantastic job, but you're not here to do their work for them; all I want is for you to ensure that they do what we want. Delegation – that's what it's all about. Which means that I can go off and do my thing, while you keep on these guys' backs and make sure they come up with the right answers. Anyway, what's changed? Before we left the States, you didn't want me to be part of the law thing. Don't tell me you're starting to rely on me!'

She'd glanced at his face, but it was giving nothing away. She allowed his question to go unanswered. The truth was, she didn't know the answer. What she *did* know was that during the week they'd been in Bratislava, delving into areas of European law about which she knew practically nothing, his presence and his encouragement had been both supportive and welcome. Only occasionally, when she deferred too often to the preference of Dr Benzes – the Slovakian lawyer leading their team – for compromise rather than attack, did he haul her back into line, reminding her that he was paying the bills and that things would be done his way.

Alone in Prague, the cat away, Sarah should have felt like a schoolgirl on holiday. But she didn't. She felt alone, and somewhat overwhelmed. She and Josh's camera crew spent the first night exploring the narrow, cobbled laneways of the Old City. They all bought Bohemian glass, and Sarah purchased an exquisite gold nameband for David, something that she'd been meaning to buy in America, but which she never seemed to have time to purchase. Here, the craftsmanship and the price were much more acceptable.

The laneways were like Fifth Avenue on the night before Christmas. Thick streams of people meandered slowly along the narrow roads, cars inched their way forward, nudging aside irritated pedestrians, and musicians walked back and forth, playing guitars and violins in return for a few coins, emulating what the tourists hoped were Bohemians. The warm summer air was full of perfume and petrol and music, a heady brew.

Sarah was fascinated by the vitality of the streets, the beauty of the shops, all encompassed in an area with such a wealth of history. Suddenly, as she was looking into a shop window, she heard bloodcurdling accusations and shouts of anger coming from a nearby laneway. Sarah looked around in horror. In New York, such anger could so easily presage the sound of gunshots, with innocent pedestrians falling screaming to the pavement. But the screams and curses hadn't affected the rest of the pedestrians, who continued to walk along calmly. And as she listened and the sounds grew closer and closer, she realised that it was nothing more than the theatre of Prague's nightlife. Then, around the corner burst a dozen or so young men and women, some garishly dressed, others looking like beggars, the men in battered suits and trilbies, the women in flounced skirts and low-cut beaded blouses. They shouted and screamed at each other at the tops of their voices, threatening, laughing, ridiculing and whistling. Sarah looked at them in astonishment. They completely ignored the fact that there were people around them, behaving as though they were isolated, not part of the crowd. And they look swarthy, unkempt and uncaring – as though they were outcasts with no dignity left to lose.

Jerry, the soundman, saw her looking at them, and walked over to her. 'They're Tziganes, Romany gipsies. Pretty fuckin' dangerous. Don't mess with them. They just spend their time wandering through Mala Strana and Stare Mesto. They don't give a fuck about you, provided you don't give a fuck about them. Good policy.'

Sarah nodded and watched them troop noisily towards the Charles Bridge. The passage they created through the crowds quickly repaired, and cosmopolitan life returned to normal. She wondered how Jerry knew about them. One day he might tell her. In the week that she'd been travelling with him and his colleague Phil, who operated the camera, she'd come to realise that they were phlegmatic, giving away no information which wasn't absolutely necessary. Sarah had grown to enjoy them. They were so different from the garrulous Joshua Krantz. They looked like a couple of American social misfits, returnees from the Vietnam war who hadn't made a smooth homecoming. They'd spent their time so far filming background shots of Bratislava while Sarah and Josh were in conference and, on one memorable occasion, had been invited into the law offices to film a conference. Dr Benzes, his colleagues and their ultra-conservative staff had shifted around uncomfortably under the heat of the lights, speaking awkwardly in monotones when Jerry's micro-phone was held towards them. Jerry and Phil had behaved with complete aplomb, treating the lawyers as though they were ingenuous starlets. Josh had explained them away by saying he was making a documentary, but Sarah knew that he was sticking the New World right up the ass of the Old. And she adored him for it.

Since then, wherever Josh went, Jerry and Phil accompanied him, filming and recording impressions, views, vistas as well as Josh and Sarah walking down streets, sitting in cafés, even their private conversations and thoughts about the day's events in their hotel bedrooms at night. At first, Sarah had been put off by them, but she'd quickly got used to their perpetual company; now she felt strange if they weren't there. And, even after a week, she still didn't know their surnames.

After their meal, Sarah said that she would wander back to the hotel to make some calls to America. The men decided to spend the evening visiting the famous Magic Lantern theatre. They parted, but Sarah didn't go straight back; instead she decided to visit St Nicholas's Church in Mala Strana, to listen to a concert she'd seen advertised on posters around the old city. The first piece was a serene Bach harpsichord concerto; its voice resonated throughout the lofty church. It was Bach as Sarah had never before heard him played. His church music was usually performed inside huge imposing concert halls, but now, for the first time, Sarah was hearing him in the intimacy of a place of worship. It gave his music a new, devotional sound.

The second piece, by Mozart, was a transcription for chamber orchestra of the *Overture to Don Giovanni*, a homage by the musicians to its first performance in Prague. This was so utterly different to the Bach and, despite the thinness of the chamber sound, it was rich, gutsy and earthy. But it was during the final work, Dvorak's *Hymn of the Czech Peasants*, that Sarah was transported back to America. In it, she heard resonances of the composer's cello concerto, which had recently launched David into such giddy national and international prominence. She should be with him now, to support him as people clamoured for his attention, there by his side to advise and console him as competing voices whispered into his ears.

But instead she was here, at the behest of a pampered and over-rich flaky Hollywood 'man on a mission', waiting for legal experts in Bratislava to get back to her and for Josh to complete his 'moment of solitude and contemplation' whatever the hell that might be.

Sarah wandered out of the church, thinking about the day. When Josh had left, she'd felt uneasy, as though she was wasting his money, doing nothing in Prague. She'd called Morrie Friedlander and told him her concerns, but Morrie had asked her the pertinent and obvious question: 'Is Josh happy with what we're doing?' She'd been forced to answer that he was indeed happy; that at the end of the week, when their business had finished in Bratislava, Josh had taken her to dinner and told her how impressed he was and how much confidence he had in her.

'There's your answer,' her boss had responded. She knew he was only counting the dollars.

It was late now, and Sarah was tired. She should be getting back to the hotel to sleep, but something in the atmosphere told her she was on holiday, and that it was okay to relax and enjoy herself.

She walked down the steep laneways of the old city of Mala Strana along the banks of the Vltava, then over the Charles Bridge. Halfway across her lighthearted mood was crushed by the spectre of the ancient hatreds she so dreaded. On the left-hand side of the bridge was a huge bronze crucifix; there was something terribly wrong about it, something out of place. Then staring closely at it, she felt a sudden shock, as if somebody had punched her in the stomach. For there, clearly and indelibly written in a semi-circle below the Cross upon which a martyred Christ was suffering, was a sentence in Hebrew. *Hebrew!* On a Crucifix! Sarah looked in horror at the defilement of her people's language. Words which Jews for thousands of years had spoken in reverence and devotion to God, the one true God, were now brutally and permanently attached to the symbol of the suffering of a Messiah for another faith. She read the Hebrew words, outlined clearly and mockingly in gold leaf: '*Qadosh, qadosh, qadosh, Adonoi t'zvaot . . . Holy, holy, holy is the Lord of Hosts.*' She felt sick at the very sight of it. It represented everything she had feared about coming to visit Eastern Europe; it was a parody of everything she believed in, everything that made her different, gave her her identity. What kind of obscenity was this, to be paraded so visibly?

Instinctively, as she always did when happy or sad, frustrated or elated, she reached up to touch her amulet. It was an anchor in the whirlwind of emotion that careened around her, a rock on which her feet sought desperate stability. Forcing her way through the slowly meandering river of people to the side of the bridge, Sarah supported herself against the railing. She felt sick to her stomach. With shaking hands, she opened her guidebook and read the story of the Jewish merchant in Prague who, in 1696, had been found guilty of blasphemy and had been forced by the city fathers to erect a statue in homage to Catholicism whilst at the same time made to pay for the ridicule of his own faith.

Reading of the humiliation, Sarah felt a profound anger welling up inside her. The numbness which she'd felt when she first saw the holy Hebrew letters mocked by the crucifix had vanished; now she felt provoked, stung by the insensitivity of those who kept the obscenity there, even polishing the gold letters so they shone in the bright light of day. They'd pulled down all the statues of Stalin and Lenin; why couldn't they have pulled down this piece of anti-Semitic mockery?

She scrutinised the faces of the tourists on the bridge. They passed the monument, giving it a cursory glance, failing like her to be outraged at its significance. Did none of these other people recognise the desecration of the Jewish faith or sense its disempowerment? Angry beyond words, Sarah examined her responses. Was she over-reacting? In front of her was exactly what she had always feared about Europe, why she had resisted going on the traditional tour when her parents had encouraged her as a schoolgirl and as a college student. Instead she had taken holidays in Mexico, Australia and Canada, countries where the government was largely free of the stain of anti-Semitism. Watching the terrifying growth of neo-Nazism, and listening to the self-righteous cant and hypocrisy of Frank Darman had forced Sarah to write the OpEd article for the *New York Times*, which in turn had led Josh Krantz to employ her, which was why she was currently in Europe, where every ounce of her being told her she should not be.

Sarah spent a restless night, sleeping fitfully. She was desperate for David, for somebody to talk to about her emotions. The following morning, judging the time carefully, she picked up the phone in her hotel room and called him.

'You're lucky you caught me. I was just leaving to go to a rehearsal.'

She checked her watch. 'At this time of night?'

'It was the only time we could arrange for all the trio to get together.'

'How's it going?' she asked.

'The usual temperamental bullshit,' he said. 'But I've noticed every time Conrad plays an arpeggio on his violin, his bow comes perilously close to Michael's ear. I'm scared we're going to have to rush him to an ear surgeon to have it extricated.'

It was so good to hear David. She'd spoken to him three or four times since leaving New York, but had been so bound up in meetings with lawyers and government officials in Bratislava that she'd forgotten how important hearing his voice was.

'I'm missing you fiercely,' she said. 'Odd, isn't it? We've been together so long and it only takes a week of separation for me to miss you badly.'

She could feel him smile across the continents. 'Well, you know what to do to make our relationship permanent,' he said.

She was so close to saying yes, it would be so easy, but living with David gave her a feeling of independence that she craved, especially after the stifling environment of her childhood. Marriage might change all that. And, at the moment, why take the risk?

'Darling, not now. Let's not get into that.'

'Need I remind you how many of your current insecurities would miraculously disappear overnight if you'd only agree to marry me.'

'David . . .'

'Hey, just kidding. It's called "advancing my own cause". Anyway, I really do have to go.'

He said goodbye and hung up. Sarah sat for a long time in her armchair, receiver in hand, staring out of the window. Her room faced the ancient and enduring River Vltava. Across the city, in the distance, were the walls of Prague castle. She felt a sudden sense of comfort as she looked at them. Last night, from the Charles Bridge and from Mala Strana, she had looked up to them, feeling overwhelmed. But here, in the security of her hotel room, twenty storeys up, paid for by a wealthy American and backed by the resources of a New York law firm a citizen of a government which kowtowed to no one nd which would fight for her tooth and nail if she was in trouble, she felt on a level with those powerful people across the river. Here she could look them in the eye here, she had substance.

It was still early in the morning, but Sarah phoned to check in with her Prague law firm. A secretary told her that the lawyer she'd briefed was researching the matter in City Records and would return her call as soon as he was able. Curtly she told the secretary to inform him that it had been two days, and she would expect answers very soon. Sarah wanted to let him know who was boss. It was a game they played in New York; perhaps it would have a different effect in the Old World.

Then she phoned the Ministry for Justice, to be told the same thing as the secretary in Bratislava had told her, though with somewhat more official aggression. Despite the fact that the Czech Republic was the most open and cosmopolitan of former Russian satellites, the ministry officials were under the impression that they could still apply Communist intransigence in their dealings with the West. This annoyed Sarah. When they told her 'it couldn't be hurried', she demanded to know why. When they said it would have to wait, she gave them a time limit. She told them she'd contact their immediate superior if they didn't move on her request, and if that failed, she'd get straight onto the country's most senior law officer.

Next she called her lawyers in Bratislava who said that they hoped very soon to have papers ready to serve on the Slovakian government. No, she told Dr Benzes forcefully. 'Soon' was not good enough. They needed to be ready by the end of the week, or she'd take the matter out of their hands. By the end of the three calls Sarah was feeling a whole lot better than she'd felt the previous night. She looked at her watch and realised it was still fairly early in the morning; she also realised that she had nothing to do for the rest of the day.

It was ridiculous. She was costing Josh a small fortune to sit on her ass waiting for other people to get off theirs. She'd given them an American shake-up in the best East Coast tradition, but couldn't judge their response. There was something serpentine, something coy and underhand in the way they tried to pacify her. Well, screw them. Tomorrow morning, first thing, she'd phone them all again to check on progress. If they didn't like it, tough! To hell with the niceties of European protocol. They were dealing with an American lawyer, and they'd better get used to it.

Her musings were interrupted by the telephone.

'Yo, Sarah.'

She smiled; it was Jerry, the soundman. She found his Southern accent hard on her ears, and knew that much of it was put on for her New York-Brooklyn benefit.

'You finished your law shit yet? Phil and me, we're going to grab a Bud. Wanna come?'

'Isn't it a bit early for a drink?' she asked. 'It's only nine thirty.'

'Time we get served, it'll be well after lunch. See you downstairs in fifteen. Oh, and bring a change of underwear.'

The phone disconnected. She was astonished. Then it dawned on her what Jerry had meant. Smiling, she dressed quickly and walked downstairs. The two men were standing in the foyer, dressed in vividly coloured tops and obscenely baggy shorts. They looked like escapees from a 1970s Beach Boys movie.

'You're going to Ceske Budejovice, aren't you?'

Jerry smiled. 'In one. Home of the Bud. Greatest beer in history.'

'Ever since I was a kid, my old man's been pumping me with Budweiser. Going to where it came from is a sort of pilgrimage,' said Phil. 'I'm going to sit in the café where Bud's made and write to my dad to tell him that his son finally came good.'

Sarah wished them a good trip and explained that even if she did drink beer, she didn't think a seven-hour return bus trip justified the experience.

Sarah had other plans for the morning, centred around Prague's old Jewish quarter, Josefov. There was a particular site that she wanted to visit there, a memory from her youth, a distant legend told to her in childhood which had become a part of her adult present. She walked out of the hotel into a beautiful summer's morning, and made her way to Josefov.

The streets were narrow and condensed, just as they were in other parts of Old Prague, but here Sarah didn't experience the same sense of alienation. Here she was amongst those buildings and artefacts which belonged to her own people, and her sense of strangeness evaporated within the walls of the old ghetto.

She found her way to the Old Jewish Cemetery, founded in the early 1400s and now Europe's oldest surviving monument to dignity in the face of unprecedented humiliation. Although the cemetery hadn't been used as a burial place since 1787, it still held an air of mourning, of solemnity and of the eternal values in which she believed. Some twelve thousand gravestones were visible, heaped abstractly and crowded together in piles; but beneath those piles of gravestones were an estimated hundred thousand more graves, buried deep in the ground, one on top of the other, a monument to the overcrowding of the Prague ghetto over the centuries.

She would allow herself the luxury of a tour when she was ready, but right now she made her way, almost by instinct, to a grave where, even early in the morning, a group of men and women were gathered, silently reading the inscription. All of the men wore skull caps, the women scarves. Being a modern American Jewess, Sarah had come without a scarf. She hoped she wouldn't offend anybody.

She walked to the grave and, through the press of people, read the inscription. It was the grave of Rabbi Judah Loew, the theologian and mystic better known as the Maharal of Prague. This was the man around whom the legend of the golem had been created, the creature without a soul fashioned from dust whose purpose was to serve the impoverished Jewish community of Prague and defend it from attack and from the blood libels so common in the Rabbi's day.

The Maharal had been feted for the creation of the golem, which could be controlled by the insertion under its tongue of an amulet engraved with the name of God. But disaster struck the community when, one day, Rabbi Loew forgot about the amulet in the creature's mouth. And so, for the first time in its existence, the creature without a soul listened to the men and women praying during a Friday afternoon service. It was enchanted by the beauty. It reasoned that it should participate, because it believed that it was Jewish; but when the doors remained closed despite its frantic knocking, the creature became infuriated and ran amok. The Jews of Prague sat terrified in their Synagogue while the golem, in its fury, began to tear apart the community in which it lived. The Jews were forced to destroy the creature before it destroyed them; its remains were reputed to be still entombed in the attic of the Old/New Synagogue in Josefov.

The legend had always had a strong impact on Sarah, just as it had affected writers such as Kafka and Mary Shelley before her. Sarah contemplated the tombstone and thought about how the legend was as fresh today, as meaningful and relevant, as it had been nearly half a millennium earlier when the Maharal had created it. She touched her amulet and wandered out of the cemetery, back into alien Prague.

# CHAPTER SIX

### Ujlak, South-eastern Czechoslovakia: 13 June 1951

Moishe Krantz stood in front of his bedroom mirror and admired himself. Not bad, he thought, for somebody my age, for somebody who's been through what I've been through. Some grey hair, but not all that much. And still handsome enough to attract admiring glances from some of the ladies – despite everything.

He decided that he should straighten his hair. He gently combed the curly sidelocks, his *payos*, as he had done every Friday night for as long as he could remember. He experienced a moment of concern when he realised that the Almighty had probably heard his little bit of vanity. The Almighty heard everything, didn't He? He straightening the greying strands and, on closer inspection, noted with disapproval that his hair was thinning more rapidly than he thought; there were fewer strands than last week. So much for his moment of vanity – the Lord had taken care of that! God gives, and God takes away. Fifty years old. Well, at least he still had his own teeth.

It was a hot night, following a blisteringly hot and airless day, and the inside of the shop had been like an oven. He had been forced to keep the door open all afternoon but even so, there hadn't been the slightest hint of a breeze stirring the leaves of the trees right outside his shop's front door. All that had happened was that a swarm of flies had found their way into the shop and spent the afternoon buzzing around, sounding like a hysterical percussion band. Business hadn't been good that day because of the weather. In fact, since the madman in Moscow went over the edge of sanity, both business and the weather had been awful.

He picked up his newly starched white shirt, freshly ironed by Vilma. God bless her. Always when he finished work on *shabbos*, his bath would be run, his clothes ironed and a freshly starched handkerchief laid out, so that when he said the Friday night prayers the old week would be put properly behind them, and all the family would welcome in their bride, the Sabbath, with boundless joy and enthusiasm. He bit his lip in anguish. All the family. All that were left! So few. He muttered silent memorial prayers for his children and his brothers and sisters. How many years were they dead now? Seven years. Seven long years since he'd returned from Buchenwald and the labour camp, and still the grief and the pain didn't grow any easier.

The last he ever saw of his younger children was in 1944. Seven terrified little boys and girls being forced to climb onto the tray of a lorry. His wife, Vilma, was forced into another lorry with other women from the village, young and old. He begged a German guard to tell him where she was going. Auschwitz, the man had said with an evil smile. It was enough. He knew he would never see her again, especially when another guard told him that he was being sent to Buchenwald. People didn't return from Auschwitz or Buchenwald. It was a death sentence.

But, by some miracle, he and his oldest son, Hermann, only stayed for three months in that hellhole which was Buchenwald. Both were strong, and because Germany needed men for the slave factories they were taken to a labour camp. Hermann was only thirteen and he almost died from exhaustion, carrying huge stones and breaking rocks with a sledgehammer he could hardly lift. But somehow, through his indomitable will, the boy survived and when the camp was liberated by the Americans, the two of them trudged their skeletal way back to Ujlak. Their shop, their family home of generations, was a nest of rats. It had been used as a urinal by passers-by. Nothing which Moishe had once treasured was left, not a *tallis*, a *yarmulka*, a set of *tefillin*, no photographs . . . all gone.

The neighbours were kind. Slowly, painfully, Moishe and Hermann ate what little they could find, or beg for, and began the process of restoring their bodies. And with their growing strength came the ability to begin repairing their home. For months after their return, father and son looked out of the window every day, hoping to see their family again. For months they wrote letters to the Red Cross and the occupation authorities in Berlin, and for months nothing, until one day a neighbour came running excitedly and told Moishe that his wife had returned. She had been seen on the main road into their village. Wasn't it wonderful!

Moishe, already dead inside, failed to respond to the news about his wife. All he asked was, 'And my children?' But the neighbour shook his head. Seven long years, yearning each day to go into their bedrooms to see them sweetly asleep, kiss their heads.

Vilma called from downstairs, rousing Moishe from his thoughts: 'Moishe, the table's set and I'm lighting the candles. Come now.' He tried to hide the emotion in his cracking voice and told her that he would be down in a moment. He fastened the buttons of his clothes, polished his shoes with a rag, straightened his *shabbos* homburg and descended the stairs to the family living quarters behind the shop. He paused on the bottom step and bit his lip, to stop himself from crying. Every Friday night, before the war, he had descended these stairs. Halfway down, he would be greeted by the joyous faces of his wife and children who would come from all over the house for the touching ceremony. He never found out what happened to his wife while she was in Auschwitz. She wouldn't talk about it; he didn't dare to ask. But they hadn't been husband and wife since her return. After seven years, life was beginning to return to him, but it was still dead in Vilma.

Anybody would have thought that their suffering under the Nazis would have been enough to last any family for a lifetime, but that madman in Moscow now was acting like another Hitler. There were stories of villagers being rounded up, of mass executions, of deportations. When a country had been so recently brutalised as Czechoslovakia had been by the Nazis, the fears and rumours of another Holocaust spread like wildfire. Panic was in everybody's throats; everybody except those who, overnight, had become good Communists. Just as, a decade earlier, some people in the village had become good Nazis. And because of those few who reported them to the Nazis, all the Jews had been taken away. And there were no Jews left now . . . well, hardly any.

It all seemed to be happening again. It was like in the old days before the war, the days of Kaganovich, when Stalin had phoned him and said, 'How many enemies of the people have you executed today, Kaganovich?' And Kaganovich had meekly replied, 'Not enough sir. Tomorrow I'll deal with double the number'. And then the next day more and more were arrested, millions of human beings. And now it was happening again.

Moishe Krantz, shopkeeper and merchant in the town of Ujlak, walked across the floor and kissed his wife and his son. The boy – because even though he was a man in body and spirit, aged twenty, he would always be Moishe's boy, his only boy – looked up and smiled at his father. Moishe tousled his sandy-coloured hair and kissed his ruddy cheeks. So precious. He looked like Moishe's grandfather, as far as he could remember. There were no longer any photographs. Only memories.

Vilma looked out through the window and up into the night sky. Already there were some stars and so she lit the *shabbos* candles and mumbled the blessing. She waved her hands over the flickering flames and hid her face in her hands. Moishe never knew what she was saying apart from the traditional blessing, but he could guess. The flames were gentle God-given lights, but he knew that every time she lit a match and ignited a candle, she saw each of her children being thrown into a gas oven, their beautiful, innocent bodies charring, blistering and burning to ash. *Shabbos* had been such a joyous event before the war. One day, maybe, he would understand why God had done it to them, why He had made the innocent suffer, why He hadn't taken the father and the mother but had left them instead to suffer and to relive the deaths of their children every day of their lives.

Vilma uncovered her face, her eyes moist, and smiled at her husband and son. 'Good *shabbos*,' she said and walked around the table to kiss the remnant of her family. The three of them embraced, just as the many had embraced before the transportation. Then, Moishe's arms hadn't been wide enough to enfold everybody in his love and protection; now he pulled them towards his body to protect them from evil.

He stroked his beard and picked up a glass of wine. He said the blessing, took off his wedding ring, washed his hands, said a blessing over the bread, broke it into smaller pieces, salted it and passed it to his wife and son. They sat down and began to enjoy a cold borscht, which Vilma had made during the day with ice purchased from the ice vendor that morning, and some hot potatoes. They ate in silence; that was the way it was these days. Not like when all his children had crowded around the table, shouting out questions about the meaning of the Sabbath. But today, it was this very silence that enabled Moishe and what remained of his family to hear the shouting outside in the street. Usually the streets were quiet in the evening. During the day the loudspeakers on the lampposts boomed out martial music, which was occasionally interrupted by radio announcements of the latest results of Stalin's Five Year plans, information about tractor production statistics or the quantity of coal extracted from the frozen wastes of Siberia. But at night, mercifully, the village's loudspeakers were turned off and the population was able to relax in the sounds of nature.

At first the shouting was distant, as though it was a family quarrelling in a nearby home. But then it grew nearer and more aggressive. Moishe looked towards his son. The two men stood and walked through the private quarters into the dark shop, still claustrophobically warm. They didn't open the door but cautiously drew aside the curtain to see what was happening. Under the streetlights, they saw people running pell-mell along the road, terrified. Moishe's mind was catapulted back to another time, a mere decade ago, when people had run along this same street, just as petrified, trying to avoid the stamp of jackboots. God Almighty, what was going on?

Hermann began to open the door but his father stayed his hand. 'Don't,' he said. Ignoring his resistance, Hermann forced open the door and walked out into the hard-packed mud of the street. He caught old Pavel Milat by the arms. 'What's happening?' he demanded. Pavel's face was red and puffed.

'Get away from me, boy. I've got to get home.'

'What is it, Pavel?' shouted Hermann.

'Get your hands off me. I have to get home.'

'Tell me what's happening!'

'Those bastards. They've come for us.'

Pavel struggled to free his arm from Hermann's grip and stumbled on up the road. Moishe had been listening and joined his son on the road. Hermann shouted to Vaclav the plumber running towards them: 'Who's coming? What's happening?' The plumber stopped, breathless, and looked sympathetically at his old customer.

'Alexander Hasek. The butcher. He's here. In Ujlak. You'd better go while you can. It may not be you he's after, but who can take the chance?' The man tried to catch his breath.

'Why?' demanded Hermann. 'I don't understand. He was far to the north just yesterday. Why is he coming south?'

The man looked in astonishment, still panting. 'You're Jews, aren't you?' Moishe didn't answer, but felt the ground move under his feet. 'Hasek! He's come for you. He's after the Jews. The Cosmopolitans.'

'Jews?' said Moishe. 'I don't understand.' But he understood all too well.

'Don't be a fool,' said the plumber as he started to run again. 'It's another purge, Stalin or something. And you know Hasek. Take my advice and get out. Quick!'

More and more people were running down the main road. They had obviously been spending the Friday evening in one of the local public houses or hostelries when the news had come through. Everybody had panicked. Maybe Hasek and his henchmen were in the next town; maybe they were already in Ujlak. Hermann ran back into the house, but Moishe stood dumbstruck in the street, trying to comprehend how this could be happening again. What else was left to take? Hermann came back and pulled him roughly by the arm. He saw with horror that his father had suddenly aged, his face was grey. It was the face of a man suddenly devastated by reality. Hermann dragged his father back into the house, and the older man followed with leaden steps. Vilma looked up in panic as they re-entered the back rooms.

'What is it?' she demanded. 'What's happening?'

'It's Alexander Hasek. They say he's come for the Jews.'

'Oh my God,' she said, her flushed face suddenly blanching white. 'Not again. Please God, not again.' She looked towards her only remaining son. 'What shall we do?'

The rumours had been current now for over a year. The arrival into the area of the Communist forces of the Czech government, the police, the army, had all contributed to the feeling of powerlessness of the citizens. There were stories about Jews being rounded up and taken. In their numbness they had never believed it could happen again; they thought they were only scare stories, started by jealous neighbours. They believed that after Hitler and the Nazis, nobody would, could possibly, do it all again. But now it was happening.

'We have to go,' said Moishe hoarsely. Vilma shook her head.

'Vilma,' he shouted, suddenly instilled with renewed vigour, realising the enormity of what was happening, 'we have to go now. I'm not waiting again for the madmen to kill us. Not this time. We've already lost enough. Let's not lose what little is left. We have to go.' He looked at his son, tears suddenly flooding his eyes.

Hermann ran upstairs, but Moishe shouted after him, 'It's too late to pack. We take nothing. We go.'

'Where?' shouted the young man.

'I don't know!' he screamed, losing control of his senses. 'I don't know. Anywhere. But away. Away from here. Now! We have to leave the house immediately. We can't wait a second.'

Vilma sat at the table as if she was riveted to the chair. She picked up her spoon to continue to eat her borscht soup, as if nothing was taking place around her. Had she understood anything he'd said? She looked strange, as if in a dream. Moishe gently coaxed her to stand.

'My borscht,' she said. 'The potatoes will get cold.' She was in another world. A world of denial.

He whispered tenderly into her ear, 'We have to go now, Vilma. Trust me.'

She continued to drink her soup, and selected a tasty potato to eat. He looked at her with bottomless sympathy and gently put his arm around her and lifted her from her chair.

She threaded her arm slowly around his waist, as if she was an invalid, and allowed him to support her as they walked towards the door. He shouted up the stairs, 'Hermann, come now. Immediately. We have no time.'

'But father, I have to take . . .'

'NOW!' he screamed. 'Do what I tell you. You take nothing. You understand me? We go now.'

The three of them paused at the doorway of the shop as the last stragglers ran past. They waited another minute for the road to be empty so they wouldn't be seen. Too many spies, too many friends willing to sell them out to the madmen, just for their crime of being Jews.

'Where shall we go?' asked Hermann.

'We could go into the fields. We can hide there until morning. Then we can make our way . . . somewhere,' said Moishe.

'No,' interrupted the boy, 'Mother can't live a night in the open fields. We have to get shelter.'

Moishe could feel the panic rising within him. His throat was constricting with fear. 'Magda,' he said.

Hermann looked at his father. Magda had been the boy's unofficial nanny when he was a baby and his parents were too busy to look after him. At the time she had only been fourteen years old herself, but even then she was the most responsible neighbour they had. She had often followed Hermann down to the river when he wandered off alone in case he slipped and fell in. She would return with the two year old, holding his hand and teaching him Czech songs. Today, at thirty-two, she had become a fervent Roman Catholic, always crossing herself. She was a good woman, a decent, honest and moral woman. Although she had only been in her mid-twenties when the men came back to the village from the Nazi labour camp, she was the first to help them, to feed them, to offer them succour, warmth and love.

Vilma nodded, appearing to have marshalled unfathomable resources to come to grips with her situation. 'Yes,' she said. 'Magda. She'll help us.'

They huddled together and crept like thieves across the street. The panic in the village seemed to have passed; houses were firmly bolted, children brought indoors. An eerie silence had descended, as though even the birds and animals sensed that something momentous was about to happen.

Magda's cottage was far smaller than their own house. Hermann knew it well, for she made the best *palachinten* in the world, hot pancakes full of steamy cream cheese and juicy raisins. For most of her life, she had been known throughout the village as one of the happiest and most pleasant young women, always smiling and politely asking after everybody's health. Sometimes she would sing as she walked to the shops. But not any more. Now all she did was make *palachinten,* look after the animals and do the cooking for old people in the village. The happy days had been before the War, when her parents were still alive, when she had been married. But then her mother and father and her husband had been killed. Now she was alone, except for her love for Christ.

They walked down her tidy footpath between the flowering rose bushes and knocked cautiously on her door. Magda opened it immediately. Her voice was harsh, deep with concern.

'If you hadn't come to me, I would have come across to get you,' she said. 'Come in quickly.'

Vilma broke down on the doorstep and threw her arms around Magda, kissing her on both cheeks. 'Shhh,' said

Magda, stroking the older woman's grey hair and whispering comfortingly in her ear. 'Now isn't the time for this. You'll hide in the barn. If they come, I'll say that I had no knowledge that you were there, that you came in around the side of the house. That should be alright for me. Are you hungry?'

Hermann nodded. Magda smiled, and tousled his hair, as she'd done since he was born. 'No *palachinten*, but there's some food from the kitchen. For God's sake eat it all. Don't leave any in the barn in case they think I've fed you.'

Magda led them around the side of the house and into the courtyard, filled with barking dogs on leashes, a goat, a sheep and a milk cow mooing in the background. She opened the door to the barn and told them to get inside and hide themselves.

Magda closed the door and hurried away, leaving them alone and afraid in the dark. Their eyes adjusted slowly to the tiny beams of light from the streetlight outside the house, which shone weakly through the cracks in the walls and the small aperture at the apex of the barn's roof. The family looked at each other, immobile, too terrified even to move in their own sight.

Five minutes passed; it felt like half an hour, and still they continued to look at each other. They had no idea of how much time had gone by. Vilma was shaking. Moishe moved silently over to her and put his arm around her, whispering consolations into her ear. 'Come,' he said to Hermann. 'Comfort your mother. I'm going up to see what's happening.'

He climbed up the wooden ladder to the barn's loft and manoeuvred his way over the straw bales until he was able to look out of the aperture. He could see the entire street. Opposite him was his house. He crouched, breathless, wondering what was going on. Up the road, he saw a car come to a stop under a streetlight. From the back emerged a short, dark-haired, slightly rotund man in his early thirties. A pistol was strapped to his waist; in his hand he carried a gold-topped baton. He was wearing a uniform which looked Russian, maybe GRU, maybe NKVD, maybe even Red Army. Moishe couldn't tell. He didn't know the Russians well enough, thank God, but one thing he was sure of: the man was Alexander Hasek, and he was no Russian, he was a Czech. A man who had risen from rightful obscurity in Prague before the Great Patriotic War to become a local despot, terrifying the entire Carpathian/Ruthenian region. A man who was a firm believer in and exponent of the authoritarian might of the Soviets. A man with a growing reputation for mass deportations, mass killings, expulsions and the deliberate starvation of anybody or any group whom he considered to be hated Cosmopolitans or anarchists denying the deity of Josef Stalin. And that invariably meant the Jews.

Moishe had heard of him only by repute, but what he saw now of the distant figure was enough to terrify him. The little man stepped away from the car; there was a pent-up power in his stance, despite his height. Hasek looked up and down the road as though he had taken total control of the village, which he had. A lorry that had been slowly following him drew to a halt behind his car. Hasek reached back into the car, removed his briefcase and took a list from it. He studied it carefully, then looked at the houses. He walked slowly and imperiously down the street until he came to number thirty-eight, the family home of Moishe and Vilma Krantz.

Moishe's heart was pounding, blood beating a staccato in his ears. God Almighty. Every instinct told Moishe to hide; he should have known what to expect, but emotion denied reason. That was why so many German Jews had died, because nobody had really believed that Hitler would do what he had said he would do. And it was all happening again. First the Nazis, now the Communists. He shrank from the horror, the terror of what he knew was going to happen next. Fear immobilised him. Visions took over from the reality before him. He heard the sound of gunfire deep within his brain, just as he'd heard it when the Germans came for him and his family. It was like a gramophone record playing over and over again. He pressed his hands against his ears to make the sound stop. He wanted to scream, but knew he mustn't. A sound would be the death penalty. He breathed deeply and tried to calm down. He removed his hands from his ears and listened carefully to the noise of the soldiers' boots marching towards his home.

When the phalanx had come to a halt behind Hasek, the little man called out, 'Enemies of the State, Moishe and Vilma Krantz. You are Cosmopolitans and Jews. You have been charged with the crime of being enemies of the people, enemies of the Czechoslovakian government, enemies of Russia and enemies of Josef Stalin and the Peoples' Soviet. Come out immediately or we will come in and get you.'

Moishe could feel tears welling up in his eyes again. Seven years ago, just seven short years ago, he had been robbed of almost everything he loved. His children, his future. Was another Hitler going to rob him now of what little remained?

'Enemies of the people, Moishe and Vilma Krantz and Hermann Krantz. Come out of the house immediately,' the little man screamed, 'or I will send in my troops.'

Moishe looked down towards his wife and son, who were huddling in the darkness of the barn, and prayed that they couldn't hear what was going on outside. Vilma, for seven years on the verge of madness, would become hysterical if she heard. Hasek turned towards one of his officers and hissed instructions which Moishe couldn't hear. The men ran inside, their rifles poised to fire at the Cosmopolitans and enemies of the people who might still be within the house.

Hasek struck his boot with his baton, like a poor man's Goering. He waited for his troops to return with the struggling bodies of the parents and the youth whom he would send for re-education to a place far away. But the troops returned empty-handed, reporting the remains of a meal. One of the troops was eating a potato. It infuriated Hasek; it was theft. He struck the soldier across the face with his baton. The potato catapulted into the road, and the man stood rigidly to attention, too terrified to flinch at the pain.

Hasek turned to his senior officer and barked further orders. The soldiers fanned out and thumped their rifle butts against the front doors of the houses on either side. Terrified people slowly emerged into the evening air, looking wide-eyed at the troops. Soldiers ran further along the road, forcing more and more residents from their homes. It was just a matter of time before they reached the barn; it wouldn't be long before he would need to say *tillum* for himself and his family. But it wasn't to be. By a miracle, somehow, the troops missed them.

By the following morning, after a night in which nobody in the entire village was permitted to close their eyes, Alexander Hasek was in a state of fury. They had searched Magda's house and kicked open the door of the barn. The men had come inside like bully boys and speared bales of hay with their bayonets. One had even climbed the wooden ladder to the hay loft and made a cursory search before urinating inches away from where Hermann lay on the rough boards, covered in straw. It was the early hours of the morning, and the soldier – a man from a nearby town – was too tired to do his job properly. His exhaustion saved their lives, but was to cost the lives of their neighbours.

The failure of the guards to find the three enemies of the State infuriated Alexander Hasek to the point of madness. He marched up and down the streets, punching terrified villagers and hitting guards in the face with his baton, screaming at the top of his lungs that he would have the entire village wiped off the face of the land.

To slake his fury, Hasek ordered that twenty men from the street be lined up outside the Krantzes' general food and provision shop. Moishe looked at the pathetic line in horror. He knew most of them; many were his friends. Some he had known since childhood. He knew exactly what was about to happen, but he also knew with absolute certainty that if he did what he wanted to do – go outside and give himself up – it would be the death sentence for his wife and Hermann. Tears ran down his cheeks as he watched his friends and neighbours shaking in terror, awaiting their fate. One had already fainted, three others were on their knees burbling confessions which Moishe couldn't hear. But he knew what they were saying; they were telling the little despot everything they knew about the Krantz family, and where they might have gone.

Alexander Hasek stood before the terrified citizens like Stalin before the mass of Muscovites in Red Square. He was as small as the great leader but today he was just as powerful. He turned from the men lined up for execution and addressed the crowd assembled on the opposite side of the street, some of the women hysterical at the sight of their husbands lined up for execution. Friends and neighbours tried to comfort them.

As Hasek spoke, everyone fell silent. The only sound was that of stifled sobs. Moishe strained to hear. Hasek might be small of stature but his voice was strong and confident: 'The enemies of the people, the Cosmopolitan family of Jews, Moishe, Vilma and Hermann Krantz, have escaped. They couldn't have done so without the help of other enemies of the people and partisans. In order to teach you villagers a lesson, I have decided that six of you, two for each Jew who slipped away, will be executed by me immediately. This is a punishment that will be borne by you and by this village and which will act as a lesson to other villagers not to side with the enemies of the people, but to do their duty and report un–Soviet activities to the authorities. Children must report their parents, parents their children, neighbours their neighbour. This is the law.'

He walked to the beginning of the row and looked at the first man. No, he was too old. He looked at the second man and the third. The fourth man had a contemptuous look in his eye. There was no fear in his face. His look irritated Hasek, who drew his pistol and shot the man through the heart. As the man slumped to the ground, blood spurting from the massive wound in his chest, a scream went up from the dozens of women standing in the crowd. The guards held them in check, preventing them from running forward. A man standing near the victim fainted.

Hasek grinned. Now, they were paying him his due respect. He marched down the line, not bothering to look at the faces of the other men, and killed five more at random. He had made his point with the first execution.

Moishe watched in horror and bit his lips to force himself to remain silent. He turned and saw Hermann had climbed up beside him. He tried to force his son away so that he wouldn't witness the scene, but Hermann fought to resist his father. The young man knew what was happening. He had been in a labour camp. He had seen thousands of people crushed to death under the heavy whips and rifle butts of the Nazis. He had buried the memory as he grew from teenager to manhood, but the sight of such hideous brutality, such insane murder, perpetrated against his neighbours was too much. He opened his mouth to scream, but Moishe put his hand over his lips and hissed in his ear, 'Shut up! One noise and we're dead.'

Hermann's eyes blinked wildly as shot after shot rang out. Only when Hasek got into his car and drove into the next hapless town did the gunshots finish. And then the wailing of the entire village began, a collective feral scream.

The Krantz family remained hidden and huddled together for the rest of that day, not daring to breathe a word into each other's ears, in case someone was standing outside the door of the barn. They strained to listen as best they could when the shooting and the screaming came to an end. They tried to differentiate the many sounds around them: there were the pigs grunting, the geese honking and dogs barking in panic – but the farmyard noises were subsumed into a surrounding mêlée. Every now and again, a woman would start screaming. And all through the morning and into the afternoon they could hear men running here and there, shouting profane curses into the air; Moishe couldn't discern the words. There were many words spoken, most in yells and imprecations, but overwhelming all other sounds were the profanities shouted into the air. So many that Moishe and Vilma became numb to their shock.

Early the following morning, the door of the barn creaked slowly open. Moishe could hardly breathe for fear; he nuzzled Vilma's head both to comfort her and to prevent her from screaming. They looked down cautiously from the loft and, with overwhelming relief, saw Magda silhouetted against the dawn. Moishe nearly cried. They were starving, they had been praying that she would bring them food, but she was empty-handed. Instead she said to them, 'I want you to go away from here. Now.'

'Magda, it wasn't our fault. You saw what happened. There was nothing we could do.'

'Just go,' she hissed. 'You and your kind have brought too much evil to this village. You're Jews. You must go. Leave this town. Leave the area. Go to Palestine or America, or wherever your kind goes. I want you out now. I've made up food for you which should last until you reach Kosice. Then it's up to you. But go. I can't . . . I won't help you anymore.'

And then she was gone. Moishe and his family raised themselves from the stinking straw, brushed themselves down and shuffled tentatively into the brightening day. The yard was empty of people. Only the animals watched them pick up the basket of food, divide the packages amongst themselves and walk out of the back of Magda's property to the laneway. They trudged their way back to the shadows of the main road to steal one last tentative look at the house which had been their family home for two hundred years, which had seen generations of the Krantz family grow and flourish, which had seen joy and unimaginable horror.

But what they noticed more than the building were the flowers that had been strewn in front of their home. The blooms covered the hideous sprays of blood that had blended with the dried mud of the road. They thought back to what had happened the previous day. Hermann began to shake uncontrollably. He had been distant, nervous, ever since he had witnessed the executions, now his tremor became manic. Moishe put his arms around him to hold him tightly, and whispered, 'Come. Come with me. It'll be alright.'

They turned into the back lanes behind the houses which belonged to their neighbours, people among whom they had lived for their entire lives. Now their odyssey was to begin. Hermann turned once more, and took one last look at his home before he and his parents began the long journey to America.

Joshua Krantz stood on the concrete pavement outside the shop, and wondered if his father, Hermann, would have remembered the house. Then it had been a provision shop with a central door dividing the two windows from which salamis, geese and ducks had hung, and in which the smell of freshly baked bread suffused the atmosphere. In front was a small copse of elm trees, making the house difficult to see from the road. Why had the elm trees been planted there, so close to the house, obliterating the view of the shop windows? It was odd. Joshua looked up and down the road. No traffic to speak of. Just old men on bicycles and young children running in the distance.

Near the shop he saw a house with a huge barn behind it. In the apex of the barn was a circular window. His father had told him that while he and Josh's grandparents were hiding in a nearby farmyard from the Communist anti-Semite madmen, they had seen their neighbours shot like dogs. Was this the barn? Was it still owned by the woman, Magda, who had saved his father's life?

Josh continued to stare along the road. The grass beside the pavement was newly mown, the road freshly tarred. An old Mercedes was parked outside the shop, obscuring the view even further. Would his father have remembered? Josh'd never know; Hermann had died two years earlier.

Well, now the son had returned.

# CHAPTER SEVEN

When Sarah arrived back at the hotel, still feeling moved by her visit to the old Jewish quarter, she found a note pushed underneath her door. She opened it and flushed with embarrassment, like a miscreant schoolchild caught by a teacher: *Sarah, I'm back. Give me a ring. We need to talk. Josh.*

Damn it! Why should she feel guilty? She had done everything possible that there was to do before taking her leisure time. She phoned his number.

'Sarah?' he asked as he picked up the phone.

'Welcome back. Did you find the house? How was it?'

He babbled excitedly, 'We have to talk. We have to go to Kosice right away. I've come back to collect you. I found the house, it was still there. You wouldn't believe it, it's a plumbing supply shop, for Christ's sake. I went inside and spoke to the people who own it. When can we meet and talk? How long before you can be ready to go? There's a flight out tonight, but I think that's probably too early. There are a couple of things I have to do . . .'

Sarah was astonished. He was babbling like a schoolboy. 'Josh, slow down,' she said. 'Why don't we meet downstairs in ten for a drink?'

In the bar, she could see the flush of excitement in his face as she walked towards him. He stood and kissed her on the cheek. It was the first time he had touched her, except to shake hands. She felt a shock.

'It was just like my father described,' he said, without any preliminary conversation. A waiter came over and he ordered her favourite drink and one for himself. He didn't even ask her.

'I would have recognised it without the guide. We found it so easily. We drove into town ... Town!' he laughed. 'It's a tinpot village. Three, four hundred families, no more ... there was music playing over the loud-speakers. Can you believe it? Loudspeakers! They're attached to lampposts in the street. They were used to play Communist slogans in the old days: *Today's production of tractors in the glorious Soviet Union exceeds that of last year's five-year plan ...*' He laughed out loud. Others in the bar looked at him. He didn't care. Even Sarah smiled.

'These days they use them for public entertainment. Rousing martial music. You know, Sarah, if I put that into one of my pictures, nobody would believe it. And storks, Sarah. There were hundreds of them, perched on top of the houses, just like you see in fairy tales. Huge nests built over chimneys with goddamn storks in them. God, I wish I'd had the crew there. It could have been like Fellini and those peacocks in Amarcord.'

He shook his head and reached over and took both her hands. His hands were warm and soft, with a powerful feminine essence. They were gentle, just like David's, but there was a strength in them which was comforting. They weren't the hands of a cellist, but they were the hands of a creator. Sarah felt another shock as he squeezed her hands between his, but not as dramatically as when he had kissed her. Somehow it felt natural.

Josh didn't notice her reaction. He carried on talking. 'We drove into town and got out of the car. There was this old drunk guy – God, he stank of vodka. Three days' white stubble on his face, and what teeth he still had were yellow. And his eyes! He was a joke. He kept blinking to try to clear his vision. The translator asked him if he knew where the old Krantz house used to be. He shook his head, said he had no idea. Mind you, he probably didn't know what day it was. The guide told him the family used to be merchants, that they sold food in a general store in town. I took out a handful of small change. Marvellous how money can focus the thoughts. Suddenly the fifty years began to lift from his mind. You could see it in his face, Sarah.'

Josh held her hands more firmly; he was transported across the breadth of the country and could still smell the alcohol on the breath of the old man. He was swept up by waves of emotion and she was caught in his vortex, a fellow traveller. She thought she ought to remove her hands from his grasp but he was holding them tightly and she didn't want to break the importance of the moment for him for the sake of something so mundane as the nature of a client–attorney relationship.

'Then the old drunk began to nod and say, yes, he remembered. He mentioned my grandfather and my grandmother's names. And he pointed to a street. It was literally three streets away; down to the end of the road, turn left and you're there. I could hardly believe it, Sarah. We drove down the very streets that my grandparents and their parents before them had trodden. All my ancestors, Sarah. Who knows? Maybe for five hundred years into the past. When Columbus was sailing to America.'

He took another drink and looked around the bar, but she could tell that whatever his eyes saw didn't register. He looked at her again and smiled. He knew he was holding her hands. He didn't care.

'But that wasn't what was in my mind. I was thinking about my father. He'd trodden the very same streets that I was treading now. I was there, Sarah, in my grandparents' village, the place where my dad was born. We turned into the street and something, maybe my dad's descriptions all those years ago, maybe what my grandfather had told me when I was a child, but something made me realise that this was the place, the actual street. It had a proper pavement and a proper road surface, not the mud my father told me about, but I knew in my heart that we were there. I told the driver to stop and I got out and I walked on my own into the centre of the street. There were no cars. It's just a hick place on the road to nowhere, thirty miles from the Ukrainian border. And I stopped and I stood outside my grandparents' home. The house where my father was born. And I knew it was mine. I knew this was my ancestral home.'

He fell silent. Sarah held her breath, not knowing how to respond as he took another sip of his drink. Although she didn't know him well, Sarah was inspired by Josh's introspection. Perhaps he was like this when he was being creative, directing one of his films. What she knew absolutely was that he was not in Prague, in this expensive modern hotel; he was still on the other side of the country, in another land . . . and another time.

His voice deepening, he said, 'I felt such a sense of anger that there were people – not my family – moving around in my house. These people had no right to be there.'

'Josh . . .' Sarah said softly, trying to interrupt. She wanted to ask what the house looked like. She looked closely at his face: it was distant, removed, as though he were halfway between trance and reality. His forehead was glistening. He ignored her interruption, not deliberately, by any means, but because he was so far away. She felt extraordinarily flattered that a man as eminent as Josh, a man whose name was known to so many throughout the world, should confide his most private and secret emotions to her. As though she was a wife or a lover. God! What was going on? This was supposed to be a client–attorney relationship, but Josh's enthusiasm was extending to areas where she felt uncomfortable. She would have to establish the limits soon, clearly but subtly.

'I couldn't cross the road, Sarah,' he continued, 'I just stood there. It must have been half an hour. Just looking. It was exactly how my father had told me. A double-fronted shop, with a door in the middle, and round the back was the entrance to the private quarters. There was a laneway or something between the houses, where my grandparents had kept a cart and a horse, but there was some crappy old car parked in there now . . . in my grandfather's laneway.

'The translator joined me and we went inside. I spoke to the guys that own it, a couple of men. One from Kosice and the other one from the village. They'd bought it from a pharmacist, who'd bought it from the State government, who'd owned it for forty years. The guys told me they'd just spent a fortune doing it up. They didn't know who I was, but I could tell they were making it clear that they owned the place. I just said I was back there as a tourist, but that my family had once owned the place. They gave me vodka. Fucking vodka, Sarah. Eight o'clock in the morning. Can you believe it?'

Sarah was beginning to feel increasingly uncomfortable with his intimacy. She wanted him to release his grip. but the look in his eyes told her that he no longer realised he was touching her.

'Josh,' she said, 'do you think that now is the right time for me to go over there? You said on the phone just before that you want us to pack and go.' The passion was still surging through his body.

'I want you to see it, Sarah. I want you to come and see my grandfather's . . . my father's house.'

'Josh', she said quietly, 'of course I'll come and see it. But you mustn't forget why we're here. Remember what it was you said to me in my office in New York? You told me it was time for a bit of good old-fashioned American-style retribution. That you were going to send in the

Marines. Well Josh, I'm your Marine. You've seen the house and that's fine, but I think we've got to retain some sense of dispassion. Do you really think it's important for me to go over? I'm sure I could be better employed in Prague. The lawyers here have only just started to get to work. I don't want the same lax attitude as in Bratislava. Unless I keep on their backs, they're going to look for a compromise solution. If you want your grandparents' house – your house – back, it's got to be done legally.'

'But I want you to see it with me. I want you to understand the importance.'

'I do understand. Truly. But I can't allow you to let emotion get in the way of due process. Sure I'll go over there, let's see it together by all means. But then you have to leave the law stuff to me.'

'You don't understand, do you, Sarah? I've found my family's home. My roots. I need to share my excitement with you.' He looked at her, clasping her hands more firmly.

'Josh,' she said. It came out sterner than she meant.

He let go immediately. 'Sorry,' he said, chastened. It was an odd experience for him. 'There are times when it's hard to think of you as my lawyer. I guess lawyers never become involved, do they?'

He sat back and sipped his scotch. She could see the dejection in his face. She'd offended him. It was the last thing she wanted. 'Josh, I'm sorry. Truly, I didn't mean to sound harsh and distant. But . . .' Her voice trailed off. He looked at her for a sign of warmth. He saw none.

Sarah felt guilty, but she had to be the lawyer. She smiled. 'Since we've come away, especially during our week in Bratislava, I've grown fond of you, Josh. You're a lovely guy, passionate, gentle, intelligent. But I'm here as a lawyer representing you. Friendship and the emotions that go with it could cloud judgement calls. I can't allow that to happen. It's too important for you that I remain dispassionate.'

He sipped his drink again. 'Is there a subtext here? Is it important for you as well, Sarah? You're a young lawyer. This could make you famous, even more famous than when you defended Darman. You're on the side of the good guys now. I understand why you don't want anything to cloud your professional judgement; your career's on the up. I'm not an idiot. But I'm a film-maker. I get deeply and passionately involved in everything I create. Every foot of celluloid that gets shown is a part of me. I'm sorry, Sarah, I shouldn't have forgotten why you're here. Of course you don't have to go. Not if you don't want to. I'll take Phil and Jerry and get them to see it through my eyes.'

Now she knew she'd gone too far, both as a lawyer and as a friend. She reached over and touched his hand. 'Of course I'll come. I want to see the house. I want to see it with you.' She smiled and her left hand moved towards her breasts and found comfort in the amulet which hung there.

## Nizna Mysla, a Bronze Age archaeological dig near Kosice. Present day.

Professor Dr Laco Plastov was so drained of energy that he couldn't even raise his voice loud enough to call across the fields for everyone to down tools and finish for the day. Eastern Slovakia's summers were getting hotter and hotter, and its winters colder and more desolate. Naked, except for a brief pair of shorts, thick-soled army boots and woollen socks, he dabbed his forehead with a handkerchief which he then wiped through his thick, curly, black hair to dry his scalp of the rivulets of sweat which ran down his neck and his temples. He licked his lips and drank from his flask of water, to which he had added a generous quantity of vodka to overcome its rank sulphurousness He swirled the liquid over his teeth and tongue to wash away the dust.

They had been on the site now for over six hours and although it was only three o'clock the temperature had become too uncomfortable for any of the young volunteers to continue. Laco, swarthy and muscular, was used to these conditions and could have lasted another couple of hours, but the volunteers – students from German, Austrian and French universities – were white-skinned and were in danger of fainting from dehydration. Laco looked at them with sympathy; they were as exhausted as spent fireworks. They began the day with prickling energy and, by the time the sun was high in the sky, they were drooping like dead flowers.

The shadecloth which covered part of the dig provided relief from the direct rays of the sun, but it was the hot wind which blew up from the valley that caused all the torment; a wind that was icy when it left the Tatra Mountains in the north, but which heated rapidly in the furnace of the Slovakian plains as it neared the Hungarian border.

Laco straightened his back and blinked the sweat from his eyes. He cleared his voice and was about to shout in German and Slovak, '*Okay everybody, that's it for today,*' when he noticed a buzz of excitement from the corner of the shadecloth where the diggers were at work.

An instinct stopped him from closing the show down. More young people appeared to be moving over to see what the excited volunteer had found. One of them straightened up, a young girl with pear-like breasts wearing a bikini bra and a tight pair of jeans. That was all that Laco could remember about her. That and the fact that she was next on his list. She looked around the site until she spotted him standing high on the adjoining hill. 'Laco,' she shouted, 'Laco, come here quickly.'

Young of body and eager of mind, Laco Plastov's energy suddenly returned as he ran like a deer down the hillside and then upwards onto the adjoining hill. He jumped down into the pit with the seven volunteers already there.

'What is it?' he demanded breathlessly. The enervation of moments before had left him, his mind was alive now. The girl nodded towards the corner of the dig site. Laco tried to discern what was lying there. Objects buried for so many millennia picked up the colours of the surrounding soil and were often hard to identify with an inexperienced eye. Other people might have missed it at first glance, but he saw quite clearly that it was a bone.

'So?' he asked. They were always digging up bones. Nizna Mysla was one of the major Middle Bronze Age digs in Eastern Europe. Dozens upon dozens of graves had already been uncovered and charted. This was just another area they were opening up. The boy who had discovered the bone looked up excitedly. 'There's more,' he said.

He was a young German student from the University of Wuppertal, who had been trying to win the pear-breasted girl's affection for the past three weeks. Lately he had been acting like a lovesick deer, all doe-eyed and limp. Laco had already enjoyed the comforts of six of the girls on the camp. The reason the pear-breasted girl hadn't given in to the boy was probably because she was waiting her turn.

Laco wanted to know what the kid meant. 'Explain,' he demanded.

'It's the way the fingers are pointing at an unnatural angle. I felt underneath and there's something odd. I think they're resting on metal.'

'Okay,' said Laco. 'Let's find out.'

He took the trowel out of the boy's hand. With far more daring than the volunteer had been confident to use, Laco scraped the earth away from either side of the bone. Terrified of doing any form of damage to whatever was below the surface, the volunteers would have used tweezers to remove each particle of earth, but, with sixteen years field experience, Laco knew precisely what was hard-packed earth and what was a potentially priceless archaeological relic. Within moments he had uncovered the rest of the skeletal hand. The boy was right; the hand was at an awkward angle, perhaps caused by earth movement over the three thousand two hundred years since the body had been placed on the hilltop, or perhaps because this was the one out of thirty graves in which a body had been buried with a full after-life treasury.

Laco scraped the earth from beneath the tibia and fibula but stopped when he felt an unusual resistance to his trowel. He looked up. All the students were peering over his shoulder, he had been oblivious to them for the last few minutes. 'Brush and pipette, please,' he said, like a surgeon talking to his nurses.

He wet the area and used a solid hair brush to remove the dampened and clinging earth until a tell-tale glitter of gold showed through.

'Brilliant,' he said to the German student, 'absolutely brilliant. Okay everybody. This could be a big find.' He stood and turned to the assembly of volunteers. Klaus, the young discoverer, was beaming from ear to ear. Although he would earn nothing more than praise from the camp that night, he would at last be the local hero and maybe Marta would notice him.

Out of gratitude, Laco went over to the boy and tousled his hair, 'You lead the team. You two,' he said pointing to two of the other boys, 'start over there where the feet should be. You might find anklets or clay figures. This could have been a woman so you might find some small female statues or small water jugs in the area. You two,' he said pointing to a girl and boy, 'try the pelvic area. You're less likely to find stuff but it could have moved over the years. You and you,' he said pointing to the German boy and a girl he had slept with the night before, 'keep working on the head and shoulders, and for Christ's sake, be careful. I want everything logged.'

The attractive girl in the bikini looked at him expectantly. He hadn't given her a job. 'Marta, can you come with me? We need to do some logging on the other area I'm looking at for next week.'

She looked disappointed. 'This is our first major discovery, Laco. Couldn't I work here?'

'I'd rather you worked on the other hill with me. I think there are going to be some big discoveries. Just a hunch, but you know me and my hunches. You never know what we're going to uncover.'

The girl nodded. The previous day Klaus would have been jealous to see his beloved Marta going off with a wolf like Laco. But today his thoughts of the pear-breasted girl were subsumed within his vision of another girl, almost three and a half thousand years older. What had her breasts once looked like? Who was she? What had her face looked like? Had she been attractive? Had she been diseased? Did she have beautiful jewellery? Why and how did she die? All aspects of the living suddenly seemed to be of little importance compared with uncovering the truth hidden by history.

By the end of the week, Laco was holding in his hands a stunning example of Middle Bronze Age jewellery: a delicately carved necklace which was the work of an ancient craftsman in 1200 BC, whose alchemy blended together an amalgam of copper and tin in a furnace. The man had worked his magic centuries before Homer and Virgil and Hesiod, before the rise of Greece, before Julius Caesar conquered Gaul, and long before the birth of the Christian God.

Laco's fingers felt the creases in its edge, the delicate whorls and striations which the ancient designer had carved there with a significance which neither Laco nor any other modern scientists would ever be able to determine with any great accuracy. Why were the symbols created in this way? What did they mean? Was the Bronze Age artisan representing the life-giving power of the sun, or the cold, gentle, calming light of the moon? Were the circles a representation of a woman's breast, the waves in a distant sea, or the ripples of a stone dropped into a still lake?

He had been drawing the latest finds for the better part of the day and his eyes were tired, his hands numb. Photography was all very well but it didn't represent the priceless items in the same emotional way that his hand and eye could represent them. No matter how skilled the photographer, photographs of archaeological treasures were always two-dimensional. What he wanted the rest of the archaeological world to see was the importance and grandeur of his find. It didn't match the sumptuous treasures of the Middle Eastern Bronze Age nor the glory of the Grecian or Trojan Bronze finds − jewellery which held centre stage in the most important museums in the world, relics which left visitors breathless in appreciation of the ancient geniuses who had lived fifteen hundred or more years before Christ.

But his find at the site of what remained of the Otomani-Fuzesabony culture at Nizna Mysla was significant by European standards. The museum of which he was the director, in Kosice in Slovakia, was attracting interest throughout the world. Historians of the Bronze Age were beginning to write to him asking him for samples for their collections. He could feel the momentum starting to build up. Since the end of the Russian dominance of his country, Slovaks had begun to look outwards at the same time as he was permitted to look downwards.

His father Maxim before him, an academic of great distinction, had begun working on the site when he was an archaeology student in 1947, but shortly after he'd begun, the dig was shut down amid the post-war turmoil. Nobody had been permitted near the site until eight years ago. Archaeologists during the period of Stalin's madness were harassed and treated with contempt by the local commissars; Laco's father, especially, a man of political ideals that contradicted the authoritarian rules and whose life was under constant threat until the welcome death of the dictator in 1953. But, by then, the region was in such disarray that undertaking an expensive dig had been impossible.

Throughout his long life, Laco's father had spoken in almost mystical terms about the importance of the dig and what might be buried there, about the treasures and skeletons occasionally found beneath the earth by farmers and adventurers, and about the crying need for scientific rigour and discipline to be brought to the investigation. For most of his life, Laco had felt his father's keen sense of frustration. It was a particular pleasure, now, to visit his elderly father's home once a week and show him the latest finds, discuss the latest results. The old man was completing unfinished archaeological work through his son. For eight years, Laco had been uncovering what his father had only ever dreamed of. Eight years, and hundreds of students, working only through the spring and summer months before the earth became frozen and gripped its treasures too tightly.

Today was another blisteringly hot day and the students were working to clear a two-foot-deep layer of modern earth from the new site which Laco had mapped out the previous week. It was back-breaking, thankless, filthy labour but essential to get below the present-day earth into the substrata that were laid down hundreds and thousands of years ago. Spades and wheelbarrows could be used to cart the topsoil and the first strata away. It would be crudely sieved in case there were any bones or objects of interest but it was highly unlikely. All the skeletons had been found below the five-foot level. Most were buried more than eight feet deep. There was plenty of time before Laco needed to return to the dig; tomorrow maybe, or the day after.

He looked up and saw Marta using a mild solution of acid and a stiff hair brush to clean away hard-packed detritus from a pot. Her profile was very attractive. She had long dark hair and an amazingly pert nose. She had none of the heavy broad features of Slavic women, her looks were definitely Western European. She could even be Nordic. But then her hair wouldn't be as dark. Maybe she was originally from Italy or the Mediterranean. Whatever, it was her breasts which most appealed to him. Of all fruit, he loved pears the best.

'Marta,' he called across the laboratory.

She looked up and smiled. She was being coy, this girl. He liked that. The others had given in too easily, but he liked that as well.

'Come over here. I want to show you something.'

She washed her hands and dried them on the laboratory towel. She was wearing a low-cut top and jeans. He enjoyed the way she moved. He really should have made a beeline for her first, before the others. But she seemed more withdrawn, and he always went for the easiest conquests first. He only had a limited time with the students — six weeks over spring, then another lot over summer. A couple of days for each girl.

'What is it?' she asked, coming to stand opposite him.

'Come around here, round to this side. There's something I want you to try on.'

She did as she was told. Laco dried the wet necklace. 'Do you want to be the first woman in three and a half thousand years to wear this?'

She smiled and reached over to touch it. He held up the necklace and shook his head. 'Let me do it. I'd like to see what it looks like.'

She bent her graceful head forward and he slipped the necklace over her head. She put her hands up but it was he that straightened her hair. The chain fell across her chest and dipped between her breasts. He looked up. He could feel her embarrassment as he stared at her.

'I'll bet you look more beautiful in it than the woman who first wore it.'

'Do you ever think of the women for whom these were made?' she asked.

'Often. I imagine them wearing animal skins or rough cloth tunics, leather thongs on their feet and wrists. Maybe leather plaits in their hair. Crude and garish paint on their bodies. The only refinement we would appreciate today would be the gold or bronze jewellery or the pendants.'

'And what did they look like?' she asked.

'Harsh. Crude. Their skin would be rough. Mottled and permanently stained from decorative paint and pigments. Not smooth and refined like yours,' he said reaching up and touching her cheek with his fingers.

'And their hair?' she asked.

'Matted. They'd make a daily attempt to comb the lice or the straw or leaves from it, but it would always be heavy and full of grease. Not light and shining and perfumed like yours.'

She reached up and took the jewellery off. She didn't want to be part of his seduction. But he stayed her hand, 'Keep it on. I want you to walk around in it. You see, at night, when I'm on my own, I dream about these women. If I can close my eyes and see you wearing the jewellery, then my dreams will be much sweeter.'

'But it's a false dream, Laco,' she said.

'How do you know? How does anybody know?' he said. 'I may be completely wrong. All we can do is to guess, and I'm only guessing at what they looked like. They may have had some herbal concoctions to make their skin smooth. They may have crushed leaves to make a sort of soap with which they could wash their hair. If they did, we'll never know. These things wouldn't last the thousands of years they were buried in the ground. Whatever they used would have rotted away. All we're ever left with is the metal objects and bones, and from these we have to build a picture of what the civilisation was like. That's why I prefer to see you wearing the necklace. It gives me greater comfort than the reality probably would.'

She smiled and nodded in agreement.

'May I take a photo of you in the necklace?' he asked. 'Not for publication, of course. Just for my personal enjoyment. So that when you go back to your university, and I'm alone for the long winter months, I'll have you to remember.'

Marta knew that it was a line he had used on at least three of the other girls. She had been wondering when he was going to try it on her. 'You may take a picture,' she said kindly. She was terribly fond of him. He was as old as her father but nothing like him. Her father was stern and rigid; Laco was a Bohemian in every way – wild, impetuous, funny, a most unusual man for a professor and a director of a museum. He had captivated all of the girls but, unlike them, she wasn't going to give in to his seductions.

'Marta,' he said, picking up his camera. 'Would you take your top off so that I can see the jewellery properly? You don't have to take it off completely. Just lower it over your nipples.'

'Laco,' she said, 'you're wasting your time. I'm not going to sleep with you.'

He looked hurt. 'I don't want to sleep with you,' he protested. 'I only want a photograph of the jewellery.'

She reached behind her neck and pulled the necklace over her head. 'Then put it on over your head. You take off your shirt and I'll take a photograph of you.'

He smiled and surprised her when he started to unbutton his shirt. She cursed herself for her stupidity. She didn't think he'd do it. 'Laco,' she said, 'I'm not going to sleep with you. I'm serious.'

'Good,' he said. 'I'm glad. I should at least respect and remember one of you girls when your time here is over.

I'm proud of you, Marta. You haven't disappointed me. Far from it. My respect for you has grown.'

She reached over and stroked his cheek. 'You're not upset?'

'Not at all,' he replied. 'It makes me even fonder of you.'

She walked slowly back to her desk to continue her work. He wondered how many more days she would be able to resist him.

# CHAPTER EIGHT

Adolf Hitler's grandson wore three steel rings in his nostril, four in his eyebrow and sported a safety pin bisecting his tongue. Wearing brass-studded leather and thick miner's boots, he and three hundred other of Hitler's offspring marched through the streets, holding placards, screaming 'Foreigners out!' and 'Hitler was right!'. The Neo-Nazis were on the move, led by the spectral figure of their long dead leader, Adolf Hitler, whose image floated high above their heads on a banner which stretched from one side of the street to the other.

The chanting was overwhelmingly aggressive, a series of animalistic screams of hatred, terrifying any resident foolish enough to venture out into the streets to find out what was going on. Police confined the marchers to the centre of the road and refused to allow them to turn left into the streets which contained hostels occupied by six thousand Turkish migrant workers.

Twenty storeys above the street, an elderly, portly man, wearing an overcoat to protect him from the cold air conditioning in the hotel, looked down upon the march in bemusement. He told the group of men sitting behind him, 'Those buffoons down there have no idea what they're doing. They're just mindless robots. They couldn't even begin to imagine how evil Hitler was, or how tens of millions of people died because of him.'

Another elderly man seated at the conference table responded, 'And Stalin was all that much better? If you had to toss a coin, old friend, which side would you prefer the coin to come down on? The side of Hitler or the side of Stalin? They were both evil bastards. They were both the vomit spewed up by this century.'

Boris Maximovich Tranov turned to look at his old friend. He walked slowly back to the conference table, to the meeting that had been disturbed by the noise of the demonstration in the streets far below. The other men, ten in all, looked at him expectantly. In front of each of them was a bottle of vodka. By the time the meeting was over most of the bottles would be empty.

He lifted a glass and said, 'Gentlemen, I give you a toast to the memory of the founder of our Syndicate: Kaganovich.'

Each of the elderly men lifted his glass and repeated the name, 'Kaganovich.' They threw the oily liquid to the back of their throats. Some picked up slices of black bread covered with eggs and caviar; others had already dined before the meeting started.

Boris Maximovich Tranov turned to his deputy and said, 'So, Colonel–General Zamov. A brief outline of the comrades if you please. How many of our Syndicate are still with us and whom do we mourn since we met last year?'

Comparisons may be odious, but when travelling they become inevitable. But a comparison between what Sarah was used to in America and what she experienced when entering Eastern Slovakia for the first time would have been futile. The country's roads, its hotels and their bare minimum levels of cleanliness bore no relationship to anything she'd ever experienced in her tourist past, let alone in the Czech Republic which she had just left, itself falling some way short of Sarah's minimum expectations for a country.

But it was in the arena of accommodation that the differences were at their most apparent. Initially Sarah was worried that she would be viewed by the men as being prissy, a typical Jewish American princess, more comfortable holidaying with her own people in the Adirondacks than with wild-eyed foreigners in the Carpathians. If she had been on holiday, then the distressed nature of the countryside, the visible poverty and the flyblown nature of the hotels, would have been taken in her stride as part of the charm of the place, the difference between here and America, a valuable adjunct to the experience of the vacation. But she was in business mode; she had a job to do. And in her professional life, Sarah hated having to accept this second-world standard.

It was impossible to compare the Hotel Slovan in Kosice with the places Sarah usually stayed in; one might as well compare a local municipal museum in the boondocks of New York State with Washington's Smithsonian Institution. As a hotel, the Slovan had never enjoyed a heyday. During the Communist regime, only the favourites of the egalitarian party were permitted access through the doors of the Slovan, and only those who travelled with the Party's membership passport could find room and board. Visitors from the West, usually German or Austrian businessmen, were rare. Why would anyone visit a town which had been asleep for hundreds of years, a town which awakened to the metallic dawn of Stalinism to find its once-medieval streets begrimed with the soot of iron foundries, its pure Carpathian mountain air befouled with the smoke of inefficient factories?

But since the disintegration of the Communist facade, Kosice in general, and the Hotel Slovan in particular, had been overwhelmed by a large increase of Western visitors: Americans, Canadians and British who demanded a standard of service which the hotel could never hope to provide. A lifetime of working to the Communist time-clock had given both management and staff a distinctly minimalist attitude to customer service and no amount of coaxing from the government or tourist agencies could make a dent in the ingrained attitudes. Customer service was an alien concept and, regardless of the irate demands from bristling New Yorkers, the staff of the Hotel Slovan continued to service these new demands in the same way as they had done when Josef Stalin was still in command.

Josh was bemused by the lack of Western sycophancy, the absence of homilies like *Have a nice day* and *Missing you already* – the McDonald's-driven standards of the American service society. Sarah was miffed, having expected a certain basic level of attention, and Jerry and Phil were in a state of shock when they arrived at the hotel and hadn't seemed to notice the indifferent service. They had been so intimidated by the totalitarianism of the customs officers at Kosice's airport, who had demanded to know what use they were intending to make of their cameras and sound equipment, that they remained silent and withdrawn until they entered their rooms.

The receptionist looked like the outer shell of a Babushka doll. She viewed the entourage with studied indifference as they and their oddly-shaped camera and sound equipment cases spilled out of the taxi and into the dusty foyer. Middle-aged men with shiny slicked-back hair and shinier suits sat in sunken club armchairs, half-heartedly reading newspapers. They stared at the newcomers with apathy, which changed to suspicion bordering on hostility when they saw their expensive clothes, luggage and equipment. With American disdain Sarah stared back at the men, who rapidly returned to their newspapers, losing interest in the only thing to have happened in the Hotel Slovan foyer that day. The men reminded her of the uncles of her friends when she was a little girl; she felt uncomfortable in their presence. She willingly joined Josh at the Slovan's reception desk.

The formalities ended, the receptionist handed them heavy metal keys on wooden fobs. Sarah hadn't seen relics like these since her holidays in Florida when she was a child, when guesthouses had windows that opened and corridors with bathrooms at the end. The receptionist nodded to the lift at the opposite end of the musty foyer. The lift-driver, an elderly man as asthmatic as the mechanism of his elevator, put down his paper and stood up. There was no friendly greeting, merely a grudging acceptance that he had to perform a duty for which he was being paid, and his expression made it quite clear that he would rather be sitting on his stool, reading his paper.

When the lift-driver saw the camera and sound equipment cases, he shook his head. In broken English, he said, 'Two I carry today. Rest you wait and I carry up the stairs lift when two I carry at home.'

The old man escorted Josh and Sarah into the metal cage of the tiny contraption. It creaked and cranked its way up to the tenth floor, where the lift operator hauled open the door and pointed down an equally musty, dark corridor in the direction of their rooms. They had to carry their own suitcases.

'Conrad Hilton would be rolling around in his grave if he could see this,' Sarah commented.

'He might,' said Josh, 'but Comrade Hilton would feel right at home.'

'How can you joke at a time like this? It's like stepping back a hundred years but without being cute. This place is a . . .' She struggled to find the right expression.

'A joke? Sure it is, but it has a charm all of its own. It's like some of the awful flicks that used to come out of Hollywood in the '50s and '60s. Some of them were so bad, they acquired a cult following. Bet you that'll happen here. When this place gets famous, people will flock here. Tell me, do you ever go to those restaurants in New York where the waiters are out of work actors and they specialise in insulting the customers?'

'No,' Sarah replied.

'Then you're seriously going to hate the Slovan. In places like this, they're not acting.'

The foyer and corridor were distressing enough, but when Sarah groped her way into her room her heart sank. This was a room which had risen to the apogee of its glory in the Age of Formica. The bathroom was little more than a cupboard with a decaying bath full of spiderweb cracks and a brown-stained showerhead that dripped with the constancy of a water-torture instrument. Sarah felt ill. If there was one matter on which she was insistent when travelling, it was that the personal hygiene facilities were of the very highest quality. A small but decent room, nicely furnished, was acceptable, especially when she was travelling on business. Somehow the Protestant work ethic had seeped into her conscience. But if the bathing facilities were inadequate, she felt drab the whole day. Not that this often happened in America, but the Hotel Slovan could not have existed in 1990s America – not outside a theme park, that is.

She sat on the thin mattress and surveyed her room. Two narrow, single, iron beds were separated by a rickety chest of drawers beneath the window. Its uppermost knobs had been lost to the ravages of time and the anger of countless guests. She reached over and forced open the top drawer. A stained and yellowing sheet of newspaper covered the wooden bottom. She recoiled and pushed the drawer shut with a shudder. Was she being too prissy again? Since landing at Kosice airport, she'd been concerned about appearing like a typical Jewish princess on her first trip away from the luxury of home. Perhaps she was too fussy. After all, this *was* Eastern Europe, a snowdrop slowly opening after the freezing Communist winter.

But this was also a place where she didn't want to be. Her heart, her entire disposition, rejected this hotel, this city, this country, this continent. It was the place where her great-grandparents and her grandmother had been born, where they came into the world full of hope and expectation, and where their village, their neighbours, the government and the entire Christian and hierarchical edifice had crushed them and their rights to a secure future. It was the country from which they had been forced to flee for their lives, leaving behind their possessions and their family history for the plunderers and marauders. It was the country full of hate for those born with the stain of being Jewish.

And so her great-grandmother, sole survivor of a hideous pogrom which killed her great-grandfather and countless other pathetic souls, had left this place and had trudged with her children across Europe, brutalised by unimaginable horrors along the way, to be welcomed by the brilliant torch and open arms of America. But, for modern American families, the barbarous reality of European anti-Semitism had been blunted by an eruption of sentimentalism, a strange flowering of nostalgia. Time had numbed the memories of families who had been dragged out of their homes and thrown into cattle trucks to be carted off to stalags or concentration camps, or tossed into the streets to be hacked to death by drunken peasants jealous of their meagre yet hard-gained possessions. American Jews no longer understood the awful connivance of the Eastern Orthodox priests in their pulpits, making thunderous sermons and telling their gullible and illiterate flocks that the Jews had murdered Christ and that until they converted to Catholicism, there would be no Second Coming and no redemption.

This Hotel Slovan, this Kosice, this Slovakia were the very places that the parents and grandparents of American Jews had been expelled from. It was alien territory, an ancient battleground littered with broken bones and bitter memories. A place of entrapment for Jews, a hard and unyielding earth. Why then this modern hunger to return? Why this recent nostalgic yearning for places which had been hated by earlier generations of their families, just because the barriers had been removed?

Sarah lay down on her bed. The mattress was hard and unyielding but at least that should ensure a good night's sleep. The traffic noise and the metallic clanking of the trams ten floors below made any further reflection impossible. She looked out of the window. Opposite was a huge grey department store with ill-lit windows and poorly illuminated stock. To the left, a muddy river flowed between concrete shoulders. Far to the right, a tall cathedral stood in the gathering dusk, the lower half of its spire lit with a yellow neon glow, the upper half disappearing into infinity; not enough money to illuminate the rest. But nowhere, as far as she could see through the dusty window, was there the brightness and gaiety of an American city. Nowhere was there an environment suited to modern living; no neon lights above shops, no attractive footpaths with bustling consumers and office workers, no noisy and vibrant theatre of the street with people calling out to each other. This was a utilitarian town, designed purely for the purpose of servicing industrial needs, with little regard for the enjoyment of those who lived there.

She was jolted out of her depression by the phone. 'Pretty crummy, isn't it?' said Josh without the usual greeting. 'Last time I was here I stayed over the road in the Centrum. I thought I'd give the Slovan a try this time. One is just as much an asshole as the other. Anyway, we won't be spending much time in the hotel. Meet you downstairs in half an hour and I'll show you the high life of Kosice.'

Waiting for him in the hotel foyer, Sarah was conscious of the eyes staring at her over the newspapers. She had chosen clothes which came as close as possible to blending in with the dress of the local population: a summer skirt and cotton blouse, sandals and a leather carry bag slung over her shoulder. Even so, her hair style, her make-up, even the confident way she stood, defined her as a modern, independent American woman. There was a dowdiness, a lack of concern for self, about most Czech and Slovakian women. Some, especially the women in Prague, were as fashionably and immaculately dressed as were fashionable women in London, Paris or New York. But most of the local women Sarah had seen wore very ordinary clothes, the sort worn by American women in the 1950s or '60s.

She stared defiantly at the men who were examining her; she refused to be cowed by their patronising attitudes. Screw them! She was here on her terms, and if they didn't like it or if they objected to her ancestry, that was their problem. The lift opened and Josh walked out. He was dressed in the same way as when she had first met him in New York: sneakers, a loose-fitting top and jeans. He put his arm around her and walked her to the doorway. She was no longer shocked when he touched her; his attitude was one of friendship. They turned right out of the hotel, crossed Rooseveltova and walked down Hlvana Ulica, the main street that intersected the city. On either side of the road were shops that sold a bevy of unexciting products, poorly displayed.

'Straight ahead is the centre of this place,' said Josh. 'There are a couple of churches side by side. One is a cathedral. Are you interested in cathedrals?'

'Of course,' she said. 'I've been to quite a few in my time. How does this one compare?'

'The guide took me in when I was here a couple of days ago. It's okay. Its claim to fame is that it's the eastern-most gothic cathedral in Europe. It sort of blends in with the baroque and neo-classical buildings around it, but nothing much is going to happen in your life if you miss out.'

She nodded. 'So why are we walking there?'

'Just to get out of the hotel. To show you around.'

'What about Phil and Jerry? Shouldn't they be filming this? What are they doing?' she asked.

'They're setting up and checking their equipment. Tomorrow morning they'll hire a driver to take them around so they can get background shots of Kosice. Then we'll do a walk down the main street. I'll need you. You sure you're not interested in the cathedral?' She shook her head. 'Good. There's something else I want you to see.'

They turned right into another major thoroughfare and right again. The streets became narrower and less busy but also more dusty. There was a claustrophobia about the place; the narrow streets were oppressive.

'Where are we going?' she asked.

'Trust me,' he said.

They continued to walk in silence until they came to a rusted, wrought-iron fence with sharp spikes atop its poles. It enclosed a drab and unidentifiable building, closed tight, locked with chains; a building that looked as if it hadn't been used for decades. Sarah looked at Josh, puzzled.

'Look up there,' he said, pointing to the apex of the building. There was a dark, dusty, circular, stained-glass window. She looked carefully and made out a mystical symbol in the middle: a Star of David, the Jewish icon which identified a synagogue.

'This is the place where my grandfather and grandmother used to come to pray. They had their own small synagogue in Ujlak but on high holidays, New Year and the Day of Atonement they would come into town and stay with friends. Hundreds of people from all around the outlying districts would come in especially. They would sit in this synagogue and pray all day, and then at night they'd come back into the community. They'd stay up until the early hours of the morning, talking about their lives and the way God was screwing them around.'

He grasped two of the iron poles, like an outsider trying to get in. He remained for a long moment. Sarah didn't know whether she ought to interrupt and, besides, she had no idea what to say. This was a private emotion that Josh was sharing with her; she felt uncomfortable.

'Josh,' she said softly, linking her arm through his, 'this is a symbol of what was. You and I are what *is*. We've moved on since this. We've no need to look back on places like this with anything but a feeling of gratitude that our parents left this place and gave us a life which is infinitely better than the one they suffered.'

'You're wrong, Sarah. You're so very wrong. Sure, we've moved on, but this is where we've come from. If you don't know where you've come from, how can you know where you are?'

'I know where I am, Josh. I don't need to see the house, or the synagogue, or the fields, or anything else which was associated with my family. Not just because it's of no interest to me; I'd positively avoid it. And avoid the pain that goes with it. Truth is, Josh, I'd be scared that seeing it would hurt me deeply.'

He let go of the railings and leant against the fence. She was still holding his arm and standing close to him. Somehow it felt natural, as though they were close friends. 'I don't understand,' he said.

She sighed. They began to walk away from the synagogue. 'I suppose it goes something like this,' she said. 'My past is based on what I'm told, on the legends, the stories, the myths my family created and the tales they've recounted. They're part of me. But the moment they become a reality – if I was to see the two-room hovels where fourteen people huddled together, or the burnt-out shell of a synagogue where they once prayed – I know that it would change my perception of my religion and my family.'

He shook his head. 'But you've been to Israel, you've seen the Wailing Wall, the Temple, the old synagogues. You've seen Hebron and Beersheba and Jerusalem. They were the places where your religion used to be . . . where it all started.'

'Sure,' she said, 'but what I saw there was impersonal. That was the history of my people. Nobody I know or love was damaged there. What I don't want to see is the personal side. I don't want to feel all over again the suffering that my family was put through. They've put it behind them, as far as they're able. They've made a new life in a new country. My responsibility to them, and to myself, is to do the same. To put the life they left behind me as well, to get on with things.'

Josh shook his head sadly. 'I started off thinking that maybe all of this would change your attitudes; that once you were exposed to it, there'd be some sort of epiphany. But there's not going to be one, is there, Sarah? We've come a long way since New York, but your thinking hasn't altered one jot.'

'No, and nor will it. These aren't idle speculations of mine, Josh, they're deep-seated, firmly rooted beliefs. I'm not likely to change them because of some sudden emotional revelation. I'm here to do a job; I'm here to work for you as best I can in order to get your grandparents' house back, to expose the government for what it did, to identify how these people treated your family. That's what I'm here for. But there's no way that I'm going to become emotionally involved in this. No way at all.'

Josh smiled. 'Tomorrow I'm going to take you to see my home in Novosad. When my father was kicked out it was called Ujlak. We'll see how you feel then.'

'Why do you care how I feel? Why is it so important that you change my mind?' She realised she sounded harsh, but she knew it was necessary. At Harvard, she'd been taught not to become emotionally involved in cases; it did neither the client nor the lawyer any good. But this wasn't some academic tutorial, some hypothetical question about torts or case law. She was in an Eastern European town with a lovely guy, listening to him opening his heart to her. But, in the end, professionalism had to win out over her personal feelings.

He hesitated before answering. Then he said, softly, 'Did you know that my major at college was in philosophy?' Sarah shook her head. 'Socrates never taught his students by giving them the answers. Instead, he pretended not to know the answers to his own questions. They worked out the solutions together. In that way, he got them to question their preconceived ideas and assumptions. But he also said that by teaching others he learned himself. I'm no Socrates, but I'm going to keep on challenging you. That way, if I ever manage to convince you, I'll be confirming everything I believe, and learning at the same time.'

Their pace slowed to a halt. The lights of the main road were still in the distance; Sarah and Josh were shrouded by the shadows of the night, ensconced in its anonymous warmth. He turned towards her and smiled. He had such an attractive face. She looked at his eyes, his lips, his hair, unkempt and uneven. There was so much about him which was attractive, and that was dangerous.

He sensed that she was thinking of him. He opened his arms; she stepped forward and he enfolded her. He kissed the top of her head and smelt the cleanliness of her hair, the freshness. She threaded her arms underneath his jacket and pulled him in to her. He had a strong muscular back, tall and straight. It was so good to feel him enwrapping her. He kissed her again, this time on the cheek. She moved her head slightly. He started to kiss her on the lips, but she moved away, a distant voice warning her that it was wrong.

'Josh,' she said. He nodded. She felt his cheek brushing hers. 'I know,' he replied.

Voices in the distance cried out, whether in pain or pleasure Sarah couldn't tell. They echoed in the empty streets. Despite the warmth of the night, she shuddered.

She wanted to get back to security. 'Let's go back to the hotel,' she said.

The drive to Novosad took them less than two hours. Once they had turned off the main artery south-east from Kosice, heading towards the Ukraine border, the roads changed from dull, predictable highways into pretty country lanes. Distant hills were crowned by the spilt building blocks of ruined castles or the remnants of once-grand manors, now people's spas or rest homes or hotels.

Excitedly Josh pointed to the chimney tops of the houses that flashed by. It was like a scene from a fairy tale. Resting on top of the chimneys were huge storks' nests, often containing two or three birds, which viewed the passing traffic with an imperious disdain. Sarah wondered how they could stay up there, their nests seemed to be perched so precariously. There were also bird's nests on top of electricity and telephone poles; the storks were everywhere. It looked quaint, but her practical side overcame Josh's romanticism: as he was waxing lyrical about the rustic charm, Sarah was thinking how irritating it must be to live with them above your head all through summer.

The houses themselves were more modern than she had anticipated and were almost uniformly clean and well-presented. Often white-washed, usually made of timber, some even had thatched roofs. Sarah didn't quite know what she *had* expected: houses made of hewn blocks of stone maybe, or even of wattle and daub. She chastised herself mentally; this was a living country, not some ancient archaeological site.

As they got nearer to Novosad, Josh metamorphosed from an ingenuous and enthusiastic traveller into a professional movie director. The change surprised Sarah.

Josh began to instruct Jerry and Phil about what he wanted. 'Okay guys, lots of ECUs on faces and reactions to get a travelogue feel. When I was here a couple of days ago, I worked out where the best POVs are along the street where my dad's house is, so that should save you some scouting time. But I didn't have time for a complete survey of the rest of the village, so that's part of what I want you to do today. I want you to see how best to capture shots of people walking around, going about their own business. Plenty of length, say aim low and shoot up to mid-hip. There's a hill overlooking the town so long shots won't be a problem. There are the usual church spires and one or two three-storey buildings. There's no city centre to speak of so don't anticipate any traffic or shots of communal gathering. And Jerry, for background noise, I'm not going to be able to give you anything more than birds twittering in trees. You might be lucky and get some local drunk throwing up.'

Jerry nodded. 'Let's wing it when we get there, Josh.'

But Josh was still in director's mode. 'Now the last time I came into town, there was music playing over the loudspeakers. I didn't ask whether that happened all the time or every hour. Have your recording equipment ready. When it happens, I want Phil to do some wild shots of people's reaction in the street, looking up at the loudspeakers the minute the music begins. Good face shots, maybe a bit of disappointment or bemusement. Maybe somebody a bit pissed off that this old-time shit's still with them. Scowls, but no fist-shaking at the loudspeakers. See what you can capture. And remember this is a documentary, everything has to be fresh. There are no actors and actresses. Think of it like you're shooting for the news.'

'So, don't you think that if the music comes on, it'd be better if Phil took shots of people ignoring it? Face it, boss, a couple of old ladies walking past a singing lamppost, ignoring the shit outta it, is gonna have a greater impact than people staring up in anger.'

Josh nodded. 'Take both, and we'll leave the dud on the cutting room floor.'

He continued to bark staccato instructions until Phil said, 'Josh, why not leave it to us. You just concentrate on what you're here for.'

'I'm here to direct a movie.'

'Sure,' said Phil, 'but you're also here to get your house back. This is background stuff, Loony Tune News, the sort of shit Jerry and I used to do every day for NBC in 'Nam. It's not the kinda thing you can direct. It just happens. Let us worry about background; you worry about your house.'

'That's why Sarah's here, guys.'

Sarah smiled at both men. The political subtext in the conversation was too crowded for her to enter.

As the car reached the border of the village of Novosad, Josh ignored Phil's advice and resumed his orders at an increasingly frenetic rate. 'I want that sign shot in ECU and then pan back for an MCU. Then a distance shot so I can edit it like we're speeding past at fifty miles an hour. And make sure you've got the side of the car in the picture so we've got a medium close up with the background as the sign flashes past. Jerry, let's get some atmosphere sounds that I can sync. People talking in shops, service inside a church, you know the routine. Phil, make sure the camera shots look like it's being held. Show someone's ass, then fly up to their heads and hold it there. Real home movie stuff.'

Phil looked at Josh in surprise. 'Isn't that just a bit corny? Sounds a bit like World's Funniest Fucking Videos.' he said. 'Aren't you a bit too professional to be making a fucking home movie?'

'That's exactly what the Network's bought. I told them it was just me and my lawyer going back home to Slovakia to kick ass,' he said. Sarah looked at him. He'd been touting the idea of the film since early in their relationship, but expressing it so bluntly came as a surprise. He didn't notice her reaction.

'This isn't a Hollywood flick,' he told his crew. 'This is me returning to my dad's home with a hand-held Sony, filled with vengeance. This is television *vérité*, Phil, not cinemascope. I want hand-held stuff all the way through the village. Rank fuckin' amateur hour. Jerry, your sound can be fairly crude. Lots of breathy pauses when we speak as if we're recording on the run.'

Josh instructed the driver to slow down and open the windows. The warmth of the summer morning entered the car. 'Damn,' said Josh. 'No music. Still we'll be here most of the day. Just be ready for it when it starts, Jerry. Okay?'

He instructed the driver where to go. They turned left off the road leading into the town, then veered right into a narrow road, then turned left again onto the road from where Josh's father and his grandparents had last viewed their house.

'Okay. This is the road. That's my house,' he said, pointing to a shop whose front windows were almost obscured by the elm and sycamore trees growing along the side of the road. His voice changed slightly. It was no longer as commanding as it had been when he was playing the movie director.

'Shit,' hissed Phil. 'How the fuck am I supposed to get a good establishment shot of a house with fuckin' trees poking through the fuckin' front door?'

He mused for a minute, then said, 'Maybe I could do a helicopter aerial shot, zoom in and pick it up from ground level with a hand-held, walking in through the trees. At least that will give it an MCU which will define the place.'

'No helicopters, no cranes, no tracks. This is a home movie, remember,' said Josh.

'Shit, man, you're going to have no frame of reference. Maybe I can thin out the trees a bit.'

'Do the best you can,' said Josh. 'Maybe try a ground level shot up through the tree trunks.'

'Nah,' said Phil, 'the lighting would be all wrong. From the look of it I'd have to open the stops too far, and without megawatt daytime lights it's gonna look shit. If I don't have an establishment shot we won't know where the fuck we are. Jesus, Josh, this is gonna be hell's own job.'

'That's why you're here, buddy. Still, I knew you'd have serious problems first time I saw the place. So I've found some people in Kosice and I've phoned a buddy in Prague so we can hire equipment and crew next time we're here. What I need now is some background shots. The difficult stuff we can do after we've got more stuff on Kosice and the area. Say a couple of days time.'

The cameraman smiled, until Josh added, 'It might go against the grain, but right now all I want from you is a hand job.'

'Excuse me?'

'I want a simple travel documentary. This part has got to be amateur night. Everything else we do – Prague, Bratislava, when we go back to pick up shots – that's going to be professional, we'll include archival material, the works. But for me, going back to my home town, this is exactly what I want. Just a hand-held camera, reasonable sound. The only time we're going to fake it is when we can't get the right image . . . like over the road at the entrance to the property.'

'Alright,' said Phil. 'You want it, you get it. But I ain't gonna be proud.'

'Trust me, Phil,' said Josh. 'You'll be proud. So will I.'

While the two men unloaded the equipment, Josh walked Sarah across the road to the shop. Sarah was beginning to see images through the eyes of a cameraman: it was dark beyond the trees, the light hidden by the thick foliage. Josh put his arm around her shoulder. In Prague, she had felt a shock as he touched her; now it felt nice, comfortable.

'If we see the man who owns the shop, just be nonchalant. He was suspicious of me when I first came here. Second time, he'll be paranoid.'

She looked at him and smiled, 'Just pretend I'm your girlfriend and you've come to show me the sights.'

But the man wasn't there. Another man was sitting behind the counter reading a paper. When they peered in through the window, he looked at them with suspicion. Sarah avoided his eyes, but Josh waved. The man waved back. They turned and walked back across the road.

'See that house over there?' he said. 'The one with the barn at the back. You can see the small window on top of it. That's where the lady hid my grandparents and my dad when the Communists came to wipe them out. Next time we're back here, I'm going to go across and introduce myself.'

'You mean she's still alive?' asked Sarah in surprise.

Josh nodded. 'In places like this, they tend to live longer than in the cities. She was twelve years older than my dad and, according to the guy I spoke to, she's still all there.'

'So why not go over there now?'

He looked over the road, up to the barn where his father had escaped death by a hair's breadth nearly half a century earlier. He was tempted. In Novosad a couple of days earlier, he'd been just as tempted, but he'd judged that the moment wasn't right. And it still wasn't.

'No. The first time I was here, I wanted to be alone. Just to see the house. The men inside the shop told me about the old woman and said I should go and see her. But I couldn't go, not then. And not now, either. I'm here to get some establishment shots. Rough cuts so we can plan more of this part of the film. Next time I'm here, maybe you and me, we should go over and see her. Talk to her. Find out what things were like. Right now, something's stopping me. Don't ask what, I don't even know myself.'

Sarah nodded in understanding.

While Josh and the crew were walking up and down the road, looking at different points of view, a policeman rode up on a motorcycle. He exchanged terse comments with their driver. He stared suspiciously at Josh for a few moments, then rode away.

By the time Phil and Jerry had walked up and down the road a dozen times, with Josh crouching one moment, climbing on the car's roof the next, stretching or bending to determine an interesting angle, lunchtime was upon them. Almost nothing had been achieved yet, to Sarah's surprise, they congratulated each other on the value of the morning's work. The afternoon proceeded in the same way: the crew moving from place to place within the dull and uninspiring town, measuring angles and points of view and talking animatedly, using abbreviations, acronyms and neologisms which she gradually came to understand from their context. Sarah hated technical jargon; always had. She had infuriated her teachers at Harvard by refusing to use jargon in her essays. They had tried to convince her that legal jargon was a shorthand way for people within the legal profession to communicate with each other efficiently. She, in turn, had tried to convince them that it was their very jargon which alienated the public from the law and made courts such terrifying places. And now here she was with people who were throwing jargon around like post-modernists at a literary conference. MCU meant medium close-up, ECU was extreme close-up; the rest, to do with stops, focal lengths and other technical matters, held no interest for her.

She trailed around after the men, wondering why her presence was necessary, and how much more use she could have been had she stayed in Kosice, or even Prague. Josh kept giving her encouraging glances, and occasionally came over to explain what he was doing and why. He squeezed her elbow affectionately, or held her hand, telling her that things were going terrifically well. She hoped she feigned enthusiasm as well as the actresses he was used to working with.

Bored beyond belief, she went to explore the village, which took her all of an hour. She returned, and waited patiently by the car for them to finish. By the time all had confessed their satisfaction with the results of the day, most of it had already gone. They consumed the sandwiches, coffee and beers they had brought from the hotel and, as they drove out of the village, Josh felt a need to apologise that there had been no street music during their stay. To add insult to injury, the car's air conditioning unit broke down ten miles out of Kosice. It was a hot day, and by the time they reached the city everyone's mood had deteriorated.

Back at the hotel Sarah took a bitingly cold shower. She had an overwhelming desire to talk to David. It was still early in the morning in America but she knew he'd be up, either meditating or practising.

'How are you going over there with the great Houdini? Has he conjured up any magic yet?' he asked.

'Right now I know more about POVs, ECUs, MCUs and tracking shots than any lawyer east of Los Angeles. Did you know that an establishment shot isn't a photo of New York society? It all sounds like so much crap, David, but they take it so seriously. I'm sure they're brilliant at what they do, but God give me strength.'

'How is all this going to help your case?'

'It's not. All it's helping me with is my relationship with the client. Nothing more.'

'Are you getting on well with him, hon?'

She delayed her answer a split second more than was necessary, analysing her thoughts. She was enjoying her closeness with Josh, the fact that he tried to involve her in his creative process, even though she was being unnecessarily derogatory about that to David. Indeed, sometimes she felt she was revelling in Josh's attention. In the beginning, she had found it confronting, but he was so gentle, so understated, that now she felt his gentle charm enveloping her.

'Yeah. He's very warm and friendly.'

David laughed. 'Don't fall for his ways, Sarah. He has a reputation.'

'David!' she said. 'What a thing to say! He's my client.'

'He's rich and good-looking.'

'Is that all you think of me?'

'Of course not, but . . .'

'No *buts*, David. He's a nice guy with a mega–ego and I've spent the last week and a half telling him I can't get involved in all his emotional bullshit about getting his family's house back. That should have put him off. He likes everything and everyone under his control, wants us all to be as committed, as emotional, as him. I'm sure that most people fall down and let him walk all over them, so I don't think he's come across someone like me before.'

'That's good to hear. You have to retain your objectivity or it'll go badly for you.'

'I know, honey. God I miss you.'

'I'll tell you what you really missed,' he said. 'Couple of nights ago, I had a phone call from the White House. They want me to play for the President.'

'You're kidding!' she shouted.

'Serious. The President's function secretary phoned me herself. Apparently the wife of a congressman was in the Carnegie audience when I played the Dvorak, and she raved to the President's wife. Hence the invite. Big stuff, huh?'

'Oh, David, I'm so proud of you. Jeez, I wish I was back there. I feel I'm letting you down, being away while things are really taking off for you. Are you disappointed in me?'

'Don't be silly. We both have careers. But I'll be seriously pissed if you're not in the audience when I play in Washington.'

She laughed. 'I might be busy that night. You know my politics and his don't meet eye to eye.'

'Neither do mine, but that's one night we'll let our political differences rest for a while.'

They talked more about the opportunities that a Command Performance could bring, which led on to a discussion of his work and hers. Sarah kept talking to extend the conversation longer than was necessary; it was comforting to hear him and to be a part of his life again.

When she'd put down the phone, she towel-dried her hair, then lay on the bed, staring at the ceiling. What wonderful news. She was so thrilled for David. In New York, she would have been on the phone to everyone she'd ever met, trumpeting the news around town. Yet here, so far away, it lost its impact. And, as was happening more and more frequently, thoughts of Josh somehow seeped into her mind. Despite what she'd said to David, Sarah was forced to admit to herself that she had warmer feelings towards Josh than was comfortable. She hadn't told David the full story; she hadn't told him about Josh holding her hand, and putting his arms around her. Or that she had enjoyed his friendly embrace. But, if she was feeling close to Josh, why did she feel so numb in front of his grandparents' house? Why did she experience academic interest only, instead of the deep emotion Josh had obviously felt? Why was she holding back? How would she feel if she were to stand outside her own grandparents' home, in a village very close to where she was now? Would she feel the same as Josh? She would never know. She would never allow herself to experience what he was going through.

They all met downstairs for dinner. The Slovan's dining room was a long chamber, which had obviously enjoyed a certain elegance once upon a time; now it was draped in red velvet curtains which smelt of the dust of ages. The meal was served by waiters wearing white jackets and gloves. It came on silver salvers. Strangely, it was delicious. They had ordered local specialities, allowing themselves to be guided by the waiter – one of the few people in the place who was outgoing and friendly. They had dumplings in a chicken soup, borscht with potatoes, schnitzel, the ubiquitous duck with red cabbage and potatoes. It was plentiful and tasty, and all four shared what they had ordered and, by the end of the meal, felt uncomfortably full.

The conversation at the table was way outside Sarah's area. It reminded her of when David and his friends got together and began to discuss the technicalities of music, or when her father and his friends thumped the table about last Saturday's ball game. The three men were caught up in the filming possibilities of the village: how they would need another car, another driver, so they could shoot Josh driving into the village and looking around the town; the special equipment they would need for interiors – lighting equipment more sophisticated than was available in Kosice, which Josh's contact would have to track down in Prague. They decided it would be necessary for them to return to Prague. Sarah was amazed that it was all taking so long. She had no experience of filming, but the seeming lack of planning astonished her. As a lawyer, she wouldn't begin a case until everything foreseeable had been tied down, yet here were three extremely professional men discussing what equipment they would need – surely something they should have talked about in America.

It was nine-thirty when they finished dinner and suddenly realised that they had nothing to do. The local television was incomprehensible so there was no point in returning to their rooms for entertainment.

'Who wants to come out for a walk?' Josh asked.

The two technicians shook their heads. 'We've got an hour or two's work to do, planning the shoot for tomorrow. You guys go off, we'll see you at breakfast.'

Josh and Sarah walked out into the humid night air of the street. For the third time in two days, they walked down the main road towards the part of the city centre that offered what passed in Kosice for nightlife. Two pavement cafés gave a neon glow to the otherwise dark area. In the warmth of the summer night, people had come out and were promenading.

It was provincial, but the sight of the old men walking slowly, arm in arm along the pavement, and the young men and women lost in each other's presence appealed to Sarah. It was delightful, she thought, probably the nicest thing she'd seen in Kosice since arriving. It was something that didn't happen often in New York. In big American cities, people had to have a purpose to their journey, a destination. Here the object was the walk itself. Sarah had a momentary desire to link her arm through Josh's. She felt close to him, and was delighted they were alone together.

'Coffee?' he asked. She nodded and smiled.

They sat facing the road. Opposite was the central plaza and St Elizabeth's Cathedral with its contorted towers and gothic archways. They sat silently, drinking their coffee. There were a hundred things Sarah wanted to tell him about herself. He spent so much time sharing his experiences with her, but whenever he asked about her or her family history, she was evasive, as though it was an area she didn't want to explore. But, since seeing him outside his grandparents' home, somehow ... indefinably ... things had changed within her. Out of her normal context – the context of lawsuits and billing hours and the preparation of briefs to lay before judges – Sarah's eyes had been opened to Josh. She saw a vulnerable man, a sensitive man, a lovely man. And the time was right to tell him more about herself. She had even been practising ways of broaching the subject. She thought she knew how to begin. She looked at Josh's profile; he was staring at the cathedral, bathed in yellow light. She took out her amulet and touched its comforting edges; its heavy golden certainty glistened in the lights of St Elizabeth's. She cleared her throat, and was about to begin to share with him her moment of greatest pride as a young woman, when a rowdy group of men walking towards them intruded into the peace of the night.

There were four of them: one, a young, swarthy attractive man with long black hair almost to his shoulders, and three others, two of them taller than the first by a head, the other the same size. They were all smoking cigarettes and laughing and talking at the top of their voices. A century earlier, they would have been identifiable as Bohemians. They reminded Sarah of the gipsies on the Charles Bridge, although they were more modernly dressed. As they passed by where Josh and Sarah were sitting, one of the older men stopped in his tracks and stared at Sarah in shock. There was no warmth in his look, no smile of recognition. He stared at her as though she was an enemy. He stared intently at her hands, which were holding her amulet close to her breasts. The others looked back at him, wondering what had made his affability disappear so suddenly.

Sarah became embarrassed. The man pointed to Sarah and barked an incomprehensible sentence in Slovakian. She frowned and shrugged her shoulders. 'Excuse me?' she said.

The man walked menacingly towards her, his finger still pointing as though it was a sword about to impale her. 'English?'

'American,' she said defensively.

'Where did you get that?' He was pointing to her amulet.

'What?' she asked. She had no idea what he was talking about, and suddenly felt embarrassed and surprised. Conversation in the café became muted.

'That artefact. Where did you get it?'

Sarah grasped her amulet. 'This is mine,' she said defiantly. She was beginning to regain her composure, after the initial shock.

'Where did you get that piece of jewellery? Tell me now.'

'Who the hell are you?' said Josh.

The man didn't shift his attention from Sarah's face, not even for a split second. 'Tell me where you got it or I'll call the police. Tell me now,' he shouted.

'How dare you talk to me like that,' Sarah said, her voice rising in indignation. 'This is mine. It's been in my family for generations. Who are you?'

'My name is Professor Dr Laco Plastov. I'm the director of the Kosice Pre-Historical Museum. This artefact you're wearing is very ancient and valuable. It dates back almost four thousand years. I want to know where you got it from. Was it stolen? Did somebody take it?'

Sarah clutched her amulet tightly. 'What are you talking about?' His words shocked her. 'Valuable? This is an heirloom. It's been in my family for generations. I have no idea where it came from but it's mine. It was given to me by my mother and she was given it by her mother.'

Josh stood. He was taller than the archaeologist. 'I think you'd better go. You're making me and my friend angry. We're not used to being treated like this. If you don't leave, I'll call the police. Now on your way, asshole!'

Laco turned, holding his ground firmly, and looked up at Josh. 'Please don't threaten me. You are tourists, you have no standing in this community. I do. This woman is wearing something that belongs to my museum. It's from this area. It's a national treasure. If it was given by her family, it was stolen by them. She has no right to it.'

'What the hell are you talking about?' said Josh. 'How can you tell it's ancient? You can hardly see the thing in this light.'

Laco looked at Josh in contempt. 'I'm an expert on Otomani jewellery. I've studied it all my life. This woman is wearing something which came from this area. It's at least four millennia old.'

The other three men now moved forward to support their colleague. But Josh was not intimidated. He had faced down street gangs in LA and boardrooms of Japanese business executives; these days very little frightened him. The two men faced each other like prize fighters. Sarah, still seated, felt uneasy.

'Listen,' she said, her voice rising in anger, 'you're creating a scene and being melodramatic. Sit down and let's talk about this. It's ridiculous. I'm an American citizen, I'm wearing a piece of jewellery which I've owned ever since my mother gave it to me on my twenty-first birthday. And her mother gave it to her. You've got no grounds for saying that you have any sort of claim of ownership, either in Slovakian or American law. You're making a fool of yourself. I'm a lawyer so I know what I'm talking about. Now, sit down.' She gave him her prosecutor's look, the one she used on hostile witnesses. It said, *don't even think about messing with me.*

It worked. Laco turned, said a few words to his colleagues, who nodded and walked off, leaving the three of them alone at the table. In the sudden silence, they realised that the other patrons were staring at them. A waiter came out and placed a cup of coffee in front of Laco.

'Now,' said Sarah, 'perhaps you could tell me what the hell is going on.'

'Firstly, who are you?' Laco asked. They introduced themselves.

'And what are you doing here?'

'We're here on business,' said Sarah. She didn't want to disclose anything at this stage.

'I've said who I am. My name is Laco Plastov. I'm an archaeologist and the director of the Pre-History Museum here. For the last ten years I've been in charge of an archaeological dig at Nizna Mysla, just outside of Kosice.

It's a settlement from the middle Bronze Age, about 1500 BC. We've dug up seventy skeletons and many artefacts; some of the gold ones are identical to the one you're wearing. When I was walking past just now and saw you wearing it, I thought you'd stolen it. I got very angry. There's a lot of pressure on us from the government to sell our collection to museums around the world because we need the funds. It's a full-time job for me keeping it together. I lost my temper. Now, I've told you everything you need to know about me. Tell me how you got this.'

But before Sarah could start to explain, Laco reached across the table and said, 'May I see it close up?'

She was unwilling, but Laco gave her a trusting look. She glanced at Josh before slowly taking off the amulet and placing it in the archaeologist's hands. Josh was ready to pounce if the other man tried to stand and make off with it. But instead, Laco looked at it lovingly.

'It's beautiful,' he said. 'It's one of the finest examples I've ever seen. Certainly the striations are much clearer than most. The whorls and decorations are stunning.' He turned it over and his body stiffened in shock. His expression changed from devotion to one of surprise. 'Good God!' he hissed.

'What?' asked Sarah.

'I must borrow this for a few days.'

She laughed. 'Don't be silly.'

'No, no, I'm serious,' he said. There was no longer any aggression in his voice. He sounded like a street trader, trying to strike a bargain. 'Listen, you need have no fear if it's rightfully yours . . . but these markings are fantastic, they're Anatolian. I don't believe it. There was never a link between Carpathia and the Hittites. This bull icon could even be a Trojan symbol. This is fantastic. The Balkans, certainly, but there's never been the slightest indication that the Otomani people had any dealings with the Hittites or the Anatolians. Good God. This is amazing.' He was raving like an excited child.

He showed them the obverse side of the amulet. 'These markings . . .' He pointed to a series of lines that Sarah had never really looked at before. 'It's an owl,' he said.

She stared at the markings and was able to make out the rudimentary outline of a bird. Had Laco not identified it she would never have known.

'So?' she asked, still puzzled.

'Don't you understand?' His voice was excited, he was almost shouting. 'It's the owl of Troy. Homer. Haven't you read the *Iliad*?'

Sarah shrugged. Josh was about to intervene when Laco continued: 'Homer talks about owls. Whenever you see a Bronze Age symbol of an owl, it almost certainly refers to Troy. You know that the treasure that Schliemann dug up at Troy was stolen from Berlin after the war, and was recently rediscovered in Moscow? Well, the latest photos I've seen show amulets and pins with identical markings to these. They were from Troy. But how did markings like those get onto an amulet found here? It's incredible. I had no idea there was a relationship between here and Troy. This is . . . I can't believe it.' He was struck dumb, fondling the amulet as though it was a saintly relic.

'Maybe,' said Sarah, 'this amulet isn't from here. Maybe it's from Greece or Turkey?'

'No!' Laco said vehemently. 'It's identical in every respect but this to the dozens I've got in my museum. I'll show them to you. Then I'll be able to compare this, and maybe I can work out what happened . . .'

Josh suddenly reached over and took the amulet from Laco's grip. He returned it to Sarah. 'Sorry, doctor. It stays with us.'

Laco looked at him with fresh hostility. 'I don't think you understand the immense significance of what you're dealing with.'

'And I don't think you understand *who* you're dealing with,' Josh said firmly.

Sarah had listened with fascination to Laco, her earlier hostility disappearing as he touched her amulet with reverence and admiration. As she replaced the amulet around her neck she saw that his eyes followed her actions jealously.

He looked at her. His eyes were those of a small child, desperately waiting for the approving smile of a parent. Sarah looked at Josh. His face was still full of hostility and suspicion. She didn't know what to say.

# CHAPTER NINE

Sarah had never been in a museum at night. There was something supernatural about it, as though the muted lights and the echoing absence of people gave the exhibits an eerie animation, a sense of unnatural life.

As they walked through the empty halls, she felt she was being watched by the exhibits in the cases, instead of the other way round; nature and reality reversed. Up flights of stairs, along corridors, through auditoriums, eventually they reached the floor that Laco wanted to show them. It was well past ten o'clock and Laco had forced two unwilling security guards to open the museum after hours. He turned on a few lights in the large exhibition hall: hundreds of exhibits in dozens of cases defined the eight-thousand-year history of human habitation in the area. But the exhibit case to which Laco led them was set into the floor, almost like a grave, so that visitors to the museum could comprehend the feelings which confronted the archaeologists when they discovered the real grave on the hillside.

Sarah looked down into the exhibit and almost cried out, her spine tingling with shock. The amulet around her neck dislodged itself from her blouse and fell forward as she bent down to get a closer look at the skeleton. She clutched at the heirloom instinctively, and shuddered. It was as though the amulet had a life of its own and was trying to return to the skeleton below.

The bones probably belonged to a young woman, Laco told them, who had been killed either by human sacrifice or during a battle. The skull, gaping and angular, seemed askew from the twisted spine. Her arms, now nothing more than long, dark, intertwining bones, doubled back on themselves, with her hands just in front of her jaw as though she was praying. Her legs were crouched, as though she had tried to get into a foetal position just before her death, a return to the safety of the womb. Womb? Sarah repeated the word silently to herself. That would mean that this . . . this thing had once been born. That it had a mother. Laco talked lovingly about the skeleton as 'her'. Yet that gave it life. And that was horrible: to think of it as once being alive meant that it had had a mother and a father, that it had laughed and walked and talked. Sarah had never been this close to a skeleton before. In American museums, they were displayed in glass cases; sanitised exhibits clinically presented for the voyeurs. Yet here the curators had laid the body inhumed, as it had been found, buried in the ground.

It was the skull that horrified her the most, grinning in death, defying the very nature of being human. How could an ancient skeleton like this ever have walked and talked and known the warmth of the sun and the sweet perfume of a flower?

Beside the skeleton of the young woman was the jewellery that had been found in the grave: the exquisite bronze dagger, its shaft once covered by long-rotted wood; gold rings which may have pierced her nose or her ears, or adorned her once-slender fingers; her breastplate, made of fine filaments of gold rope around a central brass plate, must have carried a considerable weight when the brass halter was in position; but it was the golden amulet and necklace that held Sarah mesmerised

Like mourners at a graveside, Laco and Josh held back while Sarah stepped beyond the public barrier to get closer to the skeletal remains of one of the legions of human beings whose identities have been lost to history. Both men could see quite clearly the effect the amulet was having on Sarah. Josh was stupefied; he commented that the amulet was dramatically similar in almost every respect to the one that Sarah wore and prized so much.

The more Sarah looked at the skeleton, the more her initial feelings of repulsion diminished. She closed her eyes, and imagined flesh on the young woman. She saw her in brightly painted, crude clothes, animal skins perhaps, or woven flax. She saw her not as she was now, lying in dirt, her bones stained with the age of the earth, but wandering the Carpathian hills, living in a pristine environment with furious crystalline rivers that caught the snow melt and clean air full of insects and pollens. But what most riveted Sarah's attention, the thing at which she stared most intently, was the amulet around the young woman's neck. Involuntarily she reached up and gripped her own.

'As you can see, they're identical. In the front, that is,' Laco whispered softly to Josh. 'It's in the back that there lies a difference. That proves conclusively that Sarah's amulet came from this area, probably no more than fifty kilometres away. You see, the Bronze Age was an age of great craftsmanship of metals like gold, copper and bronze, and many tribes developed their own special markings, much like the master masons who built the gothic cathedrals in Western Europe. That's why the owl symbol is so important. It's specific to Troy – Homer mentions it in many parts of the *Iliad*. It's more than a clue; it's evidence that this amulet travelled to Troy.'

Sarah shook her head and whispered something.

'Excuse me?' said Josh softly. 'I didn't hear.'

She whispered slightly louder. Her voice was harsh. 'I don't understand . . . I thought . . . My grandmother said this was made for her by my great-grandfather. She said he was an amateur craftsman, that he made it and gave it to my great-grandmother the day before he was killed in a pogrom. There was a necklace as well but, when she left her village, selling it was the only way she could raise enough money to save her life. That meant to save my grandmother's life as well. She was only a baby at the time. I just don't understand all this.'

'All this,' said Laco, sounding more officious than a moment earlier, 'means that your great-grandfather, or somebody else in your family, must have unearthed this amulet and kept it for themselves. Did you come from this region?'

Sarah didn't answer. He repeated the question.

'We came from Michalovce. My great-grandmother left in 1903 after the pogrom that killed my great-grandfather.'

'And your great-grandfather, was he only an amateur craftsman or did he do something else?' asked Laco.

Sarah snapped at him, 'I don't know. I think he was a farmer or something. I don't know these things. There was so much pain. I couldn't ask. My grandmother was a baby when she left here, for God's sake. She only remembers what her mother told her, and *her* memories were anything but pleasant. And considering that my great-grandmother died just after the Second World War, nothing's very clear from that time.'

Laco was unaffected by her manner. 'If he was a farmer, where was his farm? Was it near here?'

'I assume so,' she said. She turned and faced Laco. 'Look, all I know is the name of the town they came from. And that's only from family records. I know what you're trying to do. You're trying to get this back for your museum. Well, you can forget it. You have no legal or moral claim to it. This is mine. My great-grandmother and my grandmother's lives were saved by it. Why should you have it? Maybe my great-grandfather did dig it up, I don't know. I had nothing to do with it. But even if he did, enough time has gone by to make it ours by right.'

'Listen, buddy,' said Josh, 'if you want to call the police, do so by all means. I'm fairly well-connected in America and Sarah is a lawyer. If you try to get this back you're going to have a monumental fight on your hands. And we'll not only fight you, but we'll also take on the Slovakian government. This is Sarah's possession. Like I said, you just don't know who you're dealing with.'

'I know who you are, Mr Krantz. You direct films.'

Josh looked at him in astonishment. From the conversation in the café, Josh had assumed he was unrecognised.

'I've seen many of your films. I've seen your picture and read about you in *Time* magazine. We're not so cut off here that we don't know when we're in the presence of somebody important from Hollywood.'

'Then you know my connections and you know the shit fight you'll have on your hands if you try to get smart.'

'Mr Krantz, I don't want to get smart. Your girlfriend is wearing a priceless archaeological artefact. If it was just the same as this one,' he said, pointing down into the exhibited grave, 'it would be of great importance, but the Trojan symbols make it inestimably more so. It could open up a whole new area of study. Understand what I'm trying to say to you: what your girlfriend is wearing –'

'She isn't my girlfriend; she's my lawyer,' Josh snapped.

Unmoved, Laco continued: 'What this lady is wearing could revolutionise our knowledge of the prehistory of this area. We know there were extensive contacts with North Europe and with England. We know they got their tin from Cornwall and from east of the Black Sea. But we had no idea there was a relationship between the Bronze Age of Troy and Anatolia, perhaps even the Aegean, with Mycenae or Knossos, even the Minoan civilisation. This is fantastically important. It's like . . . like . . . the discovery of

Tutankhamen's tomb or Schliemann's discovery of Troy. Try to see it from my point of view, from the point of view of scientific research, finding out who we once were and how we once lived . . . how we developed.'

'I'm sorry,' Josh said, 'I know it's important to you, but I really can't see the big deal. It's got symbols on it that could have come from Troy. Great! But why go over the top and say that it's a major discovery?'

'For me, it is. I've been studying these people for years. I thought I knew them. I thought I knew how they lived, where they travelled, who they traded with. Now, suddenly, my whole world's been turned upside down. I must have the amulet to examine. I could have jumped to conclusions about its origin; the bull could be from Knossos in Crete, from Mycenae, or from somewhere on the Anatolian plateau. It could be Hittite – anything. Unless I can examine it, I can't possibly trace it, or tell how someone from this area could have it engraved on her amulet. It's fantastic. It's . . .' He was lost for words.

Sarah addressed him in measured, legalistic tones. 'You're not having it, Dr Plastov. I'm not giving it up. It means as much to me for my family's history as . . . as . . . the amulet belonging to that skeleton down there means to you.' She pointed into the display case.

Laco looked at her, and smiled. 'You know, Sarah, that skeleton was once a living, breathing human being. She could have been fifteen, maybe even twenty, when she died. She was from a well-to-do family – you can tell that by the artefacts buried with her. But the important thing, Sarah, is to imagine her not as a pile of bones, but as a young woman with strong limbs, healthy skin, long, black, silky hair shining in the pure air of the mountains, where she once walked and played and gathered up the herbs for medicine and food.'

Sarah had to stop herself from telling him that that was precisely what she'd been thinking only moments earlier.

But her thoughts had been musings; his were directed towards a goal. She wondered where he was going with this line of argument. It was late, she was tired. It had been an emotionally draining evening after a day spent in the hot sun following Josh around. All she wanted to do was to go to bed.

Unconcerned for her tiredness, he continued, as though addressing a jury: 'I've spent fifteen years of my life getting to know this young woman, and the seventy other men, women and children whose sacred remains we've dug up. Up until an hour ago, I thought I had it pretty clear. Every new grave we find, there are no surprises, just more of the same wonderful stuff. I've written papers for academic archaeological magazines around the world. I've refocussed the world's thinking about the Bronze Age in Carpathian Europe. People used to associate it purely with Mediterranean Greece, Turkey and Egypt, but now, Sarah, now, thanks to me, they're beginning to look to Eastern Europe as a precursor of civilisation. And suddenly I find that everything I've said could be undermined by one gold amulet with a Mediterranean bull symbol, a totem completely unknown in this region. Sarah, can you imagine what it feels like to have the whole of your life's work undermined?'

Sarah remained quiet. Josh admired the quality of Laco's performance.

The archaeologist continued: 'What about an exchange? I'll give you a magnificent amulet, plus a gold chain from my exhibit drawers – I've got twenty, thirty of them – if you'll let me have that.'

Sarah shook her head. 'This is an heirloom. I'm not interested in replicas.'

In frustration, he shouted, 'Outside of getting the police involved and having you thrown into jail, what must I do to convince you? I must examine it! You can't begin to understand the significance.'

'I understand very well, Dr Plastov. I suggest you do call the police. That way we'll finally settle this thing. I think you'll find under the Slovakian articles of ownership of property since the fall of the Communist government, and certainly with your statutes concerning limitation of time elapse for prosecution, that . . .'

'Look,' he interrupted angrily, 'you know I'm not going to call the police. This is getting silly. And let's stop calling ourselves doctor and mister. We're three people all with an interest in your amulet. Now, how are we going to resolve this?'

'Why don't I buy us all a cup of coffee and we'll talk it through,' Josh suggested. Sarah looked at him in horror. Didn't he realise the time? Californians obviously lived to the tick of a different clock.

But his calming voice immediately eased the tension between Sarah and Laco. The archaeologist spoke first. 'Let me show you the rest of the archaeological finds; we've got the exhibits here, and more downstairs in my office. Tomorrow, unless you're busy, I'll drive you out to the dig proper. We're uncovering the most amazing things.'

Sarah looked sceptical. 'This has all been a bit of a shock to me,' she said. 'I don't know about coffee. I'm pretty bushed. Sure, I'd like to see the collection, but perhaps another time. It's late. As to going out to the dig with you tomorrow, I'll have to think about that. I'm here working, and time out costs Josh money. I wouldn't feel comfortable about it. But, before we go, I need to know more about her.' Sarah nodded towards the skeleton.

Laco walked back towards the railing and peered into the mock grave. 'See the breast bone?' he said. 'Even though she lay undisturbed for almost three and a half thousand years, the fragments of the breast bone and ribs were jagged, as though they'd been speared by a sharp instrument. It could have been earth movement but it's unlikely because there were no other breakages in her bones. She was one of the Otomani people who inhabited this area. They were all over the Carpathians. We've found settlements in many places, especially near rivers or in valleys.'

'When did she live?' asked Sarah.

'About 1400 to 1500 BC. When I take you out there tomorrow – if you'll come, of course – I'll show you the burial site. It's fairly high on a hill. She was buried lying down on her right side. Some Bronze Age people were buried sitting up. We assume that the village in which she and her family lived was in the valley floor, close to the course of the river – assuming that that's where the river ran all that long ago. It's likely that it did because it's carved out a significant depression. It's different from Troy. The mound of Hisarlik on which Troy was built dates from the early Hittites to the Romans, but when it was in its heyday it had two rivers running close by it and into the sea, which was only a few hundred metres from its walls. I'm sure that you know your Homer, so you'll remember the hot and cold springs he mentions. Well, since then, the delta has silted up and the sea is now miles away.'

Sarah felt herself bridling. She'd never read Homer, and it was typical of a European to throw the lack of familiarity with the classical canon at an American.

'Perhaps you'd care to remind us of the exact passage,' she said shortly. Josh, concerned that emotions were flaring up again, looked at her in surprise.

Not appreciating her change of mood, Laco said innocently, 'It's from the *Iliad*. For centuries, scholars had speculated that the site of Troy lay just south of the Dardanelles – in Homer's time it was known as the Hellespont. They thought it was on high ground, close to what's now the village of Bunarbashi. But Schliemann was a Homeric scholar, and knew him very well. He especially remembered a passage which goes:

*. . . one hot spring flows out, and from the water fumes arise,*
*as though from fire burning; but the other, even in summer,*
*gushes chill as hail or snow or crystal ice frozen on water.*
*Near these fountains are wide washing pools of smooth-laid*
*stone, where Trojan wives and daughters laundered their*
*smooth linen in the days of peace before the Akhaians came.*

'A number of places claim Homer for their own, but it's
likely that, if he existed at all, he was born and lived near
Troy, probably in Ephesus or Smyrna, which is today's
Izmir, a couple of hours south of Troy.'

Laco had adopted a lecturing tone, as though they were
his students.

'Now Schliemann realised that the land area around the
mound had silted up over the millennia, and thought that
the hill of Hisarlik, a couple of miles inland and on a huge
promontory, was the spot. And he was right.' Laco looked
at Sarah innocently. It infuriated her.

He continued, 'Anyway, about our Carpathian skeleton
and the rest of the dig. We think that the village our
people lived in was probably in close proximity to the
burial site, so we're sure that the land looks roughly the
same as it did all those millennia ago, except for the
clearance of trees and the farming which has taken place.'

'Are there any remains of the village?' asked Josh.

Laco shook his head. 'Of course not. These people
weren't like the Bronze Age builders of Troy and Mycenae
who built wonderful stone cities. These villagers used mud
and wattle and daub and straw to build their houses.
Maybe wood. But, in most cases, all that disappears within
a few hundred years, or is used again by later generations.
Sometimes, if you're lucky, you can find evidence of post
holes, but only if the ground's very dry. No, village
civilisations don't leave much of a record of themselves,
I'm afraid. Very different from the Aegean Bronze Age
with the monumental sites they built.'

'But what about implements? Farming things. They'd still be there.'

'We've found some remains,' said Laco. 'But farming over the last two thousand years would have wiped out almost everything that was there at the time when this young lady was buried. You know, it's more than likely that your great-grandfather used to farm there. Because of that alone, I'd have thought you'd want to visit the area.'

Bertha Kaplan was more excited that Sarah was phoning her from Slovakia than she was about the provenance of the amulet. Despite the cost of the long-distance call, every time Sarah broached the subject her mother would hijack the conversation with questions: 'So what's it really like over there, where your grandmother was born? Is there anything left of the family? What about *yiddishkeit*? Have you been to any synagogues?'

'Ma, I told you I'll tell you everything about it when I come home. Meantime, do you remember anything about the amulet?'

'Sure,' said her mother. 'Your grandma gave it to me.'

'And how long had Grandma Eva had it?'

'All her life, I don't know. We didn't discuss it. And if we did, I don't remember. It's not the sort of question you ask. You just say, *Thanks, Ma*, and get on with your life. To her it meant a lot. To me it didn't mean so much, until I decided to give it to you, *bubeleh*. Then I missed it. You'll understand when you're a mother, please God.' Then she whispered under her breath, '*I should live so long*'.

Ignoring the barb, Sarah asked, 'Do you remember the circumstances of how Grandma Eva got it from her mother? Was it considered valuable?'

'It's gold, darling. Sure, it's valuable.'

'No, no,' said Sarah, beginning to get exasperated, 'I'm not talking of its value today. I'm talking of its historical value.'

'Ah,' said the mother, recognition suddenly arriving. 'Yes, it's very old.' Sarah breathed a sigh of relief. 'From what I remember, it was made by my grandfather, Grandma Eva's dad. He was the one killed in the pogrom.'

'I know that, Ma,' said Sarah. 'That's the story we've been told. But that isn't the way it appears. This archaeologist I met, he's got amulets that are identical. He thinks this one was dug up. Maybe even by my great-grandfather.'

'Dug up? What? From the ground? Nah!' said her mother. 'Not from what your *bubba* told me. She said he made it. Leastways, that's what I thought she said. Anyway, so what if he dug it up? What is it, a crime?'

'Ma, this is an amulet that goes back three, maybe four thousand years. It's of enormous historical importance.'

'Really? Then it must be very valuable. Good. We could do with some *mazel*, our family.'

'And you know nothing more?' Sarah said. The sigh in her voice told her mother the conversation was over.

'It's too late to ask these kind of questions of me, darling. Your *bubba*'s dead. My own *bubba, alev ha'shalom,* Grandma Eva's mother, died after the War and my grandfather, I never knew. The *mumsers* killed him in a pogrom. My *bubba*, now there was a woman. She walked across Europe at the turn of the century carrying my mummy and her other children. She got here half dead from starvation. Like a rake, she was. And my mother never once went without. *Bubba*, now she, you should have asked. But of course you weren't born then. So even you, with your lawyer's mind, would have found that difficult. I'm sorry, *bubeleh,* I'd like to help but I just can't.'

They said goodbye, and Sarah immediately phoned David. She recounted the tale of the amulet. His interest was far more enthusiastic than her mother's and also much less mercenary. But all she had really wanted was to hear his voice and to have his reassurance that she should allow the archaeologist access to her amulet in the name of pure academic research.

The following morning the telephone jarred her out of sleep. She looked at her watch; it was seven o'clock. Her thoughts immediately flew to America – perhaps there was a crisis. She picked up the telephone. It was Laco. At first, she didn't recognise his voice.

'Sarah? Did I wake you? It's Laco. Did you sleep well?'

She didn't answer. He was totally different to the way he'd been the previous night; now, he was chipper and posing as her second-best friend.

'I've just spoken to Mr Hollywood. He said he'd be delighted to come with me to the dig. See you downstairs in half an hour.'

Sarah still hadn't spoken a word. She continued to stare at the receiver, long after Laco had hung up. And she smiled.

Sarah and Josh stood on the pavement as a Volkswagen, which looked as if it had been old when Adolf Hitler was a boy, drew up alongside them. It coughed murderous smoke and its blotched body showed all the signs of terminal decay. In New York it would have been hauled off the road by a traffic cop. In Slovakia nobody gave it a second glance.

Laco reached over and forced open the front door for Sarah, who said a silent prayer before she climbed in. Josh, with his long legs, was forced to stretch across the back seat. The inside of the car stank of exhaust fumes and years of neglect. Sarah looked disdainfully at the floor – it was matted with earth, debris and ancient papers, all pushed aside by a previous occupant to allow some leg room. Sarah hoped that Laco couldn't see her nose wrinkling. She knew she was acting like a Jewish Princess, and she told herself not to be so silly.

If he did notice, Laco made neither apology nor excuse for the condition of the car. Rather, as they drove out of the city eastwards towards Michalovce and then south to Nizna Mysla, he began to tell them about the Otomani people.

It was an exhilarating trip. Once they were away from the monotonous stretches of the highway, the back roads of eastern Slovakia were charming. They reminded Sarah of country lanes in parts of New England, although without the grandeur of the trees. After twenty minutes of driving at high speed through tortuous lanes, Josh found himself concentrating on the hedgerows and the lie of the land because he was too terrified to look at the road. Eventually they arrived at the village nearest to where the archaeological dig was situated. It looked like any village in any part of the world, and no different to the three or four they had driven through at high speed to get there, scattering dogs and chickens and children as they thundered through.

There were the usual churches, hostelries and houses huddled together around a main square, and no sooner had they driven into the village than they were already driving out. Old men sitting on benches outside shops watched them with studied curiosity. It would be their talking point for the rest of the morning.

As Laco urged the car up the hill, it showed every sign of being defeated by the enormous strain. The windows rattled as he changed to a lower gear, the chassis creaked and, as the car slowed, the cloud of black smoke from the exhaust moved menacingly closer.

Once they had breasted the hill, he parked the car in an area cleared of grass beside the road. An army-like compound surrounded by a wire fence stretched far into the field; inside there were caravans, several wooden huts and a long bench placed strategically within four poles and covered with shadecloth. On the bench were thousands of small pieces of pottery. They looked as if they had been placed there haphazardly, but Sarah was sure that there was a carefully considered order to the mayhem.

As they walked through the open gate in the fence, Laco explained the purposes of the buildings. 'This one,' he said pointing to the first wooden shed, 'is where all objects that we find are first brought. That's where I or one of my assistants examine them and code them. We enter them in registers so we know the position in which they were found and make an assessment of what they were used for. There are cupboards in there full of more pottery than you would ever be able to exhibit in a museum. That hut,' he said, 'is my sleeping quarters, and this table is where the students wash the pottery and paint item numbers on, so that if a piece is misplaced somehow we can always trace it back. We usually eat in the fields under shadecloths. It gets very hot here in the summer.'

Sarah felt the glorious heat of the sun on her body. She was wearing light slacks and a DKNY top. She delighted in smelling the purity of the Carpathian air; it was exquisite. There was a smell of honeysuckle or possibly rose, and a hint of fennel in the air. The cacophony of the crickets and birds was overwhelming, making it difficult to hear Laco as he walked away from them, explaining the technical processes of archaeological recovery and reconstruction of the artefacts. She followed in his footsteps, listening with interest, but what really captivated her was the smell of the air. Since leaving New York, most of her time had been spent in airplanes, air-conditioned offices, or in the centre of large cities. The air here tasted like champagne.

Laco picked up items, and began explaining their age and possible purpose: a ceremonial cup, an axe head . . . it was fascinating, especially when he handed them over so that the Americans could hold them.

'See this cup,' he said to Josh, 'it was a burial cup for use in the afterlife. It was made three and a half thousand years ago.' Laco picked up a bottle of vodka and poured some into the pot. 'Here,' he said, giving it to Josh. 'You'll be the first person in thousands of years to drink from it. Don't worry, it's been well washed.'

'But it's only nine o'clock in the morning,' Josh protested.

'You're right,' boomed Laco. 'We're two hours late for our first drink.'

Josh laughed, and threw the liquid back. 'Shit! What is this stuff?' he said, coughing.

Laco looked at Sarah, 'The first man in all that time, and what does he do? Complain about the quality of the product. Typically American.'

Sarah burst out laughing. She was feeling good. Better than she'd felt since leaving New York. This was like a holiday.

Josh breathed heavily to rid his body of the vapours of the vodka, came over and put his arm around her shoulders as she turned and stared into the far distance. The hills were undulating and gentle. 'Imagine,' he said, 'your great-grandfather may have farmed here. How does that make you feel, Sarah?'

She didn't know. She ought to know, but she didn't. She felt shut off from her past, just as she'd felt yesterday, when standing outside Josh's home in Novosad, appreciating the excitement he felt but unable to share it. Yesterday, it had been his triumph, his discovery, his link with the past. Today it was hers. This was her ancestral land, the very place where those who had passed on their seed to her had stood, and worked, and loved, and felt the agony of hatred. She should feel *something*, some empathy, some linkage. She should. But she didn't. And it upset her.

Her mind flew back to her conversation with Miriam Neisser a few weeks ago. It seemed like longer, so much had happened since then. What was it Miriam had said? That Sarah was closing her eyes to the past because she couldn't see herself clearly in the future. Was this what she had been so frightened of? Confronting her past. What was her future?

Sarah put her arm around Josh's waist. She didn't think about the consequence of her actions. It was a natural thing to do – not deliberate, not contrived, just something she wanted to do, to be close to somebody she respected and admired and with whom she felt comfortable.

'It feels odd,' she told him. She needed to tell him, To have her lack of feelings appreciated by someone who wouldn't be judgemental. 'Peculiar. A bit disconcerting. I never imagined it like this, Josh. Whenever Grandma Eva used to talk to me about Michalovce and the village and this area, her words were so dark and dreadful. Of course, she was only repeating what her mother had told her, because she left here when she was a baby ... and her mother was only about thirty when her husband was murdered in a pogrom and she traipsed across Europe in order to survive. But the overwhelming impression I got about this place was of narrow, cobbled streets, dirty pavements and houses close together with people living one on top of another in disease and poverty. My vision was that there was dirt everywhere and no privacy, and you couldn't be yourself. And surrounding them, surrounding this ghetto, were horrible, hideous people who hated them just because they were Jews. People who wanted to hurt and kill them.'

'But your great-grandfather was a farmer.'

'I didn't know that. And I've still only got Laco to believe. My great-grandmother wasn't alive when I was born. She died some time around the Second World War. My grandmother was a baby when my great-grandfather was murdered. The story I was told was that he was a craftsman, a good, decent, wonderful man. You know the mythologies that grow up around people who've been martyred. But I had no reason to disbelieve my grandmother. I had no idea it was like this.' She gestured towards the landscape surrounding them.

Laco held back from commenting. This was precisely the effect he had hoped for. He'd known that once he got her to the site of the dig, that once he had invested her mind with the power and history of the place, she would change her mind. He fought back his smile.

Judging the moment, he said, gently, 'Sarah, I'm an archaeologist because I need to know the truth. My people, the Slovaks, have suffered bitterly for thousands of years. Yet we've survived. It's always fascinated me to learn who we were and where we came from, what we did, what we thought, how we reacted. By opening up the ground and digging up the past, I know who I am today.'

'I know who *I* am today, Laco,' she said, turning to face him.

He shook his head. 'Look back, Sarah. Look over the landscape. Your family trod these hills. They picnicked near that river. Your great-grandmother wore crinolines and a high-necked dress. She did needlepoint and baked moist cakes. All these things you didn't know about her, Sarah, but it was that – in part – which formed you. Isn't it important for you to know about her so that you know more about yourself?'

Sarah was stunned into silence. How had he known what she was thinking? Josh had used the same argument when they first met in New York, to no effect. But that was before Slovakia, before she came face to face with the reality of a great-grandfather and great-grandmother who had their own life, their own being, who weren't just pictures above a fireplace on a mantelpiece. It was all very well for her to be a New World theorist, pontificating about what should and shouldn't be from the sanctuary of a Manhattan apartment, where she had her identity and self-confidence. But she was out of her element now; she was out of her realm of security. New York was where she and everything about her was centred, where she walked in her own footsteps. She felt anchored in the musty comfort of her past whenever she visited her parents' home. She touched the broken swing in the garage, her old doll's pram, whenever she visited the house, just to keep a sense of order in her frenetic life, to remind her of who she was and where she had come from. That was her life. But, until now, there had been no great-grandmother or great-grandfather. Life began in America, so they hadn't existed, except in legend. Even her grandmother had always been a part of America, always firmly rooted in New York, tied to a brownstone tenement by her apron and the smell of cooking french fries or potato *latkes* and the huge continental quilts and bolsters that she used instead of sheets and blankets like all Sarah's non-Jewish friends.

But here, in Slovakia, Sarah was encountering her family's otherness. She had left New York without any personal bonds to Eastern Europe, unlike so many of her parents' friends. Now, suddenly, she was a part of everything that she found difficult and alien. She had managed to build a wall around herself in Prague and Kosice, and Novosad when Josh took his emotional bath. But here, close to where her great-grandparents lived their lives, here were her roots, tangled in the black fertile soil and perfumed grasses of Slovakia.

She walked away from the men towards the site of the archaeological dig. A dozen or so young men and women were bent down to the ground, digging or scraping, working early in the morning to avoid the full vengeance of the sun.

Had her great-grandfather stood on that hill to survey his land? And beyond, had he taken his horse to drink in that valley when it was tired and sweating from a day's work ploughing the fields? Had that copse of trees growing down by the brook been there a century ago, when her great-grandfather was a young man? How high were the trees then? Who had planted them? Did her great-grandfather see the same distant houses on the horizon that she saw now? How had he felt about their grandness compared to the hovel in which he lived? And had he brought Grandma Eva's mother up to this spot to gaze out on to their world, to smell the fennel and the rose blossoms? Had they made love here and conceived the seed which now gave birth to Sarah's doubts?

Emotion welled up in her breast. She hadn't ever thought she would feel this way, experience this depth of belonging. Yet she also felt disoriented as her two worlds came together. If her great-grandmother, the sepia woman smiling at her through the ages, had stood up here, would she – at the same age as Sarah was now – would she have felt the same thoughts? Sarah was powerful, she was a lawyer, a first-class American citizen. She could come and go as she pleased. But her great-grandmother had not enjoyed such freedom. No, she could never have had these same feelings. She would have felt cowed, overwhelmed by the weight of her surroundings, like a blade of grass, blowing this way and that with the gale-force winds of politics, anti-Semitism and ancient hatreds.

How could Sarah have been so prim, so proper, so utterly academic, dry and removed as she had been when she wrote that stupid, stupid OpEd piece saying people should never return to Europe, should have nothing to do with the Old Country? Statements like that demanded caution, wisdom, a perspective. She had told only one side of the story, had known only one side of the argument. But had she bothered to seek counsel from those who came from Europe? Had she asked those very people whose lives had been rent asunder by wars, who had been made refugees, whether they agreed with her hypothesis? No! She had coldly analysed her own feelings, had made an intellectual assessment, had come to an academic conclusion and then launched into print with a well-argued, well–documented, sophistic monologue. Damn her for her arrogance, her captious self–righteousness.

Passions were swirling around her head like screaming banshees: one moment she felt an incredible depth of elation as though she was finally home; the next she was overwhelmed by a feeling of utter horror at the terrible secrets that were buried beneath her feet, the nightmares her family had had to endure here. She felt alien, because she was a Jew in a foreign land, yet she felt she belonged also, because the Jews had lived here for five hundred years. She felt angry, because this was where her great-grandfather had been slaughtered in a pogrom, his young life ended mercilessly and brutally. And she felt peaceful, at harmony with her past, as if she could lay to rest her great-grandfather, and his parents, and their parents before them, by saying: 'I have returned. Your descendant, the woman for whom you suffered, the purpose of your living, the offspring to carry your seed into the future, has finally returned. I am here. I'm home. I'm your pride.' And she also felt deep embarrassment, because Josh had been right about her OpEd article, and she was wrong.

As though on cue, Josh walked over to her and put his hands tenderly on her shoulders. She turned around and looked up at him. They were standing close, as close as they had been the previous night. He could smell the fragrance of her hair. He didn't need to ask any questions; he knew instinctively what was racing through her mind. She smiled at him. Tears welled up in her eyes. She wanted to hug him, to throw her arms around him. To apologise. But she didn't. Instead, she shook her head gently, turned away from him and wrapped her arms tightly around herself.

'This,' Laco told them, pointing down to a huge hole in the ground, 'is the level where we have to be very careful. For the first two maybe three feet, we go at the ground with spades. The topsoil contains nothing. Most of the graves were found six to eight feet deep. But the trouble is that, sometime in the last four thousand years, there might have been a movement in the earth which could have forced artefacts or bones upwards, so we can't just go in like vandals or grave robbers. We have to move in with much more delicate equipment, like trowels and even brushes.'

Josh stared into the hole. 'How can you be certain there's anything under here?'

'I can't. Archaeology is so much a matter of luck. You know, Josh, people had been searching for Troy ever since the time of Thucydides, four hundred years before Christ. Time eventually buries all human record. Archaeologists have the job of reconstructing what used to be. Some of us – and I don't wish to sound immodest – have the ability to look at the lie of the land and imagine the same landscape as it was thousands of years earlier, probably a lot lower, maybe a lot steeper. We have the ability to look at a mound and say, *That's not natural. That was created by human beings.* Or we can look at a pile of stones and imagine it as the north or east face of a wall, the rest of which might be buried fifty feet underground. We're architects of the past.'

'So, by looking at this hill you know it's a burial site?'

'I'm not that good,' laughed Laco. 'The first of the artefacts found around here in modern times were dug up by some farmers at the end of last century, but archaeology was in its infancy then, and people had the idea that there was gold to be found under this hill. They were right of course. The peasants came from all over, just hacking into the ground. God knows what damage they did. Fortunately the local nobleman was one of the very few from the ruling classes who had an education; he'd studied science and anthropology in Paris and knew all about the new science of archaeology. So he put a stop to it before the peasants did too much damage. Then he put guards up here and he did some digging himself. He uncovered some graves, and some archaeologists came out from Bratislava and Charles University in Kosice. But then all sorts of political problems erupted and it wasn't until the mid-1930s that one of the greatest archaeologists in the world decided to resume the dig here. He was my father.'

Josh looked at him in surprise. Somehow, he couldn't imagine Laco with a father, and looking so proud of him as well.

'He did the first proper scientific analysis of the area. His diggings were over there, but they were stopped by the Communists.' Laco spat in disgust, and pointed to a nearby hill. It looked pristine, completely untouched, with earth and grass growing in profusion and crops weaving patterns in the light breeze. There was no dig to be seen, no sign of any human intervention.

Josh looked surprised. 'What do you mean, he dug there?'

'My father exposed the graves of thirty-five bodies. He got the pre-history museum started. We're still cataloguing some of the artefacts that he brought to the surface.'

Josh shook his head. 'I don't understand. There's nothing there.'

'Josh,' said Laco, 'archaeologists dig what's underground. When we've got everything out we cover it over again. There's no point in leaving a denuded hill with massive holes for people to break their necks. We might as well let the people grow crops and farm here; we're enough of a nuisance as it is, and we have to pay the farmer for loss of his profits. As soon as we've got everything out from this site, we'll put all the soil back and the farmer can plant his crops. It's the way it is.'

'So you're uncovering the crimes of history,' said Sarah quietly.

'Crimes?' Laco was surprised by her use of the word.

'The girl that we saw in the museum, the one you thought may have been sacrificed. Somebody did that to her. Somebody ended her life. My great-grandfather was killed in a pogrom somewhere around here. He could be buried anywhere near here. Throughout the centuries, throughout thousands of years, people have been murdered and brutalised, and their remains have been buried and the crimes covered up and forgotten. And the criminals just walked away.'

Laco shook his head. 'Sarah, I have no knowledge of these crimes. I'm not trying to point an accusing finger. All I'm trying to do is to bring these people back to life for our generation and those of the future.'

There was nothing more to be said. She whispered to Josh, 'Can I go home now? I really would like to go.'

They turned their backs on the archaeological dig and returned to the battered Volkswagen.

Josh thought very carefully, and in the end decided not to invite Phil and Jerry to come to dinner with Laco. The technicians were working on one side of Josh's project, and Josh felt they should be kept separate from the other side, the personal side.

When Laco arrived at their hotel, he insisted that they go to the Texas Steak House, where the hamburgers, he assured them, were as good as anything in America and the steaks big enough to fill a plate. They drove through the old part of Kosice, the part which dated back to the Middle Ages, through the busy central area, surrounded by square-shouldered buildings housing municipal offices, museums and art galleries and into the newer and more domestic part of the city. The roads were wider here, the houses modern, characterless and utilitarian. Suddenly, appearing out of nowhere like an old-fashioned whorehouse in the wrong end of town, was a neon-lit building with a garish flashing sign that read 'Texas Steak

House'. Underneath were words in Slovakian, which Laco translated as 'Steaks, hamburgers as big as your appetite'.

It was a Wednesday night and there was almost nobody in the streets. Except for the old part of town near to St Elizabeth's Cathedral, where people gathered as a community, Kosice was like every other provincial city – it closed shortly after dark.

'See,' Laco said as they entered the building, 'I told you it was like something out of New York.'

He was greeted like a long lost friend by the owner, Josef, who kissed him on both cheeks, then embraced Sarah's hand as though it was a religious icon and pumped Josh's arm as though drawing water. The restaurant was decked out like any cheap, family-oriented middle-American diner. In the States, it wouldn't have raised an eyebrow, but here it was the latest in *nouvelle cuisine* and cutting-edge decor. They sat down and examined the huge menu which, when deconstructed, offered only variations on the theme of steaks and hamburgers. The descriptions of each of the variants had obviously been written by a pornographer with pretensions to advertising: everything was *succulent* or *oozing*. It was so comical that Sarah read the entire menu. Laco instructed the waiter that everybody would have the hamburgers, and that everybody would have vodka.

Josef sat with his important foreign guests and, in an interesting dialect which approximated to English, talked about his plans for opening up a chain of Texas Steak Houses throughout Slovakia and maybe even into Prague. When Josef had outstayed his welcome, Laco whispered out of the corner of his mouth, and the owner stood, wished his only customers of the evening a virile meal and retired to fuss around the other tables, straightening the place mats, knives and forks.

'How are you feeling after the visit to the dig?' asked Laco.

Sarah shrugged. 'A bit like I've been on an emotional roller coaster.'

Laco nodded in sympathy. 'That's how I am the first time I begin a new dig. I open up an area which might not have seen the light of day for thousands of years, but I never know what I'm going to find. The ground is a repository of secrets. I feel like a voyeur when I begin to uncover potsherds and jewellery that has been buried there for thousands of years. I feel as if I'm somehow intruding into the eternal rest of the grave–owners. Each article that we uncover is like holding a piece of magic. I wash it and I look at the delicate craftsmanship which some man or woman thousands of years ago invested in the piece of pottery or jewellery. These days everything is mass produced. In those days somebody had to sit and lovingly fashion a handle, or rim, or lip. And, even better, when the object is worked in gold or copper, you can really see the dedication and the love that's gone into it.'

Without any thought towards Western proprieties, Laco reached over and held Sarah's hand. 'You mustn't be embarrassed by your emotions, Sarah. You must share them with me. I sometimes cry on a dig when I come across the bones of a small child who died of a disease, or in an accident, or who was perhaps sacrificed to propitiate some cruel God. I'm part of these people, Sarah, just like you are.'

Sarah wondered whether he had known she was in a turmoil at the dig. She had kept her back to him deliberately. She stared into his eyes. He had such beautiful, black eyes. His hair was falling recklessly across his forehead. In another life he could have been a musician, a painter or a poet, wearing the multicoloured clothes of the Bohemians, singing his beautiful melodies and making young girls swoon whenever he looked at them.

Josh reached over and took her other hand. 'Sarah's a very together young woman, Laco. Her emotions are beautifully under control. She knows what she's doing.'

Laco's gaze was broken. He looked over at Josh and burst out laughing. He sat back and said, 'So, Mr Hollywood, and what did you think of the dig?'

'Fascinating. Absolutely stunning. It never occurred to me before, but there are so many similarities, and yet so many differences, between your work and mine. My life is full of making images, creating fantasies in celluloid. Yet what you're doing is digging up real things and recreating an entire world that actually once existed. It's just incredible.'

'How do I know I'm right?' asked Laco.

Josh shook his head. 'I don't understand.'

'You say I'm recreating a real world, that I'm digging up objects and telling people what they were used for, and how these people lived and what they did. But how do I know I'm right? You create your fiction in search of the truth. Maybe I'm creating my own fiction as well. I assume that something I dig up is used as a comb; maybe it was used for something completely different. I assume that a cup was used to drink from, like the one you used today; but maybe it was used to gather blood after a human sacrifice. I can't be any more certain of its purpose than you or Sarah can. And all day I've been telling you that the people were gentle craftsmen. I've got good grounds for thinking that, all the evidence is there. But maybe there's a vital piece missing. Maybe there's a bit of the story that I haven't yet read or seen that would change everything. Maybe they were fierce warriors, maybe adventurers, maybe cannibals. I can never be certain. But each new piece of evidence I dig up, even if it's precisely the same as all the others, it's another piece of the jigsaw put together.'

He looked towards Sarah. She put her hand to the amulet.

A waiter brought three plates of hamburgers and French fries to their table. He also brought three huge glasses of beer, which he told Laco was compliments of the management.

Laco finished his vodka with one swig and took a huge gulp of beer. He toasted Josef, who was standing in the corner watching the proceedings from a respectful distance. The proprietor waved back and shouted, 'Enjoy! Enjoy! I love you. You are my friends.'

The meat was grey, over-cooked and full of white globules of fat. It would have been rejected by all but the sleaziest roadhouse in America, but Laco ate it with such gusto that they simply had to follow suit.

'You know,' he said, his mouth still half-full of food, 'what I said to you is interesting. You, Mr Hollywood, you make incredible pictures and people sit there for two hours watching your movies and believing every word your actors say. You transport them into another world. But that world disappears the minute the lights come up. Your world is somewhere up there,' he said, pointing into the air. 'My world is down there in the ground. I'm trying to make civilisations, which completely died out without trace three and a half thousand years ago, come back to life.'

'How did they die, Laco?' asked Josh. 'Do we know what happened? Earthquake? Famine?'

Laco shrugged. 'Hard to say. Certainly, as far as we can see, there were no great earth movements. There's very little geological movement at all in this part of Slovakia. Maybe a climate change, but probably not, from the records we've dug up. It's been pretty much like this on and off for at least six thousand years.'

'So what was it?' asked Josh. 'Disease?'

'Maybe. Who knows what causes a civilisation to decline? There are lots of theories, of course. Often civilisations decline for political reasons; the collapse of the central ruling organisation. When a civilisation is building up, like in Egypt or Assyria or Mycenae, it's very warlike and militaristic, and it acquires vassal cities and even states all around it. There's usually a very strong and powerful king or warlord who rules over the area and every small city around pays tribute. He offers protection; in return they give him wine, women and song. But when that central political organisation breaks up the civilisation goes into decline. All public building and works come to an end, the army and navy fragment and revolt, buildings are abandoned. New kinds of worship come in and take over from the old established cults. If the people are able to write and read, then literacy and education are usually the first thing to go. Then the economy just seems to fuck up.'

'Like America in the 1990s,' said Josh.

Sarah laughed. Laco didn't. 'Believe me, you are so close to being right, it's frightening. There are a lot of people who think we're seeing the end of Western civilisation. All the indications are there: Asia and the East are beginning to become militaristic and growing in money and influence. They're like Egypt and Rome and Mycenae in the early days. They're spreading their wings. They're frightening.'

'And you think that's what happened here three thousand years ago, do you?' asked Josh.

Laco sipped more of his beer, and looked at Sarah. Slowly he said, 'I don't think so. In fact, the more graves we dig up, the more I'm sure it didn't. But it's not just here. There's a lot of speculation of how the Bronze Age came to an end in the Aegean and the Middle East. You know, there were half a dozen of the most incredible kingdoms ever known in the region of Greece, Egypt and Turkey. Fantastic buildings, huge empires, unbelievable wealth. All at the peak of their power and influence one day . . . and within a few years – probably not more than fifty – it all came to a sudden horrible end. That's not even the blinking of an archaeologist's eye.'

'How?' asked Sarah.

Laco shrugged. 'I have my own personal theory but it's very hard to prove. It could also apply to why the graves of the Otomani people at Nizna Mysla came to a sudden stop around the thirteenth century BC.'

'What do you think happened?'

'It's going to be damn hard to prove, but it seems to fit the facts rather neatly. The trouble is, whenever anything fits facts the smallest and most insignificant of new discoveries can totally fuck you up – like your bull symbol on the amulet. I've been thinking around this theory for years and suddenly it could all be useless.'

'For God's sake,' said Josh, his voice rising in frustration, 'tell us your theory.'

'Well,' Laco said, wiping his mouth with a serviette, having finished his hamburger and fries while the other two were only nibbling around the edges. 'You have to think about who these people were in order to understand what could have happened to them. You have to understand what technology they had. They were metalworkers and craftsmen; their gold and bronze jewellery was fabulous. It still looks as modern as something made in New York or Paris today. It's just breathtaking. Have you seen the pictures of Helen of Troy's head-dress? One of your Hollywood stars could wear it to the Academy Awards, Josh, and people would gasp in wonder. You see, these people here in this area, and Bronze Age people in England and throughout Europe and in the Aegean, they had the technology to smelt copper. In fact, the Chalcolithic age began in about 6000 BC. You don't need sophisticated technology to extract copper from its ore. The metal just appears when the ores are heated over a really hot fire. But about two and a half thousand years before Christ, people discovered that if you add just a tiny amount of tin to molten copper, you get the most incredibly strong metal called bronze. A wonderful metal: hard-edged, sharp, beautiful. The problem is that tin is very scarce. Copper, you find in many places; tin, almost nowhere. The closest tin to here was in Spain, or in Cornwall in England, or east of the Black Sea. There's also been a recent discovery of an ancient tin mine in Anatolia in Turkey, which makes me wonder whether people from this region maybe did have some contact with Troy. That's why I'm so interested in your amulet, Sarah.

'You see, there were well-developed trade routes built up thousands of years before Christ. People travelled throughout the known world just to trade in tin, spices, dyes and other rare things.'

Sarah sipped her beer and stared at him in fascination. She was really interested in his description. She glanced over at Josh who also was motionless. Laco was playing to his audience. Sarah held back a smile.

'Now, because tin was so scarce, bronze weapons and armour and jewellery were very expensive. You couldn't equip a large army with it, and you could only give the jewellery to the most important people in the village or the city, and that was the situation for a thousand years. People working in a beautiful craft, making wonderful arms and jewellery, and, occasionally, for something interesting to do, going out to rape and pillage a neighbouring village. But always on a very small scale. No big armies, just local warlords, except in very rich lands like those controlled by the Hittites in Turkey.'

Josh interrupted. 'What are you talking about? What about the Trojan War? The most famous war in history, a huge army camped outside the walls of Troy. Thousands of men. That was the Bronze Age, you said so yourself.'

'You've been watching too many movies, Mr Hollywood,' said Laco. 'The force that sailed to Ilium on the Aegean coast of Turkey, just south of Hellespont, was a combined militia made up from about twenty city states under the control of Agamemnon of Mycenae. He was the brother of Menelaus, king of Sparta, and it was Paris's alleged abduction of his wife Helen which caused all the problems. But each city didn't contribute more than a handful of fighters. Put them together and you've still got a very small army. Maybe a thousand men. Homer was the greatest fantasist and bullshit artist in history. A bit like reporters do today, he built a huge story out of nothing.'

'So what happened to the Bronze Age?' Sarah intervened.

'There are theories that a new long slashing sword was made which could destroy the terrifying chariots. Suddenly, infantry could overcome horse-drawn chariots, making Bronze Age armies useless. But I have another theory. I think what happened was this: a technology that had been known about for at least a thousand years suddenly took off in a big way. Around 1200 BC, northern Europe started to smelt the most common mineral ore there is, using a new and exciting technology of making fire very hot and of dropping charcoal into the mixture. Iron had been smelted for thousands of years, but it was cheap pig iron, useless for weapons, shields or arrowheads. But, with the use of bellows, and the addition of charcoal, the Iron Age began. Suddenly, metalworkers were able to extract real iron metal from iron ore to manufacture iron swords, spears and shields *en masse*. And, suddenly, everybody could be armed. So, instead of a few elite soldiers, the Iron Age king or tribal leader could call on the strength of thousands of ordinary people. He could form a huge army, march them halfway across the continent without any real opposition and destroy towns, sack, pillage, rape, steal and conquer. Make people bend at the knee. The production of iron changed the face of the world. It enabled people to mobilise and caused mass migrations. I think that's what happened to the cities of the Aegean Bronze Age. I think they were swept out of existence by an advanced technology. The same could have happened here.'

Sarah realised she had been holding her breath, hanging on his every word.

Laco judged the time to be right for his *coup de grâce*. 'And you know what that sounds similar to, don't you? A new and terrifying technology given to a people who rose up and conquered other people? Remember 1939. Here in Slovakia and Poland and Hungary, you had peaceful nations with low levels of technological advancement. Armies which still used cavalry and swords like they did in the days of Napoleon. Suddenly Germany rises up with incredible technology, a war machine like the world has never seen before: tanks, planes, advanced weapons systems. They just sweep across this land and rape and pillage, making everyone slaves and killing tens of millions of people. History repeating itself. *Plus ça change, plus c'est la même chose.*'

Josh looked at Sarah. She was staring at Laco, her mouth slightly open. Her thoughts were on a battlefield, where an innocent civilisation was swept out of existence by the brutality of an advanced European nation. Her voice was low as she whispered, 'I want to know what these people were like'. She slowly removed the gold chain and the amulet from around her neck. Reaching over to Laco, she took his hand and placed the jewellery into his open palm. 'Tell me what they were like. Find out for me.' She held his hand, the amulet clasped between them.

# CHAPTER TEN

Autumn in Okhotsk was arguably the most miserable and godforsaken time that any town anywhere in the world ever had to endure. The Sea of Okhotsk, trapped between the Kamchatka Peninsula in Russia's far east and Hokkaido, Japan's northern-most island, froze during autumn into a murky grey sludge that oozed up and down at the sluggish behest of the tides. Vicious winds blew in from the vast Asiatic land mass, blasting the skin like torrents of biting rain, making even the act of breathing painful. It was hell on earth. Summer in Okhotsk was pleasant, if you ignored the flies and mosquitos; spring could be delightful; in winter, nobody with any brains ventured outdoors, but autumn – it was wet, cold and depressing.

And it certainly was not the time for a funeral. The ground, frozen solid, creaked open grudgingly to the grave diggers' pneumatic drills. The town's cemetery, six miles north of the outer limits, was grey and desolate, and buffeted by biting winds. The grave diggers – fat, sturdy men wrapped in multiple layers of wool and padded windproof leggings, jackets and hats – were constricted in their movements as they attempted to prise apart the ungiving earth. It took them two hours to dig the rectangular hole. They cursed and spat as their trapped body heat made them sweat like pigs. They had no idea whose grave it was they were digging, and they didn't care. All they wanted was to retreat into their hut, huddle around the wood-burning stove and feel the flush of vodka warm their skin.

A hundred metres away the priest sat in his warm office, contemplating the white stone chapel across the barren churchyard. He dreaded crossing the enclosure in the icy cold, but cross he would have to, because soon he was due to perform the ancient last rights for . . . he looked up the name on his register. He'd never heard of the old man.

The priest scurried across the enclosure to the coldness of the chapel. He turned the wheel of the radiator; there was a hiss as hot water flooded into the cold metal veins. He nodded, then shivered. In an hour or so, the chapel would be warm enough. It was a delicate balancing act: too many people in the small chapel and it would be overly hot; too few and it would be cold and unfriendly. He had no idea whether the old man had any family. Maybe he had a few relatives, maybe not. The priest would know in an hour.

The journalist looked at his watch. Another hour until it was time for the burial. He flicked through his notes to make sure he remembered everything, then looked along the length of the small office to the door at the far end. It was a half-glass, half-wooden door which revealed as much about the movements of the editor as it did about those of his staff. The journalist could see him sitting behind his desk: twelve o'clock and already his eyes were glazed with the effects of vodka, his nose glowing in the dull mid-morning light of autumn. Ozden could see its blue-red veins from his seat. Too drunk and the man would be belligerent, but just pissed enough and he might agree. It was worth one more try.

Ozden walked nonchalantly towards the editor's door. To his left, through the frozen windows of the building, he saw an oil tanker nosing its way through the slush which was the Sea of Okhotsk. For a moment, he wondered where it was going, but then his mind refocused on the job at hand. He tapped on the door. The editor looked up and scowled. 'Come,' he ordered.

'Oleg, a question,' the journalist said as he walked tentatively into the room. It stank of body odour. The power cuts and water restrictions – part of everyday life in modern day Russia – caused everybody to be irritable, but most people still managed to wash regularly. Not the editor. Ozden doubted he'd washed since the days of the Communists.

The editor looked at him in bleary-eyed contempt and nodded.

'Have you changed your mind?' asked Ozden.

The editor frowned, trying to remember what decision he'd made that required changing. The journalist filled in the alcoholic memory lapse: 'About me going to Moscow.'

'Why would you go to Moscow? What's in Moscow?' His words were slurred.

'The burial today. The old man. Remember?'

'Oh,' Oleg said, with a dismissive wave of his hand, 'he's dead. It's too late, the story's gone. Don't waste my time. Go and find out what's happening in the streets. Do your job. Don't fuck around with ghosts. I told you, no.'

'Oleg, the fact that he's dead doesn't change a thing. I'm telling you, this guy . . .'

'I said no!' the editor screamed. 'Look. Understand this. I don't want you to go off to Moscow. I know you. You'll get women, you'll run up expenses. Just get on with your job and leave me alone. Now go on. Piss off.'

His last words were so badly slurred, the journalist could barely understand them, but he certainly grasped the sentiment. Well, damn him. He would go to the funeral anyway and see what was what. He returned to his desk, angry but not chastened, and opened the bottom drawer. He took out a half bottle of vodka and swallowed three quick nips in succession. It was the only way with cheap vodka, and all he ever seemed to drink these days was cheap vodka. It burned the back of his throat and made his brain fuzzy, but it warmed his entire body through in a matter of minutes in preparation for stepping out into the freezing cold of a Siberian autumn day.

The priest stood in front of the plain wooden coffin. Its only adornments were brass handles. He had waited for ten mourners to enter the chapel before him, hoping they would warm up the cold room. He had been standing there for five minutes now, and still they were coming in, admitting a gust of freezing air and a flurry of snow flakes each time the door opened. The mourners all looked as though they had been dressed by the weather, each wearing a white drizzle of snow, which immediately turned to water in the heat of the chapel. They sat in different parts of the church, as though contact were anathema. As though by prior arrangement, or as if they were deliberately avoiding the place because of the imminent arrival of the Holy Ghost, nobody occupied the front row. By age-old custom, this was the row which was reserved for family; but the priest knew that there was no family.

The priest recognised one of the middle-aged men entering the chapel. He was surprised by the man's attendance; he was a journalist on the local paper. Surely this wasn't a burial which would attract the press. In consternation, the priest looked again at the details of the man he was about to bury. A nobody. Lived in the district for forty years. A clerk or something in the fish cannery. Must be a relative of the reporter.

The priest looked at his watch and decided not to give the mourners any more time. He was hungry and wanted to get the burial over before the weather turned any colder. As he began the mourning rites of the Russian Orthodox Church, the door opened once again. But this time, instead of admitting another frail old man or woman rugged up in old clothes, it revealed a tall, fair, muscular young man dressed in modern clothes, Moscow clothes. He looked imperiously around the chapel, as though about to issue a command to all those present in the room. For a moment the priest was put off his monotone. Others turned and stared. The attention was no longer on the coffin, but on the stranger. Here was a different face, a new face. Maybe family, but more likely not. He would have walked to the front if he were family. It was a moment of excitement, but the priest quickly lost interest in the newcomer and continued with the service.

But the journalist didn't lose interest. He knew most of the fifteen mourners by sight. All old friends from the fishing club, the hunting club or the cannery. But this stranger – here was something out of the ordinary. By the look of him, and his stance, he was powerful and rich. He hadn't been cowed by endless Siberian winters; he didn't wear the look of a man who spent most of the year indoors, drinking, smoking and waiting for the few months of sunlight to brighten up a godforsaken life. Just look at his clothes. *Where the hell was he from?* the journalist wondered.

The priest finally came to the end of the service, intoning a few words about how loved the dead one had been, how much a part of the community and how apologetic he felt that he had hardly known him in life. And then the coffin was wheeled out. The priest followed but nobody else. It was too cold. Nobody was sufficiently close to the deceased to risk standing in Arctic winds just to see the old man lowered into the freezing grasp of the earth. The mourners filed out of the church and back to their predictable lives.

All except the journalist and the young man. They looked at each other across the breadth of the chapel. The journalist looked quizzical; the powerful young man's face was unreadable. Ozden stood and strolled over to the young man.

'New in town?' he asked. The young man shrugged.

'Did you know . . . ?' He nodded towards the space at the front of the church where the coffin had once been.

'I knew Oscar.'

Well, thought Ozden, he has the right name. 'How?'

'A long story,' said the young man.

'I'm interested.'

'Why?'

'I'm a reporter. I'm doing a story on his life. I thought I knew all his relatives, but I don't know you.'

'And what is it about Oscar that interests you?' asked the young man.

Ozden didn't answer. Instead he asked, 'What brings you here from Moscow?

'So many questions.'

'How about you answer them? After all, any bastard new in Okhotsk is a story. And I'm always interested in stories.'

The stranger looked at Ozden for a long and discomforting moment. Then, surprisingly, he said, 'A beer?'

'Sure,' replied the journalist.

They walked out of the chapel into the freezing midday air. Eddies of snow swirled around the pavements, and the ice had built up dangerously, even though the pavements had been cleared by street sweepers two hours earlier.

'I have my car just around the corner,' said the young man. 'Where do you want to go?'

'There's a nice inn not far from here.'

Despite the freezing air catching in his throat and hurting his lungs, Ozden asked, 'Your name?'

'Vladimir.'

'And your last name? Do you not have a patronymic?'

'Just Vladimir.'

The journalist shrugged. He was good at getting information out of people. After a couple of beers he would know the man's name and his connection with the old Stalinist. There was a story here. It was getting better and better.

The old man had first come to Ozden's attention through a conversation he'd had with a mutual friend, a drunken old bastard who had told him that Oscar had once, in a drunken moment, confessed to being a Stalin warlord somewhere in the west near Moscow, but that somehow or other he'd managed to escape the purges. It was a fucking good story but Oscar, the old bastard, had died before Ozden could talk to him. That hadn't stopped Ozden from investigating; dead or alive, it was still a story. He'd phoned friends in Moscow, but the files had revealed nothing. He'd phoned a friend who had once worked for the NKVD, but all the information he'd got in return for his trouble was a wishy-washy denial. The files showed that Oscar had lived in Okhotsk all his life, but that wasn't true. It was classic KGB cover-up. And, since Yeltsin, Ozden no longer feared the KGB. Why was a useless old bastard being protected unless he had something deep and important to hide from his early days, from the days of Stalin?

Now that Communism was over, the files were open. He could have gone to Moscow and done the investigation himself, but his piss-weak, drunken, idiot editor wouldn't let him go over there and investigate. Fuck his mother.

Maybe this young man was KGB. He had the look. Maybe he'd come to give him the details. Stranger things had happened. The young man's car was modern, much more modern than any other in Okhotsk except those that belonged to the fat cats in the government. Even the seats were comfortable and heated. This was luxury. This man must be loaded. Now this really was a story. Why would someone like him come to the funeral of an old bastard like Oscar? The journalist gave directions: 'Turn left, then second right . . .'

But instead of stopping outside the door of the garishly lit inn, the young man accelerated the car out of the main part of town and into the woods beyond.

Ozden objected, but the young man simply said, quietly, 'I know you wanted a drink, but before that we need to talk privately. You've been making enquiries about Oscar in Moscow. You've set off some alarm bells. That's why I'm here. There's a story I have to tell you.'

'Who are you?' Ozden asked.

The young man looked at him, and smiled. Ozden sat back, excited in his certain knowledge that, for once in his life, he'd cracked a big one. At last he could go back to his editor, bang his story on the bastard's desk and tell him to get fucked. Then he'd pack his bags, leave his hideous wife and fly to Moscow to get a real job. Anybody who could get the KGB to come to Okhotsk was a real journalist.

Ozden's triumph was short-lived. As soon as Vladimir saw that they were well outside of the town and that there were no cars around, he stopped the car. Turning to Ozden, who looked at him, he pointed up to the roof of the car, just above the journalist's head.

'See there . . .' he said.

Ozden looked up. With the speed of a whip, Vladimir smashed the iron-hard side of his hand into Ozden's exposed throat. Ozden gagged, gasping to force precious air into his crushed windpipe. His hands clutched uselessly at his shirt collar as blood bubbled up into his mouth. Vladimir had seen it all before. He didn't even bother to look. The poor bastard would be dead in a very short while. Ozden's head fell forward onto his chest; a last gasp leaked blood, saliva and vomit down the front of his shirt.

Vladimir drove quickly off the deserted main road into a side road and then deep into the woods. There he opened the passenger door and manhandled the flaccid form of the journalist out of the car. He dragged the heavy body off the side of the track to ensure that it would be found within a few days. Then Vladimir pulled down the dead man's trousers. He took out a sharp knife and sliced off the man's penis, then stuck it into Ozden's mouth. Despite his years of killing, he was revolted by the act. He would never get used to it. He took a bottle of vodka out of his car and poured it over his blood-soaked hands, rubbing them to remove the last remnants of the journalist. Two hours later he was flying out of Okhotsk.

Later that evening, Vladimir phoned a man in Prague.

'Nikolai Alexandrovich, it's Vladimir.'

'Well?' said Zamov.

'Everything has been taken care of.'

'How?' asked the older man.

'Do you really want to know?'

The silence indicated willingness.

'I cut off his cock and stuck it in his mouth.'

Vladimir could feel the disgust of the older man in his silence.

Justifying himself, he continued, 'I wanted it to look like a homosexual lovers' quarrel. That's what angry gays do when their lovers cheat on them.'

'And how would you know?' asked Zamov.

This time it was Vladimir who remained silent.

'You have done well, Vladimir. Though I deplore your methods.'

The older man put down the phone and breathed deeply for a few moments. Such a disgusting way to terminate a man. Still, he was a journalist, who had started asking awkward questions about one of the brethren. Why? Half a century and people were still interested. Was there no end to their curiosity? It had all happened in the past, so long ago, another age. And now another killing.

He picked up the telephone again and dialled a series of numbers in Bratislava.

'Tranov,' a gruff voice answered.

'Our little matter is completed. The journalist's inquiries are at an end.'

'Excellent,' said the old Stalinist.

# CHAPTER ELEVEN

Laco Plastov's Volkswagen jerked its way past the sign announcing 'Novosad' and collapsed with a final shudder. For the past fifteen minutes, it had been backfiring like a farting bull, fulminating and angry with the unexpected strain of two more bodies than its usual load. Josh suggested they call a road service. Laco's response was to laugh. Eventually, he managed to restart the motor and they crawled to a garage just within the village boundaries. Laco filled up with petrol and poured some decoking liquid into the engine. When he started the car again, it coughed and vibrated like an elderly asthmatic, blew a huge cloud of grey-white smoke which filled the canopy of the petrol station and then drove away much more happily.

'See,' said Laco, 'this car is like a wife. I know her moods, her temperaments. I know what she needs. I know how much vodka to get her drunk and how much so that she's only playful. I love this old car. As the director of the museum, I'm entitled to something bigger and better but I told them to give me more money and let me keep my car. That's how I can afford Western cigarettes.'

Sarah felt herself becoming disdainful again and told herself not to be silly. Josh reached over and patted Laco on the shoulder. 'It's really good of you to come with us. You're right of course, being an archaeologist you'll have a much better knowledge of what to look for than we did on our last visit.'

'That's what most people don't understand about archaeology. They think it's digging up the ancient past. But we're just as fascinated by the recent. The line between being an archaeologist and an historian is becoming increasingly blurred. I'll give you an example: let's say we dig up World War One or Two artefacts. An historian probably wouldn't know what to do with them; they don't like to get their hands dirty. All they care about is documents. It takes someone like me, someone who doesn't mind getting his fingernails covered in shit, to really find out the truth about what went on.'

'And you really think you can uncover the facts about my family?'

'Listen, Josh, no matter what the new owners have told you, many old houses contain relics of the past. In a corner of a cellar, or in an attic, there's usually a scrap of paper or an old item of clothing, maybe even a box of letters. It's amazing how people don't throw these things away; they just store them. Maybe we'll get lucky and the new owners will have put things into a "too-hard" basket. That's what I'm good at – unearthing other people's lives.'

They pulled up outside the plumbers' supply shop. The first time Josh had been here, all his eyes had seen was a building, but his mind had invested the experience with all the emotions of a man fulfilling his family's destiny. On the second occasion, with Sarah and the crew, he'd viewed his family home as a scene in a film. But since meeting Laco another dimension had been introduced – that of the explorer, the discoverer, the seeker after truth. He now tried to imagine what the shop would have looked like when his father had left there aged twenty, the lone remaining child of a family slaughtered in the war.

The three of them crossed the road and entered the shop. It smelt of dust and vodka. It was just past ten in the morning. The man behind the counter was in his mid-forties, tall, with a broad face and a lean body. He looked up from the paper he was reading. He recognised Josh and smiled. Then his smile faded as he remembered the circumstances of their last meeting; that Josh's family had once owned his property. Why had he returned? Did he intend to cause trouble? The owner began to speak animatedly in Slovakian. Laco answered him, his voice calm and moderated, his hand gestures speaking volumes. There was no need for a translation. After an exchange of a dozen or so sentences, Laco said to Josh, 'He thinks you're trying to steal his house from him. He says that he bought it legitimately and that he's got the papers to prove it. He's frightened now that you've come back a third time. I've assured him that we're not here to dispossess him, only to look around for old time's sake.'

Sarah looked at Laco in surprise. 'But that's not true. You know the reason we're here.'

'That's why *you're* here, Sarah. It's something you can deal with. I'm not getting involved. I'm part of this community. All I'm here for is to help my good American friend, Mr Hollywood, with my genius as an archaeologist, and to help find whatever bits and pieces remain of his family. All the legal stuff you can do in Bratislava. You can get this guy evicted if you want, but you're not using me.'

'Fair enough,' said Josh. 'Let's pretend that we're here to find more about my family.' Sarah was forced to go along with the deception but she felt uneasy.

The shopkeeper shook his head vehemently when the archaeologist questioned him. Laco translated the owner's words in rapid-fire succession: 'No, there was nothing left. When I put in a new ceiling, I threw everything out. It was full of rats' nests and bird shit. The roof had caved in and was open to the sky. Storks had built a dozen nests inside the cavity. It was disgusting. It smelled foul. Anything which might have been here from the old days was rotten. I made a huge bonfire in the garden and burnt the lot. And good riddance.'

The man went on to explain that he had spent a fortune putting in a new tin roof and wooden beams. Anything that he may have missed had since been destroyed by the weather, or the rats, or used by the storks for their nests.

Laco turned to Josh. 'He's invited you to go up into the roof cavity and see for yourself, which means he's probably telling the truth. These things happen. I'm sorry.'

Laco could sense Josh's disappointment. He'd hoped to be able to find something, but it was almost certain that nothing was left. Laco said goodbye and they turned to walk out of the door. The shopkeeper said something else as an afterthought, perhaps a tidbit because he thought he'd seen the back of them. Laco thanked him. 'Have you ever heard of a woman called Magda Oloxo?' he asked Josh, outside the shop.

'I know of a Magda. She lives over the road.'

'Apparently she knew your family very well. She always talks about them. According to him, she hid your dad and his parents when there was a massacre. Do you know anything about that?'

'Sure. My dad spoke about her often. I've been saving up visiting her until I was emotionally ready.'

'Apparently she lives just over the road. Over there. She's in her seventies. The guy in the shop thought she might have something belonging to your parents. What massacre was this?' asked Laco.

They started to cross the road. Josh didn't answer, which surprised Laco. He whispered to Sarah, 'Do you know anything about a massacre?'

She nodded and whispered back: 'Apparently Josh's family managed to escape some brutal killing during a Stalinist purge of Jews. And the whole village turned against them. He's never been terribly forthcoming about it.'

Josh turned to Sarah as they neared the house. 'I should have visited earlier. I was avoiding it. I don't know why.' She smiled. She didn't know why he'd avoided seeing the old lady, either.

Laco opened the gate of the house the shopkeeper had indicated, and the three of them walked down the path. It was overgrown. The dead buds of roses, wilted in the summer heat, were brown and desiccated. Laco knocked too hard on the door. Josh felt his face flushing with excitement. After an interminable wait, it was opened cautiously by a woman in her forties or maybe fifties. She and Laco spoke in Slovakian. The woman frowned and studied Josh carefully. She was a few years older than him. Eventually she nodded and in broken English, said, 'I am pleased to welcome you. My mother is in the yard. But I ask you to be careful. She is old and very frail and has recently returned from an operation on her heart. Before I admit you, may I please ask her whether she is wish to talk to you? She might be upset.'

'Of course,' said Sarah.

The woman disappeared. Another interminable wait. The three remained silent on the porch, Josh hardly breathing with the strain. Eventually the daughter returned and said, 'My mother will see you. Please come around the house. I ask you again to be careful. She is not well. She has still a weak heart.'

As they followed her along the side laneway, the farmyard smells became more pronounced. Goats bleated and dogs barked. At the back of the house was a large yard with a central elm tree surrounded by a circular wooden seat. Close by was a table, and under its parasol an old lady sat. Her white hair was pulled back severely into a bun. She wore thick glasses, but Sarah could see from her creased brow that she was almost blind, her face searching for the visitors.

Cutting the yard in two was a two-storey barn, its apex towering over the roof of the residence. Josh whispered,

'That was the barn where my father and grandparents hid from the massacre. Unbelievable. I'm here. It's like . . .' He searched unsuccessfully for the words.

They sat down at the table. The daughter explained to her mother where the people were. The old woman held out her hand across the table. Josh reached out and took it in his own. He felt her dry, parchment skin; it was warm. The old woman said something. It sounded wheezy. Laco strained forward to listen but her daughter, used to her mother's vocabulary and way of speaking, translated: 'My mother asks whether you are Hermann's son.'

Josh nodded. The old woman, half blind, saw the movement and said something else. 'She says she has carried the guilt of your family half her life. She is so pleased that now you are here, so she can apologise and die without the stain of guilt.'

'Guilt?' said Josh.

Tears began to well up in the old woman's eyes. She struggled in her frock pocket for a handkerchief. She removed her glasses and wiped her face. She began to speak now, more clearly, but sobs caught in her throat. Laco looked at Josh and shrugged his shoulders. He couldn't understand a word.

The old woman turned to Laco and reached over to hold his hand. Ancient memories spoke through her tortured body. Laco listened carefully and nodded. He spoke to the old woman slowly. She smiled through her pain and appeared to be agreeing with what he said. They continued to talk until Josh showed his exasperation at being excluded. Laco held up a hand to silence the woman's stream of regret. He turned to Josh and explained.

'She is telling us how the Communists took over the area when she was a girl. One minute the Nazis were here – whom she calls the spawn of the devil – then when things were just beginning to return to normal and they were starting to mourn for the dead, the Communists came in and behaved just as horrifically as the Nazis. She describes it as living through a nightmare but never waking up.'

The old woman spoke to her daughter, who translated: 'My mother says that all her life, she has been a devoted Catholic. But the Communists made her forget her charity towards other human beings. She says that your grandmother and grandfather were her dear friends, and that your father, Hermann, was a lovely boy who loved her *palachinten*. It was the fear of the Communists that made her forget Christ's message to love all others. The Communists and Alexander Hasek, may God forgive him. When Alexander Hasek came and murdered the villagers, she hid your father and your grandparents. My mother used to work sometimes for your parents in their shop, selling food. She used to babysit your father when his parents had to go to Kosice on business. She says that in the massacre she was very cruel to your father and your grandparents and sent them away. She should have helped them, like a good Christian. But she was scared.'

Josh was riveted by the old lady's words. Laco and Sarah scarcely dared to breathe. The old woman's daughter continued, translating as her mother's increasingly rasping voice began to fail and falter. 'It was the day after the massacre that my mother sent your family away. She was very angry. Many of her friends were killed by Hasek. He was an evil man; he terrorised the whole of this area. Every village was frightened of him. He hated Jews. People think he collaborated with the Nazis but he denied it. He was a Stalinist.'

The old lady was sobbing now and wiping her eyes. 'My mother says she feels a terrible guilt. She told your family that she didn't want Jews in this village because it meant the death of so many of her friends. She says for fifty years she has hated herself every day for saying these things to your family. Your grandparents were good people, fine people. They helped her with money and food.'

Josh was on the verge of tears. He bit his lip to stop himself from crying, but reached over and grabbed the old woman's hand in both of his.

'Tell her, thank you. Tell her not to feel guilty. Tell her she's a wonderful, wonderful woman. Is there anything I can do for her? For you and your family?'

The daughter translated the words, smiled and shook her head. The old woman continued to sob gently into her handkerchief.

Laco said to the daughter, 'Who is this Hasek that your mother talks about?'

The daughter didn't bother to translate. 'I know very little. I was born when my mother remarried. She sometimes talked of this Hasek. He was a very evil man. Many people around here were affected by him. He was a local commissar. A man of no great consequence before the War, I believe. It was only when he became a Stalinist that he became important. From what I've been told, he was very vicious. He had a large house in another village with lots of servants. He was like a god.' She nodded towards Josh. 'Hasek came here, looking for this man's family. The story was that their families knew each other and hated each other. Hasek's father told of how your grandfather cheated him of money. So when Hasek became important, he was after them. They were Cosmopolitans or Jews or something. I don't know the full story, but when he couldn't find them he went crazy. As revenge he massacred ten village people.'

'What happened to him?' asked Sarah.

'He died or disappeared. I don't know.'

Laco asked the same question of the old lady, who responded. Laco was surprised. He asked her several other questions, until she became visibly distressed. The daughter intervened, but Laco persisted, this time more gently. They continued to talk in Slovakian until Josh interrupted: 'What's she saying, for Christ's sake?'

Laco smiled. A victory smile. 'According to her, everybody thought that this Alexander Hasek had been murdered after the purge of Stalin's henchmen by Khrushchev or Beria or Malenkov in the middle of the 1950s. It was Beria who brought Stalin's anti-Semitic witchhunt to an end. The minute Stalin died, Hasek know he was doomed because of what he had done to the local people, so he disappeared in March 1953. People assumed he was dead. There was an official hunt for him and reports came back that he'd been executed by a firing squad in a Moscow prison for crimes against the people.

'That was until twenty years ago. A man from the village went to Prague and came back and told everybody that he'd seen Hasek. That was in 1975. Apparently the people here doubted it, but the man was absolutely convinced. He swore it was true. He reported it to the local police. A week later he was found hanging from a beam in his barn. Not even the police thought it was suicide.'

The daughter shrugged her shoulders. 'It is best to keep out of these things.'

Laco nodded in agreement. Josh began to ask more questions, but Laco, almost imperceptibly, shook his head, stood and bade them a warm farewell.

Josh and Sarah kissed the old woman and her daughter, and promised they would return. Outside, walking to the car, Laco pre-empted Josh's question. 'They were scared and they knew nothing more. And we were distressing the old lady. There'll be plenty of documented evidence about the death of this man in the village records. And now that Russia has opened up and we can search their files, we can find out more information about this Alexander Hasek character.'

'You've never heard of him?' asked Josh.

Laco shook his head. 'Do you know how many warlords killed how many poor bastards during the Stalin period? Ten, twelve, maybe twenty million people were sent to gulags, or murdered on the say-so of vindictive neighbours or some piece of local filth who wanted to lick some communist official's ass.'

'But surely someone like this Hasek, someone who massacred so many innocent people in a small village, that would have to be exceptional, wouldn't it?' asked Sarah.

Laco shook his head and opened the car door. 'Only for the people in the village. And there are thousands of villages in Eastern Europe ... and nobody has any idea how many there are in Russia. It's not surprising I haven't heard of this Hasek. There would have been a thousand Haseks in Stalin's time. Most of them would be dead by now. Those who aren't are probably skulking in some corner of Siberia, scared to open the front door.'

Struggling to get into the back seat, Josh said, 'This Hasek character. Sure, he might be just another one out of the mould, but he tried to kill my father. That alone means it's something I'd have to follow up.'

Laco shrugged his shoulders. 'I thought you were here to get your house back.'

'I am,' said Josh, irritation seeping into his voice. 'But the house is only the key to opening the door.'

'Key?' asked Laco.

'Do you know how many millions of people had their lives and property taken away from them at the say-so of Stalin and the people who worked for him? Innocent people were destroyed. People like my family.'

'And mine,' said Laco.

'Yours?' Sarah asked. 'Your family were victims?'

Laco laughed. 'It's a long story, but Jews weren't the only ones to suffer.'

'I never said they were,' said Josh.

'Everyone suffered,' Laco told them, 'except the bastards who worked for the Party. The Party was everything. Join the Party and you were safe.'

'How did your family suffer, Laco?' asked Josh.

'It's a long story,' he repeated. 'Meantime, are you sure you want to follow this guy up? You could be opening a can of worms. Some things are better left hidden.'

Josh nodded vigorously. 'Any ideas how I'd go about it?' he asked.

'How would you go about it in America?'

Josh thought for a moment. 'Well, if I was researching an American war criminal, there'd be plenty of records. Social security, Department of Veterans' Affairs, Pentagon . . . I don't know.'

Laco turned round. 'Same here. It's not hard. Except when you try to search Russian files – not that they don't let you any more. Right now there are more American PhD students searching KGB files in Moscow than there are tourists, but the files are in such a state of disorder that it can take years. And if something's been hidden deliberately, you'll never find it.'

'Does that mean you're not interested in looking for him?' Josh asked.

Laco thought for a moment, then started the car, which back-fired loudly, and drove off. 'Your father wasn't the only victim, you know, Mr Hollywood. Like I said, so was my father. When I get back I'll ask him what he knows.'

He didn't notice Sarah and Josh beaming at each other. Nor did he see Sarah reaching back to squeeze Josh's hand.

Laco didn't drive straight back to Kosice as Josh was expecting. Instead, he took them to a large imposing building in the centre of the village.

'First step in the search, Mr Hollywood – local records. Officials in villages like this have nothing to do all day but keep records.'

Inside the town hall Laco asked for the official in charge of Novosad's documentation. Within five minutes, they were sitting in the office of a surprised, and somewhat agitated, apparatchik, whose last unexpected visitor had arrived two years earlier, and had grilled her on the minute details of the previous five years of town hall accounts. She continued to feel uncomfortable in the presence of strangers. The room smelt of cheap cigarettes, and the mandatory map of Slovakia was displayed on one wall, with the Czech Republic darkened to appear as though it was a satellite state.

The woman, whose name Sarah and Josh forgot the moment she introduced herself, listened to Laco's request, and immediately called for files. They were eventually brought into the room by an elderly man, who struggled to carry in his arms the two large document folios. Josh and Sarah watched in amazement. Even before Sarah had graduated as a lawyer, the entire administration of America was already computerised. Every document was available through a search program on-screen. These huge folios, that had obviously been gathering dust in an archive, were like something from an ancient library, not a modern public records office.

The records officer, her black nylon shirt reeking of stale body odour, stood and opened the first folio. She found what she was looking for after four or five minutes of searching, and incomprehensible mumbling. Laco pored over the document with her. He asked for paper and pen and took notes. Sarah was thrilled that they were able to leave the office quickly. She wanted to make a comment about the woman's body odour problem but felt it would be ungracious.

Back in the street, Laco explained that he had found the name and address of the man who had been found hanged. The official knew the family, and they still lived in the same house. 'That's the thing that most people from the West don't understand about the East. Except in the big cities, almost nothing changes. Your house, Josh — it surprised you that Magda was still living over the road. It didn't surprise me. What *is* surprising is when somebody leaves a village. That becomes gossip for years afterwards.'

They followed the instructions of the town hall official and drove to the house where the widow of the man who had witnessed Alexander Hasek's alleged resurrection still lived. At first, the old woman was guarded and suspicious, but when Laco explained that Josh was a famous Hollywood film director and was interested in the history of the area his family were born in, she opened up, pulling them all inside into the front parlour of the house.

Laco translated her excited babble: 'I was a young girl when your father left the village. I remember it; it was the day of the massacre. I remember your grandparents and your father. Oh, it's good to see you. It's really good to see you. I've seen some of your movies in Kosice. I never realised that you were the famous son. I'm very proud to have known your papa.'

Laco asked questions and translated simultaneously. 'We're interested in Alexander Hasek. Your late husband apparently saw him in Prague.'

The widow nodded vehemently. 'People deny it. They said he was mistaken or drunk. But my husband could hold his drink and he knew Hasek well. He'd worked for Hasek's family, on their house. My husband was a carpenter.' She pointed to the furniture and the cabinet in the room. 'He built all this. And much more. He spent weeks working on Hasek's parents' house and knew Alexander well. They called him to do the work because he was the best cabinet-maker in the whole area.'

Josh looked around at the furniture and smiled. Through Laco, he told the woman that the work was of a very high standard. She beamed, and continued: 'He thought that his friendship would save us when Hasek became the commissar in the area, but Hasek wasn't after us. He was after all the Jews. He hated Jews. He said they were responsible for the war and responsible for the death of his parents. He said they robbed people and were in control of the world's banks. He said killing Jews was the only thing that Hitler got right.'

Sarah's fists clenched involuntarily. The old libel. Would it never die and be laid to rest?

'He made everybody read the Protocols of the Elders of Zion. My husband read it and believed it. He was a simple man, a good man, but . . .' She shrugged her shoulders. 'My husband tried to contact Alexander Hasek when he became the commissar but Hasek ignored him. He was too important. Then the massacre . . .' The widow stopped talking and stared out of the window. 'Some of the men who were killed were my friends, or friends of my parents. I knew them all. I'd grown up with some of them.'

She shook her head and fell silent, on the verge of tears. Sarah stood and put her arm around her. Her lower lip trembling, she continued, 'They were shot down like dogs. Hasek knew some of them as well. Even people he knew he shot like dogs! With his own hands. He didn't care. He was like a god, so powerful. When he couldn't find your family,' she nodded at Josh, 'he became crazed like a madman.' She shook her head at the distant memory. 'Why?' she asked.

Laco shrugged his shoulders. 'Millions of widows ask the same question.'

The woman sighed and continued. 'Your family disappeared. We thought they were killed. I was sad because I liked your grandparents. They were kind. They were good people. Sometimes when my parents didn't have money for food, they would give credit. They never asked for the money back but trusted people.' She sighed again, deeply, and shook her head. 'So much sadness.'

Laco interrupted. 'Tell me about your husband seeing Hasek in Prague.'

The woman concentrated. 'He went to Prague one Christmas. It was 1975. He went to see his cousin who had come from Australia. They were going to travel to Bohemia. It was the first holiday he had had in years. In Prague, he is walking in Wenceslas Square when, on the other side of the square, he sees a man walking among the thousands of people. But this man on the other side – he stands out. My husband recognises him and follows him. Hasek walks towards the river so my husband crosses the square. It's a big square, he thinks he has lost him, but then he sees him again. He walks up quickly behind him and says, 'Alexander Hasek?' The man turns around and stares at him. My husband knows he's right. The man's face turns white in shock. Hasek shakes his head and says, 'No, you've got the wrong man.' He walks quickly away. My husband follows him and says, 'You remember me,' and tells him his name. He tells him the name of the village. He reminds him that he used to work as a carpenter on his parents' house. But the man starts to shout and says he'll call the police, that my husband has the wrong man. My husband says, 'Don't deny it. I know who you are. You killed my friends.' The man starts to hit him with his umbrella then runs away. A policeman came up and stopped my husband from following. He asked him what was going on, but by the time he had explained the story, Hasek had gone.

'A week later, after they had been in Bohemia and the cousin went to France, my husband returns and tells everybody in the village. People don't believe it. They think he made a mistake. Hasek couldn't have survived, they said. Not after what he did. He told the police, and the officials in the town hall. They said they'd investigate, but he heard nothing. Then two weeks later . . .' Her lip trembled and she started to cry. Sarah continued to hold her tightly.

Laco said, 'Just tell us simply what happened.'

'I am at the grocer's buying the week's food. I come home. I know my husband should be here, and I know something is wrong. A chair has been knocked over in the kitchen. I search the house and I go outside into the barn and he is hanging there. His face is blue. The police say there was a struggle, that his arms are bruised as if he was beaten. They question everybody. Nobody has seen any strange cars or people. They think it might be somebody in the village. But he had no enemies. Everybody liked him. That's all I can tell you.'

'You think it was Hasek?' asked Josh.

'Who else?' said the woman. 'Who else?'

While Laco, Josh and Sarah were talking to the widow, an old man sat quietly in his office in Novosad's town hall. It was lunchtime and he knew nobody would be in the building. He picked up the phone and dialled the code for Kosice, then the phone number of the offices of the municipal headquarters of the region. He asked for a man to whom he hadn't spoken in over three years. The man was guarded when he came to the phone.

'I have some information for you,' said the old man from Novosad, 'information about our friend. You remember you asked me to keep my eyes and ears open? You remember you said you would be generous?'

'Of course,' said the official in Kosice.

The old man told the official about the visit from Laco and his colleagues, about the files requested by the public records officer, and that the documentation they were interested in concerned the death by hanging of a Novosad resident who believed he had seen Alexander Hasek.

Igor Nemez listened with growing apprehension to the old man.

'Tell me about your visitors,' Nemez said. The old man described them as best he could, but his memory was hazy. He found it difficult these days to remember things that had only just happened. One man certainly was Slovak, the other and the woman American.

'When they entered the building, they would have left their names and signatures at the front reception desk. Am I right?'

The old man in Novosad agreed.

'Get their names and call me back. Have you any idea where they are now?'

The old man said they had gone to the house of the widow.

'And after that?' Nemez asked.

'I don't know,' said the old man.

'Are they still there?'

'I think so.' His voice wheezed in asthmatic concern.

'Good. There's one thing that you have to do for me. It is most important. Do you remember what I instructed you to do if this happened?'

'Of course,' said the old man.

'Then do it. There will be a handsome reward in your bank account tonight.'

The old man smiled and put down the phone. He went to the back of the town hall, took his old bike from the rack there and rode as quickly as his spindly legs would carry him to the house of the widow. He waited until the three visitors emerged.

'Excuse me, sir,' he said to Laco. Laco turned in surprise. Josh and Sarah looked at him questioningly, not understanding the old man's words.

'I couldn't help but overhear what you were saying in the town hall. There is a man you should speak to; the policeman who investigated the matter. He may have information for you. I was sent to tell you this.'

Laco thanked him. The old man gave the address and explained how to get there.

The house was on the other side of town. Initially, the former policeman was suspicious and guarded with Laco and the Americans, but when Laco explained that they had been sent to him by the town hall officials, he opened up somewhat. He was used to dealing with official matters. Laco explained that they were trying to determine whether a man called Alexander Hasek was still alive.

'Hasek?' said the policeman. 'No. I investigated that years ago. Nothing. Some fool of a carpenter claimed to have seen him, wasted all my time. Months of work it cost me. What foolishness are you following now?' he asked.

Laco explained. The policeman shook his head. 'Look,' he said, 'every now and again, somebody comes looking for this Hasek. My boss, God rest his soul, got fed up with it – especially after this drunken idiot claimed he had seen him in Prague – so he made me do a thorough investigation. I checked dental records with Moscow, fingerprints, everything. There's clear indisputable evidence that Hasek died in a purge in the '50s. I did my report, but the idiot carpenter refused to believe it. So I investigated the carpenter. He was an alcoholic, who could no longer work because his hands were shaking too much. He became a beggar. He even tried to sell the story to the newspapers. That was what it was all about – money. In the end, the devils of his mind took over and he hanged himself. Don't waste your time. It's all rubbish.'

Outside, Laco explained what the former policeman had said. 'Well?' Josh asked Sarah. 'You're a trial lawyer. Whose story do you prefer?'

'Gut reaction?'

'Yeah, gut reaction.'

'I'll go with the widow. The policeman's story was just too pat, too well thought out. These things happened twenty years ago, yet he remembered the details really clearly. That's a put-up job in there.'

Igor Nemez pondered what to do next. Would these things never be laid to rest? Damn, hell and blast. He unlocked the bottom drawer of his desk and took out a thin blue file. He extracted a copy of the *New York Times*, dated two weeks earlier. The article outlined the trip which Joshua Krantz, the famous Hollywood movie director, was taking to Slovakia in order to reclaim his family home which had been taken over by the Communists. Krantz! It had come full circle. Grandparents, father, and now the son.

Nemez took a sip of water to ease his dry throat. He picked up the phone and dialled a telephone number across the length of the country. An elderly man in a small Bohemian town called Cesky Krumlov answered.

'Alexander,' said the man from Kosice, 'I'm afraid I have some bad news for you. The dogs have started to bark again.'

# CHAPTER TWELVE

Sarah was lying on her bed reading a book when the telephone called her back from the perfumes and conversations of eighteenth-century Parisian society.

'Were you asleep?'

She smiled, recognising Laco's voice immediately.

'Reading. Trying to get to sleep.'

'Are you dressed?'

She burst out laughing. 'A gentleman doesn't ask a lady that.'

'You may be a lady, but I never said I was a gentleman. Are you dressed?'

'No, I'm not. I'm in my nightgown.'

Now Laco laughed. 'Nightgown! Such an upper middle class term. I sleep naked. Even in the middle of winter.'

'Dr Plastov, I hardly think this is a proper conversation to have with an unmarried female tourist.'

'Miss Kaplan, I am me. I make no exceptions for your sex or your status.'

'What do you want, Laco?'

'I'll meet you downstairs in half an hour and take you somewhere special.'

'Don't be ridiculous. It's . . .' she looked at her watch, 'eleven thirty.'

'I am a Slovak. I am not controlled by the clock.'

'I'm a New Yorker which means my clock is twenty-four hours, and I'm exhausted. It's been an emotionally draining day. Forget it. I'll see you tomorrow like we agreed.'

'You'll see me downstairs in half an hour.'

'Laco,' her voice became commanding, 'I'm tired. It's been a heavy day. I've got a conversation to have with my law firm in America first thing tomorrow morning.'

'Half an hour.' He put the phone down.

Damn his presumptuousness. She barely knew him, and already he was giving her instructions. She lay back on her bed and picked up the book. She read two paragraphs. She re-read them. The third time she realised that she hadn't taken in more than a dozen words. Her mind was on Laco's arrogance, and the fact that he was driving closer and closer to her hotel. Where would he be now? She looked at her watch. Approaching the city boundary? Driving up Hlvana Street? And, more to the point, where was he planning to take her? A sleazy nightclub full of smoke and animated people whom she couldn't understand, even when they used broken English and exaggerated hand gestures. Or maybe he really fancied his chances and was planning an evening drive to look at the moon over some deserted lake. Did he seriously think that she'd be interested in a cheap Lothario like him, a man who undressed every young woman he saw with his eyes?

She picked up her book again, determined not to answer the telephone when he arrived downstairs. She re-read the same paragraphs and realised that still nothing was sinking in. She stood and looked out of the window. Sporadic lights along the main road gave patchy illumination to the half a dozen or so people still walking along the road that late at night. The clanking trams and trolley buses had already come to the end of their day and were parked in the nearby station. An occasional car roared into and out of sight.

Sarah scanned the roads for an old Volkswagen. Damn him and his presumption! How dare he assume that she would get dressed and go out with him!

She walked across to the wardrobe. It was a warm night so she selected a linen dress. She took off her nightgown and slipped the dress on. She brushed her hair and looked at herself in the mirror. Suddenly she realised with embarrassment that she had completely forgotten to put on underwear. She stripped quickly, washed herself in cold water and re-dressed, properly this time. She selected a perfume that David had given her for her last birthday, sprayed a cloud into the air, closed her eyes and walked through it. Her mother had taught her that trick – the perfume was less overwhelming and gave men just a hint of allure.

God Almighty, listen to me! she thought. Allure! I'm almost married to a beautiful, sensitive, Jewish cellist and I'm going on a date with a crazy, chain-smoking, heavy-drinking, Catholic Bohemian.

The phone rang and she grabbed it from its cradle.

'Still in your nightgown, Mrs Hollywood?'

'I'm not Mrs Hollywood.'

'You're Mr Hollywood's lawyer. That makes you Mrs Hollywood in my eyes. I'm downstairs in the lobby.'

He put the phone down. His arrogance prickled at her. She would teach him a lesson in manners. She walked quickly down the corridor to the elevators. The old man who seemed perpetually to be on duty opened the cage for her and greeted her with a smile.

'Is late for you to go out,' he said. 'The streets are not careful.'

'I'll be alright,' she said.

He shrugged his shoulders and turned his back on her.

The vestibule on the ground floor was like the rest of the hotel, not air conditioned. It was hot and muggy after another airless summer day. She saw Laco looking at a display case, his back to her. He sensed her presence and turned. He was wearing an open shirt and faded blue jeans. He was dressed entirely inappropriately for a man in his mid-forties. This was how James Dean dressed when he was in his twenties. David would never have dressed like this.

'You look beautiful, Sarah,' he said as she walked towards him.

He put his arm around her shoulder and kissed her on the cheek. She should have objected. His arm was still around her shoulder as they walked, in silence, out of the Hotel Slovan towards his car.

'Where are you taking me?'

'A special place.'

'Where?'

'You'll see.'

They drove out of the city. The roads quickly became deserted. By now Sarah was familiar with the layout of the town and she knew they were heading out towards the airport. Laco turned right into a country lane. The headlights of the Volkswagen hardly illuminated the road ahead, yet he drove fast, seemingly uncaring. He didn't speak and neither did she. She was regretting coming with him. She hardly knew him. Yet, in the space of a couple of days, she had given him her amulet to examine – which she had never let out of her possession since her mother gave it to her – and she had traipsed with him throughout Eastern Slovakia. He was endearing and had a boyish charm. Yet there was a crudeness to him which was so . . . so what? So unlike David. He had no refinement, yet showed moments of extraordinary sensitivity; an earthiness, yet a sense of aesthetics. He was a strange and complex man.

'Laco, I think I'm entitled to know where I'm going.'

The car began to climb and he still said nothing. The road became increasingly steep and the old Volkswagen whined loudly in complaint.

'Laco!' she said, this time with more determination.

'You know,' he said, 'for centuries this land was criss-crossed by invaders. Austrians, Hungarians, Russians, Germans, Mongols. Every bastard. And yet we're a very proud people. We survive. There are many marks of the civilisations that made us what we are today, the great families that built castles and mansions all over Slovakia. We are a poor country and some of them we find hard to keep up. But there's one near here which is my favourite. You can stand on the top of the turret and see Hungary and the Ukraine and, who knows, maybe as far as Troy.' He laughed. 'I'm only joking about Troy. It's a special place, Sarah. You can really only appreciate it at night. On a clear moonlit night. I want you to see it.'

It was the oldest line in the book. It may have worked on his twenty-year-old, gullible female students but it wasn't working on her.

'Is this where you take all your girlfriends, Laco?'

'Some,' he said with disarming honesty.

'Laco, let's understand one thing, shall we? I'm here to do a job. I have a very close relationship at home. You're a nice guy but . . .'

'Why don't you wait until we get there. You may not fall in love with me but I guarantee you'll fall in love with the place.'

She smiled, and thanked God he couldn't see it in the poor illumination from the car's dashboard. The castle suddenly appeared as they rounded a bend, looming phantasmagorically out of the night. How it had been built where it was, Sarah would never understand. It seemed to be perched on the highest hill in the region, dropped intact from the sky. Those extraordinary ancient builders had managed to balance the huge Gothic structure delicately on the hilltop, like a fragile crown on a monarch's head.

Laco stopped the car in the carpark. He opened his door and, for the first time since Sarah had met him, he walked around and opened hers. It was a full moon and she could see the gloomy grey pathway quite clearly. At this height there was a cooling breeze blowing. It rustled her hair and she noticed that it blew inside Laco's shirt, opening it to expose his chest. They walked up the path and through the castle keep. Laco explained the layout of the castle's collapsed walls, the crenellated towers and where the dungeons had once been.

As they walked towards the battlement steps which led up to the keep tower, he grasped her arm and said, 'These stairs are a bit tricky, even during the day. I know them well. Let me help you.'

His hands were warm. She didn't object.

There were thirty steps in all and by the time they got to the top and looked out over the panoramic landscape she could understand why this was his favourite place. Even in the dark of a moonlight night, the view was breathtaking. Far, far into the distance on all sides, Sarah could see sporadic lights of farmhouses or the distant clusters of lights that marked out the villages. In the sky, twenty miles away at least, she could see a tiny plane heading south.

Laco rested his arms on one of the battlements. She leaned against the stone wall, alongside him.

'This castle was started in 1100 by a local nobleman,' he began, 'and finished in 1172 by his grandson, a local prince called Miroslav. He was a powerful man who had made his fortune by working very closely with the traders from the Ottoman Empire, dealing in slaves. The traders supplied him with men and women from Egypt, Africa or the Middle East and he sold them into Europe. I often come up here on my own, late at night, and stand here looking out over this view, pretending that I'm Miroslav.'

'You mean you want to be a slave trader?'

He smiled. 'No. Of course not. I just imagine myself controlling everything around as far as the eye can see, having the power of life and death over everybody. Having the people down there looking up at me in fear.'

'And you'd like that?' Sarah asked in surprise.

'No, I didn't say I'd like it. I said I often think about it. I think I'd be a very different kind of person to Miroslav; much more gentle and open with people. I would use my power of life and death for good. But it's not that part of his story which I find so compelling, it's the other part.'

'What other part?'

'It's a legend. Nobody knows whether or not it's true. I like to believe it, because it's romantic and says so much to us today.'

Sarah settled more comfortably against the battlement. Despite the refreshing wind, the stone was still warm from the heat of the day. She enjoyed listening to Laco. Like every Bohemian, he was a natural storyteller, and on their long drives throughout the countryside he'd kept Josh and her amused with anecdotes presenting his somewhat anarchistic view of life. She settled back to listen to the pleasing melody of his tale.

'For years Miroslav lived all alone in this dark castle, ruling his land. From time to time he travelled to Constantinople, but that was as far as he would go. The more he visited the fabulous church of Hagia Sophia – in those days, Sarah, it was the biggest and most prestigious church in the world – the more devout he became. The church was built by the Emperor Justinian in 548, and its name means Holy Wisdom. Each time Miroslav went in there, he came out wiser, with deeper insights into the blackness of life. Sometimes he would spend a whole day on his knees, staring up at the mosaic of Jesus Christ as the Pantocrator, the Ruler of all things, praying day by day that Christ would make him see light where he only saw black.

'Other princes went to Paris and Prague and Warsaw, and danced and feasted and felt the pleasures of young women . . . but not Miroslav. His courtiers were worried about him, as were the local churchmen, the local burghers, even the local artisans. Why? Because Miroslav was doing nothing to improve the culture or trade of his land. He was becoming wealthier by the day, but his people were falling behind the rest of Slovakia as his moods became more and more introspective, more and more bleak. While other princedoms were attracting the best poets, writers, painters, sculptors and architects, Miroslav's people still lived in the dark ages.

'So his castellan decided to do something about it. He rode off to a far kingdom and brought back for Miroslav the daughter of a distant nobleman. She was the most beautiful girl in the world, long silver-blonde hair, the biggest blue eyes, the creamiest skin and the most ravishing smile . . . enough to melt the heart of the meanest of men.'

Sarah watched him in the moonlight, and could see him warming to the fantasy. She was enjoying herself as much as he was, feeling more and more romantic as the minutes ticked by. Who wouldn't? Alone with a stunning man in the middle of a moonlight night on top of a Gothic castle, being serenaded with a tale worthy of Æsop.

'Well, the minute Miroslav saw her, he fell head over heels in love. His bleak countenance left him, he smiled, he laughed. He let the sun into his princedom. They were married within the month. He threw open this castle to the people and invited in the finest minds in Western Europe to shed even more light on this part of the world.

'For a year, everything was wonderful. Until, late one night, on this very battlement, perhaps even on this very spot, his wife was walking and there, in the sky, she saw a light. She stopped and as she looked, it grew brighter and brighter until she was nearly blinded. She fell to her knees and when she looked up, there before her was the Tree of Knowledge, from which Eve and Adam had eaten the fruits. It was suspended in the air and there was a bright halo around it. As she stared at it in astonishment, the tree slowly lost its fruit, then its branches, until just the trunk was left. And then the trunk grew two more sturdy branches, until it resembled a cross. And, with the noise of rushing wind, the Tree of Knowledge transformed itself into the very cross on which Christ was crucified by the Romans. And a deep and fearful voice from the sky said, "Woman, go and command your husband to gather up a great army and free my home, my Jerusalem, from the grip of the Saracens".

'The cross disappeared, and Miroslav's wife knew that Christ had visited her. She fell full-length onto the ground, where her husband found her an hour later. He thought she had fainted and ordered his servants to carry her down to her bedchamber. But when they picked her up, they nearly dropped her again in fear . . . because a light was shining out of her body. A halo all around her. She was unconscious, but she was smiling, as though in a rapture.'

Sarah realised she was hardly breathing. She willed Laco to continue.

'They put her on her bed and for four days she simply lay there in a trance. Doctors came from all around and all could see the halo. Despite the fact that she didn't eat or drink for all that time, her face was flushed as though she was in the best of health and she continued to smile, as though looking at the portrait of someone she loved dearly.

'On the fifth day, without any warning, she sat up, eyes bright and clear, skin glowing, and hair shining . . . but the halo had disappeared. She looked at Miroslav and said, "Husband, gather a great army and free Jerusalem".

'Now nobody spoke to Miroslav like that. Nobody. But he knew that these weren't her words; that they were the words of God. So he gathered up a great army, equipped them and marched them towards Constantinople. Fortunately, because he knew so many people, the rulers let him pass, only demanding a king's ransom of tribute which he willingly paid. And he marched to Jerusalem. There he joined up with King Richard the First of England and became part of the army which fought Saladin. He was killed in one of the battles and his army was decimated.

'For the two years he was gone, his beautiful wife held court. She was loved by the people and would spend her days riding from village to village, handing out charity and alms. At night she would host banquets at which wonderful stories were told. But as soon as the last guest was gone, she would take herself up to the battlements and look south in case the lights of torches showed the army returning, her husband Miroslav victorious at its head.

'On one of these evenings, a lone rider approached the castle gates. Miroslav's princess felt a foreboding. She called down and asked whether the knight had any news of her husband. He shouted up that Miroslav had died valiantly at the hands of his enemy. She nodded, thanked him and threw him a purse of gold for his trouble. Then she threw herself off the battlement onto the rocks below. People saw her fall, but no one found her body. It was as if it had disappeared into thin air. The country fell into disrepair, into disease, and people started to wander away, to escape the long black night which had fallen upon them. And the castle has never known the sound of laughter from that day to this.'

Laco stared out into the far distance. Sarah was uncomfortable.

'And the moral of this story?' she asked.

'Moral? It's a story. A local legend.'

'And it has nothing to do with what I'm doing here? What Josh is trying to do about getting his home back?'

Laco looked stunned. 'Do you think I'm that devious?'

She smiled. Oh yes, he was that devious. A story about Christ asking a beautiful young woman to get his home back; it was a warning. Don't mess with things or dreadful consequences will eventuate. But it was a wonderful story.

'Is that what you tell all your girlfriends when they come up here with you?' she asked.

Laco looked at her in surprise. 'You think this is a line, Sarah? It's not. I didn't bring you up here to seduce you. I'm sorry if you think I did. I came up here to share something with you. Something which is private, personal. Come on. I'll take you back to your hotel.' He turned and walked towards the stairs.

She held out her hand. 'Laco, I'm sorry. I misunderstood. Please don't go. I apologise.'

He looked at her. The moon was behind him, and she could only just make out his features in the dark. 'Laco, I'm really sorry. I . . . I . . . thought this was just a come-on. That you brought me here to try it on.'

Laco walked back, but remained distant from her. 'You've got the wrong impression of me. I know I'm a bit of a wild man and make jokes and stuff, but, deep inside, I'm a Slovak. I'm passionate and proud and I love my country. And I love fine art and beautiful music. You've made a judgement about me which is shallow. Not worthy of someone like you, someone smart and clever.'

She thought a moment and nodded. 'You're right. I have made a superficial judgement about you. I'm truly sorry.'

He shrugged his shoulders and moved closer to her. 'You are a very beautiful woman, Sarah. This boyfriend of yours in America is a very lucky man. Do you love him?'

She nodded. 'Deeply.'

'Then you're both lucky. I wish I shared your luck. My girlfriend, the real love of my life, was Yugoslavian. We met at the university in Prague when we were students together. She came with me here to Kosice, but when the Soviet Union broke up and the wars started, she returned to be part of the fight for her country's freedom. I never heard from her again. To this day I don't know what happened to her. She may still be alive. She may be in prison.' He fell into contemplation.

Sarah was speechless. She felt guilty for her own happiness. He looked so pathetic, so utterly lost. She reached over and held his hand. He put his arms around her and pulled her close to him. There was a faint smell of cigarettes about him, and a strong sense of maleness. She hadn't been held properly by a man since her last night, weeks ago, with David. It felt so good to be enfolded in his arms, to be part of his strength, protected by it. He kissed her on the top of her head, on her scented hair.

'What a beautiful perfume,' he said. 'What is it?'

'Poison.'

'Poison? It's an absurd name but a beautiful scent.'

She lifted her face to look at him. 'Laco, I don't . . .'

He kissed her on the lips. She should have pushed him away. She didn't. He kissed her again, more passionately. Oh God, she thought, I've fallen for his line. Oh Christ, what am I doing? And then she kissed him back, passionately.

Over breakfast, Josh knew that something had happened to Sarah. She was more garrulous, brighter, more communicative.

'You sound as if you had a good sleep last night.'

'Excuse me?' she asked in surprise.

'Well, you just seem very fresh and bright and alert. You seem as if you slept particularly well.'

'Yeah, sure. I had a great night's sleep. Anyway, what time is Laco picking us up?'

Josh looked at his watch. 'In about half an hour. Enough time to have breakfast and brush our teeth before we go on the trail again. Phil and Jerry are already out. I told them to get background stuff. They don't need me, they know more about that than I do. You'd be amazed how much background material you need when you're making a movie, even a TV documentary. You have to have vistas and cityscapes and close-ups of little kids eating ice-cream and garbage in the streets and rivers trickling by – a million different things to get the flavour of a city. You might only see them as an image for a second or so on the screen, but it's an image which builds up a composite picture in the mind of the viewer of where the city's at. It could take them a week of solid photography just to get ten minutes of background in Kosice and Novosad and other places.'

'And you really don't need to be there?' Sarah asked.

'Generally directors only need to be there when we're dealing with actors and extreme close-ups, when there's interaction between performers. The rest of the time a good cameraman can visualise a finished film in his mind, and Phil's just about the best I've ever worked with.'

'But you're in this film, Josh. Don't they need you walking about in the street?'

'I'm taking this movie. Don't forget this is you, me and a Sony in Slovakia.'

'And an American network has bought that?'

He smiled. 'That's only a fraction of it. The real stuff is when we get to court and you see me going in and out, and my reactions. Crowds of reporters shoving microphones in my face, archival film about Nazis and the Stalin period. And of course there's you. You'll be a star.'

Sarah put her cup of coffee down with a clatter. 'Josh, that's something we need to discuss. I don't mind being by your side, but I'm not going to star in your film. I'm a lawyer, for God's sake.'

He smiled.

She insisted, 'I'm not a movie star. I've had enough publicity with that bastard Darman. That's as much as I need for the rest of my life.'

'You'd better talk to Morrie about that then, because it's all been agreed.'

'Morrie . . . ?'

'Sarah, it's no big deal. He thought it would be good for you, for your career.'

'Josh, I'll decide what's good for my career. When lawyers start to become actors . . .'

'I don't want you to act. All I want you to do is to be my lawyer, standing on the steps with me outside a Bratislavan courthouse, telling the world about the injustices done to the Jewish people.'

She remained silent, her mood of last night and this morning completely evaporated.

'What's the big deal, Sarah? Every American lawyer fights to get in front of the camera on the courthouse steps. It's the way they get new business.'

'I have a problem with that sort of exposure, Josh. Naively, stupidly, I thought that I could keep out of the limelight with Darman. I was doing it for the principle, not the exposure. I miscalculated. I didn't realise the case would attract such international attention.'

'How could you not have realised?'

'I didn't think constitutional issues would be front-page news. I knew we'd get into the law reports and maybe the Jewish newspapers, but I didn't think I'd be harassed by the media for weeks after.'

'A Jewish woman lawyer defending a virulent anti-Semite who was accused of saying the Holocaust never happened – and you didn't think you'd be front-page news?'

She shrugged her shoulders.

'Boy, do you need some lessons in media.'

'Josh, I won't star in your film. I'm sorry. If you want to get another lawyer, that's fine with me.'

'Is it?'

'Is it what?' she asked.

'Is it fine with you? Do you want to resign the case? Do you want to leave me and go back to America?'

'I . . . That's not a fair question. I'm here as your lawyer.'

'Sarah, you know we've become friends. I rely on you as more than a lawyer. I want to share things with you.'

Her heart sank. 'Josh, we've had this conversation. While I'm here I have to remain your lawyer.'

'I understand that, Sarah, but we've moved on a hell of a long way since that. Think about your reactions at the museum, the dig. That's not the reaction of a lawyer. That's the reaction of a woman. And I was with you when it happened. That creates a special bond between people. You can't escape that bond, Sarah. It's happened.'

'And in the States,' she said, 'I have a serious bond with another man.'

'I know. You've told me. I'm not asking you to marry me, Sarah.'

'Then what are you asking me? I don't know where I am with you, Josh. You're not being fair. I haven't got all that much experience in these sorts of things. You have. You're playing games with me, with my emotions.' A tone of desperation, of insecurity, crept into her voice.

He reached across the breakfast table and grasped her arm. 'That's one thing I'm not doing, Sarah. If I was intent on screwing you, I wouldn't be playing games. I'd bring in the cavalry: the lifestyle, the riches, all the bullshit that turns young women's heads. I've never done that with you, not for a single minute. At first, I just wanted you for a lawyer. I know this is going to sound unbelievably arrogant, but when it comes to beautiful young women, I've got an address book full of them. A smorgasbord. You think some of the most incredibly lovely actresses in America wouldn't hump me if I phoned them? They'd do anything to get a part in one of my movies.

'But I've had that scene. I told you. I've had it in Hollywood and New York, in Paris, Rome. I don't need it . . . I don't want it anymore. Sure, I like sex. I've got some close female friends and we have a great time. But that's not the issue. Like I said when I first met you, I wanted you to be my lawyer because you were passionate and different and you had a transparent honesty about you which I found amazing. Truth to tell, even the first time you were with me, you made it quite clear that you didn't give a damn about who I was. All you cared about was the case, the rights and wrongs of it. A woman who could defend a Nazi because of her passion for the First Amendment, but who wouldn't take on a well-known movie director because she thought I was wrong, that's some woman.

'You impressed the shit out of me. And you were just what I needed. I was fairly clear in my mind, pretty convinced that what I was doing was right. Everyone I asked gave the same answer: "Go for it". What I needed was mental clarification. I'd been to LA lawyers and even another one in New York, big-time guys. And all I got was heavy-handed agreements: "Of course we can do that, Mr Krantz", "It's not a problem, Mr Krantz", "We'll teach those bastards a lesson, Mr Krantz".

'But when I came away from those meetings, I had a bad taste in my mouth. And then I read your article, and did some research about you and the Nazi, and I thought, someone who is patently that honest is the woman I want to fight this thing for me, because if I'm about to make the wrong move, she'll tell me.'

Sarah shook her head and moved her hand from under his until they were holding hands properly.

'Josh, you're not even being honest with yourself now. What you really wanted from me was to cash in on the publicity that I was getting with Darman.'

He laughed. 'I don't need you for PR, Sarah. Publicity follows me around like a bad smell. That's not why I wanted you. I hired you because you were a damn good, honest lawyer. I was a bit like Diogenes. When you're surrounded by bullshit, all you really want is to be with an honest person.'

'I'll always be that for you, Josh.'

He nodded, and stroked her skin lightly, fondly. 'Trouble is, what's happened since we've been in Europe is that I've grown close to you as a friend. Not just as a lawyer. And unless I'm completely fucked up in my judgement, I think you like me.'

'Of course I'm fond of you. I think you're a lovely man. You're intelligent, you're honest and you're one of the rare people I've met who's a mover rather than a shaker. You get out there and make things happen; you don't just shout about them. Big things. You follow your dream. I admire that in you. I'm proud to be with you. But being proud doesn't mean that I want our relationship to go further. I'm deeply committed to David. He wants me to marry him.'

'And have you agreed? Are you going to get married?'

Her silence was testimony to her indecision.

'You see. You like to pretend that you're committed, but you're not really at all. You're just in the relationship for convenience. You probably love the guy, but not enough to marry him. He's probably a fantastic man, but not fantastic enough for you to commit fully. You've got too much to do, too much to live for, before you get married. You're too young, you have too many experiences still to have.'

She took her hand away from his. He was intruding too deeply into her personal space and she found that offensive. 'You don't know me that well, Josh.'

But he knew he had hit a raw nerve. The look on her face told him that he was absolutely right. She probably did love David, but where was the passion?

'Sarah, I'm not asking you for an affair.'

'Then what are you asking me for?'

'A chance.'

'A chance for what?' She was desperate for the conversation to end, so she could get back onto dry land.

She didn't know what to do, whether to go further and see where things led, or to put a stop to everything now, as propriety and commonsense demanded.

'A chance to be more than a friend. To take it step by step. To see where our friendship can develop, without the crap about lawyer and client. That's all.'

She breathed deeply. Oh shit, she thought. Two in the space of twenty-four hours. How the hell am I going to explain this? And *who* the hell am I going to explain it to?

# CHAPTER THIRTEEN

Igor Nemez, Deputy Director and Assistant Chief Administrative Officer of the Council of the City of Kosice and its surroundings, greeted his overseas visitors with a warmth and openness which their time in Kosice had not led them to expect. Igor spread his huge arms as they walked into his office and, in a deep, mellifluous, heavily accented voice boomed, 'Welcome to Kosice. I am so honoured to meet the famous Hollywood legend, Mr Joshua Krantz, and his lovely travelling companion. When I am in Prague or Vienna on official business, I always take time off to see the latest Mr Joshua Krantz blockbuster. I haven't missed one.'

If it were a scene from a movie, the director would have instructed him to walk around the desk and embrace the two Westerners and their Slovakian friend. But this was real life, and instead the second most senior government bureaucrat in Kosice pumped their hands with joy at the unexpected meeting.

He spoke in cautious and measured English to Josh and Sarah, and periodically in Slovakian to Laco when he was unsure of a word. 'You are most welcome to enter my office. But to what do I have the honour? You said downstairs at my receptionist that you want to consult on a matter of business. Please, sit, so that we might drink with each other and discuss your problem.'

Laco explained why they had come. Understanding nothing of the conversation, Josh watched carefully for the official's reaction when Laco mentioned the name, Alexander Hasek. He knew enough about actors to believe that this man was genuinely surprised.

'Of course I know of this Hasek. A mass murderer. He was from Venubov. He committed atrocities in many towns in Eastern Slovakia many years ago. A monster. But dead, thankfully. In Moscow, many years ago. Why do you seek his memory after all these years?'

Josh explained: 'We've been to Kosice to have a look at my family's former home. We found out about a massacre that occurred there because Hasek was after my family. Everybody thought he was dead, killed in one of the purges after Stalin's death, but a man in the village saw him in the early 1970s in Prague. When he reported it, he was attacked and hanged in his own home. Since then, people have been too scared to open the inquiry any further.'

Igor Nemez nodded gravely. 'Ah! The horrors continue. We thought we had buried this animal. But you say he was alive in the 1970s? I will look at the records. Now, the name of this man who was hanged? Then I will find out the police officer who investigated and follow it through. Tell me, where are you staying in Kosice? How long will you be here? Believe me, we will do everything speedily, but inevitably these things do take some time. I wouldn't want you to disrupt your tourism for this. Dear friends, have you seen what our beautiful country has to offer? Dr Plastov is an old friend of the area. I'm sure he will be delighted to be our ambassador.'

It was the end of the interview but Sarah and Josh didn't move. Nemez looked at them, his smile refusing to disappear from his face.

'I'm not sure you quite understand the seriousness of our request. We have strong grounds for believing that a mass murderer is still alive. We would like to examine your files immediately so that we can find out his last address and trace him from there,' said Sarah.

'My dear young lady,' said Nemez, 'these files are long buried, just like Hasek. To bring them up from archives is difficult. Also we had a fire, as Dr Plastov may remember. It was big news at the time. Tragic. This was in 1981. Many old records were burned. Perhaps Hasek's. We haven't had the money or the staff to sort things out as they should be. It might take weeks to go through to find out his address. You are on a . . .' He looked at Laco and asked a question in Slovakian.

Laco replied to his question, 'Wild goose chase.'

'Exactly,' continued Nemez in a patronising tone, 'a wild goose chase. Is nothing here. You will ruin your holiday. Of course I will look but we are understaffed, and since the President of my country broke away from the Union with the Czech Republic and Czechoslovakia is no more, we do not have Prague's millions to pay our way. My office used to have twenty more people than I now have. I even have to make my own coffee.' He burst out laughing.

Sarah was irritated. Was this how officials had treated her ancestors – with palpable contempt, using their positions to ridicule, to diminish?

'This really isn't a laughing matter, Mr Nemez,' she told him. 'I am a member of the American bar. If I want information I call upon a government department and I use the Freedom of Information Act to get what I need. Discovery is a cardinal principle of the West. Your country is looking towards the West for its future, not the East. I would hate to have to go back to my country and tell them that your attitude was one of obstruction.'

Even then his avuncular smile remained. 'My dear young miss, there is no intention on my part to hide these matters. Hasek was a monster, but now he is a dead monster. He was killed in a purge. To prove this will cost me many weeks of time, but it is well known amongst people who know. Is it so important to you that I roll up my sleeves and go to the basement and search through the files? I have no one else to do it. You cannot do it because you cannot speak our language. Maybe Dr Plastov. He is an archaeologist. He is used to digging. Maybe you, Professor, would like to do it? I can give you the key.'

Josh intervened before Laco was able to respond. 'It's a government function. We expect you to provide the resources to do it.'

The veneer began to crack. The smile wasn't quite so wide. The eyes narrowed just fractionally. 'Mr Krantz, in your country, I am sure you have enormous power. I am sure you can tell people what to do. But you are a visitor here, a guest in my country. While I would like to help you, I am afraid that I have many priorities during my day. Yours is a priority which isn't quite as pressing as others, but do be assured, my dear young people, that it will be attended to and I will write to Dr Plastov in a month, or however long it takes me, and inform him of the results of my search. Now, you must excuse me. It has been an experience to meet with a famous Hollywood director. Perhaps I can give you complimentary tickets to visit our local theatre. They are playing tonight.'

He opened his desk drawer and took out a thick wad of tickets. He pulled off the top three and handed them to Laco. 'You may not understand much of what is said, but there is great passion in these players. It is the universal language of drama, something which you deal with every day, Mr Krantz. Now please, feel free to drop by at any time and visit me. I am always happy to have a coffee with a great Hollywood director and his lady friend, even if I have to make the coffee myself.'

As they walked down the corridor, Josh began to speak. 'You know . . .' But Laco gripped him by the hand and squeezed it painfully. The three of them walked quietly to the end of the corridor, through the heavy wooden doors and down the marble steps until they were outside. Even while they crossed the road and headed away from the main square towards the narrow streets of the Old City, Laco maintained the need for silence.

Eventually, two corners away from the City Hall, Laco hissed, 'Bastard! That fire in 1981 destroyed two toilets and the cleaners' room. The story they put out at the time was that a cleaner was smoking and fell asleep on the toilet; he nearly died of smoke inhalation. But everybody was convinced it was arson. Fortunately, the fire was put out before it damaged any records, even though they said that many old records were destroyed. But my father knew the fire chief, who told him the truth. Nothing was destroyed. Nothing.'

'So he's hiding something?' said Sarah.

'We can't just jump to that conclusion. Could be, but I doubt it. He's just a typical Eastern European official. He does the absolute minimum necessary to keep his job. As it is, he hates me. My father was the mayor between '59 and '73. He fired Nemez and half a dozen others for incompetence and laziness. They orchestrated a campaign against him and he was kicked out in the '74 elections. An old apparatchik got back in and immediately re-hired Nemez and all his cronies. But all the improvements you see in Kosice, small as they are, were due to my father. He was reappointed for a brief period in 1981 before Moscow intervened.'

'Your father was mayor?' said Sarah in surprise.

'That's how I know about the fire. Nemez was having a dig at me. My father was in his office when the fire started. The bastards locked the doors so he couldn't escape from the building. He could have been killed. But they were incompetents, and the fire went out by itself. My father was a powerful man, but even he could not stop the onslaught from Moscow. Anyway, even though he's old now, he still has contacts.'

Josh interrupted. 'Do you think Nemez was telling the truth about Hasek?'

'I have no idea, Josh, but I'll tell you one thing – we'll find out nothing more from him. In a month, two months, maybe even a year, I'll get a letter saying they made a thorough search of the records but that the last known address for Hasek was Siberia.'

'So how are we going to find out?'

'Plenty of ways. That's the advantage of being a historian and an archaeologist. I'm trained in digging up facts. You know, in many cases, journalists come to me asking me for help. I know who to ask, what to look for and where to find things.'

They adjourned to a café to make plans. 'The first thing we are going to do,' Laco said in a low voice, 'is not to mention him by name. From now on we call him the enemy, or the quarry, or T2 or something. The less we mention his name, the safer we are.'

'Safer?' said Sarah.

'Eastern Europe, especially here and the Ukraine, is still dominated by friends of the communists. The young people and the intellectuals have broken away and are revelling in the freedom; so are the nationalists, and anyone else who put Slovakia or the Czech Republic or Serbia or any of the other satellite states first. But there's still a very strong, powerful, old guard which is dormant, waiting for the new-style capitalism to collapse and old-style authoritarian communism to return, and the worse the economy becomes, the more converts they get. The Communist Party is the fastest-growing political party in Eastern Europe.'

Sarah burst out laughing. 'You've got to be joking,' she said scornfully. 'There's no way in the wide world that communism would ever be allowed to return to the old satellite states. Sure it's getting disgruntled converts, but it's burnt out. There's no power structure any more.'

Laco smiled. 'Don't underestimate the strength of the brotherhood. There are millions of people in the former USSR who would love nothing more than a return to centralised government, to stability. Not in the Czech Republic maybe, but certainly in the Ukraine, in Slovakia, in Poland, in Georgia, in the East. There's nothing too overt happening, no massive political rallies, but there are an awful lot of older people who hate what's going on and think the old communist system was preferable. They'd like to march boldly forward into the past.'

The waitress brought the coffee.

'We need to do research before we take this any further,' said Sarah.

'How do you research a ghost?' asked Laco.

'There are bound to be reports by government commissions, reports held locally in places other than the town hall, eyewitness accounts. There must be places we can look.'

'Sarah,' said Josh, 'this guy was reported as having been killed. For all we know he *may* be dead. And if he is alive, then the likelihood is he's hiding behind an entirely different identity. We won't find his name in a newspaper story.'

She sipped her coffee. 'Then how do *you* propose we find him?' she asked.

'We have an archaeologist who knows how to dig up the past, a lawyer who knows how to research facts and get to the bottom of things, and a film director who . . .' He stopped, wondering what his value to the group could be.

'Who's good at making things happen,' intervened Laco. 'You've got powerful connections. You would be amazed how somebody from America's State Department can make people in Bratislava or Prague move into action. The United States is good at bringing moral force to bear on other governments.'

'This isn't a government-to-government matter yet, Laco,' said Sarah. 'It's nowhere near. We've got a hypothesis based on a questionable sighting of a man who may be dead. Not even the State Department is stupid enough to go into bat for something like that.'

There was a long moment of silence, then Josh said, 'If we're not going to find details in government records or newspaper columns, how the hell *are* we going to find this bastard?'

'Before we decide that, Josh, there's another issue: the simple matter of whether we *are* going to trace him. We came here to get your property back from the Slovakian government, and we've got teams of lawyers working hard on it at an enormous cost. I know this is important to you, but we're in danger of becoming sidetracked.'

Josh bridled. 'Sarah, this man tried to kill my family. That takes precedence over a house.'

'Then I'll have to inform Morrie and the office in New York.'

Josh looked at her in surprise. 'I don't understand.'

'This is a change of brief for me, Josh. I'm here as your lawyer.'

He nodded slowly. 'Right,' he said, 'I just had the impression that this was our fight. I forgot you were my lawyer.'

'I'm sorry,' she said. 'I didn't mean to hurt you but . . .'

Laco asked quietly, 'And me?'

'You?'

'Sure. What's my role in this?'

Josh looked surprised.

'You're assuming that I'm just coming along for the ride. You don't employ me, Joshua.'

'What do you want?' he asked.

Laco smiled. 'A thousand dollar donation to the Museum. That'll give us food and drink for next year's dig. That's all I want.'

'Two thou, but from now on I own your heart and soul until we've resolved this matter one way or another. Now, can we get on with things? Where do we go first?'

Laco was stunned at the sudden fortune he'd been thrown. If he wanted even five hundred dollars for a dig, he had to go cap in hand to the authorities and beg. And risk almost certain rejection. But two thousand dollars. It would pay for . . . his mind reeled.

Focusing again, he began to plan their strategy. 'We'll go to Venubov. It's close to here. That's where he was born, where his family lived.'

'But how will we find his house?'

'The same way as you found yours.'

'And you think his family will still be there?'

'It's likely, but even if not, there will be people there who used to work for the family. They'll know. You'd be surprised how much servants know about the doings of their masters. That's one of the great things about the communist system where everybody is equal.'

Sarah remained silent. She was wondering why she was so incapable of reading Josh's thoughts. Before the interview with this Nemez character, he had been a man on a mission, driven by thoughts of revenge, of wrongs being righted, of the decisions of history being revoked. But now he was acting like a film director planning the next day's shoot. And she had no understanding of Hollywood.

Igor Nemez knew his approach had been wrong the moment they walked out of his office. He had thought that playing the role of the jolly official, eager to help and full of concern, would satisfy them, but they were far from satisfied. His approach should have been that of the bureaucrat: saying little, nodding gravely, taking notes and promising a hasty result. He had badly underestimated the seriousness of their resolve. It was an error he must correct immediately.

He had imagined them to be dilettantes, but there was revenge in the air. Plastov must be working for his father. How many years was it? More than twenty, and old Plastov still retained the grudge. Not the defeat at the elections but his dismissal from the directorship of the Museum, his ignominious retirement, the articles denouncing him in the local press. He had neither forgiven nor forgotten. This was Plastov's revenge. Well, nobody would attack Igor Nemez.

He had been doodling pictures since they had left; his pad was full of concentric circles, triangles and drawings. He looked at one of his drawings very carefully and bit his lip. He didn't remember when he had drawn it, nor what had motivated him, but it was a sign. He bit his lip harder. Did he have the courage? So near to retirement, so close to the end of a long career? He had his house in the Tatra Mountains, an apartment in Bratislava; he even had a time-share in Paris and enough in an account in Austria so that he would never have to think again about money. Just as long as he lived quietly during the next three years and didn't ruffle any feathers nor ripple any ponds; just as long as there was no audit of the Council's accounts; just as long as no one found out that fifty of the people who had been claiming dependency for the past ten years had been dead since the War. And they would quickly trace the flow of funds to him, and from him to his Austrian account. Damn the hide of Plastov. Damn him to hell and back! Nemez didn't need this. Not now. Just three more lousy years and he would be able to disappear with his Hungarian mistress, leaving his wife and his disgusting, grasping parasitic offspring, and live out the rest of his years in paradise.

He put his finger to his lip; his finger came away bloody. He had bitten too hard. He picked up the phone again. In the old days, the days of Stalin and Beria, he would have left the building and made the phone call from the privacy of a café, but these days the KGB was no longer operative, and the Slovakian Secret Service consisted of two retired colonels who spent their time buying lunch for chauffeurs at the American Embassy. There would be nobody listening to his conversation.

He opened his address book and found the name Vasik. Opposite was a phone number. He memorised the middle four numbers, then walked over to his filing cabinet. He unlocked it and took out an old ledger containing the names of tenants of government properties, shopkeepers, factory owners, residents of housing communes. He flicked across the pages until he found the number he wanted. The middle four digits of the telephone number of the mythical Vasik belonged to a hypothetical character he'd called Viktor Schmeidl a decade ago. Nemez breathed hard. Could he do it? It was a huge step, and desperately dangerous. The repercussions would be unbelievable if it went wrong, but it was the only way to stop their investigation in its tracks. Opposite Schmeidl's name was a telephone number. Nemez hadn't used it in twelve years, but he would have been informed by those above him if it had changed. He walked back to his desk and dialled the number.

Within three rings, a woman's voice answered in Russian: 'Baltic Fish Canneries, can I help you?'

'Igor Nemez. Kosice. Slovakia.'

'Somebody will ring you back,' she said and put down the phone.

For two hours, Nemez waited. He looked at the phone. He looked at his watch. His secretary walked in but walked out instantly when he waved his hand to dismiss her. In fear, she rang through to his desk to tell him that his next appointment had arrived. He told her to cancel. Her voice cracking with concern, she said, 'But he's travelled from Bratislava to see you.'

'I don't care,' snapped Nemez. 'I said cancel. Tell him to come back tomorrow.'

'Yes, sir,' she said.

The silence of the room enveloped him. He continued to stare at the phone. A line of perspiration at his hairline accompanied a tingling in his scalp. He ran his hands through his greying hair. Still the phone didn't ring. He tried to read, but the words swam before his eyes. How had it come to this? Why were they after Hasek? He was an old man, nearly dead. A couple of years, and Nemez wouldn't have had to lie. But he couldn't risk further investigation. Like a loose thread, it could unravel the entire fabric.

He felt himself shaking with the pent-up frustration of waiting. He prayed for the telephone to ring. When it did, he was already grey with anxiety. He nearly jumped out of his seat.

He snatched up the phone. 'Yes?'

'So many years. Are you free to talk?'

'Yes.'

'Do you have a problem?' The voice was soothing, calming.

'Yes,' said Nemez.

'A friend of mine will be with you tomorrow. Or does it have to be sooner than that?'

'Tomorrow is alright. How will I know your friend?'

'He'll know you,' said the voice on the other end of the line. He rang off.

Nemez took a handkerchief out to wipe his brow. The two-hour build-up of tension had made him shake, but he now realised that he was crying.

Sarah still felt uneasy as she put down the phone. The call to Morrie Friedlander had been anything but satisfactory.

As usual, she had been full of resolve before calling him, but had ended up bending in the breeze of his manic desire to do anything to please Josh. Sarah had told him about the developments of the past two days, secretly hoping that he would tell her that she wasn't Simon Wiesenthal, just a lawyer involved in a property restitution case. End of story. She wanted him to tell her that she wasn't permitted to go hunting ghosts from Stalin's era, but was to settle the house matter quickly, profitably and with a minimum of fuss. She had hoped that Morrie would instruct her to tell Josh that she was unable to participate in this search . . . but Morrie had defied her hopes, though not her expectations.

His first questions were those of concern: 'Is there any danger in this from your point of view? If there is, I want you out of there now.'

Despite what Laco had said, she decided to assure him that there was no danger. She didn't want to sound like a hysteric, and she knew Laco to be a weaver of dramatic tales. She was sure that the only danger they faced was that of official obfuscation.

'And Josh is quite happy with your participation?'

'More than happy,' she told him. 'Although I told him it was outside my area of expertise, he insists that I stay on his team.'

'Then do it. He's your client; do what you're told.'

'But Morrie,' she complained, 'I have no experience in this area. I'm a trial lawyer, for God's sake. I'm not qualified to hunt communist mass murderers. I don't even know which laws apply if we find the son of a bitch.'

'It's all there from the Nuremberg trials. They determined most of these matters at the time. Look, Sarah,' he told her, 'I don't want to bruise your ego, but your job is to keep Josh happy. Ours is to provide you with all the backup and support you need. He insisted on being accompanied by a relatively junior lawyer rather than a partner. But while this firm is acting for him, he'll get the best legal and personal advice we can offer. That's what he's paying the bills for.'

'Morrie,' she said, 'how long do you expect me to go on like this? Look, I've got commitments in America. I came over here for a couple of weeks at the most. It's getting on for that now, and we haven't had a peep out of the Bratislava lawyers, or even the ones in Prague. I can't get them to move their butts despite the fact that I'm on their backs every other day. I'm just doing no good over here.'

'Does Josh want you to go?'

'No. Quite the opposite.'

'Do you want me to see if David is willing to come over there to spend some time with you? I'll happily foot the bill. It's not a problem, Sarah. It's only an international airfare. He can stay in your room, so there won't be accommodation expenses.'

It was a generous offer and unexpected. It took the wind out of her sails, but she thought of her room and its two single beds. And then she thought of Laco kissing her on the parapet of a ruined castle. And just as quickly, she thought of Josh and how he would react. Jealously, no doubt. She smiled ruefully.

'No. Thanks for the offer, but it would just complicate things. But I'm serious, Morrie, I'm not going to stay over here just to be Josh Krantz's plaything ... Oh God, I didn't mean it like that.'

Morrie burst out laughing. 'I know exactly how you meant it. You're a professional lawyer, you want to get on with your life and your career. I appreciate that. Give it another couple of weeks, that's all. If you want me to phone David and see if he's got time to come over there, I'm happy. But you make *me* happy, Sarah: don't cause problems yet. You know Josh phoned me a couple of days ago?'

'No,' she said, surprised.

'He phoned to tell me that you're the best damned lawyer he's ever had. He was complimenting your honesty and your sense of dedication. He said that, despite your youth, I should make you a partner.'

Sarah beamed a smile. It was a lovely thing for him to do. She wondered if he'd still say the same thing after she'd acted like . . . like a lawyer.

'It's on the cards, Sarah. You bring in lots of work from a client like Josh as a permanent feature of your income base and you'll be sitting at the partners' table within the year. That I can promise you. And when *that* makes the front pages of the Jewish newspapers, your mother and father will really have something to be proud of.'

'Is this what's known in law as holding out an inducement, Mr Friedlander?'

'You're damn right it is, Miss Kaplan.'

Sarah lay back on her bed after the conversation, wondering how Morrie had known about David, and about her parents' reaction to her publicity over the Darman case. Jack Abrahams had obviously been talking about her. She was flattered. But her conversation with the head of the firm hadn't been pleasing. If anything she had consolidated her position in the firm by doing nothing. That's what galled her most: the fact that she felt impotent, and yet everybody was praising her powers as a lawyer just because she knew how to look after Josh. This wasn't law; this was PR.

But deep down, she was thrilled about what was happening. Josh was everything anyone could want in a client. He was passionate, he had the money to throw at causes, and he was taking her into areas which were of infinitely greater importance – and interest – than representing corporate criminals in a New York court. For professional reasons, she had to tell Morrie what was going on as well as express her reservations, so that if things did fall into a bundle, not all the blame would come back to her. But she was as excited about the direction things were taking as Josh was and, she suspected, Laco.

There was a tap on the door. She looked at her watch; it was quarter to eleven. She walked across and opened it. Laco was standing there, with a cheap bottle of vodka in one hand and half a dozen roses in the other. She was stunned, but his plaintive little-boy-lost look was the most disarming thing she'd seen in weeks. He looked like a puppy who'd lost its master. If only she hadn't smiled, she would have been safe. Her smile suddenly changed him into a wolf. He pushed his way past her, asking, 'Are you alone?'

'Laco, you can't come in here,' she said, leaving the door open. But he was already at the other end of the room, near her bed. Concerned that someone might see, she closed the door behind her. She was angry with him, with his presumptuousness.

'I want you out of here, Laco. This is wrong. Don't take any comfort from what we did last night – that was an aberration. It was the castle and you and your bullshit stories. I don't know what made me kiss you, but I'm not going to kiss you now. I want you to leave.'

His little-boy-lost look was long gone. 'No you don't. You're upset because your biggest client is pissed off with you. You're treating him like a cold fish, and he doesn't like it. He's still hurt. You've got a job to make up the damage. And why did you say that stuff about the house? You could see he was passionate. You have to learn to go with the flow.'

'Laco, my professional relationship with Josh has nothing to do with you. Now, will you please leave.'

'You're confused. You want company; you don't really want me to go.'

'Yes, I do. I'm not joking, Laco. I'll call the manager if you don't leave. I'm nearly married and I'm not going to have an affair. I shouldn't have kissed you, I'm sorry I've sent out the wrong signals and led you on, and I'm sorry if you got the wrong idea – but go!'

He put the vodka and the flowers on the bedside table and lay down full length, hands behind his head on the pillow. 'You know you're even more beautiful when you're angry.'

'Oh, for God's sake!' she shouted. 'That is the oldest, dumbest line in the book. It's nearly midnight and I'm exhausted. Piss off, Laco, before I do something serious like scream rape!'

Laco smiled and took off his shoes. This really was too much. She marched to the door, opened it and said, 'If you're not out of here in two seconds, I'll scream.'

Laco looked at his watch. Ten seconds, twenty seconds, half a minute passed. Sarah closed the door. Fuming with anger, she sat on the other bed.

'What do you want from me? Do you want to make love to me? Is that it? If we make love, you'll go away?'

He shrugged. 'I don't want to make love to you now. Not when you're angry. I want to make love to you when you're happy and passionate.'

'I won't stop being angry until you're out of this room.'

'Sure you will,' he said. 'Your problem is not that you want me to go, but that deep down you want me to stay. Your problem is that you want to make love to me but you're too scared to admit it to yourself. That's your problem.'

Sarah was furious beyond words. She hadn't confronted a situation like this since she was in school. And date-rape trials had put a stop to smartass kids trying this sort of thing on in college. In America, at least. There was only one way to deal with his arrogance, and that was calmly, dispassionately.

'That's not the truth, Laco,' she told him. 'I don't want you in my room, or in my life. I was carried away last night. I enjoyed it. I enjoyed kissing you, but that doesn't mean I'm going to give my body to you. My body belongs to me, not to you.'

'I don't want to *own* your body, I just want to rent it for a couple of hours.'

'Oh, please,' she exclaimed. 'There's no need to be crude.'

'I'm not being crude. Why do Western women make such a big deal about sex? You make it seem as if it's one of those commodities which can never be replaced once it's given away. What is it? Let's face it – it's just half an hour of shared joy. It's two people coming together to enjoy something mutual. It's not life and death. In Eastern Europe, we don't have these attitudes. Two people like each other, they make love. When they stop liking each other, they stop making love. Usually they stay friends. Okay, maybe not with our generation, but certainly my students' generation.'

'That sounds about as passionate as buying fruit and vegetables,' she said.

'So, what do you want, Sarah – passion? You want me to tell you I love you? I don't love you. I like you. I think you're sexy. I think you're beautiful. You've got a great smile, beautiful face, hair, everything. And a great mind. Very clever. And naive. That I find very erotic. Brains and naivety – a very sexy combination. But do you want me to swear love to you? Nah, if it's love you want, you've got love at home.'

'That's the point, Laco. I have love at home.'

'And is he a good lover?'

'He's kind and gentle. Not that it's any of your business.'

'But is he a good lover, a great lover? Does he make your heart stop beating? Do you feel faint when he's inside you? Do you . . .'

'Laco,' she said furiously, 'these aren't things I want to discuss; and especially not with you.'

Ignoring her, he went on, 'Is he passionate? Does he make you feel like a woman? Tell me the truth.'

It was such an '80s line, like something out of a women's magazine. Have a great orgasm . . . then you're a real woman! The '90s were way beyond that superficial, sexist attitude. But he had touched a nerve. Something which she'd buried deeply within herself. David, dear beautiful David, was sensitive and kind. But there were times when the animal in her screamed to get out, when her body ached for a thrusting, back-arching, claw-digging, hair-raising session of sweaty sex. She remained silent, frightened by her thoughts.

'He isn't passionate, is he, Sarah? Look at the words you use: gentle and kind. That's what kids are to little animals. You want a man, Sarah. You want somebody with fire in his balls.'

'And you're the man, are you?'

Laco shrugged. 'Come and sit beside me.' He patted the bed.

Her anger had given way to confusion. She had spent hours that night thinking about David. Even comparing him to Laco. He was so gentle and generous and – oh damn! there was no other word – kind. But his visceral passions were all for music.

She didn't know what made her do it, but she stood and walked across the narrow space separating the two beds and sat down beside Laco.

'Sarah,' he said, looking at her, 'I'm not saying that I'm some muscle-bound he-man. Anyway, those guys on steroids can't get it up. But I'm a man of fire. Touch me and I'll set you alight.' He reached over and put his hand on her upper leg, his fingers reaching inside her thigh. She felt her body shudder.

She couldn't let him get away with it. Her voice unexpectedly hoarse, she told him softly, 'You're really something out of the 1960s, aren't you? Women aren't interested in that crap any more. You're totally out of step. Women seek out men like my David, for their understanding, their harmony. You're so full of shit, Laco.'

'No, I'm not. Not with you. With Mr Hollywood, definitely. Bucketloads of shit. But there are two areas in which I'm totally honest: one is my archaeology, and the other is being with you. Tell me to go now and I'll go. I mean it. Say to me you want me to go and I promise you I'll get up and leave. But if you don't say it, we're going to spend the night together and you're going to have the most amazing experience of your life.'

'How do you know I haven't had amazing experiences before?'

Laco smiled. 'I know. I know when a woman has been made love to properly. There's something in her eyes. Your eyes are still full of a sort of quest, looking for but never quite finding perfection. Maybe it won't happen for you tonight, maybe not tomorrow or the next day. But spend enough time with me and I promise you it will happen.'

Her mind ached with doubt. Everything, every single part of her, said she should get up and open the door. He would go, she knew he would. But he'd touched a raw nerve. Maybe because she was lonely, so far from home, uncertain. But he was right: she was desperate for passion. David was a wonderful lover but he always allowed her to go first, never really participating with her, only ever allowing her to rise to the heights in her own dreams and fantasies. It wasn't a shared encounter: it was two people flying close together, but never quite touching.

She looked at Laco, at his mop of black hair, his day-old beard, the nicotine stains on his teeth, his curly, matted chest hair. There was so much about him that was repellent, so much that, in New York, Sarah would have rejected out of hand – his egoism, his arrogance, his assumption that he was some sort of Slovakian Don Juan. Yes, in New York, her city, she could have handled him, told him to go to hell, ridiculed him because his macho line was so ridiculous and outdated. She could have told him that feminism ruled, OK, that women were no longer turned on by smouldering Rudolph Valentinos, catching women helplessly fainting into their strong masculine arms, that his personal hygiene left a lot to be desired, and especially that she already enjoyed a relationship with a man whose sensitivity, depth, gentleness and measured responses left Professor Dr Laco Plastov for dead.

But . . . always a but! She *could* have told him all these things. She closed her eyes and tried to envisage David. What she saw in the darkness of her mind was his sensitive face smiling at her, nodding, willing her onwards. She heard his gentle voice telling her it was all right, that he didn't mind what she did, as long as she was happy. Shit! Even in her fantasies, he was considerate and understanding.

Sarah opened her eyes and looked at Laco. He was smiling, as if he could read her mind. The nerve of him! The sheer maddening arrogance! But, oh God! She wanted him. Her whole body ached to feel him inside her. To feel his passion.

She put her hand on his chest and combed her fingernails through the hair below his shirt. His body was hot. He began to say something, then fell silent. The silent assurance of the victor. His hand moved higher up her thigh; his other hand moved behind her back and gently pulled her on top of him.

Eastwards. Everything in their minds was centred to the east of Kosice. Novosad, where Josh's family had lived for centuries was south-east of Kosice. Michalovce, where Sarah's family had lived for unknown generations, where her great-grandfather had been brutally murdered in a pogrom, was north-east. Directly east was the town of Venubov, from where Alexander Hasek, mass murderer and the man who had intended to exterminate Josh's family, originated. And east of them all was the Ukraine . . . brooding, menacing, backward, historically anti-Semitic, with its infamous border where the customs officials at Uzgorod regularly held up travellers for twenty-four hours or more before extorting whatever cash or goods they possessed. It was an evil and merciless part of the world, as uncompromising as the old Soviet Union, as archaic in its attitudes as the former dictatorships in which local officials had been the sources of power, authority and government for the villagers.

Laco drove his old Volkswagen at its usual hair-raising speed, whistling a Slovakian folk tune as though he didn't have a care in the world. Sarah was reflective as she sat in the back of the car, surrounded by ancient pieces of pottery and reports of conferences held ten years ago. Josh sat beside Laco, trying to work out the atmosphere in the car. One was happy, one pensive; normally both were garrulous. Laco usually told stories as they passed buildings or monuments, bringing the history of the area to life. But the car shot past them without even a mention.

Josh was used to dealing with temperamental actors, and his radar could detect tension between actors in a film often before they realised it themselves. Broaching the subject invariably brought things to the surface before they became too deeply buried, too hurtful.

'So, you guys – how are you feeling this morning?'

'Fine,' said Sarah. Her response was too quick. Too certain.

Laco increased the pitch of his whistle.

'And you, Laco?'

He nodded sagely. 'Good. Wonderful.'

Oh boy, thought Josh. There was trouble between Sarah and their interpreter. He would need to be diplomatic to find out what the problem was and how to overcome it.

'You know, Laco, you're doing an awful lot of driving us around. It's incredibly good of you, but it must be taking you away from your work at the University or in the Museum. I know we've struck a deal, but how long can you do it without falling too far behind in your work?'

'You're a lucky man, Mr Hollywood. Three days ago, when we met, I had just said goodbye to a group of German and Austrian students. Another group arrives in two weeks' time, and then I will be busy showing them what to do and how to do it. I usually spend the time between groups cataloguing and analysing the finds. It's fairly boring routine work and I'm very fortunate because one of the German students, a pretty little thing called Marta, agreed to stay on for these two weeks and help me out. I just go in for an hour or two a day after I leave you and check on her work and make sure she's happy.'

'You're lucky she volunteered,' said Josh.

'Well, to tell you the truth, I think she's in love with me.'

The temperature in the car dropped a good twenty degrees. Not a word was spoken but Josh could feel Sarah fuming in the back seat. She couldn't be jealous, he thought. That's ridiculous. He put it out of his mind. It was too unworthy a thought. Laco could only be superficially attractive to a woman like Sarah, a woman who appreciated refinement and sensitivity – everything Laco wasn't.

They drove into sight of Venubov. It could have been another Novosad: red roofed, post-Stalinist houses built in geometric configurations, just within the town boundaries; one set of traffic lights controlling the occasional cars, whose paths crossed on the two major roads in the town; and the archetypal town centre built around a medieval square. This comprised a dozen buildings dating back to the sixteenth or seventeenth century, a church with a tall spire whose height dominated the town, a barracks-like administration building, whose bureaucrats were as stony-faced as its facade, and the ubiquitous town well and pump which the city fathers believed should be kept as a tourist attraction to give credence to the city's ancient history.

They parked in the shade of one of the taller buildings in the main square. A dozen or so people in the street, carrying panniers or cane shopping baskets, looked at them with momentary interest, then retreated back into their own lives. Laco pointed to one old woman, already bent from age and cares. Despite the heat of the day she was wearing a woollen scarf, a thick, black, woollen skirt, a black cardigan and thick brown stockings. She shuffled towards them. In her shopping basket was a loaf of bread and a small brown paper package which could have contained cheese or meat.

Laco walked over to her and bowed down towards her ear, whispering niceties. The old woman looked up into his round and attractive face and smiled. Her three remaining teeth were brown and sat at angles to each other. He introduced Josh and Sarah. The old woman nodded.

Laco asked her in Slovakian whether she knew the Hasek family. The old woman thought for a moment and nodded. She whispered something into Laco's ear. He spoke again, and she shook her head. Putting his hand into his pocket, he withdrew some money which he placed in her hand. She was startled by the amount. For Laco, it was enough for a good lunch; for the old lady, it was a week's food. She babbled her thanks.

Laco asked the same question a second time. The old woman looked around to see if there was anybody listening, then whispered something into his ear. The money had assisted her memory. Laco picked up her free hand and kissed it, then sent her on her way.

'Come on, quickly. Into the car.'

Without argument, the two Americans climbed into the Volkswagen, and Laco drove away quickly. He turned right out of the main street, then right again onto a smaller street, where he parked the car under the shade of an elm tree.

'Well?' demanded Sarah.

'She knows the family. None of them lives here any more. After Alexander was taken to Moscow, they all moved away. She has no idea where. But the family maid still lives three doors away. The trouble is, she didn't know her right from her left.'

'And where's Hasek's house?'

Laco nodded across the road. 'The big one with the tiled roof and the huge gates. Right now it's occupied by the local pharmacist. In the old days the Hasek family owned half the houses in the street, including the houses on either side where the servants lived.'

'And the maid?' asked Josh.

Laco shrugged and pointed to one house on the left of the street, and then to another on the right. 'One of these.'

He got out of the car, and the others followed him down the path of the house where Hasek's former servant might still be living. A young girl answered the door; she couldn't have been more than fifteen or sixteen. She was suspicious when she saw the three strangers, two of them dressed in expensive clothes, one – the one who spoke in Slovakian – dressed as though he had power. Laco assured her that everything was alright and told her that they were looking for an old lady who used to be the maid for the family who lived three doors away.

'Does she live in this house?' he asked.

The girl shook her head. 'We've only been here a few years,' she said nervously. She looked behind her into the corridor which divided the house, wondering whether to call her mother for assistance. 'My father is an official of the town. We were transferred here from Bratislava. He is in charge of firefighting for the whole district. Is that alright?'

Laco assured her it was fine, thanked her and the three trooped several doors to the east. This house was of the same vintage as the other, but had the feeling of being much older. The garden was unkempt, the grass overgrown, the hinges on the door rusted, the paint on the windowsill non-existent. The windows themselves were thick with ancient spiderwebs.

Laco knocked on the door. There was no answer. He knocked again. Still no answer. They turned and began to walk back along the driveway. Slowly a window opened in one of the upstairs rooms; a woman in her seventies peered out. Her face was ravaged by age, creased and careworn from a life without money for cosmetics and lotions. Her voice croaked, 'Yes?'

'Forgive me disturbing you, mother,' Laco said, 'but I am seeking somebody who used to work for the Hasek family a few doors away. I wonder if you might know her.'

The old woman stared at them and made no answer. Sarah whispered to Josh, 'It's her.'

'We'd like to talk with you,' said Laco, making the same assumption.

'Who are you?' the old woman croaked.

'I am a professor of the University. I am doing historical research. These friends are from America. They are interested in talking to you.'

'What about?' demanded the old woman.

'About the family who used to live in the big house next door.'

'What was the family's name?' asked the old woman.

'You know the name, mother,' said Laco. 'Please, let us in. I don't want to talk about this out here where gossipy neighbours might hear your business.'

'The name?' demanded the old woman.

'Hasek,' said Laco.

'I know of no one by that name,' said the old woman and began to close the window.

Laco raised his voice. Josh and Sarah had no idea what was being said, but they understood the tone of the conversation. 'I will return with the police if you close the window, and will have you taken to Kosice for investigation if you don't let us in.'

The old woman stared at him, her suspicion changed to fear. 'I am an old woman. I have done nothing wrong.'

'But you were the maid to the family. You know all about Alexander. It is important that we find him.'

'He is dead. He has been dead for many years.'

Laco shook his head. 'You know that's a lie, mother. And if you don't help us, it will go badly for you. If you do, there is much money for you. American money.'

This was the key that opened the door. 'How much?'

'Much money.'

'How much?' she demanded.

'It depends on the value of your information.'

She shut the window and they returned to her door. One minute, two, then three went by. While they were waiting, Laco quickly translated what he and the woman had talked about. 'How much shall I pay her?' asked Josh, more to break the monotony of the wait than to determine the answer.

'If you pay her what it costs you to have lunch in a Los Angeles restaurant she'll be able to live in comfort for three months. If she is frugal, maybe even a year. It's worth it for you to go without lunch.'

Josh smiled. 'Of course.'

Laco looked at Sarah. 'And you, Mrs Hollywood, what do you think about paying the witness? Isn't that against the First Amendment or one of your precious Constitutional rights?'

'Don't call me Mrs Hollywood. Not now, not ever.'

Josh was taken aback by the violence of her response and was about to ask what the problem was between the two of them, when the door creaked slowly open. The woman was tiny, and when she beckoned them inside they understood why it had taken her so long to open the door. She was crippled with arthritis: the joints of her fingers, her elbows, and her knees were so swollen that she looked like a deformed caricature from a Grimm fairy story.

Sarah winced involuntarily as the old woman's gnarled and crooked fingers pulled her inside the house. She led them into the parlour, where the fetid air reeked of the presence of cats and the absence of ventilation. The room was hot from the summer sun, and the closed windows, against which a dozen entrapped flies buzzed hysterically, stopped the stench from escaping. Three or four cats lounged on torn chairs and a settee with exposed innards. The old woman hissed at the cats but they refused to move. She swore at them then, and the four fled out the door, followed by another two or three that had been surreptitiously hiding behind the sofa. The smell of urine and stale cat food in the airless room nearly made the three visitors retch, but the old woman's lungs must have been used to it.

Sarah said to Laco, 'For God's sake, ask her if I can open a window. I'm about to throw up.'

Laco told the old lady that he would have to let some fresh air into the place. The old woman let out a crone-like cackle. They sat, and Josh thanked God she didn't offer them refreshments.

'The money,' demanded the old woman.

'First tell me your name.'

'First the money. No name. What do you want to know? Who are you?'

'What I told you was the truth,' said Laco. 'I am a Professor at the University. I am investigating events in 1951. Were you the maid for Alexander Hasek and his family?'

'It's not a crime,' said the old woman. 'I was only one of the maids. There were eight servants plus chauffeurs and gardeners. He was a very important man.'

'When was the last time you saw him?' asked Laco.

The old woman shrugged. 'The last time he came home.'

'When was that?'

'I don't know. I forget.'

'Then you get no money.'

'Alright. It was 1953. It was March. It was the first warm day we had had for a long while after the bitterest winter I can remember. Alexander had just come back from a visit to Bratislava. He was always going there for consultations. At home he was eating a meal, his first good meal in weeks, when the phone rang. He came back into the dining room and told me he had to go to Moscow. He said something bad had happened. We made up his portmanteau and his chauffeur drove him to Kosice where he took a train to Warsaw and then flew to Moscow. That was the last I saw of him.'

Laco translated the old woman's words.

'Why are you lying?' he asked quietly. The gentleness of his question gave authority to its menace.

'I am not lying,' said the old woman defensively.

'Yes, you are. We know you've seen him since. He came back here in the 1970s.' He looked closely at her face to see whether the gambit had worked.

The old woman's grey pallor turned white. She shook her head. 'No. It's not true. I never saw him. Who told you I did? It's a lie.'

'The records are open now. People can find out things. They can find out your involvement with Hasek. You are in a great deal of trouble.'

Her lower lip began to tremble. Sarah couldn't understand what was being said, but she knew that the old lady was becoming distressed. She was about to reach forward to stop Laco but a look from Josh made her stay her hand.

Laco raised his voice. 'The records show that you knew him after his supposed death. The records show that you met with him and gave him aid and comfort.'

'It is not true,' croaked the old lady, her voice breaking into tears. 'It is a lie. You said you would give me money. I only let you in because you said you would give me American dollars.'

'We will if you tell us the truth. Lie and you will be arrested and you will spend the rest of your miserable life rotting in a prison, away from your cats. They will be taken away by the authorities and destroyed. Given poison. They will die in agony . . . if you lie to me.'

More tears welled up in the woman's rheumy eyes and she began to sob.

'You have one chance of saving yourself and that is to tell me the truth immediately.'

She remained silent for a few moments, tears still in her eyes. Then she turned to Sarah and said something imploringly. Laco didn't translate it. She looked at Josh, but didn't like his face; it was too smart, too clever. So she turned back to Laco and told him softly, sobbing occasionally, 'I wrote to him. That's all. While my hands could still grip a pen, I wrote to him. That's all I ever did, I swear to you. Master, you must believe me. I am an old woman. I can't do things any more. I never met Alexander again after he left, I just wrote to him every couple of months. That is all.'

'Where did you write?'

'To his address in Moscow.'

'Until when?'

'Until . . . I don't know.'

'Think,' shouted Laco and banged the table. Sarah was shocked. Josh turned to her and frowned, warning her to keep absolutely quiet.

The woman took out a filthy grey handkerchief and wiped her eyes. 'I wrote to him until 1974 or '75 in Moscow and then after that I wrote to him in Prague. He moved there.'

'Until when did you write to him?'

'I don't know. I am an old woman. I forget things. Maybe until ten years ago. He said he was leaving Prague and that he would write to me with his new address, but he never did. He forgot about me. '

'Why did you write to him?'

'He sent me money. That is how I could still live here. I was his friend. I was his special friend.'

'What do you mean?' asked Laco softly.

'What do you think?' the woman said, her voice breaking in emotion. 'I was his woman. For years we slept together. He had many women. He was an important man. But always he came back to me, his Vera. Always he returned to Vera. Always he remembered me. Every year, until ten years ago, he sent me money to live on. Maybe he is dead. I don't know.'

'Do you have any of his letters?'

'I have them all.'

'I must take them with me as evidence.'

The old woman looked at him. Her eyes were puzzled. There was a look of pain, a depth of distress in her face.

'Will I go to prison?' she asked.

Laco smiled and shook his head. 'No, Vera, you won't go to prison. The lovers of men like Hasek don't go to prison.'

Laco turned to Josh. 'How much do you have on you in American currency?'

'About five hundred.'

'Give her a hundred.'

'What's happened? What did she say?'

'I'll tell you outside. Give her a hundred dollars.'

Josh took out his wallet and peeled off a hundred-dollar bill. The woman looked at it, frowning at its strangeness. It was a currency she didn't know. Laco explained its value in Slovakian crowns. Her eyes widened in amazement and she repeated the amount. It was a king's ransom. She reached over and grasped Laco's hand, kissing it with the fervour of a religious fundamentalist. Then she reached over and kissed Josh's hand, mumbling thanks and gratitude. Laco told her to go and get the letters.

While the woman was out of the room, Laco explained what had happened. Josh, overwhelmed by Laco's interrogative brilliance, threw his arms around him and kissed him on the cheek.

'You genius!' he said.

'It was a disgusting and despicable thing to do,' said Sarah vehemently. 'How dare you treat an old woman like that? In America, you'd face disciplinary proceedings if you were a lawyer.'

'Sarah,' said Laco, 'when in Rome . . . This woman has lived under the yoke of authority all her life. The only approach she understands is an authoritarian one. She wouldn't have responded at all had I not been heavy-handed with her. As it is, she's got enough money to live on for a year, and we've got letters which could help us trace a mass murderer. An old lady got hurt, but the end justifies the means.'

'Isn't that the excuse every tyrant has used throughout history?'

'Sarah,' snapped Josh. It was the first time he had used that tone with her. She was shocked. 'You may not like it but what Laco's done has enabled us to trace a man who killed ten of my father's neighbours and countless others, a man who got off scot free and has lived a long, free life. Unlike the countless widows and orphans whom he left behind. That's all I'm concerned about. I'm sorry this lady was upset, but she'll get over it.'

'She's already got over it,' said Laco. 'Did you see the look on her face when I gave her the money? The rest was all an act. People pretend to be scared of authority, but it never works. I don't know why they do it.'

Sarah turned and walked towards the open window. She breathed deeply to clear the rotten smell from her nose. The old woman returned, still bowing and kissing hands, and handed over a thick wad of letters, all with the same handwriting. Laco took them and they left the house.

What they didn't see as they drove back to town was a black Opel, big enough to carry four burly men, who watched Laco's old Volkswagen disappear down the road, leaving behind a cloud of black fumes. The men debated whether to follow, or to visit the old lady and find out what had been said. They decided to follow Laco's car. There would be plenty of time to deal with the old woman.

Marta was completing the delicate task of washing away the millennia of aggregation with a mild solution of acid from the bronze whorl which Laco had told her was a hair ring. Why he was so certain that a Bronze Age woman had used it to tie her hair together, rather than as an earring, which was what he had confidently asserted an almost-identical whorl to be, Marta had no idea. Still, he was the archaeologist; she was merely the student of history who had volunteered to participate in the three-week archaeological dig.

Laco's clumsy attempts at seduction had fascinated her at first. He had been through all the girls on the dig like a child let loose in a sweetshop. And he had come to her last. Last because she was the prettiest, the most sophisticated, and because he had assumed, rightly so, that she would be the most difficult to seduce. The others had fallen like overripe apples from a tree; she had retained her dignity until the very end, only falling for his naive seduction techniques when the others had all gone home and she could make love to him without the whole world knowing. At the final night's party, he had looked so crestfallen, so like a hurt little boy saying goodbye to all his playmates, that her resolve had disappeared and she had told him that she could afford another two weeks before she had to return to her University. His face had brightened, his manner had improved and he had thrown his arms around her, hugging her until he had nearly crushed her ribs.

The following day he had tried to seduce her three times, at breakfast, lunch and dinner. The day after, when she had decided that she wanted to make love to him, she had waited until he was sitting at his laboratory bench classifying a piece of pottery. She had taken off her labcoat, revealing a skimpy top and shorts tight enough to cut off her circulation. She had sashayed over to him; he had not noticed her until she was almost at the bench. His face had been a portrait of amazement, especially when she had walked seductively around the bench, knelt down, unzipped his trousers, and given him the best blow job he'd ever had in his life.

Wordlessly, she had returned to her bench, put on her labcoat again, and got on with her work. It took Laco a full fifteen minutes before he could say a thing. When he did, he asked simply, 'Why?'

'Because this time, *I* wanted to.'

Since then, they had made love every day. On lab benches, on armchairs in his small and fussy office, in his apartment, on riverbanks, and even once a back-breaking attempt in his Volkswagen. But things had changed, as she knew they would, when the Americans appeared on the scene. Marta had stood on the opposite side of the road, watching curiously, on the day that Laco had driven them to Novosad. She had wanted to see the woman, Sarah, with whom she knew Laco was suddenly enamoured. Marta knew that he would do everything in his power to seduce her. But Marta didn't mind. She wasn't in love with Laco. He was a nice man, passionate and wild, and she needed that. But she would be returning to Berlin shortly, and he would soon become just another episode in her life.

She smiled when he walked into the laboratory. He kissed her hello.

'How was the trip to Venubov?' she asked. 'Did you find what you were looking for?'

'More than that,' he said, pouring himself a vodka. 'We found an old maid of the family. It didn't take much persuasion to get her to tell us that she had been communicating with Alexander Hasek up until the 1980s. So much for his death in a post-Stalinist purge.'

Marta whistled. 'So where is he now?

'We've got all her old letters, and that means his last known address. From here on in, it'll be a detective job. But it's worth it. He was a real bastard. He doesn't deserve to live out a peaceful retirement. The Jews have spent half a century bringing their war criminals to justice. Like bloodhounds, they never gave up. But what have we done? We've spent half a century protecting ours, denying the massacres and slaughters. Well, fuck it, I'm going to expose this bastard.'

She kissed him. She had missed him, and she wanted him now. They made love, slowly, tenderly, each knowing that the following day, or at latest the day after, Marta would be leaving.

There was an animalism about Marta which appealed to Laco. She was so different from the hot and cold Sarah. On the one occasion that he had made love to her, Sarah had been all over him, kissing him, fondling him, taking nearly an hour before she was ready to release her mind and body to the joys of an orgasm, and then within half an hour, she had suddenly turned cold, like a real ball-biting bitch, sending him on his way as if he was a delivery boy. And today she had refused to talk to him properly; she had snapped at him as though he had done something terrible. Well, to hell with her. If she wanted to avoid him, that was fine. There were plenty more Sarahs in the sea. Anyway, what really appealed to Laco was the hard, driven frenzy of a woman like Marta. So demure, so refined on the outside, but when she started to make love she was like a feral beast.

Usually their lovemaking lasted fifteen minutes or so. But this time, perhaps because it was their last, she didn't stop. She tried one position on the bench, then dragged him down to the floor, then led him naked down the corridor into the Museum where she pushed him onto the desk and climbed on top. It was as though she was an animal familiarising herself with her territory, knowing that her mate had been with another and wanting to reclaim what was her own, as though she was remembering the different places, the different positions in which they'd made love, so that when they were no longer together, when she was back in Berlin, she would be able to recall every sensual detail of their last encounter.

He came loudly; she came twice in rapid succession. They lay in each other's arms, sweat pouring off them, their groins covered in the fluids from their bodies. His back was aching, a bulldog clip on his desk was pressing into his left shoulder, and he had a crick in his neck where the corner of the desk was pressing on his spine. His left buttock was pinched by the in-tray, and Marta's weight, slight as she was, pressed him into the leather desk organiser. She was almost asleep. He had to wake her or he would scream in agony. He kissed her passionately on the cheek, and she murmured, 'God, that was good!'

'Marta, you have to get up. I think my back is broken.'

She smiled and unplugged herself from his body. She sat unselfconsciously naked and dishevelled on his couch while he unpeeled himself from the knick-knacks on his desk. He opened his desk drawer, taking out a clean towel kept specially for such purposes and threw it gently at her. They walked back along the corridors still naked. If the Museum guard was watching, they didn't care. Laco was still lost in his pleasure: his body was totally relaxed and satisfied, his mind still numb from the sensations. He walked into the laboratory and opened the fridge.

'Shit,' he exclaimed. 'No beer. Oh God, I'm dying for one.'

He walked over to his clothes, in a pile on the floor, and searched his pockets for a cigarette. While he smoked, Marta washed herself at the laboratory bench, dried herself with the towel and slipped on her underwear and clothes. 'I'll go for beer,' she said. 'I could do with one too.'

He took some money from his wallet and gave her enough to buy four bottles.

'I won't be long,' she said.

She picked up the keys to his Volkswagen while Laco slowly, methodically dressed himself. God, she was good. He would really miss her when she was gone. He smiled as she disappeared out of the door. He wondered how Sarah would remember their lovemaking of last night. Sure, she'd been good, even passionate, but despite what she had told him, he knew that there had been something holding her back. She had said she had completely let herself go, but Laco knew that wasn't true. There was a part of her that was still closed to him, that she had not opened. Even when she was attacking him, kissing his chest and neck, grinding herself against his body, he could feel that there was something preventing her from moving forward. A thin cord which held her away from him, a gossamer thread firmly anchored to somewhere, or someone, in America. He had hoped to be able to snap the cord, to turn her on fully, but her attitude had been one of hostility afterwards. Still, maybe one day.

He finished dressing and sat back in his laboratory chair. He put his arms behind his head. He was tired. He closed his eyes and put his feet on the bench, breathing deeply and wondering why everything in his life was going so right at the moment.

The windows of the laboratory imploded into the room and the force knocked him off his seat onto the floor. Razor-sharp shards of glass flew across the room and embedded themselves into anything in their way. If he had been standing by the window, if he hadn't been sitting in the chair and been knocked onto the floor by the concussion waves, he would have been cut in two.

His mind reeled at the noise, and the burning-oil stench and heat of the explosion. His ears sang in agony, as though a banshee screamed inside his skull. He raised his aching head and saw the tail-end of a fireball rise above the window: yellow flames and black smoke intertwined in a vision of Hell.

'Holy Mother of God,' he gasped and ran to the window, treading on a million glass splinters which lay throughout the laboratory. On the road below he saw his yellow Volkswagen, engulfed by flames. Everything was on fire: the rubber wheels, the bonnet, the seats. And Marta was on fire, too, her body held tightly in the driver's seat by the seatbelt. She looked like a rag doll, her pretty dress, her hair, her skin burning like a torch. Only her head, knocked backwards at a grotesque angle by the explosion, stared upwards at him. It was black, stripped of her beautiful fair hair and translucent skin. It was the head of a gargoyle, like one of the skeletons he so casually dug from the ground and examined.

Laco backed away from the window and began to scream. He screamed until he had no voice left. The police found him there, crouched underneath his laboratory bench, shaking uncontrollably. Crying.

# CHAPTER
# FOURTEEN

Sarah saw Laco sitting in the foyer of the Hotel Slovan as she emerged from the elevator to go in to breakfast. The moment she saw him, his shoulders hunched, his hands supporting his head, slumped in the chair like an old tramp asleep at a train station, all the anger, all the sense of outrage she felt against him for his callous intrusion into her life, disappeared.

She walked over to him, knelt down and put her hand on his shoulder.

'Laco, what's wrong?'

His haggard face, bloodshot eyes and the day-old stubble showed that he hadn't been to bed since they had arrived back from Venubov. But this was no dawn reveller suffering the effects of Bohemian cavorting. His mouth was grim and determined, his eyes were narrowed yet saw nothing. She sat in the chair next to him and reached over and took his hand.

'Laco, tell me what's happened. What's wrong?'

'They killed a beautiful and innocent young girl.'

Sarah's scalp tingled. The blood drained from her face. 'Killed? Who?'

'I don't know who killed her. They were after me, but they killed her by mistake. She was so young. So fresh. So much to live for.'

'Tell me exactly what happened.'

Laco blinked, seeming to see her kneeling there for the first time. 'I saw her head burning. Her skin. Her hair. She was . . . she . . .' His body began shaking as he relived the horror. She stroked his head and whispered in his ear, encouraging him to talk about it.

And he did. In clipped sentences, as if the pain of explaining was hurting his body. 'After I dropped you off I went back to my laboratory where I did some work with Marta. She's the young German student who stayed on to help me with the cataloguing. She went out to get some beer. There was a huge explosion, a bomb in my car. I looked down from my laboratory window. The roof of the car had gone. She was sitting there, still gripping the steering wheel, but her body was on fire.' He shook his head as though trying to wipe the scene from his memory.

'Laco, who did it?'

'Them.'

'Who is them?'

'I don't know. We've stirred up a nest of wasps. But my poor Marta got stung to death instead of me.'

'Have you called the police?'

'They were there within a few minutes. I've been in the station all night.'

'Did you tell them everything?'

'Not everything. I didn't tell them about you and Josh. There was no point in involving you. I just told them that I was on the trail of a man called Hasek. They looked him up in the records. They told me he was already dead, that he died in 1953. I said I was following up evidence. They asked me why anyone would try to kill me for trying to find somebody who had been dead for forty years. I told them that he probably wasn't dead and that his friends or protectors had tried to kill me. The police think I'm nuts. They think the real victim was Marta. They're investigating her background in Berlin; they say she may have hidden communist, anarchist, neo-Nazi or pro-

Palestinian affiliations or something. They said that nobody tries to kill an archaeologist, but that lots of young German students die in unexplained ways. I came straight here from the police station. I didn't want to go home.'

Sarah put her arm protectively around his shoulder. 'Oh, you poor dear man.' She pulled him closer towards her.

'It's not me. It's Marta. She was so young. So pretty, so clever. She had everything, and my last memory of her is her skin burning like a torch. I'll never forget the way she looked up at me with her dead eyes. Never.'

He buried his face in his hands. Sarah was on the verge of tears. 'Laco, if they tried to kill you once, they'll try again. You have to go. We have to think about security, protection. Maybe you should get clear of this place while we're organising it.'

'We're all in danger,' he said. His voice was hardly audible in his cupped hands. 'I'm in danger. So are you and Josh. These fucking sons of bitches. You'd think they'd know their day is over, but they're still there. Still malicious and malevolent. Spectres and devils from the past.'

'Do you really think we're all in danger?' she asked.

'I think you should go home, Sarah. You and Josh. This started off as a boy scout crusade. It was a good idea at the time, but it's way beyond that now. It's caused the death of a human being. It's not fun any more. Now it's getting very dangerous.'

'You think Josh and I should go back to America?'

'Yes,' he said. He removed his hands from his face and looked at her. She was still shocked by the harrowed look in his bloodshot eyes. He put one hand on his knee and with the other, grasped hers. 'Yes, I think you should go back. I think you should get out while you can.'

Images reeled around her mind. She was suddenly very frightened. She'd slept badly. Maybe it was a precursor to disaster, brought about by the sudden transformation of

Hasek from ghoul into a living enemy, a quarry to be hunted and punished; or maybe it was that, for the first time in her life, she was confronting a reality about her own past that she had cravenly avoided. But to go back now to the security and comfort and sameness of New York when she was beginning, just beginning, to gain an understanding of the horrors of the past would be an admission of defeat, an admission that the old, black *dibbuks* – those which had terrified her ancestors for countless generations, had killed her great-grandfather – had won against her. Against her! When for the first time in all of those generations, one member of her family – Sarah Kaplan – held the power. She thought of the long lines of naked men and women, queuing to be examined by Nazi concentration camp doctors, who had the power of life and death over them; she thought of pictures she'd seen of elderly Jews in ghettos, forced by blond-haired, blue-eyed Aryans to crawl in the gutters and fill their frockcoat pockets with horse shit; she thought of the skeletal men and women, staring hollow-eyed through the barbed wire at the American liberation troops, too weak to smile; and she thought of the powerlessness of a thousand years of European Jewry, shut up and vilified and persecuted by men like Hasek. And she suddenly felt more angry than she had ever felt in her life.

She stiffened her shoulders and said vehemently, 'Like hell! A young girl has died because of us. That's something which needs to be squared. In law. With the proper authorities. Do you think I'm going to crawl away and allow myself to be intimidated by some ageing criminal, some mass murderer? Nobody is going to frighten me. I'll pull the roof down on his head. I'll go see the Minister of Justice. We'll see who's frightened of whom.'

Laco looked at her in surprise. She had such resolve, such a sense of purpose. 'And anyway,' she continued, 'do you think we're going to be safe in America now that we've uncovered this – what was it you said – this nest of wasps? They'll be buzzing around wherever we are. That's the trouble with an open border: it's easier to get in, but it's also easier to get out. Laco, I never wanted to come over here in the first place. I made no secret of that. But I swear to you that if a young girl has died because of us, now isn't the time to back away. These people have to be brought to punishment for what they've done. And if they've killed once they'll try again. The only way we can deal with that is by exposing the bastards for who they are and what they've done – now, and in the past.'

Laco continued to stare at her in incomprehension. Who was this woman? Was this Sarah? The spoilt American woman who'd rather be at the opera in New York than in the East of Europe? He looked at her with new eyes. And it helped his state of mind. It was as if a thick mist around him had suddenly lifted. But the exhaustion and confusion made him giggle.

His reaction surprised her, but before she could ask him what was funny, Josh marched out of the elevator. He was surprised to see the two of them sitting huddled together, especially after their mood the previous day. Sarah walked quickly over to him and whispered into his ear a *précis* of what she had just been told. He looked visibly shaken. He walked over and said to Laco, 'I'm so sorry about your friend, but we have to talk. Come on. I'm going to buy you a strong cup of coffee.'

They walked silently into the dining area. As usual there were twenty or thirty groups of people there; some were families who had come from America to see their ancient family roots; others were businessmen dealing in the iron, steel and coal of the area; and others still were unidentified and unidentifiable. The three of them sat at a corner table. As had been the case the previous two mornings, Phil and Jerry had eaten breakfast early in the morning, long before Josh and Sarah woke, and had taken the car to find suitable tourist places to use as background scenes. There seemed to be no end to their need for background.

The waiter poured them coffee. They waited for him to disappear, then Josh said, 'Okay, from the beginning. What happened?'

Laco told him. Slowly, cautiously, with none of his usual bravura or exaggeration. This was too serious for invention and effect; this was real life . . . and death.

When Laco had finished, Josh stirred his coffee, thinking. Sarah looked at him. Under normal circumstances, she would be the first to proffer advice, but these weren't normal circumstances.

'How dangerous is the situation for us? For you?' Josh said finally.

Laco shrugged his shoulders. 'Who can say? They have tried once and failed. There is a good chance they will try again. But there is an equally good chance that their failure may scare them off.'

Josh shook his head. 'This was a professional hit. A sophisticated car bomb like that requires resources and skill. Professionals don't give up after the first attempt; their pride, and the contract, won't let them. They'll try again, and I think we have to take that into account when we're making any decisions.'

'Decisions?' said Laco. 'There are no decisions. There is only one choice. Despite what Sarah said in the foyer, you have to go home to America. Forget these plans about your house and finding Hasek. And for me, I have to call on my resources. My father still has contacts, people who can find out who is behind this.'

'Laco,' said Sarah softly, 'what's the point of our going home? I told you, the borders are open. These bastards can come to America just as easily as we came here. If we've exposed something that they want to keep secret, then running away is not going to help. In fact, it could make matters a whole lot worse. While we're in a small area where everybody knows each other, strangers will stand out from the crowd. They'll be easier for you to recognise. But once we're back in the States . . .' She shrugged her shoulders.

'Sarah's right,' said Josh, 'but not about herself. This isn't your fight,' he said, turning to her, 'it's mine. You're going back to the States today. So are Phil and Jerry. I'll stay. If these bastards have tried to kill Laco and failed, they'll still be in the area. Let's make them the target. Mobilise your forces, Laco. You're well known in this town. Use your fame to their disadvantage. Let's get them on the run.'

It was Sarah who broke the mood. 'I'm not going back. I'm a part of this.'

'Sarah, you're going.'

She shook her head. 'Josh, I'm not. Up till yesterday . . . maybe. Today, no way. Not after what they've done. It was partly my responsibility.'

'You're off the case, Sarah,' he said pointedly. 'You're going back home. No arguments.'

'No.'

'You're fired. There! Now you're really off the case.'

'Then I'm fired, but I'm still staying.'

'Why?' he asked. 'This isn't your fight. It's mine . . .'

She interrupted him. 'Not today it's not. Like I said, yesterday, maybe. But not after what's happened.'

'Sarah, I'm absolutely serious. There's some dangerous shit going down here. Things which you shouldn't be involved in.'

'But I am involved, Josh. Deeply involved. Whoever they are, they know my name, my address.'

'Then get yourself protection in the States. But this isn't the place for you. Not now.'

'Where is the place, Josh?' she asked quizzically. 'Are we going to be any safer in New York, Los Angeles? You think people like this wouldn't reach across borders, across continents, to shut us up?'

'You're much safer in America. We can control the situation over there. I'll pay for whatever security you need.'

'Crap,' she said. 'Look at the Oklahoma bombing. Look at the way aircraft have been brought down. The FBI couldn't even protect people at the Atlanta Olympics when the whole damn world was watching. Our police and security forces are so undermanned they're next to useless. And the FBI aren't much better, not with the budget cuts and all. No, Josh, this is something we need to face. And we have to face it right here, and right now.'

'And how the hell am I going to protect you?'

'You said so yourself – hire the best help you can get,' she said. 'You've got money, you've got unbelievable resources. Do it! Hire bodyguards, for you, for me and for Laco. Everywhere we move. Hire the best investigators, the best detectives. Fly to Bratislava and force open up the files of people who knew this bastard, Hasek. Demand support or threaten to blow Slovakia apart in the media. Front-page stuff, *Time, Newsweek, Sixty Minutes, CNN*. That was always one of the fronts you were going to fight on, well now's the time, Josh. Make the officials shit scared. Believe me, the assassins will get to hear about it. One thing terrorists are shit-scared of is exposure, so we're going to make a huge, unbelievably loud noise. They think they're safe when they terrify people into skulking behind closed doors. We'll show them that we're not scared. Laco, how do you feel about that?'

He shrugged indifferently. 'Right now I just want to have a shit, a shave and go to bed for a week, and when I wake up I want to cry for my poor dead Marta.'

'Stay here from now on, Laco. Don't go back to your apartment,' said Josh. 'Sarah's right about one thing – we do need security. We've been blundering around like amateurs. A place like this must have whole armies of unemployed security agents, or guards, or militia men. People who know the ropes. I'll pay them in American dollars. Meantime, you move into the Slovan and we'll all get protection.'

Laco nodded weakly.

Igor Nemez stared, grey-faced, at the man opposite him. It was early morning, an hour before he usually left home for the office. His wife, a burly but attractive woman, was surprised by the appearance of the stranger at her door at seven-thirty in the morning. Surprised because he looked like KGB, and these sorts of early morning, unannounced visits had come to an end with Gorbachev.

Her husband ordered her to leave the room and closed the door imperiously after her. He had been in a strange and defensive mood for a couple of days now, but the appearance of this stranger explained much. Maybe there was a scandal at the Town Hall, maybe someone was in trouble with Bratislava. She returned to the kitchen to continue with her cleaning; maybe it was her husband. Good. He would be arrested, and then she wouldn't have to suffer the indignity of his running off with his mistress.

'Well?' demanded Igor. 'How do you explain your incompetence? To kill a German student will bring the world down around our ears.'

The stranger's voice was quiet, which made it all the more menacing. 'Raise your voice to me and I'll cut your fucking balls off. Do you think we intended to kill the girl? Fool! How could we have known she'd be the next driver? The question isn't our incompetence; it's why you are in such a fuss. Assassins often miss their targets – or had you forgotten? Do you think people just sit there waiting to be terminated?'

Furious, Igor shouted, 'You are supposed to be a professional. I thought the great Wet Division people never failed. Well, be arrogant if you like, but you have made life impossible for me. I was one of the last people they came to see before they went out to the old woman. They are not fools. They will tie it straight back to me . . .'

'And you will deny it. You were nowhere near the Museum at the time, you were at home with your wife, or fucking your Hungarian mistress.'

Nemez's jaw dropped and his eyes stared frantically: 'How . . .?'

'Igor, did you really think you could have any secrets? You could not be so stupid as to imagine that, because of some minor irritating changes in the government of the Soviet Union since 1991, we have been sitting on our asses. There is nothing we don't know about you and your mistress, and your bank accounts, and your nest eggs in other countries. Now, let's talk about the future, not the past, shall we? We missed the archaeologist on our first attempt. He would be a fool if he was not aware that the bomb was meant for him, and he is certainly not a fool. During his interview with the police last night and this morning, he mentioned nothing about the Americans. Maybe he is trying to protect them, or maybe he has other reasons which we don't know about. Either way, if he's smart, he'll talk to his father. We should have dealt with that old bastard years ago.'

Sarah didn't know whether to bow, or to kiss the old man's ring. The entire morning, Laco had been defining the almost mythic status of his father: Czechoslovakia's foremost archaeologist, its most important intellectual dissident, leader of the revolt by the academics against the Soviet Union's arbitrary imposition of third-rate minds to senior University posts, adviser to governments, local politician, reformist mayor of Kosice, spearhead for the move to expose Soviet atrocities after the War and especially after Dubcek's Prague Spring . . . the list went on and on.

But the sprightly old man, pulling weeds from a garden bed in his front yard, looked more like the archetypal grandfather than an icon of theomorphic proportions. He stood when the hire car drew up outside his house and walked quickly to the front gate. He kissed Laco on both cheeks. When Laco introduced him to Josh and Sarah, he bowed with mock respect and ushered them into his home.

'I have heard much about the two of you from Laco. He calls you Mr Hollywood, but I will call you Joshua if you don't mind. Your namesake was one of the twelve spies who collected information about Canaan. From what I understand, it is applicable. And you,' he said, holding Sarah's hand and showing her to a seat, 'I will call Counsellor. I understand that's the proper form of respect paid to attorneys in America.'

She smiled. He was lovely. And so was his house. Clear, light and full of the trophies of a lifetime of achievements: photos of the old Dr Plastov with dignitaries, addressing conferences, receiving degrees or awards and – most precious of all by its position in the centre of the wall – an old photograph in which he was dressed in a prison uniform, standing in a queue of other prisoners, while a Russian guard, holding a rifle, looked at them with contempt.

Dr Plastov saw Sarah glance at the photograph. 'We called that young guard the Yard Dog,' he said, 'because he was so vicious and stupid, such a Ukrainian animal. I keep that picture to remind me of our various fortunes. I often wonder what he is doing now. When I was in the Soviet re-education camp, he was a god. Whatever order he screamed at us, however obscene or infantile, we simply had to obey, or we would be beaten. We were his puppets.

Maybe now *he* is being raped and screamed at by some merciless prison guard. I can only hope so.'

She smiled. She would have assumed that a man like Laco's father would have come to accommodate the past, have found it in him to offer charity and forgiveness to his former enemies who had caused him pain and suffering. She found it immensely satisfying that he continued to feel outrage and bitterness against the perpetrators of evil.

'By the way, Dr Plastov, I'm only called Counsellor when I'm in court. Out of court, I'm Sarah.'

'And I am Maxim. So, a drink to support this unexpected and happy occasion?'

'A drink, yes, Father. Happy, unfortunately not. You haven't heard of the incident at the Museum last night,' said Laco.

It took him a few minutes to bring his father up to date with the latest developments. Maxim Plastov became gaunt and sad.

'So, old Alexander is likely still to be alive. And he is still responsible for killing people. Will these old devils never die and go away to enjoy their eternities of misery? Their grip on life is . . . remarkable.'

'Did you know him?' asked Josh.

Maxim nodded. 'It was one of those rare coincidences where paths cross throughout life. Since we were little more than children, he had always been there in the background. So were many other people, of course, but they never became monsters. That's how I know him.'

His silvery white hair fell across his broad and lined Slavic face. When he had greeted them at the gate, Sarah had recognised him immediately as an older version of Laco; she had liked him from the minute she saw him.

In his broad Slovak accent, his voice deep and slow with age, he told them: 'Many years ago we were students together in Bratislava. He was never very academic, little more than average. He was a dilettante, spending most of his time with the girls from the town. While I was writing essays, he was jumping from one bed to another. Our paths diverged when I was given a scholarship to study in Magdeburg University in Germany aspects of the Neanderthal people. He returned to Kosice, where he became a city official.

'We lost contact. I began my career in a teaching position in Bratislava. Then the War broke out, and I joined the Czech Resistance. I have no idea what he did to fight the Nazis, but after the War, while the West rejoiced, the East faced yet another hideous dictator. Czechoslovakia was the last Eastern European country to hold out against the forces of communism, but men like Hasek ensured that we were brought into line with the Russian masters by a coup in February 1948. Naturally, Alexander Hasek was rewarded for his support of the communists, and around that time, I heard his name mentioned several times. I remember it surprised me. He had always been such a nonentity. Then, with a weak government in power in Prague, Stalin easily set up his Prague puppets in 1949, and Hasek's was one of the names that began to form on people's lips: Hasek this, Hasek that.'

He settled back into his armchair, uncomfortable with his memories. He reminded Sarah so much of her great-uncle Benny, many years ago when he used to tell her stories about the early days in America.

'It's funny,' Maxim continued, 'but there was a time, just after Stalin's bully boys moved into Prague, when I thought of contacting Hasek and trying to get him to use his influence to sue for Czech independence. I foolishly assumed that he was a patriot.' Maxim shook his head sadly.

'Word soon began to spread of many warlords in the country, people who were brutalising the population. We in the resistance began to keep records, in case there was a reckoning. Because I was a historian, I was given the responsibility. I was shocked to find that one of the people on whom many of the reports centred was Alexander. Of course the reports were grossly exaggerated. They spoke of him as a monster who ate little children and bayoneted pregnant women, a vicious anti-Semite and murderer of Tziganes. Another Hitler. I read into the rumours and discounted them. This wasn't the Alexander who had seduced girls and spent his time trying to befriend everybody at the university. In those days, everyone hated Jews and gipsies; Hasek was probably no different. But a mass murderer? And so soon after the war? A man in Carpathia and Ruthenia who had the absolute power of life and death, and who exercised it as though he was a Heinrich Himmler or a Reinhard Heydrich; a henchman and confidant of the men who supported Stalin's rule in Czechoslovakia – this surely couldn't be Alexander Hasek.

'Naturally I investigated, and found them to be one and the same. I couldn't believe it. His rule over the territory, from the Ukraine to Roznava, from Hungary to the Tatras, was feudal. He set up his command not in Kosice, which was the centre of local power, but in the house where he was born. He used slave labour to build it into some sort of mansion. He forcibly removed his neighbours and controlled the entire street. There were even guardposts at either end. Only people whom he wanted to see were ever admitted. He had built his castle.

'And people from all over his domain who wanted to entreat with him had to travel to him as though on some sort of pilgrimage. They had to go to his home, where he would see them in his pyjamas, or in his bath or on the toilet. Just like England's Henry the Eighth. An absolute monarch. Anything to demean his visitors and their status. In the very beginning, people treated him as a laughing stock. But he heard the people laughing at him, and exercised a reign of terror which resulted in deaths, arbitrary hangings and mass executions in the street.'

Josh interrupted then and told Maxim of the massacre of the neighbours of his grandparents, because Hasek had been unable to find them. He explained that this was how he had become involved, and why he was so personally keen to bring Hasek to judgement.

Maxim nodded. 'Hasek terrorised the area for four years, and during that time hundreds of people were deported, or summarily executed. Any whisper, any rumour, was enough for him to drive out in his Mercedes, like some Teutonic knight on horseback, break down doors, drag terrified people into the streets and shoot them in the head. Or separate families, sending the women and children off to some camp and the men to Siberia or to the deserts of the East. Just the mention of his name sent shivers of terror down people's spines. But it all came to an end when Stalin died. Hasek ran like a frightened rabbit to Moscow for protection, fearing the wrath of the people. When I was mayor of Kosice, one of my first acts was to set up an investigation, but the information came back that Khrushchev had purged people like him. I requested his file from Moscow, but it read that he was long dead.' He looked with sad eyes at the three young people who were listening rapt to his every word.

One thousand years ago, when the original settlers first saw the peculiar series of S-bends in the Vltava River and the verdant meadows on either side of its tortuous banks, they must have thought they had found paradise. The town of Cesky Krumlov was established there, within the gentle magnificence of the Bohemian hills in countryside which now lies close to Austria and Germany. This town grew to become one of the most popular tourist destinations in Eastern Europe. The houses, many of them architectural and artistic masterpieces of design and beauty, huddled around the ancient castle with its precipitous walls and frescoed tower, like children under the sheltering wing of a parent. Any visitor arriving from Prague or Munich or Vienna would have discovered one of the most ornate and beautiful towns in Europe, a monument to the craftsman's art. Tiny boutiques set in narrow cobbled streets, all of which seemed to rise ever upwards to the central courtyard of the dominant castle, nestled side by side with ostentatious churches and pompous civic buildings. The generations of city fathers who added, century by century, to Cesky Krumlov's wonder must have pondered just how much more beautiful a town could possibly become.

And their thoughts had been echoed of late by tourists. After the war, southern Bohemia became a playground for the very few rich people of Prague. As the communist system ebbed, more and more Czechoslovakians felt free to travel and visited the town to see its grandeur. And when the wall between East and West tumbled, the once-hated Germans and Austrians flooded across the borders to re-inhabit – if only temporarily – the Sudetenland and areas south. And when the Americans discovered Prague, Cesky Krumlov was not long in succumbing to the dollar.

Most of the town's population welcomed the sudden influx of visitors, who brought money and business. Most, but not all. One elderly man, who had moved to Cesky Krumlov for the estrangement which retreat brings, didn't like them at all. He had lived there for the past ten years, purely because it was an out-of-the-way glory of a former time. Now he found that life was becoming increasingly fraught. He had come to the town without fanfare, buying a modest house on Parkan, whose front opened onto a charming, secluded *cul de sac* and whose back looked out onto the Vltava. There, on weekends, when the town was packed with visitors, he would spend hours watching the boats, and the beautiful swans that glided effortlessly across the water. Wonderful birds, swans: on the surface, they appeared utterly graceful, calm, floating languidly; yet, out of the sight of onlookers, the birds' legs were pumping furiously.

Sitting on the banks of the Vltava was one of his most blissful pleasures, giving him a time of quiet, a time to reflect on a long and eventful life. Here he was safe from the intrusion of the outside world, from prying eyes, from questions. Here he would sit for hours, with his newspapers or books, as boats plied this way and that. The old man's house was within sight of the noisy, wooden Lazebnicky Bridge where, these days, tourists by their thousands stood and stared up at the ornately decorated tower of the city's castle. The old man didn't like his peace and quiet being interrupted by tourists. He didn't like them staring down at him from the bridge, even though they were too far away to see who he was. Despite the distance, he always sat with his back to them.

The old man had his routine. Every morning he awoke to the smell of coffee and rolls, prepared by his housekeeper. He got up, dressed, breakfasted on his lawn overlooking the fast-flowing river, and then walked slowly up the hill towards the bridge. He always crossed it with head bowed, to avoid the curious eyes of tourists. Then, slowly, he passed the Church of St Jodocus and climbed the steep hill of Latran until he came to number fifty-three, a house which centuries ago had belonged to an alchemist and still bore his alchemical signs. Like so many of the other ancient houses in Cesky Krumlov, some dating back to medieval times, the alchemist's house was painted to look as though it was made from pointed blocks of limestone. It was a *trompe l'oeil* and, even after a decade of looking, these houses never failed to fascinate the old man. So much trouble just to look different, interesting. Yet he had to admit that Cesky Krumlov was a wondrous town, with its steep streets, narrow cobbled laneways, wonderful medieval houses, churches, towers and turrets and castles –

so much more aesthetic and rewarding than the dull and ordinary Kosice.

Every morning, when the old man arrived at the alchemist's house, he found a warm corner away from the bitter winds of winter, or a cool shaded corner in the blistering heat of summer, and rested from the exertion of the walk. When he had recovered his breath, he walked on to his favourite square, where a chair was always waiting for him at his favourite café. Without asking, the waiter brought a glass of water to revive him after the exertion, then a cup of coffee, a pastry and a copy of the latest magazine from Prague. And here he sat until one of the other old men of the village joined him, and they passed the hours playing chess or draughts, or talking about the forthcoming invasion of tourists, or the invasion which had just passed now that the school holidays were over.

At lunchtime, the waiter brought the old men – by now, there would be at least a couple more – toasted sandwiches, usually ham with a slice of cheese melted into it, and more coffee. The old men chatted and meandered through the local gossip, discussing whatever changes had occurred since their wanderings the previous day, and debating which event they would attend that night: maybe a concert in one of the churches, a recital in the town hall, or a lecture in the castle. And then the old man bade them goodbye, and returned more quickly downhill to his home, where his housekeeper had tidied up, made his bed and prepared his tea. He slept until about five, ate his tea, and then dressed to attend the evening's agreed-upon performance. So the day ended. And so the next day began.

Except on that one particular hot and humid Monday. When he arrived back at his house on Parkan, looking forward to a cool drink of water after which he would prepare for a Bach recital, his housekeeper met him at the front door. She looked distressed. It was a break from routine. She, like him, needed the symmetry of routine.

'What's wrong?' asked the old man.

She said nothing, but nodded inside the house. A tall, heavy-set man sat in his front parlour, a room which hadn't been used in six years. The stranger stood when the old man entered.

'Perhaps we could go outside onto your magnificent lawn and talk,' the stranger said proprietorially. He looked at the old woman and asked, 'Mother, could you bring us both a glass of lemonade?'

The stranger walked uninvited through the house. The old woman restrained her fury at his impertinence. Her employer looked crestfallen and followed meekly. It was unbelievable, for he had always been the very model of a once-powerful man, yet now that she saw him next to a man of real power, she realised what he had become. In the ten years that she had worked for him, she had never noticed a deterioration; but now she saw it clearly. She became frightened. How long before the old man died? How long before she would have to look for another job? And where would she find one as easy as this?

The two men sat on the chairs in the garden, the music of the river making their whispered conversation impossible to overhear. They sat close together. The younger man talked first; after all, he was determining the agenda. The old man studied him closely. He was forty, forty-five perhaps. He would have been a child when Alexander was exerting the sort of power which eluded him now . . . power which this man possessed.

'So, a beautiful spot you have chosen to retire to. After a lifetime of service.'

'Will you at least tell me your name? I assume you are here to kill me. I would hate to be killed by somebody who is unknown to me.'

The younger man looked at him in genuine surprise. 'Kill you? Whatever gave you that idea? If we wanted you dead, we would have done it decades ago. We don't kill people who have been faithful servants. We reward them, and ensure them a peaceful life until they pass away. Surely you understood that my mission was to protect you?'

Hasek smiled, and nodded. He wondered when the young man would return and kill him. Not now, that was for certain. All he was doing now was spying out Hasek's current situation so that he – or more likely another assassin – could return in a couple of days, or weeks, and do the deed quietly, late one night. No, they wouldn't kill him now, especially if people were searching for him. That might prompt an investigation – something Prague and Moscow would want to avoid in case the truth accidentally came out. Anyway, if this man was going to kill him, the one thing he would ensure would be his anonymity. He would kill with a massive injection of insulin during the night, or another drug, leaving only a tiny puncture hole and virtually no residue. An assassin certainly would not ask his housekeeper for a glass of lemonade.

'My name is Kyril. I am here because my colleagues failed to silence the archaeologist from Kosice. This I regret, but it is a reality which we must deal with. Hence, Alexander, we must talk about contingencies. First we need to know why this man Joshua Krantz, and his woman Sarah Kaplan, are seeking you out. Do you know either of them? Do their family names ring a bell?'

Hasek was stunned to learn of the failure in Kosice. He clenched his fist, and hissed, 'If I had been in charge, that would not have happened.'

'It is because you were once in charge that we are in this mess now. This man, Krantz, his family used to own a house in Ujlak. Now the town is called Novosad. Does it mean anything to you?'

Mists began to rise from the swamp of his memory: grand moments of triumph and power; of standing on a platform before a mass of terrified people and threatening to extinguish their lives; blissful times of potency such as he'd never known before or since, of dragging people out of their beds in dawn raids, seeing them standing shivering in the freezing streets before being transported into the maw of Josef Stalin's revenge.

Ujlak? Krantz? Just names. There were so many. He rolled the name around in his mind, trying to remember by association. But it was no good. These days, all the faces of those petrified men and women, lying on the ground, begging him for mercy, were just a blur.

'Well, old friend, he is certainly keen to find you. We were hoping you could tell us why. Think about it for a couple of days. I'll return and inform you of the details when we have decided how to respond.'

'Shall I move? Go abroad?'

Kyril shook his head. 'Any break in your routine would be noticed and cause questions to be asked. Just sit tight. We'll sort things out.' He sipped the lemonade the surly housekeeper had brought him.

'Tell me, was it Igor Nemez who alerted the Syndicate?'

Kyril nodded.

Hasek smiled. He would love to see his old friend once again. Fifteen years separated their ages, but they had once been the closest of friends. More like father and son, really. Igor had been so young, so eager to advance in the hierarchy.

'How is he?' he asked.

'He committed suicide yesterday. A tragedy,' said Kyril prosaically. He turned and looked upriver towards the ancient bridge, and beyond it to the medieval tower.

Dinner was a desultory affair. The meeting with Laco's father had been fruitful, at times delightful, but as they drove back into the city they had passed the black scars on the walls of the Museum, the windows bandaged with plastic, and the suppurating roadway where the intensity of the fire in Laco's Volkswagen had melted the road surface. All that was missing to confirm the horror of the previous night was the blackened shell of his car, now safely locked in police headquarters, being examined by forensic experts.

Laco excused himself. He was tired, he needed to rest. He had not slept since the bomb. His father, Maxim, had insisted that Laco stay with him, but Josh had strenuously argued against it. He said that Laco should stay at the hotel where they were best able to protect him. Laco, still suffering from shock, agreed to stay with the Americans.

Sarah and Josh stayed in the restaurant and talked about the ramifications, the dangers and the wisdom of staying on. Now they were less emotional, they could determine a more appropriate response. They talked through the idea of employing bodyguards, of importing security from America, of informing the CIA or the FBI, of talking to the American Ambassador in Bratislava, even – despite their bravura protestations over breakfast – of leaving the area altogether and flying home. They discussed each option matter of factly and, the more they talked, the more they became convinced that they had to see this through. Despite the girl's death, they were only peripherally involved and so were not targets, but leaving for America, however tempting, would not diminish their involvement.

Josh took Sarah's hand in his. 'You know my feelings, Sarah. For me, it's important that I stay. But I still think that you should go back.'

She smiled. 'I'd really rather stay with you.'

'I was hoping you'd say that.' He kissed her hand like a courteous old-fashioned European. 'You're a very beautiful and very plucky girl. You know, one day this is going to make a hell of a movie. Uncovering an unknown massacre by a Stalinist murderer, finding him, exposing him – it's a story every movie director dreams about. Most of the crap that lands on my desk is so stereotypical and wooden that I bin it after the first page. But Christ, Sarah, this is actually happening. This is us. It's unbelievable.'

She felt a new closeness towards him. Perhaps it was the danger that made her feel this way, perhaps the fact that in him, in Josh, lay the resources which could alleviate the nightmare. The money, the power, the connections. She leaned across and kissed him on the cheek. It took him by surprise.

'You know, the first time you visited the office, half the girls were crazy about you.' He grinned in embarrassment. 'In the beginning I thought you were so full of yourself, so Mr Wonderful, Mr Hollywood, up to your armpits with your own self-importance, living in your own insulated world. There's a wonderful line in Shakespeare where a character is constantly proclaiming his innocence; it reminds me of how I saw you at first. I thought you were protesting too much. But I was wrong, Josh. I owe you an apology.'

He put his hand gently behind her neck and pulled her across towards him. He didn't care that other people were sitting at tables, eating, maybe watching. He kissed her tenderly on the lips. She responded in a gentle and non-committal way. No romance, no passion, just friendship. It spoke more eloquently than any protests she could make. It told him the horizons of their relationship.

Half an hour later, after her second cup of the black liquid the Slovan claimed was coffee, Sarah bade Josh goodnight and went up to her room. She lay down and looked across at the other bed on the opposite side of the narrow divide. That was the bed where she and Laco had made love. It seemed like years ago. She felt a twinge of embarrassment. She had been the dominant one. He had switched on something inside her and she had almost let go. Not totally, not unashamedly, but for the first time in years, she had felt like a gipsy; she'd reacted as she had rarely done before.

At home David always took the lead, his gentle skilful hands touched her in all the right places, excited her, thrilled her. With Laco, it was different. Being alone in a room with him was so wrong, so sinful. If she was single, it would be fine . . . but now – when she was a breath away from saying 'Yes, I'll marry you' – now it was wrong. But, if she was honest, that was what excited her, that other her, that she had kept hidden as an adolescent girl growing up in her parents' home, as a university student watching her sorority classmates acting in ways they never would at home, as a graduate student watching women drifting between men as though they were trying different brands of ice-cream, and as a lawyer watching colleagues making furtive phone calls or inventing absurd excuses to explain lunchtime absences. These sorts of evidences of another side of a person's character offended her. She had never allowed her physical nature to overrule her sense of moral discipline; she had always been able to – indeed had wanted to – say 'no' when it seemed wrong. Even when a good-looking guy came on to her at a party, she felt more at ease with herself following a course which would enable her to wake up in the morning and face herself in the mirror. What other people did was their own business, of course, but when they behaved in a way which was morally loose, Sarah found it distasteful.

Which was why her relationship with David was so good and right. There was an honesty about it. They conducted themselves as if they were married and yet, as far as she was concerned, she hadn't yet committed to being married. But her sexual feelings for Laco had come as a complete surprise. He had opened her up and shown her a new Sarah, a Sarah that had always been there, but deeply buried in dreams and in fantasies. It was a Sarah that she had always kept closely controlled, one she thought she would never allow out to become a Mr Hyde to her Dr Jekyll. Never!

She thought about the events of the day. Her mind wandered towards the evening when Josh had held her hand and kissed her. God, he was a nice man. How could she have been so judgemental back in New York? He was as good-looking, attentive, courteous, decent, intelligent as any person she knew. If it wasn't for David, she would have been delighted to enjoy a relationship with him.

But then that hadn't stopped her with Laco. God, what was she thinking about? How could she have allowed herself to fall for such a transparent Lothario? How could she leave a man as decent and loving as David in New York, and within a couple of weeks be jumping into another man's arms, allowing him to kiss her, to fondle her, to invade her body? What was she turning into? She had even allowed Josh to kiss her. But it would have been wrong to deflect him; wrong emotionally, wrong in every way. And she hadn't wanted to. She enjoyed him holding her hands. She enjoyed touching him. She missed being touched.

She stood up, straightened her hair and walked down the corridor. She knocked on the door of another room. No response. She knocked again. The door opened and Laco's tired face looked out at her. He looked drugged, and surprised. The moment she saw him, Sarah regretted her action. He would think her so cheap. What could she be thinking of?

'Hello, Mrs Hollywood,' he said. He sounded half asleep.

'I just came to see if you were alright.'

'Come in.'

'No. No, I won't. I just came to see if you were alright. If there was anything I could do.'

He held the door wide open. She shrugged and walked into his room. It stank of cigarette smoke. And beyond that, of cheap alcohol. 'Laco, I really didn't come here for any other reason than to . . .'

He put his arms around her and kissed her. 'I'm glad you came,' he whispered into her ear. 'I was asleep and not asleep. I was having dreams. I need someone to hold.'

'Were your dreams about Marta?' she asked as they sat on the bed. He nodded. 'She was your lover?' she asked.

'What a strange way you have of putting things. What do you want me to say? I seduced her. I took her flower. I de-virginised her. I made her into a fallen woman. There are so many stupid metaphorical expressions that people invent when they're frightened of sex. Sarah, she was a grown-up woman. She wanted me. I wanted her. We screwed. We would have parted the following day and never seen each other again, but we would always have remembered having a good time. I tried to tell you, the first time we were together, that sex is no big deal. It's not a huge commitment. Maybe for you, but not for me.'

Sarah shrugged her shoulders and whispered, 'I'm confused, Laco.'

'I've shown you a side of yourself that you're not sure about, haven't I?' She nodded. 'I thought so. You enjoyed it so much when we were together, and then the following morning you were like a bear with a sore head. Obviously I touched something in your mind which upset you, maybe embarrassed you. I don't know. If I did, I'm sorry.'

'I thought I was sorry too. But if I was really sorry, I wouldn't have come to your door just now,' she said. 'Oh shit! Maybe I'm not sorry at all. Is there a difference between being cheap and exploring sides of your personality that you don't understand?'

'Not now,' he groaned. 'Don't start that Freudian stuff with me. I'm too tired.'

She smiled, and pushed him back onto the single bed.

'Too tired to make love?'

'Yes,' he said. Her face fell. 'I'm too tired, so I'll just leave it all up to you.'

# CHAPTER FIFTEEN

The move was as swift as it was unexpected. Dr Maxim Plastov arrived as they were eating breakfast, and said, 'Can you pack and check out of the hotel within the next fifteen minutes, please.' It wasn't a question, it was an instruction.

Josh asked the obvious question, 'Why? Where are we going?'

'Just do what I ask you, please. All will be explained.'

Nobody moved. Not even Laco.

The elder Dr Plastov spoke softly. 'During the night I have been making arrangements for your safety. You, Joshua, have also been making arrangements, which we must discuss. My arrangements have already been completed. Although I have had friends guarding this hotel front and back all night, it obviously isn't safe. There are too many places where an assassin can get in. Please, my friends, come with me as soon as possible.'

It didn't take Sarah long to throw her clothes together into a suitcase and bid goodbye to a bathroom which, despite days of regular use, was still as incommodious and unwelcoming as it was the first time she had seen it. Josh found his packing just as easy. Laco had nothing to pack. Phil and Jerry took much longer because of the volume of equipment they had brought with them.

The fifteen minutes' warning from Dr Plastov became a gathering downstairs at the Slovan's reception area forty-five minutes later. Josh paid the entire bill on his credit card and everybody trooped outside into the hot, fume-laden summer air. Standing either side of the Slovan's pavement canopy were two tall, stony-faced, solid-looking men. Anybody with a modicum of knowledge would recognise them as security men, and it was obvious that they were scanning the immediate area. Sarah felt like a public dignitary, walking through a barrier which protected her from the public.

A small motorcade of four cars awaited them. The leading car, a shining black, heavy-looking Eastern European model which neither Sarah nor Josh recognised, had its engine running. A man jumped out from the front passenger seat and opened the back door. Sarah looked at Dr Plastov, who smiled and nodded encouragingly. She got in. Josh followed. Laco sat in the seat closest to the pavement. His father jumped into the back and pulled down a seat so that he sat facing them.

The car pulled effortlessly away. Josh turned to see Phil and Jerry being escorted into the car behind. Their guardians collected their equipment, which they had been forced to leave on the pavement, and climbed into the last two cars.

Dr Plastov tapped proudly on the window, 'Bulletproof glass. Armour-plated doors. It took a bit of getting. What do you think?'

Josh nodded. 'I'm impressed. I don't think I could have done that quite as easily, even in New York.'

'Sometimes the streets of Eastern Europe are a lot more dangerous than New York, or even Chicago in the time of your gangsters.'

'Is this really necessary?' asked Sarah.

Dr Plastov gave her a fatherly smile. 'The only time you will know whether it is necessary, my dear, is when it is too late. I pray that nothing happens to us from now on, in which case this elaborate precaution will have been unnecessary. But I am not prepared to take such a risk. Not with somebody as important as you or Joshua.' He looked at Laco and smiled, reached over and gripped his knee, 'Or my son.'

'Where are we going?' asked Josh.

'To a safe house. I have been arranging it during the night. The car wasn't a big problem. It was driven here overnight from Bratislava. It was used during the communist regime by the head of the Slovakian internal security division, but since his demise it has been lying idle. Friends of mine in the government were happy to furnish it on loan. The President of Slovakia and key ministers all have this sort of car. Giving it to me was no problem.'

'And the house?' asked Laco.

'That was more of a problem. It took quite some organisation. I had to think of certain criteria for a suitable safe house. When I was in hiding from the Nazis and later the Stalinists, I stayed in barns or derelict places. But such places are not suitable for you. So, what to do? I had to find a house big enough to accommodate you all. It had to be in very large grounds so that guards posted at vantage points could see people coming from miles off, and had to be easily protected so there were no buildings nearby where assassins could hide. But, most importantly, it had to be unoccupied. The last thing we would want is to expose an innocent Slovakian family to danger. So the obvious place was Romberk Castle.'

Laco looked at his father in surprise. 'You're joking.'

'This isn't a matter about which I would joke.'

Sarah looked at Laco. 'What is this place?'

'Perhaps you'd better tell her, Father.'

'It's a castle. A very nice castle, as castles go. For my taste, it's a bit ostentatious, but I'm sure you won't object. It belongs to the National Estate. The castle manager used to work for me at the town hall. When I was dismissed I found him this job. He's still grateful.'

'A castle!' said Sarah.

'Only the best for friends of my son.'

'What kind of castle?'

'A castle,' said Dr Plastov, shrugging his shoulders. 'A castle is a castle. What more can I tell you? It's set in a thousand acres of beautiful countryside. It's sixty kilometres west of Kosice. It's closed for renovations at the moment, so there are no tourists. It has attractive apartments where, from time to time, the President of Slovakia and his guests stay. When there's a need, he allows important dignitaries and visitors to stay there if they find themselves in this part of the country. When important government people come from Bratislava to visit Kosice, they sometimes spend a weekend there. It has a very small staff to look after it when there are no tourists. And it has wonderful security because it contains State treasures – great artworks, magnificent suits of armour, gorgeous frescoes and one of the most important collections of porcelain in the country.'

'And the swords! Don't forget to tell them about the swords.'

'Ah, the swords,' said Dr Plastov, in response to Laco's excitement. 'The last baron Romberk was a fanatical collector. He travelled throughout Europe, buying swords. He claimed to have examples of cutlasses, broadswords, scimitars, fencing swords, épées and God knows what else from every battle since Anglo-Saxon times. Probably nonsensical, of course, but that was his claim. They are displayed in the Great Hall. They're very valuable.'

'Where is the baron and his family?' Sarah asked. 'Aren't they in residence?'

'The last baron is currently resting peacefully in his family vault and has been since 1921. The castle was built by Count Vok of Romberk in the thirteenth century. It's mentioned in a scroll from the time of King Wenceslas in 1250. And it passed from father to son for several generations until it was conquered, then it went backwards and forwards from owner to owner. In 1870, a very wealthy Prague grain merchant bought the title and the castle from the last son of the family – an impoverished, alcoholic gambler. Once he got the money, the son began taking opium, and eventually died in a Parisian brothel. Anyway, the merchant became the new baron and it and the title stayed in his family until the last baron died without issue. Since then it's been taken over by the State and is part of our heritage.'

The motorcade was travelling west, parallel to the Hungarian border, along Highway E571. At the small town of Roznava, the car turned left and drove south. Since leaving Kosice, Sarah had been fascinated by the manoeuvring of the cars. As though by instinct, their driver would slow down at seemingly irregular intervals, allowing another car to overtake. Then again, without any obvious indication, he would accelerate past two of the cars in the motorcade to become the leader again. What looked like a game of cat and mouse was in fact a series of stratagems to defy anybody who might be attempting to interfere with their progress or shoot at them as they were driving.

'Perhaps we should go and speak to Igor Nemez again,' said Josh. 'He wasn't particularly helpful the first time, but I'm sure he could be persuaded to open up the files, especially after the attempt on Laco's life. Maybe this time he won't be quite so obstructive.'

Dr Plastov shook his head. 'I am afraid Igor will be of no further value to you. Or to anybody else. His body was found in his garage yesterday afternoon. He gassed himself.'

Sarah felt a prickling beneath her arms. Her scalp tingled as the blood drained from her face. 'He's dead?'

Dr Plastov nodded. 'It looks like suicide. His wife told the authorities he came home very agitated and went to the garage to do some work. He didn't appear again, and after a couple of hours she saw smoke coming from the garage. She found his body there. A rubber hose was attached to the car's tailpipe.'

Instinctively, Sarah grasped Josh's hand. 'That's terrible. That's . . .'

'Yes, it's terrible,' said Dr Plastov. 'He was a collaborator, a fool and a weakling, and had all the usual vices, but it's a terribly lonely way to die.'

'Why did he commit suicide?' asked Josh.

'Because,' said Laco, 'he was deeply implicated. Obviously he knew something or was covering up.'

'It's a bit more serious than that,' said his father. 'Some unknown faces have been seen around the Town Hall since your visit. Men who looked like leftovers from the bad old days. According to a friend of mine in the Town Hall they made two visits. Afterwards, Igor was very shaken, very frightened. The police interviewed Igor's wife. She says that men of the same description turned up twice to speak to him at home. I don't think you have to be a genius to put two and two together. Your visit about Hasek frightened Igor. It's one thing for somebody from Slovakia to ask; even these days he could probably still cover things up with intimidation tactics. But an American lawyer and an American film-maker are a lot more frightening for a man in his position. Your visit would have meant the very real danger of exposure, and that would have put a lot more pressure on him. My view is that he called in Department K.'

Sarah looked at Laco, who shrugged his shoulders.

Maxim Plastov explained, 'Remember in Kafka's book, *The Castle*, there was a character identified only as K. We never know his name. Well, some literary spy gave the name K to the Wet Division of the Czechoslovakian Secret Police. They were responsible for political assassination, for getting rid of irritants to the State. Naturally, after 1991, we thought they had been disbanded and returned to whatever swamp they'd originally crawled from, but obviously Igor Nemez retained some contacts. After your visit he must have called them in. Hence the untimely death of the young German student. They weren't aiming for her; they were aiming for you, Laco. I knew that it was far more serious than just a threat, which is why I had to organise all this overnight.' He waved his hand to encompass the motorcade.

Then he turned and pointed to a castle in the distance, nestled snugly into a beautiful green valley. 'And that, ladies and gentlemen, is Romberk Castle. May I present to you your home for the next week or so.'

Sarah looked at the distant edifice. It was exquisite, breathtaking. It looked like every child's fantasy castle, an image dreamed up from reading fairy stories. Turreted towers, crenellated walls, the entire edifice was large and haughty, but somehow had a lightness of style, an airy quality to it. Even from a distance. Were she a tourist she would have been thrilled. But in the current situation she felt anything but happy.

His florid face, and the occasional drool of spittle that gathered like a white pustule at the corner of his mouth, were clear indications that Boris Maximovich Tranov was drunk. His partiality for schnapps with a beer chaser became legendary in diplomatic circles when he was Second Secretary at the Russian Embassy in Washington during the 1980s. He had drunk a number of American Secretaries of State, plus their assistants, plus their acne-faced, weak-kneed Harvard or Yale crew-cut mother's boys assistants, under more tables in more receptions in more embassies than any other diplomat in the history of Washington. Chinese, Taiwanese, Korean, Polish, Hungarian, British and many other diplomats from many other countries used a lexicon of excuses to avoid parties at which the Second Secretary was host. His receptions always began with toasts to *détente* and to peaceful cooperation between East and West. But the diplomatic *canapés* never seemed to absorb the alcohol and the toasts just kept coming. While he was still standing and toasting at the end of the night, his guests were slumped in their chairs, lying on the ground, or occasionally retching surreptitiously in corners.

Tranov retired from the diplomatic service in 1991, a woolly mammoth unable to acclimatise to the warmth of a new era. Moscow wasn't the town he had known as a boy and so he chose to settle in Bratislava where, as a diplomat, he had spent wonderful years after the Great Patriotic War until 1953, when Khrushchev's new Secretary of State ordered his transfer to an asshole country in Africa, which no longer existed. A few years of quietly hiding from the power elite in Moscow and keeping his nose clean had enabled his rehabilitation and an old friend, a part of the network, had cautiously suggested his return to base. It was the era of Khrushchev's forays abroad, when he strutted like a peacock on the world stage, and a time of confusion and revisionism in Russia . . . a time when the past, the immediate past, was being examined to find out who was responsible for the misery of the people. Khrushchev began the process with his denouncement of Stalin at the Party Congress in 1956, and continued the following year with his dismissal of Molotov, Malenkov and Kaganovich. Then others in the Kremlin began looking for someone to blame for all the terrible things which had happened under Stalin.

It was in Moscow, in 1957, that Tranov, along with other diplomats and apparatchiks who had worked closely under Stalin in the satellite nations, had been called to a secret conference in a dacha on the Black Sea. There he learned about the Syndicate. Tranov had never considered that such an operation, similar to the Odessa Syndicate for former SS men, or the Rat Lines, might be necessary for people such as him, but the more he listened, the more he understood the need for the Syndicate, and from then on he was a convert. The people in the Baltic, in Czechoslovakia, Poland, Hungary, the Ukraine, in the Asiatic East, people who had been loyal servants of the Kremlin, who had carried out Stalin's instructions to the letter, did not deserve to meet with their fate in a hysterical revisionist purge. Sure, Stalin was nuts at the end. Everybody knew that. But people were only carrying out orders.

At the end of the weekend on the Black Sea, Tranov returned to Moscow. He felt as if he possessed a Masonic handshake, a Knights Templar book of instructions, a secret ring, or any other paraphernalia that signified membership of a cabal — a cabal dedicated to protecting ordinary men and women whose only crime was that of loyalty.

The warmth of the Hotel Perugia in Zelena Street in the Old City of Bratislava was exacerbating the effects of the vodka. In the old days, in the embassy in Washington, where he had facilitated new identities for members of the Syndicate, he had been able to drink like a man. These days, because he was getting on in years, he drank like a girl. Just a few glasses and he was giggling. The indignity of it all!

His companion eyed him humorously. Colonel-General Nikolai Alexandrovich Zamov, an old Stalinist warhorse who had survived Beria, Khrushchev and Brezhnev, the insanities of that birthmark-tainted lunatic Gorbachev, and then the drunken, womanising madman Yeltsin, was on a business trip to Bratislava. He had looked up his old friend. And, as they had done each time during the past ten years that Zamov had made this business trip, they left Tranov's office at eleven o'clock for lunch. It was now four o'clock in the afternoon and not a morsel of food had passed into their stomachs. Just enough alcohol to sail a battleship.

'So, you old bastard,' said Zamov. 'What news of Bratislava? How are things in Bratislava?' He was repeating himself and slurring his words badly. People were staring. 'How's your life in this asswipe of a toilet, Bratislava?' He started to giggle. By the time the manager of the hotel came over to politely ask the two old gentlemen to leave his hotel, they were in each other's arms, tears pouring down their florid cheeks, roaring with gales of laughter as each new word defined another era: Stalin, Beria, the Kremlin.

How they found their way back to Tranov's apartment was a mystery. The following morning, Tranov's housekeeper found him and his old colleague sprawled in the entrance hall. She was within an inch of calling the police to investigate a double murder, when the deep guttural moaning from within the pile of clothes alerted her to their identities. She recoiled with disgust, and tried to work out how to remove them to their beds to continue to sleep off their stupor.

By lunchtime, the two men were able to discuss the reason for Zamov's visit, although their croaking voices were kept *sotto voce* out of fragility rather than secrecy.

'Remember Hasek?' asked Zamov, somehow finding the strength to massage his temple.

Tranov shook his head and regretted the movement instantly. There was a large pool of viscous liquid inside his skull which kept swirling even when he was still. It made the act of thinking painful. 'Hasek?' He rolled the name around his tongue. 'Hasek? Should I?'

'No more than any of the other comrades. All of them loyal to Stalin. Now accused of crimes against the people.'

Tranov's eyes narrowed. 'You said nothing about being here on Syndicate business. I thought this trip was to deal in armaments.'

'This is more urgent than in the past. There wasn't time to inform you through the usual channels. There's been a serious fuck-up by Division K in Kosice.'

'Division K!' Tranov roared. 'Why the fuck wasn't I informed? Who authorised the use of Division K?'

'A sprat called Nemez. He's the local mayor or something like that. He panicked.'

Tranov nursed his aching head. The aspirin hadn't even touched the sides. 'This Nemez, is he one of us?' Zamov nodded. 'Then why didn't he follow procedures? There's a clear protocol. Any investigation about one of ours is reported to the Cell Leader, who assesses its risk. Then, if he believes it warrants action, he reports the matter to me. I decide whether to call in the Wet Brigade. Not some poxy local politician.'

'I know, comrade,' said Zamov. 'But this Nemez character was approached by an American lawyer and her client. The client's name is Joshua Krantz.'

This time Tranov recognised the name. 'The film director?'

'Apparently he was looking for his grandparents' house in some shithole near Kosice, a town called Novosad. Somebody there told him about a clearout by Alexander Hasek who was looking for some Jews. Unfortunately they were this Krantz's grandparents and his father. When Hasek couldn't find them, he got angry and went too far, publicly executed a dozen or so villagers. Now Krantz is acting like a bounty hunter from the Wild West, searching out Hasek to bring him to trial.'

Zamov rustled in his briefcase and brought out a wad of photographs which he threw contemptuously onto the coffee table between them. Tranov scanned them cursorily. Some were of a young man and woman walking in a city, some of the same man and woman and another Slavic-looking man in a village somewhere. Others were of an old car with shadowy figures inside.

Tranov put down the photos and shook his head in wonder. 'But there would have been a cover story, surely? Dead in a purge, a suicide, something like that?'

'Of course there was. The files are in order. Krantz will find nothing if he gets that far.'

Tranov felt relief sweep through his body. 'What story did we use to cover for Hasek's death?'

'Khrushchev cracked down on Stalin's lieutenants in the Warsaw Pact countries in '53. He brought them to Moscow for re-education. The files show that, for a couple of years, this Hasek character was a clerk in Svobodnyy.'

'Where the fuck is that?'

'Way out East, within pissing distance of the Chinese border. Then the files show that he was recalled in '56 when Khrushchev denounced Stalin. During the purge Hasek was transferred for further re-education and is buried somewhere in Siberia.'

Tranov nodded. 'So there is no way that his current whereabouts can be discovered.'

'You can never be one hundred per cent sure. That's why I'm here. And it's because his cover story was constructed so tightly that we have a problem now. If Nemez hadn't panicked, the Americans might have forced open a couple of local files, hit a brick wall, realised they were forty years too late and gone back to America. But because the idiot shat himself in his pants, they are now convinced Hasek's still alive. Why else would Nemez have killed himself? So they believe that their lives are in danger, and they've gone to ground somewhere in Slovakia. Maybe even over the border in Hungary. We've lost sight of them.'

'What do you mean, gone to ground?' Tranov felt his throat constricting. He pushed the button near the fireplace to call the woman to bring coffee.

'Exactly that. It's a complicated story, Boris Maximovich. It involves a local archaeologist and his father, and a number of other elements which make the whole scene into a nightmare of bungling and miscalculation. The archaeologist is the other man you see with them in the photographs.'

All remnants of the jocularity, the bonhomie, the fellowship of the previous day, evaporated in that instant. The drunken old sot who had fallen asleep in the doorway was replaced by the cold, calculating director of an ultra-secret cabal, set up to protect those who had faithfully served Josef Stalin until the very end. The man who speared Colonel-General Zamov with his piercing eyes had survived countless investigations through his caution, cunning and his extraordinary political antennae. 'Nikolai Alexandrovich, you had better start at the beginning and give me every detail, no matter how long it takes.'

It took three hours. The old woman brought several refills of coffee, as well as plates of black bread, red caviar, rolled herring, chopped egg yolks and goat's cheese when she assumed their bellies needed food. They drank and ate without giving her a second thought, so deeply immersed were they in the conversation. When every detail had been retraced for the tenth time, Tranov stood and massaged his back, then the base of his skull.

He looked at Zamov with disgust. 'The archaeologist survived the first assassination attempt, and a second one would see a federal investigation, not just local police. And this whole thing started because Nemez panicked and committed suicide, with the aid of an adrenalin injection from Division K. What chance that the coroner will find he didn't gas himself to death?'

'None,' said Zamov, shaking his head. 'We have put enough money in the coroner's account to keep him quiet.'

'Well at least you've done something right. Holy mother of God, this is a fucking disaster. Why wasn't I informed from the beginning? Don't you understand,' he shouted, 'these things must be knocked on the head when they're little pimples! Otherwise they grow into huge pustules and then it's a total disaster. For forty years, we've been covering our asses, hiding our comrades, making sure that our people didn't suffer as the SS did after the Great Patriotic War. The last thing we need when our comrades are old and weary is for them to be paraded before the world's media like Nazi war criminals. Have you seen the old men they're dragging out in Canada and America and Australia? Men who can barely walk, let alone stand trial. And all for following orders. I will not have that happen to our comrades.' He stabbed a finger at the seated Zamov. 'From now on, I take over this operation personally.' Zamov nodded. 'The first thing we have to do is contain the damage. We've got to think as though we're them. Put ourselves in their shoes. Forget the American Krantz and the woman. They don't know shit. They don't even know what time the bus leaves. The real problems are the Slovaks. The father and son. What were their names again?'

'Plastov,' said the Colonel-General.

'The problem is them. We have to deal with them.'

'But we can't,' insisted Zamov. 'This Krantz person is too famous. There would be a media outcry if his companions were assassinated. Besides, he could simply replace them with somebody else local. Let's face it, old friend, there aren't all that many people favourably disposed towards us. He would have no shortage of volunteers to help hunt down a Stalinist henchman.'

Tranov nodded. 'Okay. Then if we can't touch them, we have to think through what methods they will employ to track down Alexander Hasek. We will have to anticipate every move they might make, and, before they make it, we are going to have to deal with the people who have the information. You know what that means? Starting at Cesky Krumlov and working our way back. Ring the bell for the woman and ask her to get paper and pens. We are going to work out the trail they will use to get to him and determine where we can break it.'

Paradise must have looked like this. Sarah closed her eyes. She let her imagination wander around the landscapes of old woodcuts in medieval books or the vivid colours of the Renaissance mind. Despite the vivid sunlight, she saw bucolic scenes of rolling hills, gentle streams meandering through glades, lambs frolicking with lions, unicorns on distant hills, Adam and Eve decorously naked with the leaves of trees covering their private parts, and the sun dappling the ground. She was sitting on a hillock a hundred yards from the castle entrance. Her knees were bent and her chin rested gently on them. Her skirt was gathered modestly underneath, as though she was holding herself in protection. The wind, perfumed from the orchards hugging the river, blew strands of her black hair into her eyes. It was a perfect summer's day. An American New England summer's day. The wind, the scent of the fruit blossoms, the stillness of the day and the noises of insects were all America: the American childhood spent on a perpetual holiday with her parents, the delights of youthful memory. She squeezed her eyes more tightly, lay back and felt the hot sun warming her face. It was an erotic feeling. She drifted into her favourite memories: a holiday in Florida, her first ride in Disneyland, the ovation she got when she was elected class president at Junior High.

A cloud fell across her closed eyes. She opened them; Josh was standing over her, dark and mysterious.

'Do you want to be alone, or can I share some time with you?'

She smiled and patted the ground beside her. 'Come lie with me and be my love,' she said. 'My favourite line from Christopher Marlowe, one of my favourite poets.'

He lay down. She couldn't feel his body but she could feel his presence.

'I just deliberately misquoted,' she admitted as she turned to face him. 'The real word isn't "lie", it's "live". The whole stanza goes:

"Come live with me and be my Love,

And we will all the pleasures prove,
   That hills and valleys, dales and fields,
   Or woods or steepy mountain yields."
I didn't want you to think I was asking you to live with
me.' She grinned. He smiled back.

'It's beautiful verse,' he said. 'And I'll bet this is as
beautiful as the scene Marlowe was looking at when he
wrote the words.'

They lay silently, looking up at the enormous sky,
relaxed now after the initial tension of arriving two hours
previously. The estate manager had hugged and kissed
Laco's father profusely on seeing him, and had promised to
show the others around in the afternoon. In the meantime,
he had given them permission to make themselves at home
and to wander the grounds. Laco and his father had fallen
into a deep conclave, talking over some matters of
immediacy which were pressing on Laco's mind, and so
Sarah had wandered alone to this Elysian spot.

'Sarah, there's something I've got to ask you. You don't
have to answer, but . . . Last night I phoned your room to
see if you were okay. And I phoned you again this
morning, before breakfast. There was no reply.'

'Are you keeping tabs on me?' she asked quietly.

He didn't reply. He had his answer. It was all he needed.
He lay back down on the grass and stared up into the
canopy of the trees above.

'Why are you sleeping with Laco?'

Sarah closed her eyes again, this time more tightly,
squeezing them until it hurt. 'It's hard to explain,' she said.
'I'm not even sure I understand it myself. It's so unlike me,
so unlike anything I've ever done before. There's a part of
him which has found a part of me.'

'He's only going to hurt you.' He reached over and held
her hand.

'Josh, don't. Please don't. You're not being fair. When
I wake up in the morning and think about what I'm

doing with Laco, I just can't believe it. But when I'm in the middle of it, it's like a whole new side of me takes over. It's as if I'm in the middle of a suppressed dream. Suddenly there are new colours, new sensations, things I only ever thought existed for other people. He makes my body come alive in ways which I can't comprehend. I can let myself go with him because he doesn't give a damn, because he's only interested in screwing and not in being deep and meaningful. If I had a relationship with you, it would become more complex and go deeper and deeper until I'd have to make the choice between you or David. And that's a decision I don't ever want to have to make.'

Josh lay quietly for a while. Then he slowly stood, without looking at her, and went back to the castle. For the first time in her life, Sarah felt deeply unsure about what she was doing.

When she returned to the castle, the others were sitting in a semi-circle around a vast mahogany desk in a crimson room. The room was lit by two chandeliers whose jewels scintillated in the brilliant late-afternoon sunlight pouring in through the windows. Suits of armour, roundels of swords, and cabinets of porcelain and silver testified to the room's antiquity. Even the uncomfortable chairs on which they sat, whose arms were made from the antlers of deer shot by one of the castle's owners in some dim age, attested to the exclusiveness of their surroundings. Sarah deliberately chose a chair away from Josh. She didn't look him in the eye. She couldn't.

Maxim Plastov assumed leadership of the meeting by choosing the chair behind the desk. He began by welcoming them, and hoping that their tour of the castle had been fruitful and enjoyable. Before he was able to continue, Josh interrupted.

'Forgive me for breaking in here, but there's a matter of great concern to me that has to be resolved before we begin.'

Sarah looked at him in horror and cringed in her seat, fearful of what he was going to say. Was he going to expose her in front of all the others? But she audibly sighed with relief when he spoke.

'I began this whole ordeal by my quest for justice. Sarah is peripherally involved and, even if she doesn't want to be, I'm afraid that circumstances have kinda taken over. Laco is deeply although involuntarily implicated, for which I owe him an apology. But neither Phil nor Jerry are central characters in this whole thing. They are here to help me make a film, but that seems to be secondary at the moment. The last thing I want is for them to be harmed. So far we've kept them up to date with what's happening, and they've gone along with it. But we're getting into the big stuff now, and before anything else goes down I want to give them the opportunity of withdrawing. And I think that the same thing has to apply to you, Maxim. You've come to our aid, but it's not your fight. It's ours. Sarah and I have talked things through at length and, although we're far from happy about it, we're prepared to face whatever danger may be forthcoming. But this is my fight, not anybody else's, and if anybody wants to clear out before it gets too late they'll be sent on their way with my very best wishes and no recriminations.'

Jerry snapped his fingers. 'Gary Cooper in *High Noon*. John Wayne in any movie about the Second World War. C'mon, Josh, give us a clue.'

Everyone joined in the laughter. Phil interjected, 'Josh, we've talked this whole thing through, and we're staying. This is news, man. A once-in-a-lifetime. Jerry and me, we were too young for Vietnam, but between us we've lived in LA and Chicago and New York City. Compared with that, ain't nothing these mothers can throw at us would scare us. You trying to keep us away from the news story of the year? Get real, man.'

Josh nodded to the two men in gratitude, and handed the meeting back to Dr Plastov.

'You have happened upon this by accident,' Maxim said. 'My own research is far from finished. I had intended to publish in a couple of years time, once I'd had more opportunities to continue my research in Moscow. But it is now important that I open up to you precisely why it is that I have gone to great lengths to protect you from the hornets' nest you have stirred up. There is an expression which is used in American movies, I believe' – he looked at Josh for agreement – '"You don't know what you're dealing with". Well, my friends, in this case, I'm afraid that you really don't.

'I want to tell you about a group which we've known about – or at least which we've suspected has been in existence – for about forty years. Nothing has been publicised about them, nothing has been mentioned in books or magazines. I am not even sure that the secret service agencies like Britain's MI6 or America's CIA or even Russia's KGB knows anything about them. To be perfectly frank, they might not even exist at all. Our only way of determining their existence was by a process of elimination. That is part of the research which I have been conducting since the collapse of the Soviet Union, when my colleagues and I were allowed access to KGB and NKVD files.

'We – by whom I mean people who were imprisoned or exiled under Stalin, and who survived – began to wonder why so many of the monsters who had committed those atrocities went unpunished. Of course Stalin was denounced by Khrushchev three years after his death, but the crimes of those who were Stalin's henchmen went unpunished. Why? Because we were behind the Iron Curtain. It was all very different in the West after the Second World War. Simon Wiesenthal set about hunting down Nazi war criminals, and the world quickly learned about the Odessa Group, which was set up in the closing months of the War to spirit SS monsters away to a new identity and a contented retirement. Without the help of the governments in South America, especially Chile and Argentina, they would have found life more difficult, but they were resourceful and would have found a way.

'But nobody in the West cared about the citizens of Russia, or the peoples of Hungary or Poland or Romania or Albania or Czechoslovakia or Bulgaria, or the other poor bastards who were the victims of Stalin's insanity.'

Sarah, agog, had to interrupt. 'Maxim, are you saying that even today there's still a group of Stalinists who are hiding and protecting those guilty of mass murder during his reign?'

Jerry whispered to Phil, 'Told you there'd be a ball-tearing story here.'

Dr Plastov nodded. 'I am not saying anything so specific, my dear, because we have no direct evidence of its existence. But then we have not seen anti-matter in space, although science tells us that it exists. The likelihood is that many of our home-grown monsters were sucked up in the vortex of Moscow in the early years of Khrushchev's rule, and before anyone had even thought of show trials or retribution, this group had doctored files in the archives to show that these men had been purged or re-educated, and had died in the process.'

'But you have no evidence,' Sarah continued. 'You're only assuming it. Surely . . .'

'Surely what, Sarah? Surely during Khrushchev's rule, when the Soviet satellite nations like Czechoslovakia and the others were looking towards freedom, I should have marched into Moscow and demanded access to their files? Let me remind you of the situation in Czechoslovakia in the 1950s. There was terrible repression. The communists' economic policies almost bankrupted us. There were imprisonments, executions, people sent to labour camps

. . . if you even breathed the word "democracy" you suddenly disappeared. How could people like me possibly have gone banging on the doors of Khrushchev's Kremlin, demanding access to KGB files?'

'But surely,' said Sarah, 'in 1968 when Dubcek liberalised things, you could have found out? And there would have been files in Prague or Bratislava or somewhere.'

Dr Plastov laughed. 'How could I have access to those files? They were controlled by locals who answered to Moscow. Alexander Dubcek was a local hero. We loved him, worshipped him. But it was the era of Leonid Ilyich Brezhnev, and he was Stalin's protégé. When Dubcek turned his back on Moscow and began to look towards the West, Brezhnev sent in the tanks. Fourteen thousand party functionaries and half a million party members who refused to renounce Dubcek's proposition of socialism with a human face became toilet attendants or road sweepers. Professors and teachers and journalists and other intellectuals became the target of Gustav Husak, the bastard who was put in place of Dubcek and the most totalitarian president we have ever had. Again, we were forced to meet in secret and whisper behind locked doors like frightened rabbits. Hardly the time, Sarah, to march to Moscow and shout, "Hey, Leonid Ilyich, let me see your dirty underwear".'

Sarah nodded. 'I'm sorry. I'd forgotten how hideous life was before Perestroika.'

'But since then, since the beginning of the 1990s, we who are still alive have been doing a bit of auditing. That is why we have come up with this idea that there simply has to be a covert group operating to protect these people. People like the man you believe responsible for the massacre at Ujlak, Alexander Hasek.'

'But why?' asked Josh. 'Why couldn't they simply have disappeared? There were tens of millions of people who went missing. You said so yourself.'

'True, but they were little, powerless, ordinary people. People whose crime was to have vindictive friends or neighbours who reported them to the Party. The men like Hasek would have – should have – been arrested during the anti-Stalin purges by Khrushchev and certainly by those who were nationalists within the satellite countries. But it's as if a lid has been clamped down on the nest of snakes.'

'How can we find out about it?' asked Sarah. 'If it's true, then the whole world should know.'

'The best way is by finding Alexander Hasek, and then working backwards to determine who is protecting him,' said Maxim.

'How?' asked Josh.

Laco, unusually quiet in deference to his father, intervened, 'The letters we took from his maid. They were written to an address in Prague. It was a post office box, but at least it gives us a district and a place to start. And who knows, maybe . . . just maybe . . . we'll be able to find out who used to rent it in 1986, which was the date of the last letter.'

His father nodded. 'Laco and I have read all her letters. They are exactly as you would expect them to be, bearing in mind who wrote them. Full of gratuitous thanks and blessings for his continued thoughts and support and assuring him that there is a warm bed if he should deign to return to her home. Nothing, however, from him. Quite how he kept in touch we don't know, except that her last letters to him, the ones in '86, became frantic. She begged him not to break communications, not to move away, to continue to send money.'

'Did she mention in her letters where he might be moving? Did she indicate any future address?' asked Sarah.

Dr Plastov shook his head. 'Sadly, no. It was obvious that he was deliberately keeping her in the dark.'

'So,' said Laco, 'it's off to Prague for us, as soon as we can arrange suitable security and protection. Meantime, you guys stay here and enjoy your rest. Make the place your own.' He smiled broadly. He enjoyed being facetious.

Sarah looked at Josh, and then at Phil and Jerry. They were all wondering what Laco meant. 'What do you mean, "stay here"? We're not staying here. We're going to Prague. This is our problem. Not yours.'

Laco began to say something, but fell into silence, as his father told her gently, 'Sarah, this is very much our problem. You are Americans. If this man Hasek is still alive, then he must be brought before the Slovakian people to atone for his crimes. The people he murdered were Slovaks, the crimes were crimes against us. You and Josh are only involved in an indirect way. You came to reclaim the Krantz family home. I applaud your decision. Former citizens who owned properties and who were expelled because of their politics or religion or ethnicity should, by right, be permitted to reclaim their property. But you are not involved in bringing one of our criminals to justice for crimes he committed before you were born. Please, children, leave Hasek to us.'

'But we *are* involved, Maxim. Because of us, because we stirred up this nest of vipers, a young woman is dead. Laco could have been killed, and a city official has committed suicide.' Josh shook his head to try to clear the bad dream. He looked across at Sarah, who nodded in agreement. 'The reason we've stayed isn't because we're particularly brave or because we're on some crusade to right the wrongs of the world. Don't you see, if we don't stay and clear this mess up, it's just going to follow us to the States. To wherever we are.'

Maxim glanced at Laco, who gave a surreptitious shrug. 'But what can you do? You don't speak the language, you don't know the country, you have no idea of our history or traditions. If anyone in the street talks to you, you will be exposed immediately and endanger everyone else. The dangers are immense. How can you possibly be of any help in tracking down this man?'

There was a moment's silence before Sarah said quietly, 'Don't confuse the issue by introducing trivial problems, Maxim. Look at the big picture.'

Everyone burst out laughing. It was a good time to break for coffee.

The two old men pored over the notes they had spent most of the day writing. It had been a long day, the need for detailed focus not helped by each man's headache. But at least by the end of the day, everything was coming together. They had drawn the line that could connect the Syndicate to Hasek, Hasek to the time he had lived in Prague, and those who had known him in Prague to the Americans. Which meant that they could now control any further danger of Hasek's exposure, and their own.

Tranov stood and walked through the French doors into his tiny courtyard. He stood there in the brilliant late afternoon sun, unzipped his trouser fly and urinated generously over his tomato plants.

'Since I've been doing this,' he said to Zamov, 'they have gained fantastically in size and colour. Trouble is, now I can't eat them 'cause they taste like shit.' He burst out laughing at his own joke.

He walked back into the room and rang the bell. 'Enough with the coffee and the biscuits. Now we'll have some vodka.'

Zamov's jaw dropped. After last night, he didn't think he could *look* at a bottle, let alone drink from it.

Without a thought for his friend's liver, Tranov picked up the conversation where it had ended before he went outside to relieve himself. They had been discussing where to begin the operation to clean up the mess left by their Wet Division, Department K, in Kosice.

'Their next logical move will be into Prague. From tomorrow morning, someone will be waiting at Prague Airport for a flight from Kosice.'

'But if we've lost them, they could be anywhere. Out of the country, even. How will we know which flight they'll be on? And they could drive for all we know.'

'Wrong! They are still in Slovakia. Even though there is a border crossing from Slovakia to the Czech Republic, it is not the same as going to Hungary or the Ukraine. They would not have risked crossing a dangerous border. Don't forget they are being accompanied by two Slovaks, the father and the son archaeologists. They certainly would not have gone eastwards to the Ukraine. There are hold-ups there for two or three days. The customs guards are the most corrupt in the world. They won't let a car move without payment. So the Ukraine is out of the question. Which leaves Hungary. Possible. But again unlikely. They won't cross a local border with the American film director. Think about it. Think about what would happen when a man as famous as Krantz waltzed into town; the gossip would spread like wildfire . . .'

'It didn't in Kosice.'

'Kosice isn't Hungary,' said Tranov. 'Hungary is cosmopolitan, Kosice is fucking Middle Ages. Do they have a cinema?' He allowed the question to remain unanswered. 'And finally, their third option is by road. Again unlikely. Somebody like Krantz would demand immediate transport. Road would take them days and add the risk of being spotted. No! We'll stake out the airport. They may arrive tomorrow. More likely the next day. But we'll be there. Now, who's the best man we have in the Wet Division?'

Zamov shrugged his shoulders. 'Slatkin. He's ex-Statni Bezpecnost. His father was deputy to Jindrich Vesely who ran Department K after the Moscow take-over in Prague just after the War. The son turned out to be excellent, and loyal. He worked his way up and quickly became one of the best Wet men working in Czechoslovakia. Slatkin was head of the Wet Division of the St. B until it was closed down in '91. During his time, he worked all over Europe. He's worked with the East Germans and the Romanians as well as with the KGB and the GRU. He's good.'

'Excellent,' said Tranov as the woman walked in with a tray of vodka already poured into glasses. Zamov admired her instinct. She had been bringing coffee the whole afternoon, yet now she knew the time was right to bring something stronger. He picked up a glass and passed it to his seated colleague.

'To Prague,' he said as they clinked glasses.

Drinking coffee, Josh said, 'There's somebody I want to bring over from the States. Somebody I've used many times. Somebody who will be of enormous benefit, I promise.'

Ever the lawyer, Sarah demanded details, but Josh just smiled and shook his head. 'Trust me on this one.' And so the meeting came to an abrupt end.

Josh retired to his ornately furnished bedroom, set aside from public view and reserved for people of great importance who stayed at the castle as guests of the President. He opened his address book, picked up the phone and dialled a long series of numbers.

'Josephine, it's Josh Krantz. How you doing?' he asked. There was a squeal of delight at the other end of the phone. 'I want you to drop everything and get your ass over to Slovakia.'

'Slovakia! But that's so far from Los Angeles!'

Josh gave the address and instructed total confidentiality. Not a word to be said to anybody. He said he would transfer twenty-five thousand dollars into any bank account nominated for just two days' work, and an all-expenses-paid holiday in Paris on top. Again, Josephine squealed with delight. And for the whole of the following day, Josh was like a cat with the cream.

Life for Maxim was more fraught, however. Accompanied by two security guards, he left the castle that evening to return to Kosice in order to clear up matters related to tracing the post office box in Prague, and to begin the process of reactivating contacts in Moscow, or diverting existing ones, just in case it was necessary to trace Hasek back to the Centre.

Laco relaxed, swimming in the pond and walking around the grounds of the castle for most of the day. Sarah read a book that she had promised herself she would finish by the end of her trip, and Josh spent the time in the library, enjoying the beauty of the ancient volumes, whose leather covers and faded gold spines gave him the feelings of permanence and security which he suddenly craved.

They ate lunch together, *al fresco*, the manager and his wife setting up a table of delicious food on the *loggia* with its panoramic view of the undulating grounds adjoining the castle. The afternoon was spent in studied and focused relaxation. Josh and Sarah went for a long walk and talked about any subject other than the complex intertwining of their relationships. Laco examined the roundels of swords and suits of armour and envisaged a life led in medieval castles, a life without cigarettes and rock music. In the evening, Maxim Plastov returned from Kosice with news that his colleagues in Prague had done some interesting groundwork and may have some useful information when they journeyed there within the next few days. They spent the night playing a board game and by common consent, went to bed early.

It took two days for Josephine to arrive, by a whole series of circuitous routes that Josh had specified when he had phoned her in Los Angeles. By the time she did, tempers were beginning to fray. Everyone had demanded explanations from Josh but, irritatingly, he refused to bow to pressure. It was just past eight in the morning when a car approached along the minor roadway which fed the two villages close to the outskirts of the castle grounds. It slowed, checked its directions and turned into the castle's driveway. The security guard hidden amongst a thicket of trees at the entrance warned his colleague, three kilometres away, stationed on the castle steps. A general call was made to all of the other guards securing the grounds. They quickly moved inwards to protect the castle and its occupants. The guard on the steps walked quickly into the conservatory where the Americans, Maxim and Laco were enjoying a relaxing breakfast. He whispered into Maxim's ear, who then announced to the group, 'A car is approaching the castle. It is a tourist car with a chauffeur in front and somebody in the back.'

'That's Josephine,' said Josh with a grin from ear to ear. 'She's arrived from Austria. Wonderful!'

Phil and Jerry looked at each other in horror. 'You asked Josephine to come here?' said Jerry in surprise.

'Who else?'

'Oh for Christ's sake, Josh. Not Josephine!' Phil was stunned. 'Last time I saw her, she nearly raped me.'

'Who is this Josephine?' Sarah demanded.

'The best make-up artist in Hollywood. I use her whenever possible. Her ability is unmatched – she can transform anybody into anything. With her bag of tricks she could even make Phil look like a middle-aged Chinese woman. As long as we keep our mouths closed no one will be able to recognise us. Same goes for you guys,' said Josh.

Laco, Phil, Jerry and Sarah all objected at the same moment, but Maxim held up his hand like a schoolteacher quelling a noisy class. 'I think it's a very sensible decision. The people we are dealing with are ruthless and extremely dangerous. Once we break cover, we're going to need all the help we can get, especially in the area of disguise.'

They looked out of the conservatory window as the car pulled up. What emerged was a tall man, young and drop-dead gorgeous. Sarah looked at Josh quizzically.

'I thought you said . . .'

'Meet Josephine,' he said, as the man walked up the steps of the castle and into the Great Hall, followed by the chauffeur carrying two suitcases and three substantial pieces of hand baggage.

Maxim and Laco remained sceptical and silent until Josephine was ushered into the Conservatory by the estate manager. The man who walked in was even more gorgeous, muscled and tanned close-up. Sarah thought that he must spend hours every morning preparing his appearance before he emerged into daylight. And not only was he stunning to look at. He was beautifully dressed in a casual, yet precise manner. His shirt and slacks looked manicured. How he could have travelled from LA to Austria, and then into Slovakia, and still appear breathtaking was beyond her understanding.

But the moment he opened his mouth, all the superstructure of masculinity disappeared. He espied Josh and screamed, 'Josh, you little darling. You didn't tell me you'd bought a castle. But in the back of beyond, *bubeleh*. Oh! It's sumptuous. And I even get a holiday out of this. I can't believe it. But you're a really naughty boy, and you've got me into a lot of trouble with the boys and girls back home. I've let a lot of people down because of you, y'know. *Chutzpah*. I don't think I'll ever get another studio job. What was that awful book? *You'll Never Work In This Town Again*. Anyway, you owe me, because I was all set to do Streisand for this new movie she's doing – oh! such *dreck*. All about a mixed marriage and the effect it has on a girl's relationship with her parents . . . girl! You hear that? I had to make her look like an eighteen-year-old. Streisand!! Then the girl grows up into a mother, and guess what? You guessed it, her daughter falls in love with a *goy* and the shit really hits the fan. Anyway, I had to phone her up and say "Barbra darling, I'm afraid you'll have to get someone else, Josh needs me". Well! That woman's language was unbelievable. Fuck this and fuck that and you'll never do my make-up ever again you fucking Jewish fairy, and who does that fucking Joshua Krantz think he is. Oh, it was bloody. I cried for three minutes.'

He acknowledged everybody else in the room by waving a hand in their general direction. He saw the two other American men and squealed, 'Hi, Phil! Hi Jerry', then threw his arms around Josh and kissed him on both cheeks. 'Now you're going to have to square this with Barbra. You know how long-term temperamental she can be and I think she's going menopausal, but I could be wrong. And you've also got to phone up and talk to Bobby De Niro. I promised him I'd do the scar shit for one of his up-and-comings. The guy gets a glass in his face and the make-up artist he's using has made him look like Bela Lugosi playing Frankenstein. So,' he said, turning and pointing to the two Slovaks at the table, 'who are these dear people? And why did you make me come through London and Vienna to get here? Such a *farblondjet* route, darling.'

'Josephine,' said Josh. 'I'd like you to meet Maxim and Laco. They're very good friends of ours.'

'Hi,' he said, but turned peremptorily back to Josh, ignoring Sarah completely.

Josh noticed Sarah's reaction, and said, 'And this is a dear friend of mine, Sarah.'

'Hello,' he drawled in his voice specially reserved for attractive women. 'So why am I here, honey-bun? What's it all about?'

'Josephine, we all need make-overs. We're doing a home movie and we need to look different.'

He looked at Josh sceptically and smacked him on the hand. 'That's bullshit, and you know it. Honesty in all things, Joshua Krantz. Now, tell me the truth or I won't do it. I don't do weddings or barmitzvahs, y'know. I'm a movie make-up artist, which means I've got to get into the heart of the character. Cut the crap and tell me what I'm dealing with here. Do you want me to make you look evil like Dracula, or shall I blend you in with the countryside and make you look like a tree? If you don't level with me, Josh, I'm not going to be able to do the job.'

Josephine could tell from the looks passing around the table that everybody was being particularly cautious. He turned around towards the ensemble and announced, 'People, you brought me into this. You made me one of the team, so don't treat me like an outsider now I'm in town. I know there's something funny going down because of the way this man made me get here. Don't breathe a word, Josephine. Don't come straight here, Josephine. This is *X-Files* meets James Bond.'

'Josephine,' said Josh, 'there are things going on here that it's better you know nothing about. For your sake.'

'Bullshit, Joshua Krantz. And don't patronise me like I'm an old fairy godmother. You of all people should realise how much a part of any movie the make-up artist has to be. You can have an actress bursting into tears in a deeply emotional moment but if the shades of her make-up are wrong, it could ruin everything. It has to give the right support to the feeling. Same with hair. Now, I have to know precisely what it is you want to convey if I'm going to be of any use to you. It's either that or I don't even bother unpacking. Josh, you're being a naughty boy. You have to trust me.'

'Josephine, it's not quite that easy. There's some really heavy shit going down here. We're all involved, but you don't have to be. By telling you the details, we could involve you and that's the last thing I want to do.'

'Oh bullshit. I'm an old movie queen. I love being involved. Now you just tell Josephine what this is all about.'

Josh told him as much as he needed to know. He said nothing about Hasek nor about the deaths of two people, just that they had uncovered some information that people didn't want them to know, and in order for them to continue looking the only safe way was to change their appearances.

'Okay,' said Josephine, satisfied. 'That sounds good. So we're dealing with the need for concealment, rather than creating a mood or an impression. Now, let's have a look at you.'

He looked from one to the other until he arrived back at Josh. 'Hmmm. This isn't going to be easy, is it? She,' he said, pointing at Sarah abruptly, 'I see as a Russian mother. Maybe we could add a couple of pounds to her tits, thicken up the lips a bit, ruffle the hair, maybe a head scarf. No, no, too *babushka*. Maybe something a bit startling, out of the ordinary. Yes. Hair pulled severely back to accentuate the Slavic cheekbones and maybe a scarf looking a bit like a bandolier. Shoulder to midriff. That way we could really go to town on the tits. Put a couple of small pillows in there to make her look like she's had fourteen kids.' Sarah flushed in embarrassment but chose to remain silent.

He pointed to Laco. 'Him we have to make old. The father, we have no problem. We make him look ten years younger and he'll be gorgeous. We'll put some nice colour in his hair, get rid of the bags under the eyes. You'll look stunning,' he assured Maxim. 'But the son, my God, have you been hitting the bottle recently? Slept in a car for the last couple of weeks, have we?'

Laco was stung by the impertinence, but Josh signalled for him to remain quiet. Josephine continued, 'I think with you we'll make you into an American businessman. That way, nobody will notice the debauchery. Good suit, polished shoes.'

He turned to Josh. 'Have you noticed how dirty the shoes are around here? I couldn't believe it. The moment we crossed the border from Austria, it was as if everybody had just left the farm. Men and women. Don't these people have any pride?'

He turned back and spoke directly to Laco. 'American businessmen always have nicely polished shoes. But I don't think we'll put you in a tie. I think maybe open collar. Maybe a nice pullover, a bit 1970s. Relaxed and comfortable. Before the Age of Greed.'

He looked at Phil and Jerry and tutted. 'I think you boys have to stay out of sight. Not even George Lucas and a week of computer morphing could make you two look anything but bums. Maybe that's the trick. Maybe I'll make you look more like bums than you already are.'

'Josephine,' snapped Phil, who had no difficulty with Jews or gays, but still couldn't come to terms with a Jewish gay.

'Okay, okay, what I'll do is roughen you up a bit. Change your hair style, hair colour, maybe make you both into middle-aged German students. There's a lot of them about at the moment. I wonder what their daddies did in the War! So,' he said, turning to Josh, 'where's the wardrobe? Where am I going to get all the props from?'

# CHAPTER SIXTEEN

The Slovakian matron walked cautiously, as if in considerable pain, as she lumbered her way along the airbridge at Prague Airport after the two-hour flight from Kosice. She grasped eagerly onto a handrail wherever there was one, her labouring body straining against the inclines and declines which are a feature of the long walkways of modern airports. The rheumatism in the old lady's back was hurting her more now than ever, and she walked with a pronounced sway, each step an agony after the confinement of the economy class seat.

She pulled her headscarf looser around her neck as the summer sun streamed in through the huge airport windows, making her uncomfortably hot. Eventually she got through passport control and walked slowly down more of the airport's corridors, stopping every couple of minutes to massage her hip with her free hand. She struggled with the old, heavy hold-all that contained her few private possessions. Younger, fitter, stronger people walked rapidly past and beyond her. She muttered a few sullen imprecations at their rapidly receding backs.

She pulled her suitcase, an old grey one with a red strap to hold it together, off the conveyor belt and struggled with it through customs and out into the crowded and noisy public concourse. She looked hopefully to see if her daughter was awaiting her, but she was not there. The old woman cursed the Lord under her breath, and her daughter's meanness for not picking up her aged mother.

Her thick and creased stockings were making her legs sweat. She could use a good bath when she got to her daughter's place, if she ever got there in this crush of people. She had no hands free to negotiate around other passengers or their well-wishers and had to mumble loudly and cough to make her way through. And she had no hands free to clutch her amulet and feel its comforting warmth, as she had done almost every day in New York since she had been given it when she turned twenty-one.

The old Slovakian woman waited patiently in the queue of other passengers, sitting on her suitcase and massaging her back before the bus arrived. She put her luggage on the bus and paid the fare, saying 'Praha' to the driver, who nodded and waved her to a seat at the back of the bus. The old woman fixed her scarf again and looked around surreptitiously, to see if she could find her travelling companions. But they were so well-camouflaged by Josephine's extraordinary make-up that they blended into the crowd and were invisible even to her.

The bus pulled away and Sarah felt a profound sense of relief. She wasn't experienced in the world of espionage – it was as alien to her as a weekend with Kalahari bushmen – but she would have sworn on the Bible that she hadn't been spotted. Nor was she experienced in the craft of acting, but Josh's direction of her as an old woman had given her an insight into the character she was portraying. So good a director was he, that after half-a-dozen attempts she swore she could feel the pain of lumbago radiating across the expanse of her back.

The plan was for each of them to travel by different means into the centre of Prague, and then to lose the suitcases which had been provided for each of them. The real luggage – their clothes, equipment and personal items

– were being driven to Prague at break-neck speed, along with Josephine, in two cars by the security guards. They would all rendezvous in an apartment belonging to a friend of Maxim Plastov's, a Professor of Cultural Studies and Semiotics at Prague University. It was situated in the Old City, a few streets from the Vltava and within spitting distance of the famous Republic Square.

After the bus had spent an hour weaving through the tortuous traffic of inner-city Prague, it finally snorted to a halt at the terminus. Sarah collected her baggage and left the noisy and crowded building. She continued to play the part of an elderly woman, walking slowly away from the terminus and into the mass of people in the street. She had been assured by Laco that nobody in Prague would bother to offer her any assistance, so she wouldn't have to use any Czech. And indeed, nobody tried to help her. But then, nor would they have in New York or Paris or London.

She walked arthritically around the corner, into a small maze of streets where she found a laneway full of closely parked cars, but empty of people. She had been instructed to sit on her suitcase and wait there for three or four minutes before moving on again, to pretend to be tired and recovering her breath. The air was hot and she was sweating fiercely under the coat, scarf and the make-up. But instead of moving on to find a quieter location to change, Sarah decided that this place was as good as any. When she was absolutely certain that nobody was following her, and the streets continued to be devoid of people, she quickly opened the case, took off her coat and scarf, unpeeled the creased skin she had been wearing on her cheeks, forehead and throat, and threw them into the case. She took out a mirror and some acetone-based make-up remover and began the job of getting rid of the gum Josephine had used to stick the second skin to her face. She stopped in the middle of what she was doing and looked up and down the road again. There was still nobody coming. She took a brush out of the hand luggage that she had carried with her on the plane and pulled it through her tightly lacquered hair, rearranging it into a style more suitable to a young woman. Josh had been insistent that they didn't remove their make-up in Prague Airport, but waited until they were in the city. Now she fully understood why. People in a city are too busy and rushed to bother about the needs of the elderly. She vowed to remember the lesson when she returned to America.

In Kosice, they had worked out an arrival strategy. For them all to arrive at the house at the same time could be a disaster. The major risk for them was the journey to the apartment after removing their disguises. A staggered arrival time for the group would minimise the risk. It was a measure insisted upon by Maxim. Rather than all arriving at the safe house in their make-up and disguises, they were finding different places to ditch their identity in the centre of Prague so that they could walk away as new people. The double blind was the best chance they had of evading any surveillance.

Sarah slipped off the stockings, put on new shoes which she took from the case, and a pulled a bright red top over her head. She looked at her reflection in a window over the road. She looked like a tourist. Great! She put the hand luggage inside the case, closed it, strapped it up and stood it against the wall of an apartment building. She walked quickly away.

Re-entering the mainstream of pedestrians, Sarah felt suddenly exposed. It was an uncomfortable feeling. Disguised as an old woman, she had felt no such sense of visibility. It was comforting to hide behind a mask, to have people look at you but not see the real you. To present an image to the world and have nobody know who you were and what you were thinking. But without the make-up, without the mask, she was herself and she felt vulnerable. She walked quickly into a coffee shop and sat at a table deep inside for an hour, before judging the time right to catch a taxi to the safe house. By the time she got there, Phil and Josh were already in residence. They grinned at her. They were waiting for Maxim, Laco and Jerry, who should be arriving over a period of about two hours. Over a glass of red wine, they mused about how swiftly and yet professionally the arrangements had been made.

'Do you think Maxim used to be in the Secret Service or something? I mean, Christ, he knows all the tricks,' said Sarah.

'He didn't think about Josephine. That was Josh. Fucking beautiful,' said Phil.

'I guess everybody who was against the government had to play the part of the spy. Let's face it, in those times you had to be covert all the while or you'd be denounced and then you'd be dead. Still,' said Josh, 'nothing's impossible. I've got to admit, Josephine was really one out of the box. She's something else, isn't she? You looked older than your own grandmother, Sarah. And the way she made me look like an over-grown English schoolboy was just brilliant. You know I should get her in earlier on my flicks. With her imagination, she could create characters I hadn't thought of that would add a real tingle to a film.'

They continued to drink their wine in the large and exquisitely furnished apartment. The owner was obviously a man of means. The rooms were musty because they hadn't been lived in for quite a while, but the furnishings were sumptuous, right down to the flocked wallpaper and the King Charles feather design used to hold the wall-lights. There were four bedrooms, which made the apartment huge by Prague standards, though relatively modest by those of upper-crust New York. Sarah would have a room to herself. Josh, Laco and Maxim would sleep in another room; Phil and Jerry in the third. Which left a room free for Josephine to sleep on her own. Much as they enjoyed her company, nobody felt sufficiently comfortable to volunteer to share. And the guards, when they arrived, would take turns sleeping just inside the doorway and finding an observation spot outside.

By early evening they had all arrived and exchanged stories. The feeling in the apartment was like that of being on safari or part of a *Boys' Own* adventure. If there *was* a group dedicated to protecting Stalin's monsters, and its members were trying to stop them reaching Hasek, then Maxim had ensured that they had done as much as was humanly possible to protect themselves. Except for the overblown resources of the CIA, there was almost nothing else that could be done. The following day Josephine and the guards would arrive, so she could create all-new identities for them, enabling them to go out into the field with a sense of purpose and dedication.

By evening Josh was desperate to get out of the apartment. He had been in Prague several times before and loved the electricity of the city. He asked Maxim whether he should risk the exposure. It put him in an unusual position: for most of his working life these days, Josh had almost total control over people's lives in Hollywood; he never needed to ask anybody's permission to do anything. Yet now he was asking his new father-figure if he could go out for a walk. A week ago he would have ridiculed anybody who had tried to tell him this was the way it would be.

'I think it would be a very bad idea, Joshua. The less we go out, the less chance there is of our being spotted.'

'But we can't hole up in an apartment for days on end. We'll all go crazy. I agree about the need for security. Totally. But Prague's a big city; the chances of our accidentally being seen are one in a million.'

'Are you willing to take the risk?' asked Maxim.

He thought for a moment. 'Yes, frankly, I am. It's not a real risk. Sure, the airport was dangerous, that I agree with. That was a natural place for us to be. But the more you think about it, the more this group has to be in hiding itself. They've been underground for forty years. They can't suddenly come out onto the streets in the middle of Prague . . .'

'Josh, that's not how it works. This group has unknown resources. We have no idea what sort of people they can call on. They might have half the police in Prague carrying your photographs. If you want to go out, then go up onto the roof. Many Prague apartment blocks have rooftops where you can stand and look out over the city. Take up a book and a candle, and relax. It's what people in Prague did before the age of television.'

Maxim looked at the young man in sympathy, but his face gave no sign that he was willing to bend. Not when lives were at stake. Despite who Joshua Krantz was in America, Maxim was in charge in Prague.

Josh said to Sarah, 'Do you fancy coming onto the roof with me?'

She looked at Maxim, who shrugged his indifference. She smiled and nodded. Since their talk on the lawn that first day at Romberk Castle when Josh had told her that he knew she hadn't slept in her bed the previous night, he had been nothing more than courteous. The pleasant personal relationship which had been blossoming since they were thrown together seemed suddenly to have evaporated.

On the roof, they searched the lights of the city immediately below them and managed to identify Revolucni Street. From there, they were able to follow the geography of the city, knowing that to its south was Republic Square. They were quiet as they stood and admired the beauty of the city. In the distance was the old castle. From their height, it looked to be at their level. Its imperious walls overlooked everything.

Sarah stood close to Josh physically, but had never felt further from him. She knew their relationship had changed forever. It saddened her, because she was the catalyst. 'Josh, do you want me to answer your question? The one you asked me the day we arrived at the castle.' She wondered whether he'd know what she was talking about, whether it was in the forefront of his mind, as it was in hers. By his response, she knew immediately that it was.

'Hey,' he said, 'it's none of my business. I have no claims on you. We're nothing more than friends. Period.'

'But I've hurt you. It was the last thing I wanted to do.'

'That's okay,' he said, shrugging his shoulders. He sounded so indifferent that she was hurt. She'd hoped for his indignation, his censorship, even sarcasm — something she could defend herself against. But apathy? How can one fight apathy?

She threaded her arm through his and felt the warmth of his body. There were so many things she wanted to say to him, so many thoughts she wanted to share, but he was closed off to her now. No longer available as a shoulder to cry on. She peered through the jungle of buildings to the open space of the Staromestske Namesti below, the old town square towards which almost all visitors to Prague gravitated. The brightly coloured houses around the square presented baroque facades but the buildings were much older than they looked, many dating back to the Middle Ages. The square was brilliantly lit on all sides, and was noisy with the sounds of café talk, tourists and bells ringing the hour in the multitude of churches around Prague.

The Old Town Square was where all roads in Bohemia ultimately led and where merchants from all over Europe gathered to ply their trade. To their left was the fifteenth-century astrological clock which every hour produced a spectacular puppet show as the clock's figures danced to the same tune every hour of the day and night. On the other side of the square, garishly lit by a floodlight, was the wonderfully Gothic Tyn Church, looking spiritual and ethereal, light and white. Tourists called it a wedding cake. Try as she might, Sarah couldn't think of a more apt description. And close by, they managed to catch a glimpse of the colossal monument to Jan Hus, a symbol of Czech nationalism on which was written Hus's most famous dictum: 'Truth prevails'.

A sudden increase in the noise of traffic far below forced Sarah to raise her voice as she turned to Josh. 'We have to talk,' she said. 'There's a distance between us that I want to close. You disapprove of something I've done. Okay, let's talk it through. You've been avoiding the subject but we can't any more. Not if we're going to work together.'

'I don't disapprove, Sarah. I have no rights in the matter.'

'Please don't treat me like I'm some stranger. We're friends. Good friends. I value you as a friend.'

'Why? You made it damned clear from the beginning that all you wanted was a client–lawyer relationship. I was the one who pushed it too far. You were the one who put me in my place. You've got what you want. What's your problem?'

'But I told you in Slovakia how fond I am of you, Josh. I said you were more than a client. You were then, you are now. And I hope you always will be.'

He shrugged. 'We all make choices, Sarah. You've made yours.'

'Josh, you're sounding a bit like a spoilt schoolboy who didn't get his way. When you suddenly came into my life, the last thing I was looking for was a relationship. That's what you were offering. I want you to be my friend, not my lover.'

'Is that what you said to Laco?'

She bridled. The truth hurt. There was no way of avoiding the issue. Quietly, she told him, 'No. I wanted him for my lover, not my friend.'

Sarah felt his body wince. This was the nub of the problem. It was exposed, raw. It had to be faced.

'Josh, I've had a few lovers in my time. So have you. How many of them have you retained as a friend? How many would you seek out for their comfort, their counsel? Laco is gauche, childlike, fun, silly – none of the things I'd ever look at twice in New York. He's a temporary diversion, someone who's opened up a new side of me, something which I'd buried. And which I'll rebury when I get back to solid ground. I've slept with him twice. I won't be sleeping with him any more. I won't give him a second thought. He's passed his use-by date for me. Been there, done that.'

Josh shifted uncomfortably. If this was a movie, he'd know how to direct the scene; but he was one of the players and he didn't know what was coming next.

'But you! You're a very different matter. I want to be with you. I value our relationship.'

'Sarah,' he said, holding up his hand, 'some heavy stuff's going down right now. We're both at the end of our tethers. Frankly, this isn't a particularly good time to talk about it.'

'I think it is, Josh. I think we have to resolve it.'

'Resolve what?' he asked. 'There's a great guy you're going to marry in New York. You've got everything you want. Where's the issue?'

'The issue is that I've hurt you. You're anything but a fool. I know you're hurt because I've been with Laco. There's an anger that wasn't there before. A disapproval. I've hurt you. It was the last thing I ever wanted to do.'

He laughed, and reflected for a moment before answering. 'Do you know how different it is for me to be hurt? This might sound incredibly crass and arrogant to you, Sarah, but for years women in the States have been throwing themselves at me just to get a part in one of my movies. After a couple of decades, you get pretty fed up with it. The last thing you want is just another screw, even if the girl is drop-dead gorgeous. All you want is a relationship. Told you it would sound crass,' he said, seeing her disapproval. 'But you gotta remember that nobody dares say no to the great Josh Krantz for fear that I could fuck up their career forever. How do you think that makes me feel, Sarah? Big? Tall? Powerful? Godlike?'

She remained silent. He felt her body loosen, just a fraction. 'It makes me feel small and weak and trivial. And that's the truth. Why should I wield such power, just because I make fucking films? That's why I found you so attractive. You're not Hollywood. It's actually refreshing to be hurt. It brings me back to the real world. Does that sound odd?'

She squeezed his hand. 'No, it doesn't. It's part of the growing process.'

'Now you're patronising me,' he told her.

'I'm sorry.'

She looked at him. He really was a very attractive man. She could understand why so many women fell for him. 'Another time, another place, Josh, and I would have fallen for you big time. Marriage. Kids. The whole works.'

'It's refreshing to hear that I haven't lost the rattle when I walk,' he told her.

She felt relaxed and comfortable. She thought about David, so far away, and pondered what he would think if he heard her talking like this, discussing things in a way which had never been a part of her language or thought processes in the whole time since the day they'd met. And she thought of Laco, who didn't give a damn about thoughts and feelings, but was a magnet for those instincts within her which she'd been forced to bury since the day she'd discussed them with her mother just before she'd gone out on her first date. And then she looked at the tourists wandering carefree in the vast expanse of the Old Town Square, and up to the eternal battlement towers of the Tyn Church, which had overlooked for centuries the failings and foibles of the multitudes who passed below its ancient embrace; and she realised that in the vastness of time, her peccadillos were of very little consequence.

The following day, Maxim and Laco spent much of their time on the telephone calling in favours, reminding people of their existence, asking questions. The American contingent read newspapers, drank coffee, watched television and hung around.

The event of the day was the arrival of a tourist minibus outside the front door. Josh, looking down from his fifth-floor bedroom, was concerned about who owned the vehicle and why it was suddenly parked outside their apartment. He was about to warn the others when the moment of concern gave way to feelings of profound relief: Josephine stepped out of the back and carefully tidied her clothes. Josh opened his window in time to hear her saying in the high-pitched fury of a disgruntled Californian to her uncomprehending Slovakian driver, 'For God's sake, haven't you people ever heard of springs? Do you know how rough it is in the back of one of these things? Jesus H. Christ, you should try it one day instead of just standing there smiling!'

She walked upstairs like a princess arriving at a reception, leaving the others to collect the considerable equipment from the back of the van and haul it into the lift. When she had kissed everyone in sight, Josephine waltzed into the lounge room and announced, 'Thank God you didn't drive, darlings. You'd be sitting on piles instead of assholes. One minute we were doing marvellously. We stayed at the sweetest little inn somewhere around Brno, however you pronounce it. Absolutely gorgeous, fourteenth century, though I think it could do with a bit of a make-over. Bed was a bit soft and the furnishings looked like they'd come from a charity warehouse. Anyway, we stayed at this sweet little place and were having a marvellous time. I felt quite the madame. And then, at some hideous little stopover place called Pruhonice or something, we get rid of our beautiful limousine with real leather seats and hire that heap of crap parked out front. I mean, what are these guys into, for God's sake, sado-masochism? I've heard of security measures, but no matter what the danger, you still have to arrive in style, don't you?'

Maxim, the only one who had refused to kiss her, solemnly shook hands with Josephine and congratulated her on the brilliant make-over job for their arrival into Prague, which appeared to have fooled everybody.

'What did you expect, honey-bun? Even your mother would have the hots for you when Josephine gets to work. Anyway, I've been thinking of how I can send you lovely people out tomorrow. I've got plans for each and every one of you now I know you better. You should see what I have in store for you, Laco.'

She walked over and dug Laco playfully in the stomach, knowing it would irritate him. Laco's suppressed homophobia was on the verge of being unveiled to the group. Sarah bit her tongue to stop herself from laughing.

'Anyway, where's Josephine going to sleep? I've had a long journey and I'm really tired and I need to recharge my batteries. So, where's my bedroom?'

Maxim bowed deferentially and pointed towards one of the corridors. As she walked out, she turned and said, 'And who am I going to be sleeping with? Sarah, I suppose. The only one who thinks she's totally safe. But what happens if all this gay stuff is just a cover-up, honey?' She gave a malicious wink, then made a theatrical exit by turning, kicking up her heels and disappearing.

Laco was fuming. Josh walked over and said quietly into his ear, 'He means no harm. He knows that you have a problem with gays and he's making fun of you. Just forget it.'

'I have no problem with gays,' said Laco. 'Just with him.'

'No, Laco,' said Josh. 'You have a problem with gays.'

He walked away into the kitchen. Laco had to admit that Josh was right. Homosexuality was still a taboo subject in Eastern Europe, and he did have a problem with gays. In the closed confines of the apartment, it was his problem to deal with.

The following morning, Sarah was transformed into a dumpy American college student with acne scars on her neck and chin. Her puffy eyes and the red veins on her nose showed she experimented with cocaine, and her nicotine-stained hands and yellow teeth showed she was a heavy cigarette smoker. Josh became a middle-aged American student from the mid-West, with brown hair streaked with grey, cut short back and sides but slightly long at the front and on the crown. Laco was dressed as a Spaniard, hair jet black and parted just to the left of the middle, olive, swarthy skin, blackest of black eyebrows and teeth punishingly white. His overweight stomach was carefully hidden by an oversized cotton shirt. When he saw himself in the mirror for the first time, he was amazed at Josephine's skill. An 'Olé!' slipped from his lips out of respect for the way his entire persona had changed at the behest of her talented hands.

Laco and Sarah's task was to approach the post office for information. Their story had been carefully constructed. Sarah was an American student who had fallen in love with Laco when he lived in Oregon and had come to visit him in Prague many years after their initial affair. Prague was where her family had originated before they moved to the States, and she was now trying to trace her grandfather, whose last known address was a box at the post office. They already knew who to ask for at the post office. One of Maxim's friends had done the groundwork and identified a clerk in the records division who would be willing to open the older ledgers for a consideration.

Given the all-clear by the security guards on the street, Sarah and Laco emerged from the apartment building: an acned, dumpy and somewhat unattractive American student accompanied by her Spanish-looking Czech lover. They set off to the Stare Mesto district in Central Prague.

Josh and Maxim headed for the castle, where they hoped to be able to search the records to find out if Maxim knew anyone who had been in power at the time when Hasek was controlling south-eastern Slovakia.

Laco and Sarah walked to the nearest tram station and stood in the line of morning commuters. People were reading newspapers or talking to friends and the streets were crowded with city workers. Even so, Sarah felt a sense of unease. 'I feel incredibly conspicuous,' she whispered in Laco's ear.

He gave a look, indicating that she should remain silent. He didn't want their conversation to be overheard.

'It's better we talk quietly, like lovers whispering into each other's ears,' she said. 'Lovers talk, they don't just stand there staring into the distance.'

He thought for a moment, then nodded.

She whispered again, 'This thing is so like Mata Hari, I feel like I should have a rose between my teeth. God, it's hot under this make-up. How do actors survive a full day on a set?'

He put his arm around her and kissed her on the cheek. It surprised her. 'Like you said, it's what lovers do. Anyway, it's my Spanish blood. I can't keep away from you.'

Laco looked surreptitiously at the people standing nearby. Nobody in the queue seemed to notice them, or if they did they paid no attention.

'Something's been bothering me, ever since we left Kosice. I was thinking about it last night,' Sarah said. 'How come Vera has still got all the letters she sent to Hasek? It never occurred to me when we first found them, but surely she wouldn't have kept a copy of what she sent off to him?'

'That didn't occur to us either until we began to read them. The answer is in the very last letter she sent. What happened was that she sent each letter off to the address at the post office every month for years, and then, just before the last one, the whole bundle was returned to her by Alexander with a huge cheque. He must have phoned her or communicated in some other way, because we never found a letter from him, and she would undoubtedly have kept such a letter. We think that he told her he was moving away from Prague and there could be no further correspondence between them. He wanted all of his letters returned. If she did this, he would give her a huge final payment — a payment that would last her the rest of her life. Presumably she bundled them all up and sent them off to him.

'It was her last letter that gave us the clue; it was different from all the others. In all her other correspondence, she was fawning and obsequious. Then she got this threatening letter from him — offering money for the letters he'd sent her — and next thing she knows, all her correspondence is sent back, neatly bundled, with a large cheque and obviously an instruction telling her to piss off and not bother him again. So the very last letter she writes to him is totally different. It's a letter of anger, complaint and insult. A letter from a woman spurned. She's heartbroken and furious at the same time. A dangerous combination. And the worst thing is that he sends that letter back too. Throwing his contempt in her face.'

'Surely it would have been more logical for him to burn them. If he was closing off that period of his life, why did he take the risk and send them back to her?' Sarah asked.

Laco shrugged. 'Who knows? Until we find him, nobody can answer that for sure. But think about it. Is it really so odd? They were lovers since both of them were little more than children. He must have felt a great deal for her. Maybe he couldn't destroy the one person that kept the bond between him and a past life. Maybe she was a lifeline.'

Sarah smiled at the simple humanness of the situation, and could identify with it. 'But that still doesn't explain why Alexander would have sent back her mail. You'd think, with all the precautions he'd taken, that he would have destroyed it all. He was using a post office box so nobody could trace him and yet he sends back the one thing that we've used to start us on the trail to find him.'

Laco nodded. 'Father and I discussed that. I think it goes something like this. In 1953, Stalin dies and Hasek knows the game is up and the good times are over. He knows there's a good chance of retribution from the areas he's ruled. So he escapes to Moscow. Then he notices that the temperature for Stalinist apparatchiks is getting colder and colder by the day. He works out, not unreasonably, that Khrushchev's henchmen are going to come looking for him. So he contacts, or is contacted by, this secret group of men, dedicated to hiding Stalinists. They give him a new identity. They give him money. These allow him to escape. In 1956 or '57 he disappears and he leaves the Soviet Union. Maybe he goes straight to Prague. Maybe he goes to Hungary, the Ukraine.' Laco shrugged his shoulders. 'I don't know. But at some stage after that, probably around 1964 or '65, which is when Vera's letters began, he comes to Prague. It's been ten years since he was operative. He might have a new face or have grown a beard but mainly he's feeling secure, safe. He's got money. He's got a new career or profession. And he's got powerful friends who will ensure that anybody who tries to trace him is eliminated. He's confident. He feels infallible.' Sarah nodded. It was all beginning to fit together.

Laco continued, 'But when you're cut off from your past, there's a strong yearning for the security that it gives. And so he sends a private secret message to Vera. He tells her to be absolutely confidential, not to make waves, not to say a word to anyone in the village, but asks her to write to him and tell him how she is. To tell him what's happening in the village. Maybe even to keep her ear to the ground and find out if anybody is still talking about him. We know that's the tone of his inquiry by the very first couple of letters she writes, promising him to keep his secret and to tell him if people are asking questions. And then he begins to send her postal orders. Money which she desperately needs to keep her going. Maybe he feels guilty about her, I don't know. Maybe they've had a child together. Who can say? Anyway, this situation goes on from 1963 or '64 until 1983. I don't know whether he ever went to see her. Her letters certainly don't say that she had any contact with him, but then in 1983 all her letters come back plus a lot of money. It's like he's spurning her. And so her last letter is furious. It's like hell has no fury. She says the money he's sent her is hers by right, that she'll send him back the letters he's sent to her, but that's not the end of it. She's his woman. She has rights. She threatens to come and look for him no matter where he goes. She tells him that she will always love him, that she's never touched another man. It's pathetic, really.'

'I still don't understand,' whispered Sarah. 'That doesn't explain why he'd take such an enormous risk in sending back the letters.'

'To you, it's an enormous risk; to him, it had a different importance. I guess he thought that after thirty years, nobody would care any more. Nobody would bother. He didn't count on you and Josh . . . and my father.'

She squeezed his arm tightly. 'Don't leave yourself out of the equation, Laco. Without you, we wouldn't have got this far.'

The tram arrived. He realised that she hadn't heard what he'd said in response. He was glad. He had whispered that, without his involvement, a beautiful young student called Marta would still be alive.

They boarded the tram and sat in a seat towards the back. The smell of perspiration and unwashed clothes wafted towards Sarah. Prague people didn't wash their clothes nearly as often as Americans did, and the stench was overwhelming and offensive. Had this been the perfume of all cities before dry-cleaning came along? She glanced down at people's shoes and noticed for the first time that they were uniformly dirty. She smiled. Josephine was right. Funny how somebody as observant as Josephine could make a simple, yet eloquent statement about her society that Sarah's normal powers of observation hadn't encompassed. She now realised that Americans' fetish with clean shoes was a fashion statement; Prague people just used shoes to get from place to place.

They trundled in the tram to within one hundred metres of the post office in the Stare Mesto district. Alighting, they walked over to the gateway of a house where they stood, appearing to speak in earnest conversation. Laco looked up the road. Sarah looked down. When they were quite sure that no car had followed them, they walked arm in arm into the post office. Apart from the signs written in Czech, it looked like any post office in small town America. There was a musty smell of old letters, year-old posters on the wall, a ceiling fan stirring the air in desultory, asthmatic sweeps, cages behind which post office clerks dealt stamps like croupiers in return for crowns proffered by punters.

They stood in the queue and waited their turn. The middle-aged woman behind the counter looked at them and said peremptorily, 'Yes?'

Laco said, 'We were told to ask for Vaclav. Could we speak to him, please?'

The woman frowned. In a routine day of selling stamps, money orders and licences for everything from dogs to television sets, questions about staff were enough to interest her numbed mind. She turned to look for Vaclav, who was sitting at a desk in a far corner behind her. She called him, then nodded towards the gate at the far end of the counter. Sarah and Laco arrived there at the same time as Vaclav, a balding, middled-aged archetype of a post office functionary, the sort of administrator without whom the slow-grinding wheels of the organisation would not have turned. He looked suspiciously at the Mediterranean-looking man and the plain, young female tourist.

'Yes?' he said.

'Vaclav, we were told by Wladislaw Neumann that we could talk to you about this young woman's grandfather.'

Laco kept his voice low so that his question could not be overheard by the woman clerk, who was glancing suspiciously in their direction. Vaclav shook his head. 'Excuse me? I know nothing about this. Who are you?'

'Perhaps we can talk inside your office, or maybe we could go outside for a cup of coffee.'

'Tell me who you are,' he said suspiciously. 'I know nothing about this Wladislaw Neumann. I am busy. Tell me what you want.'

Laco leaned closer and whispered, 'A man called Neumann approached you a few days ago and asked if we could have a look inside your records. You said that we could, for a small consideration.'

Vaclav suddenly remembered the unusual conversation with the researcher from the University. His eyes shot over to the clerk, and then he beamed a smile and threw his arms around Sarah, surprising her by kissing her on the cheek. He pumped Laco's hand as he turned to the woman clerk, saying, 'My cousin's daughter from America! I've never met her before. Come in. Come in, children.'

The woman clerk smiled a greeting, lost interest and turned back to her customers. They followed Vaclav to his desk, where he said urgently, 'This could get me fired. We must all be very careful. A man approached me three nights ago as I was leaving the post office. He told me somebody needed to do honest research into our records for some degree he's taking. And that he would pay me two hundred American dollars just to look at old records. My wife needs an operation . . . and the stuff's so old, who gives a damn any more.' Laco translated softly into Sarah's ear.

Vaclav bent down and took an envelope out of a drawer which he put on the edge of the desk, being careful to open the lip in her direction. 'Don't do anything until nobody is looking. When I tell you to, put the money in here. Don't move until I tell you or you'll be seen.'

He raised his voice again and asked Laco in Czech, 'So how is our cousin? Tell me all about New York. One day I am going there myself.'

It was all too theatrical. Laco began to talk about the joys of Central Park and New York City, but Vaclav simply wasn't listening. He was watching the backs of the heads of the clerks who were dealing with customers. When he was absolutely certain that they weren't being observed, he nodded to Sarah, who took the pre-arranged two hundred dollars and slipped it into the envelope. Vaclav's hand shot out and the envelope disappeared back into his desk drawer as quickly as a snake strikes at a bird.

'Now,' he whispered, 'who is it you want to find out about?'

'There's a man called Alexander Hasek who rented a post office box here up until 1983,' whispered Laco. 'We need to know his address.'

'1983,' said Vaclav. 'Those records are in a ledger in the back room.' He stood, telling them loudly that he was going to get his cousin's last letter from his locker, and left them sitting alone at his desk, feeling vulnerable.

A few moments later, he returned with a large ledger. He opened it. 'What was the box number?' he whispered.

'One hundred and eight.'

Vaclav flicked the pages until he came to the box number. 'Who did you say owned it?' he asked.

'A man called Alexander Hasek.'

Vaclav shook his head. 'No, that's not correct.'

'He could have been using a different name,' said Laco.

'It's not a he. It's a she.'

'What?' said Sarah, as Laco translated. The woman at the counter looked around. There were perspiration beads on Vaclav's forehead. The sooner this was over the better. Vaclav scribbled a name on a piece of paper and pushed it across the top of his desk. Laco looked at it and shook his head. 'I don't understand.'

'This is the name of the woman who owned post office box 108 in 1983.' He flipped back a page, 'And 1982 and 1981.' He flipped back several more pages. 'She took it out in 1977.'

'Who owns it now?' asked Laco.

'After 1983 it changed hands and became the box for Dr Feodor Lipzin, a lawyer.'

'What date did he take over the box?'

Vaclav told him. It coincided with the date of the last letter Vera had written. Laco thanked the clerk and they stood. Sarah moved around the desk and kissed him on the cheek, saying in stilted slow English so that all could hear, 'I will tell mother all about what you look like. She will be so excited.'

Leaving the post office, Laco and Sarah ambled slowly up the road arm in arm, anxious to discuss their findings but knowing that it would be preferable to remain silent. When they were sure nobody was following, Laco took out the piece of paper.

'Olga Polemska,' he said. 'Who the hell is Olga Polemska?'

Back at the apartment they looked up the name Polemska in the phone book. This time it was agreed that Maxim and Sarah should go to see her. There were seven Polemskas in the book, but only two who lived within a reasonable distance of the post office. They phoned one and a recorded message of a gravel-voiced man told them: 'This is Oskar Polemska. I am not at home, so leave a message and I'll get back to you.'

They phoned the other. A man answered. 'I wonder if I could speak to Olga Polemska, please?' Maxim asked.

There was a long moment of strained silence. Then, softly, the man said, 'I am sorry. Olga is no longer with us. She was my grandmother. She was knocked down by a car and killed two days ago. Were you a friend?'

'No, no,' said Maxim, shocked. 'It was a business matter. Please forgive my intrusion.'

He put the phone down. Everyone was looking at him in surprise. 'I am afraid our friends have got to Olga Polemska before we were able to. She was killed two days ago.'

Sarah sat down heavily on a chair, in a state of shock. A feeling of torpor settled on the room, until Sarah said, 'We're going to the police. We have to. Enough people have died. That's it!'

Maxim shook his head. 'For all of the reasons which you know, I am afraid that going to the police is the one course of action not open to us. Who do we talk to? And about what? How do we know that it is safe? I am afraid our only course of action is to find Hasek, and to do that we must go to the Polemska house to try to find what connection she had with him.'

'But why can't we bring in the authorities, for God's sake?' Sarah shouted. 'This isn't the day of Stalin. The Czech Republic is an open government. The Czech President isn't a communist. This is a group acting outside the law, killing people. They're criminals, for God's sake, not political ideologues. We're not equipped to handle this sort of crime. You two are archaeologists, he's a film maker, they're technicians and I'm a lawyer. What the hell do we know about this sort of villainy?'

Maxim calmed her down in his gentle and self-effacing way, reminding her that the problem wasn't with the Czech President but with whomever it was within the government or law enforcement authorities that was supporting this covert group. 'They could not be acting without some form of inside help,' he told her.

'They have obviously worked out in advance what they think we will do, and are now pre-empting our movements. This is not a bunch of old men sitting together and talking about the good old days; this is a vicious and evil cabal which is either paying men who are currently in the security or police forces to protect them, or still has enough contacts in government to ensure its work is done. If this network exists, it could be all over Europe – Russia, Hungary, Latvia, here. Who knows?' He shrugged his shoulders. 'The point is that we are in a strong position to expose it. But if you are worried about the risks to you, then I fully support any decision you might make to leave and go back to America. But nothing is going to stop me and my son from exposing these people for what they have done and what they are still doing.'

'I also think you might have forgotten that they're not just killing other people,' said Laco, 'but they tried to kill me. They know me, where I work, who I associate with, what I look like. They're not going to stop trying to kill me after one failed attempt. My only way to save myself is by exposing them. It's a problem which my father lived with throughout much of his life when he worked for the Resistance and then as part of the liberalising forces in this country. I thought since the downfall of communism that I was safe.' He shrugged his shoulders. 'I'm not. I have to do something about it.'

Sarah looked at Josh, who told her gently, 'These bastards have got to be shown up for what they are. Pure and simple. But you're not involved in this. You're a lawyer. You're here on a job. You just return home and nobody will think anything about it.'

She looked around the group. Everybody was staring at her. She felt isolated. 'What about Phil and Jerry?' she asked.

'Hey, man,' said Phil, holding up his hands, 'we're not walking out on this gig. We talked last night. We want to stay to see the action.'

Sarah shook her head. 'I'm not saying I should go back to America. I don't want to walk out. But we're just not equipped to handle this. There must be somebody in authority we can trust. It's up to the authorities, the police, the government, to expose these people. Maybe even the media. Maybe we should call in the newspapers or television like we do in America.'

Maxim laughed. 'No matter where you go, my dear, who can you go to that you trust? Sarah, you keep on saying that we are on our own but you do not realise how many people are working in the background on this. People that you don't know exist. Men and women whom I have known for decades and whom I trust, and who trust me, implicitly. People who are academics in universities, or former government officials who still have access to records, people in Moscow whom I worked with while I was involved in the administration in this country, people in Prague. People everywhere. You would be amazed at what is going on in the background.'

'But it still comes down to us taking all the risks, Maxim.'

He nodded. The oppressive silence was compulsive.

'Alright,' she said softly. 'Maxim and I will go and see this family. We'll take it another stage further. But let's pray to God that there are no more deaths as a result of what we're doing.'

The following day, in fresh make-up and disguise, they knocked on the door of Olga Polemska's house. The windows were closed. The front door was draped in black; a wreath adorned the door handle. The house itself seemed to be mourning the death of its owner. Maxim was dressed in a style much older than his years and had been transformed by Josephine into a bent and elderly man, someone who might have been part of the late Olga's society, a colleague or intimate. Sarah was dressed as his granddaughter.

The door was opened by a middle-aged woman dressed in black, who looked questioningly at Maxim and Sarah. Maxim bowed and said in a low and gravelly voice, 'Please forgive me for intruding on you at this time of tragedy for your family, but I have come to pay my respects.'

As is the way in a house of mourning, the door was opened wide. They walked inside. The house smelled as though it was unoccupied, and was hot from the windows being shut in the summer heat. The woman showed them into the fussy front room which was obviously reserved for special occasions. Unusually, Olga Polemska lived in a house. Most of those who lived close to the centre of Prague lived in apartment blocks. Sarah and Maxim sat and sank deeply into the large, understuffed armchairs allocated to them.

'You knew my mother?' asked the woman.

Maxim shook his head. 'Regretfully, not personally, but I am from the Society for the Care of the Aged. My granddaughter here is from America. She is setting up a similar society over there. It is our job to visit the homes of the elderly to ensure that they are secure in their retirement. Did your mother not mention our conversations over the phone?'

The woman shook her head. 'She said nothing, but then she was forgetful. You knew she had Alzheimer's?'

'Of course,' said Maxim. 'It was a tragedy. She was so vibrant in her younger years.'

The lady nodded vigorously. 'She was amazing. All those years working and still she brought up four children. And a widow for thirty years as well. She was a remarkable woman.' She picked up a handkerchief and dabbed her eyes.

'It is very hard to come to terms with a death as tragic as this,' said Maxim. 'Did they ever find the man who was driving the car?'

'No,' she said. 'The police think he may have been a drunk. He swerved on the pavement as she was standing there. She should never have gone out. Sometimes, I had to come over here to find her. She couldn't even find her way home any more. She was in the way of the car when it mounted the pavement. The driver just drove off. They found the car. It was abandoned. The owner had reported it stolen that morning. We have no idea who killed my mother.' She sobbed bitterly into her handkerchief.

'But in one way,' said Maxim comfortingly, 'her death was swift and merciful. The Alzheimer's would have reduced her to a fraction of what she used to be as a younger woman.' The woman nodded silently.

'Where did your mother work?'

'At the Charles University.'

'Ah,' he said, nodding. 'She never told us. She kept that side of her life very quiet.'

'I don't understand why. She was very proud of her work.'

'She taught there?' Maxim asked.

'No,' the daughter said, 'she started off as a secretary and then she became the department administrator. Nothing happened in the department without her knowledge. Nothing at all. She organised examinations, visiting lecturers, the pay of all the professors, conferences. There was nothing my mother didn't organise. She could still be doing the job if it wasn't for the Alzheimer's.'

'Tragic,' said Maxim. 'Which department did she work in?'

'The Department of Ancient History and Archaeology,' the daughter said.

Sarah hadn't understood a word of the conversation, and was shocked when Maxim's elderly face drained of blood and he seemed to sink further back into his chair.

'An archaeologist?'

'Who knows?' said Maxim. 'All we know is that she was the administrator of the Department of Archaeology at Charles University.'

'And Hasek was a member of the department? An archaeologist?' Laco said in shock.

'We don't know,' repeated Maxim. 'All we know is that a woman called Olga Polemska who was the administrative assistant in the Department of Archaeology had a post office box to which Vera regularly sent letters. That is all we know. Start to finish.'

'But who would she have been collecting letters for,' said Josh, 'if not Alexander Hasek? She must have known him.'

'Which is why she is dead,' Maxim commented.

'But the trail doesn't end there,' Sarah interrupted. 'We have to assume she knew him. It's also fair to assume that she probably didn't know anything about his background. From the type of woman her daughter described – deeply religious, passionate about Czech nationalism, part of the crowd who cheered on Dubcek in 1968 – from all of these things she would be the last person you'd expect to hide a mass murderer.'

'So if she's dead, how do we get to the truth?' asked Josh.

'Through the university. We find out who she worked for. Who she associated with. I mean, think about it,' said Maxim, 'she was collecting letters month by month for someone. You would only do that for your boss, wouldn't you? Our next stage is to go to the Archaeology Department. Fortunately I know a lot of people there. It was never my university but I have many friends who either used to work there or who still do. As do you,' he said to Laco.

'Of course,' said the younger man. 'I regularly correspond with four or five people there about the work I'm doing in Slovakia. I know these people, I've worked with them for years, I've attended conferences with them. Not one of them would hide a Stalinist. Not one.'

'How do you know that?' said Josh. 'How do you know who's on the payroll?'

'Josh,' shouted Laco, 'I know these people! You can't work with people all your life and not know them.'

Silence dominated the room again. Despite his vehemence, nobody truly believed what he said.

# CHAPTER
# SEVENTEEN

Boris Maximovich Tranov massaged his aching groin. He seemed to be putting on more and more weight these day and his trousers were no longer as comfortable as they had been. In fact, they were hell. They were cutting into his crotch and making his balls throb. Christ! He'd have to go to the tailor soon or his ears would be ringing.

But then, wasn't that the case with everything in his life. Just when other men his age were able to sit back and reflect on a long and satisfying life, his was full of traumas and uncertainties. How many years did he still have to live? Five, ten at the most. What the hell! He thought back to a book he'd been reading in bed the previous night. Something about an Englishman, Thomas Hobbes. Dry old bastard. But one thing he'd said was true: the life of man was solitary, poor, nasty, brutish and short. Now, there was a man he would have enjoyed spending an evening with. What a miserable old piece of dog turd. Stalin would have loved him.

Tranov had been musing for some years now about life and death. His mortality was becoming increasingly apparent with the rising frequency of the death of his peers. People whom he had gone to school with, joined the Komsomol with, had become leaders in the Stalin hierarchy and the Communist Party with, had worked with as administrators all across Stalin's empire, and enjoyed their company in diplomatic circles around the world. But, nowadays, all he seemed to hear were reports of their deaths. '*We come to mourn the death of . . .*' All the while. Death, death, death. Who would mourn his death, he wondered?

His wife had been dead these twenty years. Mind you, her death had been a release. A young woman when he had married her, she had turned into a harridan, demanding and scurrilous. She had cost him at least one promotion by being undiplomatic at a Kremlin reception. After her death, he'd gone wild, screwing everything in sight. He'd even managed to be suspended from the embassy by his boss in Damascus for screwing the wife of the English ambassador. If he'd screwed the Ambassador, he'd have earned the Order of Lenin, but the wife was one of those frightfully upper-class English women with no tits who deserved to be skewered.

Sex wasn't fun any more. It was too much hard work, too much sweat. These days he had to pay for it, but he felt sorry for the poor bitches who had to work so damn hard to get him up. They certainly earned every crown he paid them. He especially liked the Russian ones. There were a lot of Russian whores in Slovakia these days. They were the ugly ones, of course. The attractive ones were working in Germany or the Middle East. Not that they were proper whores. They were just single women who wanted a life or a husband and who badly needed to earn money, or they were agricultural workers or divorced women. Women were erupting out of Russia by the bucketload and selling the only thing they possessed in order to get money to live on. And why shouldn't he take advantage of them? But he had only done it a few times. It was like screwing his daughter.

His groin really hurt. He walked to the window. God, it was so fucking hot. Was this the hottest summer on record? The sun was merciless as it shone through the French doors of his apartment. He looked at his tomato plants. Shit! They'd grown another two centimetres in girth. He could see it from here, but they tasted like piss to eat. What was the use?

'Are you alright, comrade?' asked Zamov.

Tranov turned around. 'Yes. Just thinking about things.'

'So what's your answer?'

'I'm sorry, comrade, I'm distracted at the moment.'

'Problems?'

'No,' said Tranov. 'No problems. Just . . . it doesn't matter. Ask your question again.'

'I asked you what we should do now that the old woman is dead. What happens now?'

Tranov's mind refocused on the problem. 'Are the police satisfied that it was a hit–and–run accident?'

'Absolutely,' assured Zamov. 'They have no witnesses to the termination, and our man drove away and dumped the car before anybody saw him.'

'Good. So we've broken the nexus between the old woman in Kosice . . .'

'Vera.'

'Yes, her. We've broken the link between her letters, Hasek and the university.'

'Correct,' affirmed Zamov.

'So there is no connection between the old woman in Slovakia and the old woman Olga?'

'None at all,' said Zamov, shaking his head vigorously.

'You are absolutely one hundred per cent certain?'

'On my life, comrade, there is no way they could have traced one woman to the other. They will never find the link. Never.'

'You are sure that this old woman in Slovakia didn't say anything to them?'

'Not a word.'

'She didn't mention the past, or that she knew Hasek?'

'Not a thing. She was so frightened she pissed herself. My guys found out everything from her. She admitted that she was visited by them, but she swears she told them that she didn't know anything about Hasek. She told them she had never heard of him. She sent them away empty-handed.'

Boris Maximovich Tranov looked at his old comrade, his eyes narrowed in fury and disgust. 'You're such a fucking idiot, Zamov! How ever did you get to be a colonel-general, you piece of horse shit? You stupid imbecile.'

Zamov struggled out of the chair and shouted, 'How dare you!'

Viciously, Tranov spat, 'And how dare you endanger the lives of all of our comrades by your sloppy stupidity and by the people that you employ. So the old woman Vera told them nothing, eh?'

Zamov shook his head in anger. 'Nothing. I'm telling you. I debriefed my people . . .'

'Your people,' Tranov interrupted, 'your people couldn't find shit in a dog kennel. I sent one of my men back to see her the day after yours had been. He wasn't quite so polite. It didn't take much to persuade her to tell him everything. Do you know what that sweet little old lady's done? She's only given them a fucking bunch of letters she wrote to Hasek over a twenty-year love affair. You fool! A bunch of letters!'

Zamov's body seemed to drain of energy, his face turned a chalky white. He sat back heavily in his chair. 'Letters?' he said weakly.

'Letters,' shouted Tranov. 'Fucking letters. Letters written by the old woman to Hasek. Letters sent to a box in a post office near the Charles University in Prague. They took them away, Comrade Colonel-General. They've got them in their possession. Our whole Syndicate could be blown sky-fucking-high.'

'But how? I don't understand.' All his previous bluster left him like air leaving a deflating balloon. It was impossible. 'Why would Hasek write letters? He knew the rules.'

'His, thank God, were destroyed. They've got the old woman's. She wrote them to him. She was his lover.'

'Then . . . then how did the Americans know where to go? How does . . . ? If he didn't send her letters . . . I just don't understand, Comrade.'

Tranov towered menacingly over the bent form of his old colleague. 'I'll explain it simply, Nikolai Alexandrovich. In words of one syllable so that your pathetic mind can follow me. Hasek was paying the old woman money. In order to keep it secret and so that we didn't find out about it, he set up a post box in his secretary's name. He used his secretary from the university to collect the letters for him. Do you understand what I'm saying, Comrade Colonel-General, or should I get my housekeeper to explain it to you? The box was in the woman's name. That is why we didn't know anything about it. That is why I had her terminated. It's called *me clearing up your mess*. Your sloppy ways have endangered this whole organisation of ours. The Syndicate could have collapsed if I had listened to you.'

By now Zamov had recovered some of his composure. He was stung by his colleague's words, but security was his responsibility and he had clearly failed. The only way now was to ensure no more slip-ups. 'So where are they? Where are the archaeologists and the Americans?' he asked.

'Probably in Prague by now. I've got men stationed at the airport, but it's been so long since these bastards saw the old woman in Slovakia, my guess is that they have somehow slipped into Prague already. I've got people at the post office, at the university, people looking at the registers in all the hotels, but they could have gone anywhere. We will find them, though. Trust me, we will find them.

'And I'm afraid,' he continued, 'that dear old Alexander Hasek also has to meet with an untimely end. In such a way that his body never reappears. His house has to be stripped of everything that ties him back to us. I no longer trust him. He has forfeited his right to be a member of the Syndicate. In fact, we are so compromised that I might order his termination immediately. He is a liability we don't need. Now, Comrade Colonel-General, may I suggest that you get your old bones over to Prague and direct operations from there. I've put fifteen men at your disposal. I suggest that after the last flight from Kosice or Bratislava into Prague tonight, we pull them out of the airport and assume that our quarry has entered the city by road. I want those people found, Zamov. I don't want any excuses, any apologies, or any more fuck-ups. I just want them found. Do I make myself absolutely clear?'

Zamov swallowed and nodded.

The next two days were frustrating for everybody. It was impossible to go out for a walk without spending an hour being made up by Josephine. And even then, all they could do was to venture to a nearby café for a drink. After learning how Olga Polemska had met her death, it had become obvious that, even if there had been a scintilla of doubt about their existence, the group protecting the Stalinists was no longer a speculation but a horrible reality. With common consent, Maxim had laid down the decree that all future investigations by them must be viewed as life-threatening. There would be no more guessing. Every approach, every decision, had to be considered from the perspective of its danger to the group and to the individual. Maxim had spent much of the previous morning on the telephone, talking at great length to colleagues in Prague, Bratislava and Kosice. When the others asked him what was going on, he used the same expression of denial: 'It is better that I tell you *when* it has happened rather than during the stages of its happening.'

They read books, newspapers, played games of Scrabble and watched an awful lot of television. Neither Josh nor Sarah were permitted to make international telephone calls, not even to assure those in America that they were well. Maxim was concerned that international calls could be traced and that, if the group was as well-resourced and intelligent as he believed, it would already have identified those numbers that Josh and Sarah were likely to ring. With modern telecommunications bugging equipment, it wouldn't be a difficult matter to establish the source of the phone call from Prague and the address from which it was made.

As evening fell on the second day of their incarceration, the security guard in the hall announced that a man was at the elevator gate on the ground floor and had pressed the level for their apartment.

'Is he alone?' Maxim asked. The security guard nodded. 'I think it's a colleague of mine. There's no need to worry.'

The doorbell rang a few moments later. The man who entered the apartment was a short, lean, middle-aged man. He walked over to Maxim and embraced him, kissing him on both cheeks. Maxim introduced him to the group as Richard. No second name to ensure his anonymity.

'Richard and I were colleagues for many years. He is currently in the Archaeology Department at Charles University and has agreed to help us.'

Suspiciously, Laco said, 'How much have you told him?'

Richard held up his hand. 'I know as little as I need to know and I want to know no more. These things are best if they are held tightly to the chest. My old friend Maxim asked me to determine for whom the late Olga Polemska worked between 1977 and 1983. She worked for a lot of people, but only eight of them were permanently attached to the University. Three of them were full professors who held the chair of Archaeology in those years. There was rapid movement at that time. She also worked for five senior lecturers, of whom four attended the University for the entire period. One of them went away on sabbatical in 1981 so I've discounted him. I have made out a list,' he said, taking a piece of paper from his inside pocket. 'And I have put the last known addresses of these people on to the list. Two of them are still at the University, though in the last stages of their working careers. I have highlighted them in blue. The others have either moved to other universities, into professorial chairs, or have retired or gone into other areas of study.'

Maxim took the list and scanned it. He nodded and shook his friend's hand. 'Richard, you have no idea how valuable this is. You are an absolute wonder. Did you take any risks?'

Richard laughed. 'When you investigate the files of others in a university department, people automatically think you are doing so to advance your career. That's university politics for you. Anyway, I am sure the sooner I leave here, the more comfortable you will be.'

He kissed Maxim on both cheeks again and nodded to the others. He moved over to Sarah and kissed her left hand gently. 'Perhaps under other circumstances, madam,' he said.

She was flattered. For days, she had been seen in public wearing a usually unattractive mask. Now she was herself, not wearing any of Josephine's make-up. She blushed at the compliment.

When Richard had left, they examined the list he had given them. Maxim and Laco agreed on a methodology of approaching the academics. But one thing needed to be done before any further progress was made on their quest for Hasek: security. The following morning Maxim left the apartment early in order to organise an increase in the number of security people who were protecting them. The firm he had commissioned in Kosice told him that it was impractical to send more personnel and gave him the name and address of an outfit in Prague. It was a company that specialised in protecting local and visiting businessmen from kidnap and ransom, a growing menace as it became a new source of revenue for the Russian Mafia. The firm, Executive Security, was located in Legerova Street, on the opposite side of the city.

Once Maxim had gone, the atmosphere in the apartment quickly became tense, as it seemed to be doing with increasing frequency. The large group of people, the confined space, the uncompromising and unremitting heat of Prague in the summer – all exacerbated the tensions. Even Phil and Jerry, usually apathetic and laid-back, had become tetchy since arriving in Prague, demanding access to the English-language newspapers, or a different television channel. Sarah, never the most pliant of people, fought at least three times a day with herself to refrain from snapping over some trivial infringement like someone not pulling down the toilet seat, or dishes being left in the sink instead of being washed. She thought they must be the same sorts of tensions that lead to the final break-down of marital relationships on their last legs, and wasn't surprised that the apartment in Prague was infected by the same cancer. After all, they were surrounded by unseen enemies, in personal danger and in a foreign land. Only Laco seemed to be in his element, treating each day as another adventure.

For Sarah, this life was a throwback to her days in college. She had hated dormitory life, hated the constant, cloying, claustrophobic company of others. Not that she was a loner. She enjoyed living with David, but their life together was that of busy people coming together in a relationship of convenience. Despite their love, they lived in a way that allowed both maximum enjoyment. They usually saw each other only in the evening – often the late evening – because he was performing, or she was at a client dinner or a meeting of the Women's Lawyers Group or one of the innumerable campaigns to which she had subscribed her name and talents. Sarah enjoyed her privacy. She enjoyed being intimate with herself, spending time in the bath, or reading on the toilet, or walking naked through her apartment. It was her liberation from the strait-jacketed behaviour expected of her as a lawyer. But in this apartment, living with this strange and intimate contact with six men she barely knew, she had no safety valve. And there seemed no end in sight. It was a prison, and she was anything but a willing inmate.

The nights were terrible, but the mornings were hardly better. And this morning was worse than yesterday. During breakfast they all seemed to miss Maxim's gentle paternal control, his calm authority. Comments were made, opinions expressed, which led to minor misunderstandings and irritated looks. Josh commented on the threatening clouds, saying that maybe a rainstorm would break the heat and humidity. Nobody responded. Sarah, weighed down by the silence, said tersely that if she didn't leave the apartment soon, she'd be a nervous wreck. She had meant to express the opinion of them all but instead it came out as if she was whingeing, a spoilt princess railing against the world. It was Laco's *sotto voce* comment, made to his cereal spoon, which created the explosion.

'You seem to be a wreck already. Why wait?'

She looked at him acidly. 'Excuse me?'

'Nothing.'

'No! You said something about me being a wreck already. What was it you said?'

Josh intervened, 'Sarah, it was nothing.'

She looked at him angrily. 'No! Laco made a remark about me being a nervous wreck. I think I've been pretty calm under the circumstances. Do you think it's pleasant being a woman, locked up in a flat with a bunch of men who don't have the same standards of . . .' She left the remark hanging in the overheated atmosphere.

Phil looked up from his slice of toast. 'Same standards of what, Sarah?'

She remained silent.

'I asked you a question. Y'know, Josh might be willing to take all your lawyer crap, but I don't have to. Shit, woman, you've been a fucking pain in the ass since the minute we got banged up in that castle outside of Kosice. Now I don't mind you insulting me 'cause of my dress or my looks, but I sure as hell mind you insulting my personal cleanliness. It's not my fault we can't get away from each other. Quicker I see the back of you, the better.'

Sarah looked at him in fury. She realised that her face had flushed red, with anger and embarrassment. She looked at Josh, who returned her look in sympathy. Laco wouldn't look at her at all, he just continued to eat his cereal. Jerry obviously supported Phil's remarks, and was wearing a snide grin. But it was Josephine who tipped her over the edge. Her face said that Sarah was being a stupid, insensitive Jewish–American Princess.

Sarah swallowed, dabbed her lips with a serviette and left the table. As she walked towards her room, Josephine, who had been silent throughout the growing drama, commented, 'What she needs is a good fuck.'

It was intended to be heard and to hurt. Josh looked at her in fury. Only Laco and Josephine finished their breakfast. The others had lost their appetites.

Josh followed Sarah to her room, and walked in without knocking. She looked like a little girl who had just been scalded. It surprised him: she was always so self-assured, so much in control, that he'd assumed she'd be full of righteous indignation and bluster. But she was on the verge of tears. He held out his arms. She tried a brave smile, and almost fell against him, feeling his arms enclosing her in their security. Josh held her tightly and felt her body releasing its tensions into his solidity. She didn't sob, she merely put her arms around him and hugged him. He kissed the crown of her head.

'I'm not normally like this,' she whispered. 'I used to get like this before I went on the pill: PMT. It was murder for me and everyone around me. This is different, though. I don't understand what's happening to me. It's as if I'm a different person, reacting to things that I'd happily overlook in real life. In the office, there's this woman, twice divorced, one son a schizophrenic, the other on drugs. She's in constant fear of a phone call from the police telling her either or both are dead. She's always snapping at people for the most trivial reasons, wrong type of envelopes, unreadable handwriting from one of the lawyers, y'know, small-town bullshit that ordinary people would just ignore.'

She looked up at him and asked softly, 'Am I becoming like her?'

Josh kissed her again. 'Yes. But then, so am I, so are Phil and Jerry – we all are. It's the situation. All cooped up together, never knowing which way to move. Just go with it.'

It was nice holding him so close. Comforting. So different from Laco. She'd not been close to anyone since their last days in Kosice. It was how she was with David when she came home from visiting her parents, or when there had been a drama at the office, or, more recently, when she'd come home from a day with Frank Darman, and needed David's strength, his honesty, his warmth, to give her the ability to carry on.

Holding Josh, Sarah realised that she had missed the warmth of a man's body. She reached up and pulled Josh's face down towards hers. She kissed him tenderly. Then passionately. They kissed until they heard a movement outside in the corridor, and separated like miscreant schoolchildren. It was all so innocent. They smiled at each other, co-conspirators in a game of hide and seek. 'Do you think Josephine's right?' she whispered. 'Is my problem as simple as needing a good fuck?'

Josh turned to leave the room. 'The question you have to ask yourself, Sarah, is not what you need but who you need it from.'

Maxim arrived back in the middle of the morning, smiling broadly. 'It's amazing,' he told them. 'Being an archaeologist, I don't move in these circles but the way things are these days it makes you realise how crazy our world is.'

They looked at him, anticipating his explanation.

'You should have seen the place! Huge poster-size photographs on the wall of cars sliding around in some skid pan or other, photographs of men wearing bulletproof vests looking like James Bond, Coca Cola bottles sounding and feeling as if they're full of liquid but actually holding hidden microphones to record conversations, Pepsi Cola cans that are miniature safes, exploding key rings that blow off your hand the minute you put the key into the ignition of a car. I have never seen anything like it. Has the world gone completely mad?'

Josh smiled. 'I guess we're more used to that sort of thing in LA than you are here. But it all sounds pretty much standard equipment for America.'

'It's not the sort of life I want to lead,' growled Maxim, 'but it's a necessity at the moment. Anyway, we have two new security guards in addition to our existing people. They will be staking out the entrance to the roadway. They have also offered other services which I haven't taken up yet, but it is good to know they are there. Services like bugging equipment for phones, long-distance radio microphones and parabolic dishes which pick up and record conversations as far as a mile away. Let's just hope we will not need them.'

He sensed tension in the atmosphere and wondered what had happened while he was absent. He was worried about the confinement of these Americans, who normally treated freedom as a right. Deprivation had never been a part of their experience and so they treated freedom of movement as though it were the same as eating and breathing. From what Maxim had read, it was a bit different in Los Angeles and Chicago where ghetto dwellers were often confined to their homes because of the violence on the streets, but here in Eastern Europe, freedom of movement and freedom of assembly were cherished rights, more often taken away by oppressors than granted to a repressed people. Eastern Europeans were used to sitting huddled in their houses, peeking from behind tightly closed curtains, shutting out the world. He had been worried that the Westerners would not last long in confinement, and from the atmosphere on his return, he thought his fears had been justified.

His musings were interrupted by a knock on the door. One of the security guards had met a courier delivering a parcel downstairs. He handed it to Maxim, saying that unless he knew the handwriting, it should be X-rayed to make sure there was no explosive device inside. Maxim carefully turned it upside down and saw that it had come from an address in Moscow. 'No,' he said, thanking the guard, 'I was expecting this.'

The others crowded around to see what it was. He told them, 'Some days ago, while you were in the castle, I returned to Kosice. From my office I phoned a colleague of mine who now lives in Moscow. Although he is an archaeologist, he was also closely associated with security services over there. I asked him if he could get information on Alexander Hasek from the old files. Let us pray it was worth the risk he took.'

Maxim ripped open the parcel and extracted four bulky, green, manila folders. By the look of them, they dated back to the War. The typed text looked as if it had been keyed on an old mechanical machine; the indentations from the keys were visible on some pages. The text was written in the Cyrillic alphabet. Maxim read it with difficulty. He spelt out the words, 'Hasek. Alexander Alexandrovich. Born Hungary, September 3, 1921.'

'Hungary!' exclaimed Sarah. 'I thought . . .'

Laco smiled at her. The earlier tension between them had eased the moment his father reappeared. 'The border was always moving. One minute it was Czechoslovakia, the next the Ukraine, the next Hungary. Towns sometimes had four different nationalities in the same decade.'

Maxim began to decipher the first file. The wafer-thin pages, almost transparent with age, were official documents attesting to Hasek's membership of the Communist Party in Hungary and then in Slovakia. There were papers attesting to his membership of the Komsomol and the Stalin Youth. Most of the documents were the routine records of a young man who joined many bodies and organisations, yet who was never reported by his leaders or superiors as outstanding in any particular field. Even as the leader of a small patriotic cadre, he was replaced after only two months by a second-in-command when the group revolted against him.

Maxim flipped through the later pages of the first file fairly quickly, then opened the second folder. Involuntarily, Laco shouted out, 'Yes!' There, staring at them from a file which hadn't been opened in decades, was a photograph of Alexander Hasek. He was dressed in a dark suit, a shirt with a high white collar and a tie which didn't quite meet the high button of his shirt. His face was shining with cleanliness, his hair slicked back and he was smiling at them through the passage of time. He was probably in his early thirties.

'So that's the bastard,' said Josh. 'Do you recognise him?' he asked Maxim, who nodded slowly.

'Oh yes. I remember this face. Handsome devil. All the girls were in love with him when we were at the University in Bratislava. Of course he was younger then, but just as handsome. He has one of those faces that blends in with a crowd. In this photo, he looks like every other Czech or Slovak you'd meet in the street. I would never have dreamt that the boy I knew all those years ago could go on to willingly murder people. One wonders what makes a man so evil.'

Sarah recalled a class she had attended as an undergraduate with Ruth Warshinski. They had discussed the work of Hannah Arendt and her concept of the banality of evil. Looking at the black-and-white faded photograph of Hasek, a man who appeared as ordinary as her next-door neighbour, she truly understood for the first time that men who became monsters were frighteningly ordinary.

They found other photographs in the file. Hasek at a meeting of satellite communist nations; Hasek in 1951 when he was appointed head of security of Carpathia; Hasek dancing with an anonymous blonde at a gathering of fat and confident looking men; Hasek reading a newspaper in a café, whose wall posters showed that it must have been somewhere in Czechoslovakia.

'It will take a long while to go through this file. My Russian never was all that good,' said Maxim.

'I don't understand something,' said Josh. 'If this group that you're talking about exists, how come Hasek still has a file? I would have thought it would have been removed and destroyed.'

'I don't know the answer to that,' said Maxim. 'Maybe they tried and couldn't get access. Maybe they forgot.' And then something occurred to him. He pulled the fourth and final file out and turned immediately to the end. He smiled and nodded.

'Here's the reason,' he said, holding up an official-looking document, stamped and embossed with authority.

'It is a certificate attesting to the death from pneumonia of Alexander Hasek in 1956 at a re-education camp in the administrative district of Yakutskaya in northern Siberia. That explains why the files were allowed to remain there. After all, why destroy the file of a dead man? That would have been too dangerous. Anybody who investigated Hasek and found that the file had been removed or tampered with would have become suspicious. Leaving it in place was a lot cleverer. If the subject is recorded as dead, the investigation comes to an end.'

Josh reached back into the second file and took out the photograph of the young Hasek. Josephine looked over his shoulder. 'Is that the motherfucker we're trying to find?' she asked. Josh nodded.

'You know what's amazing?' she said. The others looked up and examined the photograph. 'The lips. The bastard's got no lips.'

And Josephine was right. Although Hasek was smiling, his lips were so thin his face looked as if it was dissected by a scar.

For the first time Sarah examined the photograph carefully. She looked at the man's gaunt face, his cheeks, but it was when she saw his eyes that her heart nearly stopped. They were the eyes of her grandfather. It was as if she was looking at a photograph from the mantelpiece in her grandmother's old apartment. Josh noticed her reaction. 'What is it?' he asked.

'He reminds me of someone I know,' she said softly.

'Yeah,' said Josh. 'He looks a bit like my dad as well. It's amazing how monsters resemble ourselves. How ordinary they look.'

# CHAPTER EIGHTEEN

Katerina Trebon sat with her back to the open window, enjoying the mild breezes that blew in to stir the paper on her desk. She listened to the noise of people in the corridor, students walking to lectures, girls giggling, youths making crude remarks. If only the professor would come back from his lunch, she would ask his permission to take the rest of the day off. Her headache was numbing. It had now spread from the crown of her head to just above her left temple. She didn't normally suffer from headaches, but the constant high temperatures Prague was experiencing and the pressure of getting everything ready for the forthcoming examination schedule had made her unusually tense. As had the pressure from her husband to leave her job, and then the news of the sudden death of Olga Polemska. It was all too much. It was making life too difficult.

She looked up expectantly when the door opened, hoping to see the tall, aristocratic form of her professor. Instead two burly men in ill-fitting suits walked in. Something about their manner immediately frightened her.

'Yes?' she said.

'Katerina Trebon?'

'Yes.'

The first man took out a badge and showed it to her. It looked like a policeman's badge. 'Prague Homicide.'

'Yes?' she repeated, puzzled.

'We are investigating the death of your former colleague, Olga Polemska.'

'Yes,' she continued to say. She couldn't think of anything more intelligent.

'How well did you know Olga?'

'Very well. I worked with her for ten years before she was forced to retire. She was developing dementia so she was asked to leave. Why? What is all this?'

'We believe there are circumstances about her death that warrant investigation.'

'Homicide?' she said, shocked. 'You mean, she was . . . ?'

'We are in the very early stages of the investigation. Not a word of this must be spoken about outside of this office. Do you understand?'

'Of course.'

'Was anybody interested in Olga or her career or activities say a month before her death? Was anybody asking questions about her?'

'Why? Why do you want to know?'

The other man spoke for the first time. 'Please, just answer the question.' The first man was a bully, but this man – his authority truly frightened her. She had grown up under the Stalinists and even to this day she knew not to question authority. Poor Olga had been different. She was always trying to buck the system. But not Katerina. Not for anything.

'There *was* somebody who was asking about her, ' she volunteered unhesitatingly. 'I remember clearly because it surprised me at the time. One of our senior lecturers, Doctor Reikhardt Steerbaum. He's been with us for about twenty years. A very inoffensive man. We hardly ever see him in administration, he just turns up to lectures and nothing much more. He came in here a few days ago and asked if he could look up the personal files of people who used to work in the department.'

'What has this got to do with Olga Polemska?' the first man asked.

'He mentioned that he was only interested in the files of people who had worked here in a senior capacity while Olga was the administrative assistant – the position that I now hold. Since her retirement, that is. He told me that the people must have worked here from 1977 to 1983. I thought nothing of it. I let him see the files. There's nothing confidential about them, they just show periods of service and academic records. All the professors and teaching staff earn the same money, so there was nothing he shouldn't have seen. Have I done the wrong thing?'

Her head was thumping with pain. She massaged her temple. 'I didn't know it was the wrong thing to do.'

Ignoring her discomfort, the second detective said, 'Tell me about this Reikhardt Steerbaum. Let me see his file.'

She stood immediately and withdrew Steerbaum's personnel records from the filing cabinet behind her. The detective opened the file and made some notes, then closed it and pushed it back across the table.

'You are to say nothing, Katerina, absolutely nothing to anybody about our visit. This is a homicide investigation. Anything you say which affects the course of our investigation would force us to arrest you as an accessory. Do I make myself absolutely clear?'

Her jaw dropped in shock. She shook her head. 'I won't say a thing, I promise. Not a word. You have my word on that, I swear.'

The men left as quietly as they had entered. Katerina quickly pulled open her desk drawer and took out a towel. She held it over her face and vomited.

The main living room was unnaturally silent. Maxim and Laco were poring over the list of people who could be

Alexander Hasek. Occasionally they spoke animatedly in Czech. Some of the names they knew and could identify. Others were strange to them. But no one, not even known colleagues, was discounted. Sarah walked into the room and glanced over Laco's shoulder. He didn't appear to notice her, just continued talking to his father about the likelihood of particular academics having a dual personality, an inner covert life.

When the group were all gathered after breakfast, preparing to face another long and empty day, Maxim brought immediate relief from their confinement.

'I think,' he told them, 'that it is less unsafe for you to go out now than once it was before.'

Everybody looked at him hopefully, but remained silent.

Jerry was the first to speak. 'Could you say that again?' he asked.

'It is less unsafe now because we have two additional security people who will be able to trail your movements. Before, as you know, I could not happily allow you out because that would have left us without security. But these two additional men can shadow our movements and according to the experts at Executive Security, their presence will be unknown to you and they will be able to spot whether you are being followed.'

Sarah breathed a sigh of relief. 'You mean we can go out and walk by the river? Go to the old town square? Get out of this place?'

He smiled. 'You can indeed, my dear. But I would most strongly suggest that you allow our young make-up friend to assist you in changing your image. Not the full disguise, of course, just a subtle change of appearance. Maybe different clothes, a scarf over the head – anything that changes your image from the photographs they undoubtedly hold of you.'

'Yes!' she said, clenching her fist. 'Well, I don't know about the rest of you, but I'm going for a long walk around Prague. Then I'm going to get an icy cold beer in a café, followed by a strong cappuccino, followed by another beer and maybe a toasted cheese and tomato sandwich. Then after that, I'm going to get another beer.'

The idea of being free to wander the streets again, to leave their luxurious prison and do what other human beings took for granted was almost inspirational, like listening to a rousing choir in a church.

Phil was just as happy. 'I'm going to do what you're gonna do, but in another direction. And hold the cheese sandwich. I'm going to find the best BLT in town and order three. And Jerry, I love you like a brother, but we've been locked up together for too long and I need space, man. Space and freedom and privacy. So follow me and I'll kill you.'

'Follow you? You gotta be kidding. I want as far away as possible.'

Maxim listened to their good-natured banter then, like the father that he was rapidly becoming to them all, said, 'I don't quite know how to tell you this but we only have two additional guards. This means that only one person or a couple can go out at any one time. I'm afraid you will have to take turns.'

They looked at him in disbelief. Then Sarah said softly, 'I think Phil or Jerry should go out first. I've been pretty hard to get on with. It's the least I can do.'

'Excuse me!' interrupted a high-pitched, nasal voice. 'But did anybody happen to include me in this conversation? You're all deciding what's best for everybody, but did anybody remember that I'm a human being too? What about my needs?' piped Josephine. 'I've had better times with diarrhoea than I've had cooped up in this shithouse, nowhere apartment with a bunch of weirdo humourless straights. If I don't get some action soon, I'm gonna go zippo.'

'Why don't we draw straws?' said Laco.

'We don't have any,' said Sarah, fishing in her pocket. 'But I've got a coin. Why not do heads and tails?'

Maxim agreed to toss the coin. Sarah, Josh and Jerry chose heads. The rest chose tails. They looked eagerly at the coin as it landed on the floor. It was heads. 'Yes!' exclaimed Sarah, realising too late that her delight was at the expense of others. Maxim tossed again. Sarah was the only one to chose heads for a second time. She got to go out.

'It was fixed,' grumbled Josephine.

Sarah looked hurt. 'Am I really causing that many problems?' she asked, her voice reflecting her distress. Josephine realised she'd gone too far, and came over, put her arm around Sarah and kissed her on the cheek.

'When your ass is being bit by alligators, it's hard to show the nice side of your personality. Once we're outta this, it'll all seem like a bad dream. Meantime, don't take us mothers too seriously.'

She smiled at the young man's homespun wisdom, then asked, 'So who wants to come with me?' She looked at Josh and then at Laco.

There was an awkward moment, then Laco said, 'I have to stay here with Father. We need to examine the list and make some phone calls to try to identify which one, if any, of these people could be Hasek. Whoever makes the calls has to speak Czech, so I guess if you're going to go out with somebody it should be Josh.'

She smiled and kissed him on the cheek, then went into her room to do her hair and dress for a walk through town. It seemed odd that Laco had simply deferred to Josh. In Kosice, he would never have done so; he would have fought for his own way. He was irresponsible but forceful. His reasons for staying sounded valid, but as she brushed her hair, Sarah realised that there was more to it. She realised that Laco was saying he understood Sarah's growing closeness to Josh and he was happy to make room for it. He was telling her that their brief romance was over, that the circumstances had changed. That now he was his father's son, and such behaviour wasn't proper in front of a man he revered.

Sarah realised she was smiling. It felt such a huge relief. The last thing she needed was a possessive scene with Laco, especially now that their lives were in such flux. He was great fun and terrific in bed, but she had to use logic and not emotion now, and start thinking about her true needs, not just her desires.

Josephine went to work on both Sarah and Josh. In ten minutes, she had transformed them into a couple of students out for a stroll. What she could do with limited props and a minimum of make-up was extraordinary. Sarah and Josh bade the rest goodbye and walked out the front door. Sarah felt like a student on her first day of vacation. They sauntered down the five flights of stairs and nodded to the security guard who was sitting just inside the apartment block's front door. Then they walked down to the main thoroughfare. Where before they had felt oppressed walking along the streets of Prague, for fear of what might be hiding in the shadows, now they felt as if they were enclosed within a shell of safety. Sarah turned and spotted a man walking twenty metres behind them. He was as inconspicuous as any inhabitant of the city, yet his presence gave her an enhanced feeling of comfort and security.

'One of the guys is behind us,' she said to Josh.

He nodded towards a man leaning against a post box on the far side of the main road. 'There's the other,' he said.

As they made for the tram stop in the main road, clouds of petrol fug wafted over them. Sarah smelled the air and winced. Looking around, she noticed that even the buildings seemed to be suffering from decay. They were covered with an accumulation of grime and dirt, which years of neglect by the city authorities had allowed to remain. Such a shame, she thought. A beautiful city, an emerging jewel, whose gleam was hidden by the catastrophe of modern life. And the noise of modern living: all around them car horns were blaring, tyres were screeching, people were shouting. She wondered how Prague must have sounded to Franz Kafka. But then he had had different forces which oppressed him.

Sarah forced herself to snap out of the melancholy mood she felt herself falling into. This was a short and well-deserved holiday: she was on vacation from her apartment and the people she'd been cooped up with for so long now, and she wanted to enjoy herself. The tram came almost immediately and they jumped on board. They were somewhat surprised to see one of the guards at the back of the tram, the other already seated at the front. How had they moved so quickly?

While Josh and Sarah were setting off for the sensuous delights of a beer, Maxim and Laco were busy examining the names of the people on the list Richard had given them. Maxim phoned the Prague Institute of Archaeology, the governing body for all digs and archaeological explorations in the region. He knew most of the people there and his call was greeted with great enthusiasm and *bonhomie* by the director, who accepted without question his request for complete confidentiality.

After an hour, the director phoned him back, as instructed, from his private line and gave the information that Maxim wanted. Three of the people on the list had died in the last eight years. Even if Hasek was one of them, there would be no way to establish that their journey was at an end. The other five, however, were still alive and their last known addresses showed that they all still lived within the Czech Republic. The director provided addresses and phone numbers for four of them; the fifth had left no forwarding address or contact details.

It was Laco who phoned the first man on the list. He introduced himself as the Prague correspondent for *The*

*Washington Post* newspaper in America. The elderly man on the other end of the line was surprised by the call. 'How did you get my number?'

'From the university, sir,' Laco said. 'I called the Department of Archaeology and asked for an expert in the Otomani people. I was given your name.'

'Me?' said the man. 'But I have never studied the Otomani. My period of interest was long before them. I am an expert on the early Chalcolithic period, many thousands of years before the Otomani. What idiot at the university gave you my name?'

'I'm sorry, sir, there does appear to be a mistake. I was told that in 1953 you led a major dig in Eastern Slovakia into the Otomani people.'

'No, you have the wrong man. From 1950 to 1953 I was a research student in Prague. I didn't go anywhere near that area at all. My work was in Bohemia, on the German border. You have the wrong man, I'm afraid.'

Laco crossed his name off the list, recounting the conversation to his father.

Maxim phoned the next name on the list with the story that he was preparing a book on ancient history in Middle Europe and would like to use an article that the learned doctor had written in 1952 about work he had undertaken on an archaeological dig in Eastern Slovakia. The doctor denied authorship of such an article, again expressing regret that they had called the wrong man. In 1952 he had been in America at the Smithsonian. But he begged Maxim to be allowed to contribute an article on another topic.

The third and fourth academics were eventually contacted and gave similar alibis. This left only the fifth man, who had supplied no forwarding address or contact details. The two men poured a couple of glasses of vodka and sipped them slowly.

'Well,' said Laco, 'unless Hasek is one of the three that is already dead, or unless you and I have been completely taken in by one of the four people we've just spoken to, it looks as if he could be our fifth man.'

Maxim nodded and looked again at the man's name: Jaroslav Demek. He took out an address book and searched for a name, then dialled the number next to it. It was answered within moments.

'Reikhardt,' he said, 'it's Maxim.'

'Maxim, old friend. Was my list of use?'

'It was of great use. In fact, I think we have come down to somebody in whom we might be interested. What do you know about Jaroslav Demek?'

'Demek? Good God!' he exclaimed.

'What's wrong?' asked Maxim.

'Nothing. Only he is the last person I would have expected you to be interested in. He was a nothing: lazy, stupid, vapid, an embarrassment to the department. He worked for many years in the same job. A totally mediocre intellect, never wrote anything, contributed anything. We used to avoid him in the staff room. We used to joke that when he walked in at coffee time, the IQ of the room fell thirty points. Demek was one of the hangover appointments from the days of the Russians. Naturally he wouldn't have held on to his position had it not been for Moscow placing him there to keep his eye on the rest of us. He was probably KGB, responsible for holding the party line. He certainly wasn't liked by the staff or the administration and was never particularly popular with the students. I'm trying to think. He left so many years ago. I remember he and I sometimes quarrelled about the nature of archaeology, but his arguments were thin, silly even. Why on earth do you want to talk to him?'

'I have my reasons, Reikhardt. Do you happen to know where he is?'

'No idea, I'm afraid. He left the department at the beginning of the 1980s as I remember. I think the Professor would have risked Moscow's ire and kicked him out anyway because there were so many complaints from students about his incompetence. Do you know, people actually used to avoid his lectures. Sometimes he spoke to empty lecture halls. Anyway, he was around retiring age when he left.'

'And you have no idea where he went?'

'Absolutely none. He's the last person I would have stayed in touch with. Do you want me to try to find out from the secretary tomorrow?'

'No! No, don't! Don't do anything. We will follow it up from here. Thank you. You have been a tremendous help, as always.' Maxim put the phone down.

Eight kilometres away, in a van parked close to Reikhardt Steerbaum's apartment, two technicians looked at a series of numbers on a small electronic switchboard. They smiled at each other, then phoned Colonel-General Zamov. When he heard the news, Zamov breathed a sigh of relief. His first action was to trace the location of the number that had made the call to Steerbaum's telephone, using an electronic keypad connected to a reverse phone directory. He made a note of the location, then picked up the phone to call Tranov.

Josh was the first to wake, the first to come out and make himself breakfast. And, for reasons he couldn't fully pin down, he had the feeling that the atmosphere in the apartment was already markedly easier. It was as though it had been spring-cleaned. The walls didn't seem as close, the windows somehow seemed cleaner. Even the air was less thick. His walk around town with Sarah had been a breath of fresh air, and when they came home they were like a couple of kids returning from camp. They described the crowds, the smells, the traffic. And despite the fact that they had all only suffered a couple of days of incarceration, everyone hung on their every word, living their pleasure vicariously. So much so that, to the chagrin of their security guards, Josephine, Phil and Jerry demanded that they be allowed out immediately.

Josephine had been a scream. She and the two technicians had taken themselves to a nightclub in the old part of the town where a meal of roast duck and red cabbage had failed to absorb the beer and vodka they had plied her with all night. So as not to frighten the locals, she abandoned her sashay and walked into the club like a man, speaking with a deep gravelly voice, casting in-your-face looks at waiters and smouldered at a corner table like Rudolph Valentino. But the mask slipped as the alcohol did its work and Josephine's true self – a woman desperate for freedom and recognition – burst out. As the music grew more insistent and the mood of the room more relaxed, she climbed onto a table and began to sway her hips to the tune of the gipsy quartet. She was all the rage – the musicians encouraged her with increasingly erotic rhythms, and the other patrons looked on in approval, clapping, cheering and whistling. The club's manager even sent over a complimentary bottle of vodka, but by the time Josephine had sampled that, she was throwing up in the toilet and her good humour had worn off. She begged Phil and Jerry to take her home.

While the others were out Sarah took the opportunity to talk to Maxim. He had been so busy arranging things and investigating the academics that she had enjoyed no more than a few minutes of private conversation with him. She found him in the lounge room, relaxing and reading a book. When she approached him and asked if he would like to talk, Maxim put down the book and smiled. Their conversation was a delight, ranging over their lives, their ambitions and their frustrated hopes. Sarah found it was wonderful talking to an elderly man; it reminded her of the joys of talking to her grandfather.

'My son tells me that you possess an heirloom which was found in our area,' Maxim said. 'An amulet. It has a Trojan bull symbol. I would like to examine it, with your permission.'

Sarah removed the amulet from around her neck and handed it over to Maxim. She felt so differently to when she had first handed it over to Laco. Then she had felt she was being attacked; now she was sharing something which was precious to both of them.

Maxim looked at it carefully, turning it over lovingly in his hands, smiling all the while. 'Very interesting. Very precious. Laco is right. This is of great importance. It could give a whole new meaning to the study he is doing.'

'He's fascinated with the Bronze Age, isn't he? All those wonderful cities and the great romance of the heroes. He's been telling me about it. It's fascinating.'

Maxim nodded. 'The time of the birth of mankind's first attempts at true civilisation. And the time of his myth-making. Before he lost his innocence and became modern and intellectual.'

Sarah frowned. 'But from what he's told me, the Bronze Age *was* an age of intellect. The beginning of writing, the sculpting of fantastic statues, and monumental building construction, new ways of working with metals – surely that's intellectual?'

'You know, my dear, we often use words without thinking and yet we still manage to come to a deeply perceptive meaning. The ancient Near East is often called the Cradle of Civilisation. Have you ever wondered why it is called a cradle? Because a cradle is where you put babies while they are embarking on their first experiences of life apart from their mothers, when they're just beginning to struggle to find their feet. For centuries, historians thought that modern man should be dated to the age of Homer, about 750 BC. Before that was pre-history, and ancient, protohistorical man. But at the end of the last century archaeology began to grow as a science, and we realised that there were civilisations around long before the blind bard.

'From the age of Homer on humankind became incredibly sophisticated. Democracy, civil law, philosophy, empirical science, history all erupted from that area of genius within a matter of a couple of hundred years. But few people, Sarah, wonder what existed beforehand. Before Homer, for hundreds of years, there was a long dark age, an age which even now we know almost nothing about. And before that dark age there was the Bronze Age – the age of the creation of myths. The Greeks expanded their minds through rational thought and deduction, but the people of the Bronze Age worked through images and dreams to express their fears and feelings and hopes. The Greeks appeal to our conscious mind, but it was the men and women of the Bronze Age who gave us our myths, our very own dreams. It is they who were the creators of our imaginations. That, Sarah, is why Laco and I are uncovering the Bronze Age, because it represents a side of our humanity with which we modern, sophisticated intellectuals have lost touch. Rejoin the two sides of our nature and we will be complete.'

Sarah reached over and gently clasped his hand.

The following morning, everyone arose still feeling chatty and energetic from their outings. Everyone except Josephine, that is, who looked haggard and world-weary. As they were eating breakfast the telephone rang.

Maxim was expecting no calls. He picked up the receiver cautiously, as if the call were an alien intrusion.

'Dr Plastov senior?' asked a cultured Czech voice.

'Yes.'

'I have a message to give you from Dr Reikhardt Steerbaum. He apologises for not phoning himself, but said you would understand. He has asked me to assure you of the urgency of what I am about to tell you.'

'Where is Dr Steerbaum?' asked Maxim.

'He is currently in the Records Department of Charles University. He telephoned me to tell me that he has found something of enormous importance which he must share with you.'

'Why didn't he phone me himself?' asked Maxim, suspiciously.

'He said specifically that he could make no contact with you for reasons of security, that you would understand. That is why he asked me to call you from my apartment.'

'And you are . . . ?' asked Maxim.

'I am a colleague of his. Look, I feel very uncomfortable about all this. I don't want to get any more involved than I am at present. Reikhardt sounded very mysterious. I have agreed to pass on a message and that is as far as I am willing to take it. If you are not interested then we will discontinue this conversation immediately. I have upheld my assurance to him. I have no further need to be involved.'

'Please don't hang up,' said Maxim urgently. 'What is his message?'

'He wants to meet you in a café,' said the anonymous stranger. 'He has found some information going back into the past in which you will be very interested.'

'And where is this café?'

The man gave explicit directions. It wasn't four blocks from where they were. 'He asked if you could meet him there within the hour.'

'If you speak to him again,' said Maxim, 'tell him I will be there.'

'I won't be speaking to him again. Whether you turn up or not, Dr Plastov, is your problem. Not mine. I don't like doing what I'm doing. It's underhand. I don't usually deal with people in this way.' The man disconnected the phone.

Maxim put down the receiver and looked at his colleagues. He recounted the conversation. One of the newly arrived security guards listened carefully and asked for Steerbaum's phone number. He picked up the phone and dialled. There was no response. He dialled the academic's mobile number; it had been redirected back to his apartment. Again there was no response. The security guard was obviously concerned.

Sarah and Josh were cautious, but thought that Maxim should go to the café. Laco, on the other hand, suspected something evil in the phone call and begged his father not to go. Instead, he volunteered to go in his father's place. But it was the security guard who exposed an area of concern that none of them had considered. 'He wants to meet you within the hour,' he said, in broken English. 'This isn't enough time for us to mount a surveillance operation. He must know that. He is clever. He and his colleagues may already be there waiting for you. There may be great danger. I think you should not go.'

Josh walked to the window. 'But if whoever it is already knows our address through our telephone number, then surely they would have come bursting in here hours ago. It can't be a trick. Obviously this Reikhardt guy has unearthed something which he thinks is of use to us. He's taken the precaution of going through an intermediary because he's scared that his phone might be bugged. It sounds reasonable to me. I can't see your problem.'

The security guard said to Maxim, 'He wants you there within an hour. Let him wait. Go in an hour and a half. In the meantime, I'll go over there as a customer. My colleague will follow you in.'

But Sarah perceived another problem. 'Hold on a minute,' she said. 'If two of you go, that leaves us here with only two guards. If there really is a problem, then that's a hell of a lot less support than we might need. If these people do know our location, this way they're going to find it a whole lot easier to break in. They could be setting us up.'

'It's a risk,' admitted the security guard. 'I will contact my office and discuss it with them. Meantime, I am not letting Dr Plastov walk into the café without two people there. That is clear.'

He gave instructions to the other security men and left the apartment to walk quickly to the café. Maxim sat nervously finishing his breakfast, mulling over the conversation. There had been something about the indifference of the telephone caller that had sounded forced, almost false. Something that he had said, some nuance which Maxim couldn't identify, yet which unsettled him. Or maybe he was being too introspective. If a friend asked him to make such a phone call, he would be concerned for the welfare of both parties. But that was him. Maybe this man, this colleague, wasn't such a close friend. There were too many intangibles. It was all too difficult.

He looked at the clock. The call had ended half an hour earlier. It would take him ten minutes to walk to the café. That left less than an hour. Hopefully, when he arrived at the café, he would see Reikhardt and that would put an end to all his fears. Reikhardt would give him the information, shake hands and leave. And they would all meet back here within an hour, laughing at their neuroses and their naive conspiracy theories.

Maxim found the time passing slowly. He read, he talked, he listened. The others treated him differently than they had before the phone call. Now they skirted him as though he was a condemned man about to go to his execution. Eventually the guard looked at his watch and nodded. Maxim stood, kissed his son, shook hands slowly and deliberately with each of the others and kissed Sarah on both cheeks. As he left the apartment, he said, 'I will see you back here in an hour. Don't worry. Just lock yourselves in and remain calm.'

The atmosphere of the previous day, the tension and hostility, resurfaced. Their brief holiday was over.

The Café Bedrich was large and noisy. Even from the outside, Maxim could see that there were dozens of commuters still breakfasting before going to their offices. Waiters wore white aprons; waitresses caps on their heads and lace sleeves. The cashier sat at the door on a high stool, holding up an impatient line of office workers waiting to pay their bills and leave. But she methodically checked the additions of each of the waiters to ensure that the total of the bill was correct and the café was not losing out on any income.

The entry door was propped half open by a chair. Maxim walked in. He had been instructed by the guard not to look around for the location of the other security guard, who would already be seated inside, surreptitiously scrutinising every customer, but to find a seat deep within the café away from its street windows. Or, alternatively, to go to the table of his friend Reikhardt, if indeed he was there. The aroma of warm cakes, coffee and fried eggs greeted him. It was a heavy and unpleasant experience after the delightful breakfast he had already enjoyed. He looked around at the dozens of people at tables, slopping bread into their food to lap up the juices. He felt his stomach churning from the smells, but in truth he was nervous with anxiety. He scanned the room quickly; Reikhardt was nowhere to be seen.

Maxim chose an empty table near the opposite wall. A waiter came over and he ordered a coffee. The security guard who had accompanied him from the apartment sat at a table in the far corner by the window. Maxim examined every face. Nobody seemed to be interested in him. They were all talking animatedly, laughing, smoking, drinking coffee or concentrating on their meals. In another corner, opposite the guard who had accompanied him, was the first security guard. Maxim looked away quickly so as not to acknowledge him. He waited. The coffee arrived and he sipped it slowly. Still he waited. As the minutes passed, his anxiety grew. He began to feel nauseated.

Only a week ago, he reflected, his greatest anxiety was whether to plant roses or nasturtiums in a particular bed in his large garden in Kosice. Now he was a potential assassination target, a fall guy (is that how Josh would have described it?) for the insanity of others. Why had he started all this? Why had he and his colleagues begun opening the files of the Stalinists to see what lay inside? To bring an evil old man to justice? Wasn't there a case for letting old wounds heal? So much for a happy retirement, he thought.

A woman at a table on the other side of the room stood and began to walk slowly towards him. He failed to notice her. She was as nondescript as any woman in the café, an office worker, a secretary or manager. She was dressed in a dark blue suit with a white shirt and her skirt was unfashionably long. Her hair was pulled back in a severe bun; it was turning grey. She was in her forties or fifties, and would have been easy to miss in a crowd. She carried a coat over her arm and was looking at the bill the waiter had just given her, adding it up carefully as she walked slowly and deliberately through the tables. She mouthed the cost of each item she had eaten silently to herself, her lips moving slightly.

She hesitated just before reaching the cashier, then decided she wanted to go to the toilet. She asked a passing waiter, 'Where is the ladies'?'

The waiter was balancing two plates in one hand and a cup of coffee in the other. He nodded curtly in the direction of a door at the far end of the café, close to Maxim's table. The woman began to walk towards the ladies'. As she reached the table before Maxim's, Maxim looked up at her. She smiled at him; she had a gentle smile. As Maxim smiled back, the woman's head exploded. Maxim stared with utter incomprehension and horror.

What was happening? The woman's mouth, that had smiled pleasantly at him a moment before, was no longer there; it was a gargoyle's grimace. Her brains splattered against the hissing coffee machine, her hair, eyes and part of her nose hitting the back wall and the mirror above where Maxim was sitting. Diners were suddenly splattered with the blood and insides of the woman's head. It was surreal. Only the massive explosion from the gun and the concussive waves in the air affirmed that the situation was horribly real. And then the screaming began.

Maxim recoiled in horror as the headless body pitched forward, crashing on top of two men huddled together over croissants and coffee. Nearby customers tried to escape the horror, screaming as they witnessed the tall figure pitching forward onto the table, then rolling heavily onto the floor. People outside who had heard the noise but had not yet taken in the horror also began to scream.

Maxim's mouth was fixed open in horror as he stared at the grotesque torso at his feet. He drew away and started to shout in terror. Then he felt a hand grip him viciously on his wrist and pull him up and away from the gargoyle. The hand dragged him past tables, pulling him half-falling, half-scrambling towards the exit. The cashier was no longer sitting on her stool; she had fallen backwards onto the floor and was screaming. Men and women were running out of the café, yelling in fear. The security guard pulled Maxim with the speed and strength of a locomotive. Maxim's heart was beating so fast he thought it would burst. Visions filled his mind; visions of that hideous torso, once a woman, now a thing, an inanimate shape. He shut his eyes, but could still see vividly the half of her head still attached to her body. He had seen skeletons. Buried in the ground. Dry. All his life long. But nothing like this: she had been alive a moment ago, not millennia ago. Suddenly he needed to vomit. He fell to his knees and threw up on the pavement. His overriding thought was that he hadn't managed to reach the gutter. Passers-by would have to walk around his vomit. He felt ashamed. What would people think?

The guard pulled him aggressively back onto his feet. 'Please!' he shouted. 'Please. I am ill.'

'Sorry. No time. We have to get back to the flat,' said the guard. 'God knows what's happening back there. We have to go now. Pull yourself together.'

'What do you mean? I don't . . . What is . . .?'

'Dr Plastov, that woman in the restaurant had a machine pistol under her coat. You would have been cut in half if we hadn't killed her. Now we have to get back to the apartment. Our cover has been blown. We have to go *now*. Pull yourself together. This is the life and death situation we warned you of.'

'But . . .'

'Shut up! You will do what you are told!'

Maxim wiped his mouth as the security guard dragged him to their car. He nodded meekly and got in the back.

# CHAPTER NINETEEN

Laco was furious beyond belief, frightening Josephine when he screamed at the security guards for their incompetence. 'That's it!' he said, also shouting in the direction of his father, his anger encompassing everything. 'That is all I am going to stand. I want you away from here immediately. Josh, will you please arrange for my father to stay in a hotel in Paris or London or *somewhere*.'

'Of course,' Josh said without hesitation.

Maxim nodded and said softly, 'I have been as much help as I can be. The sight of that poor woman . . .'

'Poor woman!' screamed Laco, his shock and anger taking no heed of his father's desire for calm and silence. 'That bitch was going to kill you. If these men hadn't got to her first, you would be lying dead on the stinking floor of that café. They had no right to permit you to go in the first place. Now they have made you the target. I won't let them succeed. I want you out of Prague tonight.'

He turned to one of the security guards, a man who had taken control of the actions of the others. 'Can it be arranged?'

The man nodded. He knew that Laco's anger at him was merely a reaction to the shock of seeing his father walking back into the apartment, old and grey. 'Of course your father's disappearance can be arranged,' the guard told him. 'But we don't have enough time to do things properly like organise for a false passport. So when he gets to London, we'll have to find a hotel that will admit him without registration until we can arrange things properly. I will notify our London people to meet him at the airport.'

Laco continued to sound agitated. 'I want a man to travel over to London with him.' He turned to Josh, who nodded immediately.

The other guard wasn't listening. The moment Maxim and his guards had arrived back from the assassination attempt, four more employees of Executive Security had hastily arrived at the apartment, responding to the urgent calls as they ran from the café. Like the others, these were tough men, barrel-chested, unsmiling, determined. The breast pockets of their jackets bulged with guns; they seemed unconcerned about the need to hide them. Three men guarded the street entrance while the fourth was stationed with the two original guards upstairs.

'Sir,' the head guard said to Laco, who was beginning to calm down, 'before we make any other arrangements for your father, we have to think of the safety of the rest of you. We have to leave these premises. The perpetrators telephoned here. They must have access to a reverse telephone directory, so they will already have the address. They planned the assassination attempt just around the corner, so it's doubtful that they will risk another incident so close. They will know that the police are swarming in the area. But they will be watching, that's for sure. So we must leave now. There are cars outside. Pack now and we leave immediately.'

Sarah said, 'But if they're watching, they'll just follow the cars, or they'll be able to trace the number plates or something.'

'Madam, this is my job,' the guard told her sternly. 'All has been arranged. Please pack quickly so we can go.'

They left the apartment within ten minutes, passing through a phalanx of men to reach the convoy of cars parked outside the building. The motorcade drove away urgently yet smoothly, blending into the lanes of traffic at irregular intervals until only an expert would have recognized that each car was part of a convoy.

The lead car, carrying Maxim and Josh, turned into Washingtonova and drove quickly, turning left towards Wenceslas Square. Suddenly, and without warning, the two passengers were ordered to leave the car and enter a large department store. They did as they were told without any questions. Josh looked back but couldn't see Sarah or the others. The two men walked quickly into the store, under the aegis of two security guards, and found themselves amongst a large crowd of shoppers. An attractive young woman walked up to them, greeted them with a smile, and said, 'Follow me immediately'.

Again, they did as they were told. Josh looked around: the security men who had been guarding them were no longer by their side. The young woman led them purposefully towards an escalator. They ascended and followed her to one of the store's exits which led to the car park. Josh put his arm through Maxim's. He was concerned about the old man; he was still in shock and had been given no time to recover. And the pace of the young woman didn't allow for dawdling. She escorted them to a nondescript car, opened the back doors and hustled them inside. She drove the car quickly up the car park ramp instead of downwards towards the exit. Josh wondered what was going on, but the young woman was too intimidating to contemplate questioning her. At the fifth level, she screeched to a halt opposite a large silver BMW in which two men were seated, turned to them and said simply, 'Out!'.

Maxim and Josh were bundled into the BMW, which then accelerated down the ramps and out by another exit.

They emerged into the laneway behind the department store. Driving down Vodickova, Josh leaned forward to talk to the driver. But before he could say anything, the taciturn man in the front passenger's seat turned and introduced himself.

'My name is Felix. I own Executive Security. Before you ask, each of your companions has undergone precisely the same diversionary tactics as the two of you have just enjoyed, only in other shopping districts. They are now travelling on different roads, in different cars, to a private house that we use to make clients disappear. They are perfectly safe.'

'How did you organise things so quickly?' asked Josh with profound admiration.

'It is a contingency plan which we put into practice many years ago. It is foolproof because nobody, not even the FBI or the CIA, could marshal sufficient on-ground instant manpower to follow half a dozen cars going in different directions. Even if they could, taking you into public places, like the department store, and changing cars twice would make it totally impossible to follow you.'

'I owe you my life,' said Maxim. 'I'm very grateful.'

'Sir, I owe you an apology. You owe me nothing except money. It was my job to protect you and my organisation let you down. I shall be having severe words with the guard looking after you. He should never have allowed you to enter the café. It was a stupid move, and one that could have resulted in your death. The first rule of Executive Security is the anticipation and neutralisation of danger.'

'But he did,' insisted Josh. 'Before they left, the guard explained the situation to your office. He anticipated that Maxim would be endangered and neutralised it. You can't blame him. We insisted that Maxim go to that damned café.'

'My staff have absolute control over your movements while they are protecting you. If they say no, then it's no.

My man should have insisted that the meeting not take place. The caller would most certainly have phoned again. And then we would have given him an alternative location, a meeting place in an area which we would have sanitised beforehand. It was an unforgivable breach of our professional duty to our client, for which he will be punished.'

'But he saved . . .'

'He killed a woman and he endangered our client. He caused the attention of the police to be focused upon us. None of which would have been necessary had he contacted me for advice rather than relying on a junior member of my team. This was a client's life at stake. For that you bring in the boss, not a glorified office boy. That is why I am here personally now. We slipped up. Thank God it wasn't disastrous for you, sir, but believe me it won't happen again.' Felix turned back to look through the windscreen.

They drove through the outer suburbs of Prague. Josh had no idea where they were. On a hilltop overlooking the city, with a television mast behind them, the guards stopped the car. Felix dialled a number on the car's mobile phone. It was answered by a woman; she sounded like the company's receptionist. Felix said a few clipped words, then turned to Josh. 'I am monitoring the progress of our other mobiles. We are all being followed at a half-kilometre distance by observation vehicles. If, somehow, the progress of any one of us is being monitored, the observation cars will determine it. We even have observers posted up there,' he nodded in the direction of the television tower, 'in case we are being pursued by helicopters.'

Josh smiled. It was all so stunningly professional. It was the sort of chase sequence he might have used in one of his films, except that here he was the lead actor . . . and there were no stunt men. He asked facetiously, 'And what if we're being tracked by satellite?'

'The roofs of all of our vehicles are covered with the same carbon fibres which are used by the USA's Stealth Bomber. They are effectively radar-proof and can't be tracked by heat-sensitive cameras, even at night. And, in case they are using telephoto lenses in satellites, we have been weaving in and out of streets and roads which are heavily tree-lined to obscure our progress.' Josh decided not to be facetious with Felix in the future.

A series of voices erupted out of the telephone's speaker. 'Good,' said Felix, instructing his driver to head towards the safe house. 'They've lost us.'

'You've lost them!' Tranov screamed down the receiver. 'What do you mean, you've lost them? How the fuck can you have lost them? What sort of an operation are you running up there? You moron! You were staking out the apartment, you told me your top assassin was in location at the café. Now you tell me she's dead, and you've lost them! What do I have to do? Hold your fucking hand? Find them!'

'But Comrade . . .'

'Silence!' Boris Maximovich Tranov thought for a moment. In the forty years that he had been charged by Lazar Moiseyevich Kaganovich to protect comrades from the de-Stalinization process instigated by Nikita Khrushchev, he had not lost a single soul. Now, just when he was thinking of decommissioning the organisation, packing up his identity in Bratislava and retiring like any other ageing bureaucrat to a dacha on the Black Sea to die in warmth and security, the end was turning out to be inglorious.

'Kill Hasek,' he told Zamov and hung up the phone.

Maxim Plastov had undergone a metamorphosis like a butterfly turning into a caterpillar. When they had first met him, he had been sprightly and alert, with a perceptive and imaginative mind. Yet the traumas of the past week, and especially the horrifying death of the young woman whose mission had been to assassinate him, had aged him in the space of a moment. He was now an old man, humble, bent, stumbling, rambling. The spark which had set him apart from other elderly people had been extinguished.

Sarah took him outside the house for a walk in their new garden. It was a large house with well-kept lawns at the rear, enclosed by high, impenetrable fences. Josephine immediately dubbed it Alcatraz. In the back garden, Sarah and Maxim ambled along the pathways, smelling flowers and examining the buds on trees. They conversed on a range of topics, but Maxim kept interrupting his speech with comments like *I don't remember*, or *I think it was like that* or *I'm not certain*. Sarah felt so terribly sorry for him. She was worried about him. She had invested in him the same emotions she had felt for her grandfather. Their private talk about mankind's origin, his concern for her welfare, the tender, gentlemanly way in which he kissed her hand – she felt as though they were related somehow, even if very distantly. He understood her so well.

Felix interrupted their stroll, saying, 'Come, Dr Plastov. Make your goodbyes. We go.' And he returned to the house just as abruptly, leaving Maxim and Sarah in a state of surprise.

Maxim kissed Laco farewell and waved meekly to the others. His eyes were unfocused, looking beyond them at a place that was somewhere else, in another time. He didn't give Sarah a farewell kiss. His mind was ... elsewhere. They watched the car drive him down to the heavy solid iron gates, and then through them and out of sight. Maxim was gone.

'Where's he going?' asked Josh.

Felix said, 'We're driving him to Kladno. There is a small commuter airport there. A Cessna will take him over the border to Dresden. Unfortunately we will have to use his real passport, but from there he will fly on a scheduled plane to Paris. Our colleagues there will take him to a safe house. He will be given new papers there, and in a couple of months he should be safe to return to the Czech Republic, or even Slovakia, provided he goes nowhere near the east.'

'But what about his house, his garden? Most of his friends are in Kosice,' said Laco. Felix looked at him sadly and shook his head.

It had only been twenty-four hours, yet the mood at breakfast the following morning was much colder. The atmosphere in the room was sombre, as though the cobbled-together family had suffered a bereavement. The stresses and strains that they might have anticipated did not seem to be there; rather there was a sense of shared purpose, of commitment, as though each wanted to finish the job which had been left incomplete by Maxim's departure.

Except for Josephine. She was adamant that she would be leaving today, as early as possible. 'Babes, there's nothing more I can do. It's not fun any more. Anyway, the time for make-up is gone. *Kaput*. Over. They know who you are and what you look like. If only there had been time for me to put a new face on poor old Maxim before he went into that café, things might have worked out differently. But you know what they say: send 'em away with a great exit. That's me. I'm going back to LA today.'

Josh interrupted. 'I promised you a holiday in Europe. Why not take it before you go back?'

She looked at him in love and admiration. 'You'll still foot the bill, even though I'm walking?'

Josh shrugged. 'Of course. You've done a brilliant job. More than we expected. It's not your fault things have gone wrong.'

She ran over, and kissed him passionately on the lips. And kissed him. And kissed him. Eventually, he pushed her away. Reluctantly she unzipped herself from his body, saying, 'Such a waste. If ever you decide to go gay, let me be the first.' And with that, she went to her bedroom to pack.

Watching her leave was like watching a firework burning out. Whenever she entered a room, she created a *frisson* of energy, an electrifying presence. Her fun and rapid-fire repartee intimidated, entertained, delighted and often irritated the others, but there was never a boring moment when Josephine was around. Now her sudden absence felt like a heavy hand falling upon the company. Sarah, probably more than the others, would miss her. She'd miss her bitchy comments, her devastating one-liners, her ability to prick the bubbles of pretentiousness which were so often a part of the portentous mood that had developed since the troubles began. Even though many of the barbed comments were against her, Sarah had come to realise that most – not all, certainly, but most – were not meant personally. Rather, they were clever mood-setters or mood-breakers. Josephine had that rare Oscar Wildean quality of commanding a room by her very presence. Sarah was sure that things would be much more boring from now on.

Josh sensed the mood and looked over at Phil and Jerry. 'Before you say anything, you're staying. I need you to find an editing facility and give me a half-hour compilation of what we've done so far. Everything. Especially the car chase sequence. That way, if anything happens, at least there'll be a record.'

Sarah smiled. 'So that's why you've been pointing cameras at everyone?' Phil and Jerry nodded.

'I don't follow,' said Laco.

'These guys have been shooting ever since they arrived. They've got an almost complete record of what's been going on,' Josh explained.

'I've seen them filming but I didn't realise . . . You mean?'

Phil nodded. 'We've got almost everything, Laco. We've been shooting footage of all the shit hitting the fan. Even the car chase. We've got so much footage we could put together a three-hour documentary that'll grab you by the curlies.'

Sarah was impressed. 'You guys are good. I was too involved in what was going on. I didn't realise you were still shooting.'

'Thanks,' said Jerry, accepting it as a compliment. 'The technique we were using was the same as that used by hard news photographers. Low-slung cameras shooting from the hip, people running towards cars like they were escaping, angles sometimes off-centre, close-ups of people talking which we took hidden behind greenery or doors so that the immediate foreground looked like out-of-focus shadows. Serious stuff. Once we've compiled and edited it, it'll be a gut-buster. Especially centered around someone as well-known as Josh. It'll look like a cross between a CNN report from a battlefront and an Eastern European travelogue.'

'How long before I can have a rough-cut edit?' asked Josh.

Phil shrugged his shoulders. 'Can't tell until I have a proper look at all the footage, but give me a couple of days and I'll have something for you to look at.'

Josh put his arm around Phil in gratitude. Phil backed away. 'Hey! Back off, man. I saw you kissing Josephine. Just say thanks, Josh. No kissing, okay!'

# CHAPTER TWENTY

Maxim's departure affected everyone, and they all reacted in different ways. Laco suddenly felt as if the weight of responsibility for the group was now resting on his shoulders. His father was a natural-born leader, confident, quietly commanding respect; others tended to follow wherever he led. But Laco never had been a real leader. Even leading an archaeological dig, he was always the joker, the prankster, the Romeo, the good guy that everybody liked. But the people on digs were kids straight from university; these people were adults, each used to leading, not being led. His father would be a tough act to follow, but he had to try.

'Jaroslav Demek,' he said while the others were sitting around the table, musing on their own thoughts. They looked at him, trying to place the name, forgotten in the confusion, danger and anxiety of the past twenty-four hours. 'Jaroslav Demek,' he said again, his voice deeper now, stronger. 'Now, more than ever, we have to find him.'

At first his words were measured, but they slowly grew in intensity. He stood and paced around the table. 'Jaroslav Demek – it's such an ordinary name. Could be a street sweeper, a government minister, anyone. But he is the man who has driven my father from his country.' Laco walked to the mantelpiece and picked up a small statuette.

He examined it intently, watched closely by the others. He put it down. 'We have to find that bastard so we can all get back to a normal life. Especially my father. You know what he should be doing now? Pruning his roses. The house always smelled of roses, like walking into a perfume factory.' Anger seeped out of his every pore.

Sarah wanted to say something, but understood that the last thing he wanted was dialogue.

'I know he's a mass murderer. I know he kicked out your family, Josh. But now he's reached across the years and he's managed to kick my father out of his own country. The country he fought for, was imprisoned for. Believe me, I'm going to pin that bastard's neck to the wall. I'm going to castrate the swine. I'm . . .' He clenched his fists in anger.

Since Maxim's departure, Sarah had wondered who would come forward to fill the breach and direct the group. Josh, the natural director of operations in LA, felt out of context here. And he was too distracted, unfocused, making a huge effort to pull himself together. Sarah herself would have taken on the role, but was also still feeling shell-shocked, and Phil and Jerry, of course, were peripheral. So it was Laco, consumed by fury, striding around like Napoleon, who was deciding their tactics and strategy. Yes, it should be Laco, she thought. 'This Jaroslav Demek,' she said. 'He was one of the names on Richard's list?' Laco nodded.

'You said that he was the most likely suspect to be Alexander Hasek.' Again, Laco nodded.

'How do we find him?' she asked. 'He's already changed his name from Hasek once.'

Josh was galvanised out of his dejected mood. 'The first thing is to get Felix outside to check all the records for a Jaroslav Demek. If that fails . . .'

'Precisely,' said Laco tensely. 'How the hell do we trace a man who's simply disappeared from sight? No forwarding address, no contacts. We can assume that he's managed to sink deep into the slime.'

Josh thought for a moment, then said, 'He's an old man; he'll need continued support. What about pensions or social security or membership of associations or something? If this *is* the guy we're looking for, we know from his letters that he needs to maintain ties with his past. Maybe it gives him a feeling of security.'

'Brilliant!' said Laco. 'Social services.'

He walked to the door and asked Felix to join them. They explained the position carefully to him, holding back no details, openly trusting the man who had already proved that his job was to save their lives. Felix listened carefully without taking any notes.

'It will cost you extra,' he said, once Laco had finished explaining in a mixture of Czech and English.

'Fine,' Josh nodded. 'Money isn't an issue.'

'To you, Mr Krantz, it's not an issue. But so far, you have worked up a bill of tens of thousands of crowns. All we have is a contract signed by Dr Plastov senior, who is no longer here. No money, not even a deposit. There was no appropriate time to mention it before, but now, I think, is the moment. This new sort of search you are talking about will take much money. It will involve a lot of computer time and hacking into government files. Then there's the danger . . .'

'Felix,' Josh interrupted, 'I'll organise payment of your full bill immediately plus I'll put another fifty thousand US dollars into your account in case there's any shortfall.'

Felix smiled. 'You will forgive me being so mercenary but it is an occupational hazard. Much of our work comes from governments. They start off by telling us money is not an issue to protect their public servants or government ministers and that they are using us because the Czech security services are a bunch of idiots. But when it comes to having our bills paid, the delay is – how shall I say – frustrating.'

As the meeting drew to a close, Laco had a sudden idea. 'Archaeologists, even morons like Hasek, can't leave their subject alone. They have to know what's going on.'

Sarah looked at him in interest. 'So?'

'So he'll still want to be a member of the Archaeological Institute or subscribe to the *Journal of Czech Archaeological Digests* or the *Journal of the Ancient World*.'

'But if he's changed his name from Demek, or whatever Hasek now calls himself, how will we be able to trace him?'

'That's what Felix is there to do. I'm just giving him a lead.'

Felix smiled again. He had a thin, knowing smile, so different from the open warmth of Maxim Plastov. He stood, his tall, angular body graceful but also powerful. Sarah wondered how old he was. He looked young enough to be in his thirties, but his lack of impulse, the way he deliberately considered everything before coming up with pat answers, put him into his forties. An enigma.

'What we will do,' he told them, 'is find out when he cancelled his subscription in the name of Demek. Then we will investigate the names of all new subscribers for a couple of months after that. We are not talking about *Playboy*. I doubt there will be many names on the list.'

Sarah watched him leave the room. She was concerned. Her experience as a trial lawyer had brought her into close contact with inquiry agents, private detectives and the like, and she had found most of them to be lacking in moral backbone. They would do anything for a buck, work for anyone, no matter how sleazy, no matter what the cause. She found it difficult to trust any of them with anything but the vaguest details of whichever case she was working on, suspicious that they would sell whatever information they were given to the highest bidder. She felt that way about Felix now, and would continue to do so until he proved otherwise. She determined to remain distant, to observe him carefully and to ensure that he acted in their interests at all times.

The man who once was Jaroslav Demek nursed a brandy, watching the Vltava flowing swiftly at the end of his garden. For days now he hadn't been able to concentrate on anything. He'd even missed a couple of trips to town, citing ill health as the reason. The real reason, however, was the visit he had been paid by the agent of the Syndicate. *Don't worry, Alexander. Everything will be fine, Alexander. We'll look after you forever, Alexander.* Bullshit. Filthy mealy-mouthed rubbish. Condescending, patronising, dangerous shit. The sort of thing he used to say to victims before he put them to death in the old days, so their minds suddenly focused on the possibility of survival and they didn't scream and shout and cause problems. So they were coming to kill him. All because of those letters he'd written to Vera. He often thought of her; such times were the few occasions when his loins still stirred. Loins stirring – what a silly expression! What was wrong with saying that thinking about Vera gave him one of his very occasional erections. She was so beautiful in the old days, a young serving girl with the eyes of a doe, soft and big and innocent, and full breasts. He could still remember the feel of her nipples, hard and mysterious. She had taught him how to be a man, shown him what parts of her body responded to his touch, and what she did to him he would never forget. He had only been a boy, fourteen or fifteen, but she had awakened the man in him.

He had lived a long life and his early life, before the collapse of Stalinism, had been one of privilege, luxury and excess. Excess in food, in wine, in women, in power. Even when he was with Vera, there were other women, dozens of them, maybe even hundreds. He had forgotten. Women who flaunted themselves, threw themselves at him in party rooms or after meetings or at dinners held in his honour. Husbands used to whisper into the ears of their wives, and the women would somehow seek him out and whisper, in their turn, into his ear: *I want you tonight, Alexander . . . Alexander, we don't know each other but I'm hungry for your love . . . Alexander, I'm so attracted to your power. I want you to take me.* It was all a pretence, a farrago of illusion, lies and role playing. He had been the beneficiary, yet whenever he took these women to his bed, he closed his eyes and imagined they were Vera. Unclasping their dresses and feeling deep into the moist warmth of their bodies he felt Vera's breasts, Vera's slim waist, Vera's firm, round bottom. And as he entered these women, women whom he had long forgotten, he imagined he was entering his beloved Vera and he would grow hard and potent. And the women who came to him would realise that they may have been reluctant actresses in the beginning, but when he made love to them, they enjoyed the benefits of a real man.

He had screwed many women more beautiful than Vera, yet she was the only true relationship in his life, the only woman he ever thought of in terms other than contempt. And now she had turned and bitten him on the neck like a blood-sucking vampire. He had sent her a fortune fifteen years ago, enough for her to live on in comfort for the rest of her life. She was his responsibility and he hadn't let her down.

Why had she betrayed him? It must have been Vera who had told this Krantz person about him. If ever he survived, if he walked free from this, she would be the first to go. Despite his love, despite their child, he would wreak his revenge. He would happily go back to Kosice, travel the thirty kilometres to Venubov, sink his fingernails into her throat and extinguish the life from her, watch her struggle and gasp and see the spittle come from her mouth and the life leave her eyes. Or would he? Would he be able to kill the woman he'd loved all his life, even if she had betrayed him? How could she have done it? Was it because he hadn't married her, even though he had loved her . . . still loved her? Did she even love him enough to betray him? Or did she hate him more? He took another sip of brandy to calm himself.

He would be ready for the Syndicate when they came to terminate him. And come they would. If he had been in charge of the Syndicate, he would have issued the order without compunction. 'Hasek has broken the protocols. Hasek must die.' But they had forgotten who they were dealing with. He wasn't some small-town apparatchik; he was Alexander Hasek, the ruler of eastern Slovakia, the man everybody feared, the Stalin of the South. Let's see them try to take me down, he thought. He stood and walked slowly into the house. He checked each room: there was a Luger in the front room, a Smith & Wesson he'd stolen from an American soldier in the back room, and in the attic a couple of Kalashnikovs. And for when he went outside, he had a Beretta. Then of course there was his secret weapon: although it was the tourist season and there were many new faces in town, he had employed a group of locals to warn him of anybody approaching the Parkan. The bastards wouldn't get within a hundred yards without him knowing. Then why was his hand shaking?

The following day, his housekeeper took a phone call from a neighbour who lived near the beginning of the street on the hill, close to the old wooden bridge across the Vltava. She put the phone down and said to Hasek gravely, 'A man is standing on the bridge looking in this direction. He has been standing there for about an hour. He isn't a tourist.'

Hasek nodded. 'You know what to do,' he said.

The woman nodded solemnly. 'And you assure me there is no danger?' she said.

'Absolutely none. He is just a journalist wanting information about me. I told you, they're doing an investigation on fraud in the university department. I had nothing to do with it but they think that I was the mastermind. Do you think I would live so modestly if I had stolen millions from the department?' He laughed out loud, a wheezy, dry sound. 'You've known me for years. I am the last person you could imagine defrauding anybody. It's what I told you – they have confused me with somebody else. Now, you go like I told you and take a look at this man. Come back and tell me what he looks like. Make sure he doesn't see you.'

She nodded and left the house. Hasek waited for her shadow to cross the curtained window, then walked as fast as his elderly legs would carry him into the front room. He took the Luger from its hiding place and ensured its magazine was full of bullets. Slipping out the back of the house as surreptitiously as he could, he took a pathway invisible from the bridge that led between the water and the back of his neighbours' houses to almost directly underneath the bridge. There he was able to look up, immune from the gaze of those above. He could hear dozens of people walking over the wooden slats and the occasional drum roll of a car crossing over. He walked to the other side of the bridge and ascended the stairs that led from the river bank to the main road. He called on all his reserves of memory on how to remain inconspicuous while viewing an area. The lessons he had been taught in Moscow when he was a Komsomol youth were so long ago . . . if only he had listened more attentively. Peeking out from behind the stone stairwell, he saw dozens of summer tourists looking around them at the eternal delights of his town. Normally they were an irritant, but today they were camouflage, a godsend. On the right-hand side of the bridge, standing as he had anticipated she would, visible and obvious, was his housekeeper. She was so conspicuously watching the man that even from behind Hasek could see him shifting around nervously. He was wearing grey slacks and a fawn knit top, and his body was broad-shouldered and muscular. He looked powerful. Even a casual observer would have noticed a bulge in his trouser pocket, but only Alexander Hasek realised that it was a gun. The woman had done her job. He had sent her to act as a decoy, to alert the man to the fact that he had been spotted. If his predictions were correct, the assassin should walk away and contact his headquarters for instructions. Then Hasek would act, just as he had acted in Slovakia when his enemies had mounted challenges to his authority.

The assassin turned and blended in with other tourists walking across the bridge. Hasek followed to determine whether the man was alone or had company. He turned right into Latran, past the Church of St Jodicus then into Nove Mesto. It was difficult to keep up with him; Hasek was anything but fit. He ducked into shop doorways and shadows wherever possible. Only twice did the man stop, once to light a cigarette, another time to tie his shoelace. Each time he turned to look behind him to see if he was being followed. He must be very confident, thought Hasek. Or very stupid. The techniques were obvious, even to a child. Turning a corner into a small street, the man got into a parked car. Without hesitation, without allowing himself time to get frightened or to have second thoughts, Alexander walked towards the car as quickly as his old legs would carry him. He was certain now that there were no other assassins sent to kill him; if there had been, the man would have rendezvoused with them before getting back into his vehicle. One lone assassin – ha! The Syndicate must hold him in very low esteem. Fancy sending a single assassin. If Hasek were running the group. He would never allow such monumental arrogance . . . or professional sloppiness. He stood just behind the car, catching his breath, aware that he was visible in the driver's wing mirror. But it didn't matter. It was too late now, he was in control. The man hadn't noticed him. He was too busy talking on a mobile telephone, absorbed in the conversation. The window was open; Hasek stuck his face and hand through it. The conversation on the phone stopped suddenly, mid-sentence, and the young man looked around at Hasek in shock. Hasek thrust the Luger viciously into the assassin's chest and pulled the trigger. Blood spurted everywhere, but he didn't care. His only concern had been the roar of the gun, but that was muffled by the man's clothes and body. The little side-street was empty, Hasek was grateful that nobody was passing by. The dead man's head fell forward, his eyes still open, staring into infinity. The phone dropped into his lap. Hasek picked it up hesitantly, as if it was contaminated.

'Hello,' he said, in a hushed undertone. There was silence on the other end of the line. 'Hello,' he said again, this time more insistently.

Softly a man answered. 'Who is this?'

'Hasek.'

Dead silence. The man was thinking, searching for something to say. Hasek smiled. He was in charge again. He loved it.

'What was that explosion? Where's Piotr?'

'Dead. I have killed him like you sent him to kill me. That was the explosion you heard, your man being terminated. By me. Now, who are you?'

'Hasek? You are making a terrible mistake. That was Piotr. He was your friend. He was coming to warn you that you are in danger, to take you to somewhere safe.'

'Bullshit,' yelled Hasek. 'Don't treat me like a fool. You sent one of your assassins to kill me.'

'Old friend, this is not true. This is a lie. The last thing we want to do is to harm you. Believe me, stay where you are and I will come and see you personally. Have you really killed Piotr?'

'Ask him yourself,' said Hasek, laughing, as he threw the phone into the dead man's bloody lap and walked away from the car. He took out a handkerchief and wiped the blood from his clothes as best he could. He would attend to it as soon as he got back to the house. Then his life would have to take a very different direction. He saw with pleasure that there was still nobody in the empty side-street. The assassin might stay in the car forever, and that wouldn't be long enough as far as Hasek was concerned. He knew the people of Cesky Krumlov; thousands would walk past the car without bothering to look in. 'Ah,' he thought, 'the wonderful indifference of people.' What was even more surprising was that, as he walked away from the killing, he realised that, for the first time in years, he was enjoying a hard erection.

His plan now was to do some urgent packing and move to another house he had arranged to live in when he first arrived in the beautiful Bohemian town. He had made the arrangements precisely in case anything like this happened. The new place wasn't nearly as comfortable or as pleasant as his current house, but at least it was safe. It was ironic: he had set up the safe house to protect him from those whom the Syndicate failed to stop; he had never expected for one minute that he would need to protect himself from the Syndicate.

It took Felix less than a day to establish that a man called Jaroslav Demek had cancelled his subscription to two archaeological magazines on the same day of the same month in 1983. And that a man called Martin Witten had established a subscription to both magazines the following day. In itself it wasn't unusual, except that he was the only new subscriber to both magazines during that week.

'How did you manage to get the information from them so quickly?' asked Sarah.

'Do you know anything about computer hacking, madam?' asked Felix.

'Just that it's against the law,' she said tartly. The others moaned. Sarah felt the need to say, 'Sorry guys, but once a lawyer, always a lawyer.'

Felix refrained from commenting. Instead he answered prosaically, 'It's illegal here too, but we try not to let the law impede our activities too severely. We in the Czech Republic are rapidly catching up to you in America when it comes to computer security.' He withdrew a folder from his briefcase and handed a computer print-out from it to each person. It was a series of lists with several names highlighted. 'These lists,' he said, 'contain the names of all new subscribers to both magazines in the six months since Demek resigned from the University. We have checked every name. During the time we are interested in, many of them were students or young to middle-aged lecturers in university departments throughout Europe; some in America, a couple in Australia. A few of them, however, may be interesting and worth following up if we draw a blank on the name highlighted in blue. This is the one that stands out most clearly. The subscriber to both magazines is a man called Martin Witten. Plain Mister, not Doctor. He now lives in Cesky Krumlov, having moved there in 1983. He is on the electoral roll in the council district and is receiving social security payments. He also receives a regular monthly payment, far from modest, that is paid out of a bank in Prague which receives it from a bank in Helsinki which receives it from a bank somewhere else.'

Felix smiled. The rest knew that there was something coming. 'The payments originate in Moscow,' he said.

'Moscow!' exclaimed Laco.

'It appears that when Demek retired from Charles University no allowance was made for payments for social security or any other retirement benefits. It was as if he ceased to exist. That in itself is nothing short of extraordinary. The man obviously wanted to get lost.'

'How did you find out that these payments were coming from Moscow?' asked Sarah.

'Computers these days are wonderful things. They tell us so much that others don't want us to find out. We have a very good friend in one of our major banks here in Prague. He gave us the access codes for the bank in Cesky Krumlov. When we looked into Witten's account, we found evidence that a regular amount is paid to him on a monthly basis. It was a very simple job to source it back to the sender. As I said, it originated from a bank in Helsinki, a fairly well-known front that the KGB once used to pay its agents — when it had money . . . and when it had agents. The bank is still partly owned by Novodny Bank in Moscow.'

'So, it's pretty certain that Hasek is this guy, Martin Witten?' said Josh.

Felix nodded. 'I can't be a hundred per cent certain, but it would be surprising if he wasn't.'

Laco stood and walked over to the window. Unlike the castle they had stayed in outside Kosice, with its sweeping views of lawns and forests, the view from here was of a brick wall. He said, 'So now we know the name of the guy. It'll be easy to trace him. The question is, what now? Do we arrest him and put him on trial? Do we tell the police to arrest him? Do we . . . I don't even want to think about what else we could do to the bastard.'

Sarah looked at him in amazement. 'You mean you haven't thought through the most important facet of this whole scenario?'

Laco shrugged. 'What do you mean?' Josh and Felix looked puzzled too.

'Guys,' she said, 'we're on the trail of a mass murderer. For all we know his crimes could be covered by international war crimes legislation. Once we've got the bastard behind bars, there will be witnesses to subpoena, statements to take, a whole raft of legal things. But first we've got to put him under legal restraint. We can't begin to bring proceedings until he's formally accused. And that means once you've found him and got the police to arrest him, I have to sit down with people from the Justice Ministry in Prague and work out what section of Czech or Slovak legislation to charge him under.'

'But we're not at that point yet, Sarah,' said Felix. 'Our first job is to find him, isolate him and restrain him. Whether we do it ourselves or we bring in the police is something we should consider once we get down there.'

They stared at each other, each unwilling to concede a single point. The others could feel the tension crackling between them.

'Excuse me, you two,' Laco interrupted, 'you both seem to have forgotten that because of this bastard my life has been turned upside down. An innocent young woman, whose only crime was working for me, has been murdered, other people have died too and my father is in hiding in Paris. I've got a personal interest here as well. I want to see the bastard swinging from a lamppost. Maybe I'll hand him over to the authorities . . . or maybe not.'

Felix held up his hands. 'Before we start deciding how we're going to execute the delivery of this person, wouldn't it be better to find him first? From what you've told me about this covert Stalinist organisation, he will be on their hit list by now. I would certainly be putting him there if I were running the show. He may be dead already, or he may be a shell of an invalid, gasping away his last days in a wheelchair. I think you have to find out *what* you're dealing with before you determine *how* you're going to deal with it.' It was a sensible way to conclude the meeting.

'Sarah? Sarah, is that you?' His voice sounded as though he was shouting from inside a huge tin can.

'David, I can't speak for more than a couple of seconds. I'm frantically busy. I have to hang up almost immediately. But I want to know how you are and how everything is at home.' Sarah was shouting, praying that he couldn't hear the stress in her voice.

'What do you mean you've only got a couple of seconds? You haven't contacted me in over a week. I've been going frantic. I phoned your hotel in Slovakia and they told me you'd checked out leaving no forwarding address. I don't hear a thing from you and now you tell me you can't spend more than a couple of seconds with me! What the hell's going on? Morrie's going ballistic. He's been phoning every day asking if you've called. He thinks you've abducted your client – or worse, that you've been kidnapped or something!'

'David, for God's sake! You're sounding like my mother. I've only got a few seconds because we're rushing to catch a flight. We haven't been in contact because we've been running from place to place . . .'

'But your Prague and Bratislava law firms have been unable to contact you as well. They've been going crazy. They don't understand what's going on. One minute you're putting enough pressure on them to break their arms, the next you disappear into thin air.'

Sarah reached up to her breast and fondled her amulet, distressed at the grief she'd caused him. 'I know. I'm truly sorry, especially for not being in touch with you. Are you okay? Is everything alright?'

'Fine. Nothing's changed. But what about you? How are you? Tell me what's happening over there . . .'

Felix looked up from his monitor. The wave sign on one of the impulse signal detectors was beginning to show an interference pattern. He looked at Sarah, and ran his finger swiftly across his throat. Sarah nodded.

'Gotta go, darling,' she said, interrupting him. 'My flight's just about to leave. I'll call again as soon as I can.'

Felix disconnected the call.

'Were we tracked?' asked Sarah.

Felix shook his head. 'You weren't talking long enough. But somebody was just beginning to monitor the conversation.'

'Who?' she asked.

'I don't know. Could have been Czech security, the CIA or the NSA, or even our unidentified friends.'

Sarah was distressed by the conversation and wanted to think about something else. 'The NSA?' she asked Felix. 'Remind me who they are.'

Felix smiled. 'It stands for the National Security Agency – America's eyes and ears on the world. They're at Fort George G. Meade in a huge complex on a thousand acres of land between Washington and Baltimore. They used to monitor all telephone calls, faxes and radio signals into and out of America, but now, with satellites, they monitor just about every conversation that takes place between every country.'

'So why did you cut me off?' she asked. 'It could have been anyone. Not even someone interested in us.'

'True, but the one thing which this beautiful piece of equipment can't do is tell us who it is listening in to our phone calls.'

Boris Maximovich Tranov listened gravely to the news. The man giving him the information had been a war hero, a full colonel–general in the Soviet Army, a man who had stood eight people away from Brezhnev reviewing the May Day parade, a man to whom thousands of officers had once paid obeisance. Yet today, Nikolai Alexandrovich Zamov stood before his lifelong friend and colleague like a penitent before a priest. Gone was the shouting and raving; that was reserved for when mistakes could be corrected. It was now too late, much too late.

'What do the police say?' asked Tranov.

'Murder by person or persons unknown. It was a Mafia-style hit, so they are making assumptions that it was a cross-border assassination: German crime mob catching up with an escaped hood and doing its dirty work in the Czech Republic.'

'Did he have papers?'

'Of course not. He was clean. So was the car. Austrian registration.'

Tranov nodded. 'And the phone?'

'It won't take the police long to find the numbers he called before he met his end. Fortunately, we were using a diversion cut-out in Prague, so the nearest they will get to us is an office in Havelska Street manned by a couple of technicians and lots of computer and telephone switching gear.'

'And there is no chance it can be traced back to your telephone?'

Tranov asked the question with contempt. He had been assured that there was no chance of things going wrong – no chance at all – yet just about everything had gone wrong.

'No chance at all, comrade. It is switched from Prague to Moscow then to St Petersburg. Finally it comes through to me, wherever I am. For the police in Cesky Krumlov to trace the call to me, they would have to follow the thread and that is impossible. Of that I am sure.'

Tranov grunted and scratched his crotch. 'And in the meantime, Hasek has gone into hiding. Have we been to his house?'

Zamov nodded. 'Strip-searched the place. Clean as a whistle. Just books, papers, magazines, photographs. No letters in any drawers. The books have no names in them. We've checked them all. And we've been over the place from top to bottom.'

'Any names on the backs of the photographs?' asked Tranov.

Zamov shook his head. 'None. There is no way of knowing who was living there.'

'You said you found magazines. News magazines, dirty magazines?'

'Only archaeological magazines,' Zamov replied. 'Nothing of importance.'

Tranov felt a prickling under his armpits and in the back of his neck, sensations he had felt with uncomfortable regularity of late. 'You don't buy archaeological magazines over the counter in some Cesky Krumlov newsagency. You subscribe to them.'

'But . . .'

'Which means that his name and address appear on their subscription lists.'

'But his new name: Martin Witten. Not Alexander Hasek, or the name he used in the Charles University, Jaroslav Demek. There's no way he can be traced . . .' Zamov's voice trailed off. He had made that assumption too often in the past.

Tranov looked at him in total contempt, as though he had a terrible disfiguring disease. 'And you think that will stop these Americans, do you? The way they have been uncovering our operation, they must have the entire CIA working for them. It will take them no time to realise that the man they are after is Witten.'

He breathed heavily, exhaling his contempt and frustration. 'I am going to Cesky Krumlov myself. I want every available man to back me up.'

'But what about the search for the Americans?'

Tranov looked at the man with even greater disgust. Quietly he said, 'If they are not there by now, they will arrive within the next day or two.'

He stood and scratched his balls properly. 'Thanks to you, we are now in greater danger from them than they are from us.'

# CHAPTER
# TWENTY-ONE

'You are a Jew?'

His question was so matter-of-fact, yet so packed with implications, that in the noise of the car, Sarah wondered if she had heard him correctly. Either way, the question took her completely by surprise.

'Yes,' she said, sounding more defensive than she had intended. In politically correct America only a backwoods, rabidly right-wing redneck would have framed such a question.

'Then you will be interested in this place. In the fifteenth century, the Lords of the Castle granted many rights to the citizens. Among these was a freedom from Jews. They said that no Jews were allowed to reside in the town. Interesting, yes?'

'No!' said Sarah.

Felix shrugged and continued staring through the front window as the car carried them slowly towards the outskirts of the town of Cesky Krumlov.

Sarah listened to the timbre of her voice, the way in which her anger – and her defensiveness – was showing through. For a moment she was concerned that her over-sensitivity might make her sound like her mother. A Christian only had to use the word 'Jew' around her mother and she automatically assumed that person to be an anti-Semite. Sarah had once been just as oversensitive. Many years ago, as a teenager, if she heard anyone talking about Jews and Judaism, her ears would prick up, her hackles rise and she would take on the defence of her nation. Now it rarely bothered her, except in situations when she wasn't fully in control.

'So,' she asked, forcing her voice to remain neutral in tone, 'where does the name of the town come from?'

Without turning, Felix replied, 'Krumlov is from the German "Krumben ouwe" which means a place on a crooked-shaped meadow. As you can see from the shape of the hills, the Vltava winds and bends, nearly trapping the town like an island. You will see what I mean when we get inside the old part.'

'And Cesky?'

'It means Czech. It was added in the mid-fifteenth century by the Vitkovitz family.' He remained silent for a few moments. 'Sarah, my English makes me a bit abrupt. I know this, because I've been told so before. I think that I insulted you by asking if you were a Jew. Yes?'

'No,' she said dismissively.

'You are sensitive, though.'

'No,' she said again, this time more demonstratively. And then after a few seconds said, 'I used to be. It comes with the territory of being a member of a minority.'

'But in New York, Jews are in the majority. When I ask you, are you a Jew, I don't accuse you. Just like you say to me, are you a Czech. I say yes.'

'It's different for you, Felix. Czechs haven't been persecuted throughout history.'

He shrugged his shoulders. There was so much she didn't know about Czech history, but now was not the time to tell her.

They drove across an old wooden bridge, which Felix informed her was called the Lazebnicky and dated back many hundreds of years. The driver slowed the car because of the masses of people in front of them and proceeded along cobbled streets upwards into the Svornost Square, where children in colourful costumes were performing a medieval masque for the tourists. Sarah wanted to stop and look but knew it would not be possible. Felix had insisted on maximum security. Instead their car drove along the narrow, convoluted street system directly to the Hotel Ruze where, the previous night, Felix had organised for several suites of rooms to be booked for them. They drove into the arched entryway which opened out into a large courtyard. A porter came running out to stop them from going any further. He spoke rapidly to the driver. Felix translated: 'Because of congestion he says that it is impossible to park in here. He insists that we drop off our luggage then park down the hill, closer to the river. That's what he thinks.'

Felix smiled at the man and whispered a few urgent words. He took out his wallet and surreptitiously handed over a fistful of notes to the porter, who smiled, saluted somewhat incongruously and ushered the car into a private driveway within the grounds of the hotel.

'Money,' Felix said to Sarah as the car pulled to a halt. 'The universal language. I told him there would be four other cars and that we have booked six rooms. We won't be disturbed.'

When she was shown into her room, Sarah felt the same frisson of delight that she had experienced when she first saw her room in the castle just outside Kosice. It was a wonderfully ancient and atmospheric room dominated by a four-poster bed with a thick gleaming-white duvet and a canopy made of red velvet. She walked over to the window: the lead mullions separating tiny squares of almost opaque glass gave it the feeling of an Elizabethan fantasy. When she opened it, the view was onto the ancient courtyard. Looking closely at its architecture, it was now obvious to her that the hotel was an old monastery that had been converted. On the courtyard wall opposite her room was a magnificent sundial. She looked carefully at it, trying to define the meaning of its symbols. In the middle of the dial were the letters SOL, and numbers in Roman numerals from one to twelve were written around its square face. Yet also in the middle of the dial, there seemed to be an entire esoteric alphabet of astrological and numerical symbols that she'd never seen before. Felix had told her that Cesky Krumlov had once been a centre of mysticism and alchemy in the Middle Europe of medieval times. This sundial must be one of the remaining artefacts, an attempt by the monks to gain greater knowledge of the hidden world, the world outside of Christianity and the New Testament.

She turned back from the window and started to unpack her suitcase. How David would have loved this hotel, this town. From the little she had seen of it so far, it was glorious; everything they had talked about for a honeymoon, if ever she got around to accepting his offer. And then, almost as though it had a will of its own, her hand found its way to her neck, where her amulet brought her back to a feeling of who she was and what her life was really all about. Was it about chasing mass murderers around Eastern Europe, or was it . . .?

There was a knock on her door. When she opened it, Laco walked in, kissing her gently on the cheek as he entered. 'What do you think?' he asked. 'Pretty special, eh? Bet you don't have anything like this in America.'

'It's wonderful,' she agreed, 'but this whole thing is so incongruous. Here we are on the trail of a mass murderer in one of the most beautiful towns in Europe. It's like searching for the black heart inside a beautiful body.'

'Very eloquent,' he said. 'And talking about eloquence, have you heard from Mr Hollywood?'

She shook her head. 'He wouldn't be in touch with me yet. He was going to start editing this morning. I don't expect to hear from him for a couple of days.'

'I don't understand why he stayed in Prague,' said Laco. 'I'd have thought that of all times this would be the one when he'd most want to be present. After all, this is the reason he came over here.'

'No, it isn't,' said Sarah. 'We came over here to get his family's home back.'

'Okay,' said Laco. 'But things have changed. In Slovakia and then in Prague, he was . . . what do you call it when a man wants to go out and get things done?'

'Gung-ho.'

'That's it. He was all gung-ho to catch this bastard Hasek and now, just when we're about to put our fingers around his neck, he backs off and stays with Phil and Jerry to do editing. I don't get it. What's the reason?'

'You were there when he told us. I don't know anything more myself.'

'Well, I guess we'll find out as soon as it's finished. Meantime we have to find this piece of filth. Felix said to meet him downstairs. I came to get you.'

He turned and began to walk out of her room, then hesitated. 'Sarah,' he said, 'we need to talk.'

She looked at him, a frown creasing her forehead.

He spoke softly. 'I don't know whether I should say this. I've been tossing it over in my mind: *Leave it alone, Laco . . . No, you must close things off between you, Laco.* So it's important that you know I've spent the past week or so thinking that what happened between us in Slovakia was over. I've been trying to put it out of my mind. I know that for you it was an aberration, and I thought I could put it in a box and forget about it . . . but I can't.' He hesitated.

She looked at him in wonder, unsure of where he was going.

'It was wrong, Sarah. Wrong of me. Wrong *for* me. I behaved in a way which was . . . '

'Laco, why are you saying this? We've come a long way beyond what we did in Kosice.'

'And you can forget about it?' he asked.

She nodded vigorously. But then slowly shook her head. She was unsure that he would understand, and was scared that an agreement, however tacit, might open her up again to an approach from him. He saw that in her eyes. They told him that she wanted a guarantee that none of their misdemeanours would ever come back to haunt her.

'Laco, what we did – it was wrong for me as well. I'm deeply committed to David in New York. I don't know why I did it. But all thoughts of it must end. Now.'

'For you, it's easy. For me, not so much. I'll only forget you when you go back to the States, when you turn your back on Europe and me and everything which you leave behind. Sarah, if you decided to stay in Slovakia, or anywhere in Europe, I would chase you until I caught you. You are a fantastic woman – I said it before and I mean it. You're wonderful, brilliant, passionate, beautiful. Everything a man like me could ever want. You're what none of the other girls are. You are a wife.'

'Is that a compliment?' she said, stifling a laugh.

'Oh, yes,' he said. 'You know me, I screw around. But I never let myself get emotionally involved. I know you despise me for it . . .' She began to interrupt, telling him she didn't despise him, but he put his finger to her lips.

'Yes, you do. You think I'm crude and crass and a cheap womaniser, but none of the other women I've had have held my interest for more than a couple of days. They were just conquests. There's only been one love in my life, I told you about her. I don't know where she is, she could be dead for all I know. Since I lost her, I've used women only to boost my ego. I was too frightened of real relationships in case I got hurt. But you're different. The first time we made love, it was a conquest, I admit it. I wanted you, badly, but just for my ego. But the second time, when you came to my room after Marta was killed, you understood my needs, you truly did. You were like a wife. I saw you in a different light and I became scared of falling in love, of having a relationship. I knew you were committed to your man in New York. I wanted to draw away. You took the decision from me – you became cold and harsh. I tried to shrug off what we'd done, but I keep coming back to you. My mind is always thinking about you, about your goodness, your brains, your beauty. I think if you stay around, we will have a relationship, a real one. Maybe I'll even ask you to get married. My father is always telling me to. When I kissed him goodbye before he left for Paris, he whispered in my ear that I should pursue you and marry you.'

'Your father said that?' Sarah said, surprised.

'I told you, he's the most intelligent man I've ever known.'

They met in the restaurant. It was the middle of the afternoon and there were no diners left in the room. It was like a huge cavern, divided up into a number of different eating and drinking areas, each separated by narrow archways, and had originally been the monks' cellars where huge vats of wine and sherry were stored. Felix chose an area away from the restaurant's doors at the rear of the basement. Two of his men were stationed at tables near the entrance to prevent anyone getting close. Sarah, Laco and Felix were joined by three of his security operatives; one was the attractive young woman who had escorted Maxim and Josh from their car in the department store in Prague. Her name was Goshia. Sarah was transfixed by her gentle beauty. For once Laco didn't seem to notice.

'We know where he lives,' said Felix, 'in the Parkan which is just down below here. It was an easy job to trace the house. It is completely empty and seems to have been so for a least a day, though there are no signs of him having packed and left. All his clothes and personal stuff are still there. Shaving gear, pharmaceuticals, underwear. There's even a glass of water still by his bedside. There are no recent pictures for us to identify him, so all we can rely on are the photos you showed me from forty years ago. It makes identification difficult, but we'll do our best.'

Laco said, 'Maybe he's left because he knows we're onto him. Maybe someone in Prague has phoned and told him. This group that's protecting him, maybe they've spirited him away.'

Felix shook his head. 'One of my operatives found out that there was a Mafia-style assassination in the streets yesterday. A man sitting in his car was shot through the heart with a bullet which the police think came from an old gun, probably a wartime German Luger.'

'So?' said Sarah.

'The dead man had no identification, the police have no idea who he was. However, it seems to be too much of a coincidence. I think he was a hit man sent by the group to finish off Hasek. But Hasek got there first.'

Sarah reacted like a defence lawyer, 'That's a quantum leap in assumptions. Hasek's an old man. You said yourself he could be in a wheelchair. We have no idea that this murder was anything to do with him and if it was, how does an elderly man overcome a healthy, fully-trained killer?'

Felix nodded. 'You could be right. I've got no facts to back me up. But, on the other hand, it's too coincidental. Hasek himself might not have done the killing, he might have hired a bodyguard for all we know. But it still seems likely that the unidentified man was something to do with this group and Hasek. This is a small town, a tourist town. Mafia-style murders don't happen here. They happen in Prague or Moscow. If I was leading this group and Hasek had compromised its integrity, my intention would be to eliminate him. Let's face it, because of his mistake with the old woman and the letters, we've not only traced him but we're on our way to exposing the group. The only sure way of not getting beyond him and invading the secrecy of the cabal is for him to die. I think that the man in the car was sent to kill him; it is a reasonable hypothesis until proved otherwise.'

'Then,' said Laco, 'if there's been one assassination attempt and it was yesterday, Hasek could be miles away by now. He could be across the German or Austrian border, or in Switzerland – anywhere.'

Felix nodded. 'True. But we need to take a good look around town before we leave. And the other thing we need to do is to talk to people who knew him. That might give us a clue as to where he's gone.'

Boris Maximovich Tranov looked up at the circular bell tower of Cesky Krumlov's castle: it was a wonderful structure, delicately painted as a *trompe l'oeil* to make the white stucco look like huge blocks of limestone, fitting together as snugly as the blocks that made up the Egyptian pyramids. Halfway up the circular tower, a dozen or so people walked around the observation area – tourists with cameras or binoculars strung around their necks like badges of office. Higher up, clocks on each of the four points of the compass showed different times and above them again, higher still, the metal cupola rose precipitously to yet another observation area and a flagpole that could be seen for miles around. Tranov sat drinking beer in a corner of the large Svornost Square in the centre of town. Dozens of cars were parked around the periphery of the square and in between the parking areas hundreds of tourists were eating and drinking in fenced-off café areas. He watched them with disdain; they were like sheep in an enclosure. In the centre of the square noisy children were performing an irritating dance for the tourists; a silly and commercialised deference to the town's need for new visitors. The sun was hot, even though he was sitting at a shaded table, waiting for news. It was his third beer. Soon he would need to find a toilet. Unlike at home in Bratislava, he wasn't free to piss over tomato plants in order to get rid of his anger. He decided to have another beer, but not to wait until he got back to his hotel before going to the toilet. The bathroom in this pox-ridden café was probably down at the bottom of some dark, slimy basement, stinking of the collective piss of a hundred tourists, probably Germans.

A tall, thickset young man walked across the square. He wasn't a tourist; he was one of Tranov's security men. He walked straight over to Tranov and sat down. 'They are in the Hotel Ruze, having a beer in the basement. I couldn't get close enough to hear what they were talking about. They've got muscle protecting them.'

Tranov nodded. 'Much muscle?'

'Enough to give us serious trouble.'

'And Hasek?'

'I've got a dozen men trying to find out who knew him. We may have to break a few old bones to find him, but don't worry, we *will* find him. That I promise you.'

'You'd better,' said Tranov. 'If they get to him first, we will all be swinging by our necks, you and your men included. They won't just be after us of the old guard, they'll be after the entire cadre.'

'Then why don't you let me terminate them? We could force them off the road into the river next time they drive out. If we ensure they all drown, the police will be none the wiser. Or I could put a remote bomb in their car and explode it when they are fifty miles out of town, or even put a bullet through one of them with a telescopic viewfinder from a kilometre away. By the time they hit the pavement, I would be driving out of town. Nobody would know it was me, it would never be traced back.'

Tranov smiled. His men were so different from the incompetents trained by that idiot, Zamov. He reached over and patted the young man on the hand. 'You may be right. I may have to order you to deal with one of them if they get too close . . .'

'They couldn't get much closer than they are now, for God's sake, Boris Maximovich. They are in the same town. And it is not exactly a place the size of Moscow. Look at it,' he said, waving his hand contemptuously across the landscape of the town square, 'one good fart and you'd stink the whole place out. We can't help but run across them in the next day or two. I don't think we should wait, comrade. I think we should take them out surgically. That's my advice.'

Tranov shook his head. 'No, Vladimir. The police from Prague are here in droves because of what that bastard did when he terminated Piotr. They are terrified that Cesky Krumlov is in the centre of a gang war.' He laughed at the absurdity of the notion. Then he said to his young comrade, 'Do everything in your power to find Hasek, but do nothing in the Hotel Ruze.'

'But what if they find him first?'

'Then, and only then, will it be time for surgery.'

Sarah was quite content to allow Felix and his men to do the searching. In her heart, she knew that Hasek was no longer in Cesky Krumlov. She wouldn't have stayed herself, especially if an assassination attempt had been made on her. In a way, she thought, it was a pity that the assassination attempt hadn't been successful. She had been thinking about Hasek, what he looked like now. Was he like those pathetic old men dragged before war crimes tribunals, grey and emaciated, covered with liver spots? Protesting their innocence. They claimed to have been innocent pawns in a chess game played out at levels of authority far above their own. They were wheedling, spent, old people, hollow and empty. Yet Sarah had gone way beyond any feelings of empathy for these people: she had examined their crimes, she knew exactly what they had done. She had seen the evidence of their evil. And Hasek was no different. Through him, hundreds – maybe thousands – of people had been brutalised, dispossessed, tortured and murdered. She dreaded seeing him. She dreaded confronting old Europe, the Europe she hated with a passion.

But maybe now she would never have to confront him; if he wasn't dead, he had probably disappeared down some rat hole. Europe wasn't like America. In this part of Europe – central and hemmed in by numerous borders – Hasek could easily have escaped to Austria, Germany, maybe even Hungary. In America, he would have had to cross State boundaries, and the FBI or some other Federal government agency would eventually have caught up with him. Which was Sarah's problem. Assuming that he *had* crossed into another country, there would be the question of extradition to deal with, which meant treaties between one country and another – things she simply wasn't certain about. So part of her morning had been spent calling government agencies, finding someone in the legal department who could speak English and asking questions. She had received no straight answers, of course, only further questions: *Why do you want to know these things? Who are you wishing to extradite? The person you are interested in, what crime has he or she committed?* To each question, she had been as non-committal as possible, but by the end of a frustrating morning, she'd got virtually no further than when she started. She realised she would have to contact the Prague law firm she'd commissioned in the matter of reclaiming Josh's house in Slovakia, which shouldn't be such a problem now they were out in the open.

By mid-morning the following day, after further frustrations in trying to work out legal procedures in the event of arresting Hasek, Sarah began to understood how wise Josh had been to remain in Prague editing his film. The searching, the investigations, the pounding of pavements being done by Felix, Laco and the security men was as frustrating for them as working out legal matters was for her. Felix had left two men with her, but they were taciturn, spoke little English and were more intent on guarding her front and back than spending time talking to her. By the end of her second day in Cesky Krumlov, Sarah had decided to play the part of the tourist. It was such a pleasure to be out of the hotel and walking the streets. Even a hotel as wonderful and romantic as the Ruze could eventually become boring when it was constantly viewed from the inside of a bedroom.

Walking along the cobbled streets of the town, she was drawn by a gravity like force to the castle on top of the hill. Flanked by her bodyguards, she walked slowly over the old wooden bridge that crossed the fast-flowing Vltava. She asked one of the guards if he knew anything about the bridge. He nodded. 'My family visit here when I was boy at holidays. Bridge called Lazebnicky meaning bath house. Many centuries ago, people of Krumlov went to house on bank of river near here for shave and bath and haircut and leeching to let blood for disease. Story is that son of Emperor fell in love with daughter of barber and after wild orgy murdered her. Citizens could do nothing because of importance of boy. Father committed suicide, mother drowned herself in grief. Not a pretty story.'

They passed the Church of St Jodicus and its extraordinary fourteenth-century spire, then walked slowly up the hill, rising inexorably towards the tower of the castle, that looked more like a minaret from an Arabian mosque than a symbol of medieval European power. The castle itself was vast. Over the course of six centuries, forty buildings and five courtyards and parks had been constructed along the length of the prominence that overshadowed the town. Sarah stopped outside the outer entrance and took out her guidebook to read about its provenance. But before she had read more than the first sentence, one of her guards put his arm around her shoulder and pulled her roughly to the side of the road. She was shocked by the abrupt move and told him to get his hands off her. He continued to manhandle her into the doorway of a house outside the castle walls.

'What the hell are you doing?' she demanded.

'Quiet!' he whispered fiercely.

Sarah stopped complaining immediately and suddenly became nervous. She looked back in the direction they had come from. She couldn't see the second guard. He had left them quietly and was already ambling back down the road like a bored tourist, looking into the windows of the shops which served the needs of tourists.

'What's happening?' she whispered, a note of panic creeping into her voice.

'Could be nothing. An old woman has been following us since we left Hotel Ruze. Maybe something, maybe nothing.'

Sarah held her breath and watched from the safety of the doorway as the second security guard strolled casually along the street. He passed a group of tourists who were talking noisily and laughing, then an old lady who was struggling breathlessly up the hill. The bodyguard's movements were so fluid that at first Sarah thought he had somehow missed seeing the old woman. Yet as she passed him, he slowly backtracked to follow her. As the old lady drew close to where Sarah was skulking in the doorway, the guard put his arm around her, pulled her further into the doorway and kissed her passionately on the cheek. He whispered into her ear, 'Please excuse, I must hide your face.'

The old lady passed the young couple and gave them a disdainful look. The moment she had passed, the guard unclenched his embrace and said somewhat incongruously, 'Thank you very much.' He continued to hold Sarah tightly as he watched the woman lumber painfully up the hill.

As she approached the first entrance to the castle keep and the bear pit, the old woman realised that her quarry was no longer in sight. She stopped and looked around slowly, still failing to find Sarah. She stood stock still in the middle of the road as other tourists passed her by. Even observing her from behind, Sarah could see that the old woman was out of breath, sweating and breathing heavily in the warm air. But she continued up the hill for another few minutes.

Sarah whispered to the guard, 'What do you think she'll do?'

Before the guard could answer, the old lady shrugged, as though in defeat. She turned and walked slowly back down the hill. The two guards escorted Sarah out into the roadway and stood on either side of her in the middle of the street. The old woman was gazing at the ground, her face florid, her breathing short and gasping, but as she come closer to them, she sensed a presence. She looked up and saw Sarah standing between two burly men and her exhausted face registered shock. It was the final proof the guards needed that she was following Sarah. One of them walked up to her and said something in a low and obviously menacing voice. The old woman shook her head violently, but he grasped her arm and pulled her down the hill towards where Sarah was standing. The first guard questioned her, the second translated for Sarah: 'He asks why she is following you. She says she isn't. He says she is a liar and she will be damaged if she continues the lie. She says she was instructed by her employer to give you a letter. She says she knows nothing.'

'Tell him not to be cruel to her,' said Sarah.

'He knows what he's doing,' said the guard. 'We need to frighten her.'

Sarah's thoughts flooded back to an old woman in Venubov and Laco's cruel and imperious interrogation techniques. This old woman smiled at Sarah apologetically, looking for some sign of human warmth. She felt intimidated by the guards. Sarah smiled back and the old woman relaxed visibly. She spoke to Sarah; again the guard translated: 'She says she is very sorry to be following you. Her life has been very bad since the trouble started.'

'What trouble?' asked Sarah.

'The trouble with her employer,' translated the guard. 'Life was very pleasant and easy and then this man came from out of nowhere and since then her life has been terrible. Her employer is hiding. She doesn't know what the future holds. Her family depends on the job.'

'Who is her employer?' asked Sarah.

'Martin Witten,' replied the woman softly. But the name resounded in Sarah's brain. Martin Witten! She fought her desire to shout out in joy. She had found a direct link to Hasek, all on her own. She forced herself to bite back a smile. Felix and the others, all of them local professionals in one way or another, were out searching for Martin Witten and Sarah, trial lawyer and New Yorker, was the one to have found him.

'She has a letter for me?'

The old woman reached into the shopping bag she was carrying, but the guard clamped an iron fist over her wrist. She gasped in shock and pain. The other guard lifted the bag off her shoulder and opened it carefully. He took out a letter, which he gave to Sarah, then searched the bag. He shook his head and gave it back to the old woman. Sarah ripped open the letter. It was written in English:

*Miss Kaplan,*
*By now, you know that I am not Martin Witten, I am Alexander Hasek. I'm in hiding from the Syndicate; I assume you know about that. They are here to assassinate me, despite the*

fact that I have been a loyal member of the Party and follower of Stalin's orders. To survive I need your help. Either you will help me or I will die and you will know nothing. I know that you are backed by strong forces; the Syndicate too is very powerful. Your job must be to expose them, not me. The Syndicate wants revenge. You want justice.

This woman is my housekeeper. She does not know where I am, so do not follow her. Simply tell her you are willing to meet me and I will contact you again.

*Alexander Hasek*

Where previously Sarah had been fighting feelings of smugness, now an overwhelming feeling of dread descended upon her shoulders. It was as though she was holding a letter from Adolf Hitler himself. She suddenly felt sullied by touching something which he'd touched. In her hands she held the letter of a mass murderer, and he was treating her as a confidante, a friend. She looked at the old woman, but her eyes bore no signs of understanding. She was a go-between not an ambassador. She looked at one of the guards, and said yes in Czech.

The only phone call Felix would allow her to make was to the number Josh had given them for the editing suite in Prague. Josh simply had to be there when they met Hasek, Sarah demanded. She owed it to him as her client, as a friend and as somebody whose family had suffered. Felix re-read the note for the eighth time.

'The Syndicate,' he kept mumbling to himself, 'could be anybody.' He turned the letter over carefully in his hands, treating it with the respect and delicacy he would pay to an archaeological relic.

'It could be half a dozen old Stalinists, a unit of the KGB, half the people in the Kremlin. Even people who still work in Hradcany Castle. I don't recall seeing this name mentioned anywhere in documents about the time of Stalin. Must be top secret,' he told Sarah.

'But it looks as if Maxim was right,' she responded. 'We've now got proof that there *is* a group of old guard Stalinists that was set up to protect their comrades.'

Felix nodded. 'So it seems.'

'Then what do we do now?' she asked.

'I'm afraid we have to wait for Hasek to call us. One of my men followed the old woman after she gave you the letter. She went back to her house and has been in there ever since. Another team put transmitting microphones on her windows and bugged the phone, but so far nothing. No calls in and no calls out. It seems that the old woman is in there alone. She occasionally mumbles to herself but it's nothing much.'

'So Hasek isn't there?' said Sarah. Felix shook his head. 'No. He is obviously hiding in a pre-prepared house, using the old woman as an intermediary. She doesn't know it, but we are guarding her in case the Syndicate tries to terminate her.'

'Terminate her!' said Sarah, shocked by the matter-of-factness of his words.

'It looks to me as though the Syndicate have sent assassins down here for a mopping-up operation,' said Felix. 'Pure and simple.'

'That's very clinical.'

Felix shrugged his shoulders. 'We are at war, Sarah. These men are going to take no prisoners. They are fighting for their survival. They have remained underground for over forty years. You don't maintain that level of security without some very sophisticated measures and complete lack of conscience. Hasek was the odd man out; he slipped through the net by breaching their tight security and sending those letters. It was a link to his past. For that offence, they have tried to assassinate him. Just as I would under the circumstances, as well as everybody connected with him.'

'Then why do you keep saying that Josh and I aren't in as much danger as the others?'

'It's a judgement call. Laco and Maxim were the ones who were at serious risk. They're locals; they would be listened to by the authorities. But it would be an extraordinary measure to try to terminate you and Josh. The repercussions for them would be unthinkable. If a man as famous as Joshua Krantz were assassinated, even the White House would get involved. The whole edifice would collapse around their heads. They're not fools. They know it.'

'You make it seem as if we're immune.'

Felix smiled. 'Let me tell you a very short story. When I was little more than a boy, I used to go hunting in the Tatra Mountains with my father. One day we found a trap that had been set by an old woodsman. There was a leg still inside it. Nothing else, just a leg. It belonged to a wolf. The wolf had obviously sprung the trap and, in his efforts to get free, had bitten off his own limb. You can't even begin to imagine the pain that would have caused. Yet he suffered that pain for his own safety. If these guys are in danger of exposure, they will kill you and Josh and me and the Czech government to escape detection. The closer we get, the more danger we are all in, Sarah. That is why I'm increasing the number of men guarding you. They will be here in the morning.'

Josh arrived very late that night, expecting to see Alexander Hasek strapped to a chair with a spotlight blinding his eyes. Instead he found the group waiting around in frustration. He read the letter and beamed a smile of congratulations at Sarah. 'And he hasn't been in contact since?'

'Not a word,' she said.

He turned to Felix. 'What do you think?'

'I think this thing is bigger than you, Sarah and anybody else thought when you started the investigation. This is a major conspiracy against the people of Eastern Europe, conducted over decades. Either that or we are all being played for idiots by a homicidal lunatic.'

'It's unbelievable,' said Josh, as he sipped a bourbon to recover from the frantic drive south from Prague. 'I came over here intending to get back my family's home, just to prove a point. To prove that we could make those bastards who have sinned against us atone for the crimes they committed. And look at this,' he waved Hasek's letter in the air. 'We've uncovered a conspiracy that we can't even begin to fathom. It's unbelievable!'

'Epic,' said Sarah.

Josh frowned.

'Face it, Josh. This could become the greatest film you've ever made. This is Oscar material. Would you do it as a documentary or as a movie?'

'Sarah, I'm not doing this for my career, or to make money.'

'I know.' She realised that she'd gone too far and had hurt his feelings. 'But you have to admit that all the elements are there.'

'Sure. But this is different.'

'Why? You brought Phil and Jerry across to make a documentary. It's gone in a different direction, but it's still NBC material. It's – what's the best way of describing it? – gripping.'

'What's got into you?' he asked. She looked embarrassed. 'Sarah, you know I've been in Prague editing. I didn't expect to come here to find you all self-righteous and sanctimonious.'

She felt herself flush. 'Josh, I was the one he contacted. I was the one he decided to give the letter to. Do you understand what that means? He thinks of me as some kind of a friend, a comrade. But I'm not his comrade, I'm his enemy. I detest him and everything about him. I feel dirty that he's singled me out.'

'Like Frank Darman singled you out,' he said softly.

She said nothing. She knew he was right.

Josh looked at Felix. 'When do you think we're going to get the call?'

'Whenever he wants to,' said Felix. 'Right now, he's calling the shots.'

'But why?' asked Josh. 'You've got a huge number of men here. Why can't we just scour the town?'

'It doesn't work like that,' said Felix. 'He's made the first move. He's contacted Sarah through the old woman. And when she gives him his answer, he'll be in contact with us. Believe me, it's the only way. Hasek will have so many fail-safe systems in operation that we won't even be able to get close to him without him knowing. All he'll do then is run down a rabbit hole.'

The following morning, while they were eating breakfast, one of the security guards came into the cellar and whispered into Felix's ear.

'A boy has just delivered a message to the old woman's home,' Felix reported. 'She walked upstairs, opened a window and shook a towel outside as if she was shaking dust from a rug. It is obviously a sign to Hasek saying that you are willing to assist him. His house must be within telescopic viewing distance of the old woman's.'

'So?' said Laco. 'Doesn't that mean we should be able to track him?'

'All it means is that within the next hour we should hear from him.'

The atmosphere at the breakfast table changed from optimism about the future to excitement about the present. 'Should I go back to my room?' Sarah asked.

Felix shook his head. 'We are not puppets to be pulled by his string. He is a murderer. He will wait for us. If we give in too quickly, he won't give us as much information.'

Nonetheless, Sarah finished her breakfast quickly and returned to her room. Felix accompanied her. It was a small room; the day was already hot and she opened the window onto the courtyard to allow a breeze. Felix was silent as he sat there, reading a paper, waiting. Sarah sat on the bed looking through a law journal she had brought with her from America. It was the fourth time she'd read it from cover to cover yet she was still taking in less information than she would have done in her every-day, pressured New York existence. When the phone call did come, Sarah nearly jumped out of her skin. She reached over to grab it but Felix held up his hand. He allowed it to ring six times and before she picked it up he told her, 'Keep him on the line as long as possible.'

'I will,' she said quietly.

'Miss Kaplan, I think you know who this is.' His was the voice of age, thin, tending towards reedy and asthmatic. A wave of disgust passed through her body. She felt the same way as she had during the conversations that she'd had with Frank Darman when she was preparing her court case all those months ago, as if just by talking to him she was being tainted.

'I got your letter,' she said.

'I know, the old woman told me. There is a house in a district called Sidliste Plesivec, to the south of the city.' He gave her the precise address and continued, 'The man guarding you will be able to find it. Come in one car. Just you, Krantz, the archaeologist Plastov and the man guarding you. Nobody else. Is that clear? If anybody else is there, I won't be.'

'There's no need for these precautions. Nobody knows we're here.' She heard him laugh. It was more like a wheeze.

'You are currently being watched by a group of assassins led by Boris Maximovich Tranov, once a diplomat in America, now head of the Syndicate. They have at least a dozen men in town. Your every step is being monitored. Your security people must find a way to lose them.

'I know Cesky Krumlov and I have thought this through very carefully. I suggest the four cars you arrived in all leave the hotel at precisely the same time and drive in different directions. I suggest that each of the cars intersect at different points around the city and change passengers. Nobody who follows you will know for certain which car you are in. However, when you approach the address I have given you, I will have a vantage point enabling me to know who is in the car and whether or not you are being followed. Understand, madam, my need for caution – my life is in danger. I will not allow anybody to come near me unless I am certain of who it is. If these security arrangements are breached you will never have the opportunity to see me or to hear what it is that I know.'

'And when we do see you, what is it you have to tell us?'

'Information that will make you a very famous young lawyer and your friend Mr Krantz a very happy young man. You will be heroes, believe me.'

'Why should I believe you? Why should I trust you? How do I know you don't intend to endanger me? How do I know it isn't a trap?'

'You are trying to delay me so that your security can trace this call. I didn't expect that sort of naivety or stupidity from a woman of your obvious intelligence. Be there in two hours.' The phone disconnected.

Sarah put the phone down and began to relay the information to Felix. 'Don't bother,' he said holding up his hand to stop her speaking, 'it's all on tape.' He looked at his watch. 'I think we were unlucky.' As he was speaking a man knocked on the door. Felix got up and answered it. He returned and said to her, 'Another thirty seconds and we would have had his location. Damn! If my guess is right, he was phoning from close by. He will already have left there and will be watching us from a vantage point right now. This man is not a fool. He has been planning these exercises for years. He has thought through every scenario. What else is there to do when you are a retired mass murderer?'

They went into Felix's room and played back the conversation. Josh listened carefully to every word. Sarah was surprised at how tense, how hesitant, she sounded on the recording.

'Do you know this man?' Josh asked when the tape had been played through a second time. 'Tranov? He sounds like one of the Marx Brothers.'

Felix replied, 'I have no idea who he is. It won't take long to find out his details, though. We have a very good relationship with the local CIA man in Prague, he should be of assistance tracing Tranov, the diplomat. If he was KGB it could take weeks for us to find him from the files. The Lubyanka in Moscow isn't exactly Grand Central Station. These days it's possible to find things out, but you still have to get past the Moscow bureaucracy. Still, it would be very useful to have pictures of this man so that we know who is watching us.'

Josh looked at his watch. 'We have one and a half hours,' he said.

Tranov listened with growing apprehension as Vladimir defined the events of the morning. 'So his housekeeper signalled to him?' Vladimir nodded.

'A towel out of the window. I can't believe it would be that stupid,' growled the older man.

'Why stupid?' said Vladimir. 'It's actually very sensible: it's visible from miles away if you have binoculars and it doesn't rely on electronic communications so we can't bug it. There is no way we could have spotted him watching her signal.'

'What about the group in the Hotel Ruze, what's happening to them?'

'There has been a lot of activity in the hotel. We are paying the switchboard operator, who told us that the girl got a phone call. After the phone call, according to one of the maids, they all went to the room of one of the men and held some sort of a meeting.'

'And we have no idea what the phone call was about?'

Vladimir shook his head. 'Unfortunately no. Regardless of what we pay, the switchgirl won't allow us to bug the switchboard.'

'And you're letting some kid stop you?'

'At the moment, it is all we can do. There are more than a hundred rooms. We can't bug them all. I have a man working on the incoming lines into the hotel, but it still means listening to every call. This will take time.'

'After the phone call and the meeting?' asked Tranov.

'An hour went by with no movement. Then suddenly they all rushed out of the hotel and climbed into their cars.'

Tranov nodded. 'Your assessment?'

'Hasek contacted the girl and they have arranged a meet. We are following them, naturally,' said Vladimir, 'but four cars left the grounds of the hotel and drove in different directions when they got to the main road. We could only follow two of them. We followed the one with the girl and the American man; another of our cars is following the security chief and the young archaeologist.'

'And the other cars?' asked Tranov.

'Full of security men.'

'They are doing a cross-over manoeuvre. You will lose them on the second switchover. Shit! Keep me posted.'

'Of course,' said Vladimir and returned to the control room in his hotel, just beyond Svornosti Square.

Two of the convoy of cars met half an hour later in a suburb north of the town in a street called Skolni. They switched Laco with one of the security men in less than eight seconds in a road tunnel out of sight of observers, and the cars drove off in different directions. In the eastern suburb of Horni Brana, the other two cars met up and Sarah and Josh jumped out of their original car and leapt into the new one. Again the cars parted from each other at breakneck speed. Vladimir's security team tried to keep up with what was happening but by the second and third exchange, they were totally confused and were forced to report their failure.

Vladimir heard the news with a sense of almost painful despondency. How was he ever going to tell Tranov that they had lost them? But Tranov already knew.

The man was as nondescript as the house he was waiting in. Sarah was shocked at the ordinariness of him. He was small with a wizened, almost gnomic appearance, and was wearing a white shirt, black trousers and a dark striped tie. Had he not been wearing a black beret as well, he would have looked exactly like a retired Swiss bank manager on vacation. She stared at him in disbelief. Was this the personification of evil? Was this man truly a war criminal, a mass murderer, somebody who had killed at least ten men without the slightest sign of remorse just because he couldn't find Josh's family? He looked like somebody's grandfather. He had a gentleness and softness about him, almost a warmth. So totally different from the images she had amassed in her mind from his deeds. He bowed low as their car pulled up.

Sarah looked at Josh to determine his reaction. He was staring at the old man, eyes intently focusing. Laco's mouth was set in a thin sneer, his nose wrinkled in revulsion. So why was she so totally divorced from emotions of hatred? Sarah stepped out of the car. Alexander Hasek smiled at her. Involuntarily, she smiled back. Josh, then Laco, alighted from the back, Felix from the front. They stood on the pavement in awkward silence.

Felix broke the embarrassment of the moment by asking, 'Aren't you concerned about being seen? We weren't followed, but your security seems somewhat lax, just standing in the street.'

Hasek smiled. 'One of the cars following you has now returned to the centre of town. The other is cruising around, trying to pick up on your trail. You have been watched by my scouts. They are all men and women in their seventies, but they like playing my little games with me. It has given them something to do, a sense of purpose.' It was good to show off how professional he was, especially to another professional. 'Shall we go in and have some tea?'

They followed him into the tidy small house. Laco and Josh held back. Sarah could sense how uncomfortable they were.

'I can't bring myself to treat him like some long-lost uncle. He's a fucking mass murderer, for God's sake,' said Josh. 'If he'd had his way, my grandparents and my dad would have been shot and I'd never have been born. I can't just walk calmly into his fucking house and deal with him like we have something in common.' He was working himself up into a temper, an emotion he'd been restraining with all the excitement of the diversionary tactics since they'd left the hotel. 'Instead of drinking his fucking tea, I should be putting my hands around his scrawny old neck and throttling the life force out of him. He's the man who wanted to kill my dad!'

Laco put his arm on Josh's shoulder. 'I know how you're feeling. Because of him, my father is now in exile. He was nearly murdered. And a young woman is dead. But this man is only one of hundreds, maybe thousands, of others that the Syndicate is protecting. There is a more important purpose to our visit and that is to find out who is behind the group. And to expose them.'

Josh nodded, much to Sarah's relief. They walked into the house. Despite the heat of the day, the house was cool. It smelt of fresh lavender and was brightly decorated in pastels. The wallpaper in the front room where they congregated was patterned ivy, as though it was climbing the wall. It was a very feminine house, not one which seemed to belong to an elderly man. Anticipating the question, Hasek said, 'This is the house of a lady friend of mine. She has nothing to do with the purpose of our meeting. After you leave here, I shall immediately move into a different place. As you can see, I have thought this whole thing through very carefully. I have had this escape route planned for years – I just never thought I would need to defend myself against the very people who have been responsible for my safety.'

Sarah studied him more closely now they were seated. He possessed all the signs of old age: his neck was knotted and too small for the collar of his shirt, he appeared to be shrinking into his clothes, there was a noticeable tremor in his left hand, which was covered with liver spots and discolorations of the skin, his teeth were even and white and obviously false, his limbs were thin and ungainly as he sat uncomfortably in the armchair, and most noticeable of all, his eyes were rheumy, bloodshot and seemed to be full of tears. But they were also the eyes of a man who entertained infinite knowledge. They were wary, cautious, suspicious eyes, the eyes of the hunter not the prey. And it was this which differentiated Alexander Hasek from Yossi Kaplan, her grandfather. It was this which gave her the grounds to begin to hate him.

Sarah took the lead. 'Well, Mr Hasek. You've called us here. I suggest you state your business.'

Hasek nodded. 'First, may I congratulate you on finding me. Not that there's much left to find, just an old soldier, a man who faithfully followed the orders of those in authority. But be that as it may, your search has brought you here and it is important for me to know the purpose of your mission.'

'Our mission,' said Josh, 'is to . . .'

Sarah interrupted urgently, 'Mr Hasek, you will understand that Mr Krantz is particularly upset at the present time. It is necessary to keep our conversation on an even keel if we are to get anywhere . . .'

'I know you, Mr Krantz. From your films. I've even seen a few. But why are you after me? Something to do with a house in some small village in Slovakia, I believe? What has this to do with me?'

'I'll tell you what it has to do with you, you bastard . . .' Josh began, looking angrily at Sarah for deflecting the force of his venom. Right now, he didn't give a damn about consequences. This was his moment in court, his first opportunity to say the things he'd come to Europe to say. 'You're the motherfucker who murdered ten men in Novosad because my family escaped before you could kill them.'

Calmly, Hasek asked, 'And this Novosad. Where is it?' His tone was so matter-of-fact, like a teacher questioning a student, that Josh suddenly found his anger thrown into abeyance.

'It used to be called Ujlak. It's near Kosice.'

'And was it part of the Hungarian, Ukrainian or Slovakian republics at the time?'

'What does it matter? Are you telling me that you can't remember killing ten men yourself, single-handed, with a Luger? Have you killed so many people with your own bare hands that you've forgotten turning the village upside down, lining up the men from the village in the early hours of the morning and walking down the row, killing any man you didn't like the look of?'

'Josh,' shouted Laco, cutting into Josh's diatribe.

Alexander Hasek stared at him unresponsively, as if waiting for the waves of hatred to pass. 'We are not going to get anywhere if you carry on like this. Your young woman told you to keep calm. I suggest you do so, or else I will terminate this interview and you will get no further with the information.'

Furious, Josh shouted, 'And I'll have you arrested for murder, Hasek. Don't think you can bargain with me, you son of a bitch.'

Hasek merely looked at him as a father might look at a tantrum-throwing child. Then he shifted his gaze to Laco. 'I'll ask again. Why precisely have you been trying to find me?'

'To bring you to justice,' said Sarah calmly. 'To enable the authorities to arrest you, and try you for mass murder.'

'Ah!' said Hasek. 'Now we have it. But of course, you're not going to do that, are you. Because you realise that there is a much bigger fish to catch. And let's face it, I was only following orders.'

'That's the Nuremberg defence, Mr Hasek. It didn't work then and it won't work now.'

'But it's true, my dear. I was a mere pawn, a cipher in the vast Stalinist bureaucracy. I was sent orders on a particular day; I didn't think to question them, I merely carried them out. To have refused or objected would have meant my immediate deportation and death, and my replacement with someone infinitely more vicious. You may consider my deeds as an act of charity; I was merciful when it was possible, when others may have been brutish. Make no mistake, in those days, a refusal would have meant my "re-education", and I'm sure you know what that meant. It happened to many of my colleagues; I had no intention of allowing it to happen to me. Call me a coward if you will, but blame Stalin or Kaganovich or Beria for the murders of millions of people. Not an insignificant apparatchik like me.'

Josh turned on him in fury, but Laco intervened, 'So tell us, who are these people, the Syndicate?'

'Do you seriously expect me to divulge all the things I know without your guarantee of immunity from prosecution? Oh no, Dr Plastov, I need assurances from you before I will be willing to tell you more.'

A silence descended on the room. They had all been expecting it, of course, but it was different when they heard it from his mouth.

'What precise assurances do you want, Mr Hasek?' asked Sarah.

'Immunity from prosecution. If you find you are unable to grant it because you don't have the authority, a sworn undertaking that you will reveal nothing of my whereabouts. Secondly, I want to be relocated to Australia. I want my airfare paid plus one hundred thousand American dollars and a new passport in a name I'll give only to the forger.'

'You know that we're not in a position to grant any form of immunity from prosecution. We have no standing in law in the Czech Republic or any part of Europe,' said Sarah.

'And,' said Josh, 'even if we could, why the hell should we? You're a fucking murderer, for God's sake!'

'Mr Krantz,' Hasek said patronisingly to the younger man, 'such emotion. Such anger. How do you know it was me? You know nothing about those times. There were thousands and thousands of men and women like me. It was an existence like the lowest levels of Dante's *Inferno*: children reporting on the crimes of their parents, neighbour reporting neighbour, Christian reporting Jew, the thin reporting the fat, the short the tall. If you had a grudge against somebody, even for the most trivial reason imaginable, you could have them spirited away never to be seen again. If you owed somebody a tiny amount of money, you need never think of repaying it. People who were part of the Soviet system had fantastic power, the power of life and death, and yet you dare to accuse me of being a monster just because I was like everybody else.' He spoke so calmly, so evenly, that even Sarah, an experienced trial lawyer, went some way towards comprehending what life must have been like in those days.

It was Laco who broke the spell. 'My father never gave in. He never capitulated. He was never one of you. That's why to this day he is one of the most respected men in the whole of Slovakia. Can you say that, Hasek? Evil like yours flourishes when good men stay silent. My father can hold up his head in society and say, "Here I stand. I can do no more". But can you?'

Hasek wheezed a laugh. 'Interesting that you should quote Martin Luther. He was a rabid anti-Semite, I'm not. I was only ever following orders. Didn't matter whether they were Jew or Catholic or Moslem. Now Stalin hated Moslems. Did you know that? Not many people do, yet during and after the Second World War he forcibly deported and resettled over one and a half million people, most of them Moslems. It was pure genocide. Volga Germans, seven nationalities of Crimea and the northern Caucasus, the Tatars, Kalmyks, Chechens, Ingush, Balkars, Karachai – you name it, he deported them. Millions starved to death. That was genocide, my dear Dr Plastov, real genocide. But not my actions. I was only ever the smallest fish in a huge and hideous pond of villainous, murderous monsters. I'm not the one you want. And I've already admitted to being a coward. What more do you want from me?'

Sarah could see that things were beginning to get out of hand. 'May I remind everyone that we're here for information on the Syndicate. May I also remind you that everybody's life here is in danger because the Syndicate is currently searching Cesky Krumlov for us. They have no hesitation in killing those who oppose them, so I suggest that instead of recriminations we concentrate on finding out more about them so that we can become hunters instead of the hunted.'

'My conditions?' Hasek asked.

Sarah looked at Josh and Laco, then at Felix. His face remained impassive. 'Before we discuss agreeing to your conditions, we have to know whether they're possible. Felix, is the passport a difficulty?'

He shook his head. 'Simple. Just tell me which kind. French, German, Swiss? I'll need a recent photo. After that, it's between him and the forger we'll use.'

'And I'll pay the forger,' said Hasek. 'Just give me the money.'

'Australia?' Sarah asked.

Again Felix answered, 'I suppose it will present no problem. We will need to hack into the Foreign Affairs department in Canberra and backdate a visa application made from Bratislava or Vienna or somewhere. It's not a big deal. Aside from that . . .' He shrugged.

Josh intervened, realising that the conditions were already being agreed to without discussion. Sarah had taken the decision out of his hands. She had been unemotional and legalistic in the interview with Hasek. He had lost his cool, and consequently had lost his ability to lead the discussion. In anger, he told the group, 'We'll agree to the conditions except the hundred thousand. I'm not paying him a cent.'

Hasek thought for a moment. 'Provided the other conditions are put into operation immediately, I have no problems. It was a negotiating gambit. Do I have your word on all the other matters? You, especially, Miss Kaplan. As a lawyer, do you swear to abide by the agreement?'

Sarah nodded. 'You have my word.' She winced. She had just done what Dr Faustus had done. Was this how he had felt?

'Then,' said Hasek, clearing his throat, 'let me tell you all about the organisation which was created to protect those of us who were loyal servants of the State. Let me tell you about the Syndicate.'

# CHAPTER
# TWENTY-TWO

Sarah closed the file and felt the anger seeping out of her pores. She was catapulted back to those awful interviews with Frank Darman where he had laid out document after document, photograph after photograph, showing wartime atrocities, mounds of skeletal Jewish bodies, their mouths open like gaping wounds, the living dead staring from behind the wire of a concentration camp. She had forced herself not to show emotion as Darman, using a voice of conservative intellectualism, explained what the photographs truly meant: that those millions of people did not die by the agency of gas but from diseases caused by over-crowding; that the horrors had not been perpetrated at all, and that the gas chambers were there to burn clothing, not bodies.

She shook involuntarily. It was the past revisited. Hasek's account of mass murder, of genocide, of the horrors perpetrated under his command by Stalin's NKVD or the Army or by nationals in the Soviet satellite was different only in detail from the obscenities of Nazism. Had she reacted like this when she was sitting through the Darman trial, listening to those old men and women recalling the nightmares their young lives had been as they were experimented on by concentration camp doctors? No, she hadn't. In the courtroom it had all been so clinical, so legalistic. Evil cocooned by the niceties of civilised argument. But this was so different: here she was touching evil, in direct contact with it, a part of it. Sullied by it.

Guards had been posted outside the door of Felix's suite, in the corridor, in the courtyard where their cars were parked and at both ends of the road in which the Hotel Ruze was situated. As far as could be determined, the area was sanitised. Yet safety and security were no longer considerations in the forefront of anybody's mind; they had been replaced by deep-seated feelings of revulsion, arising from the documents they were reading.

The three folders from Hasek contained photographs, documents, reports, memoranda, certificates and lists. Dozens of pages of lists. For the convenience of those who did not speak Czech, he had thoughtfully translated the important sections into Russian and English. It was as if this had been a labour of love for Alexander Hasek, a task which must have taken him many weeks and into which he had poured his heart and soul. Sarah could see the pride with which everything had been done, the care that had been taken to amass the details, to prepare the brief. Yet, in the end, what was it? A litany of criminal activity, a paean to a life spent in turning thumbscrews, in reducing people to the level of non-existence, expunging them from the record of human essence. This *curriculum vitae* in itself would have been evil enough, but it wasn't what really interested the others. The second file contained graphic details of other crimes against humanity committed by other Alexander Haseks, other local warlords in different parts of Stalin's empire. Here were photos of dead or dying men, women and children. Here were lines of naked or semi-naked people, brutalised simply for the crime of being. Here were carefully compiled lists of atrocities committed by these other men – and occasionally women – in the name of Stalin and the progress of the Soviet empire and its peoples. It was a litany of horrors from 1935 onwards. Substitute the names and they could have been local Nazi *gauleiters*. But it was the third file that caused them the greatest consternation. This file contained no photographs, no horrors, merely documents which dealt with the Syndicate, its origins, and what it was today.

Laco looked up after the initial scrutiny and took a few deep breaths, like an athlete recovering from a race. 'Kaganovich! Who would have believed it? I thought he died or had been deposed or expunged when Khrushchev began the process of de-Stalinisation.'

Felix shook his head. 'So did many people. And others hoped so. But he was the great survivor. Nobody knows for sure when he died but there are reports that it was in 1961. Someone even reported that he saw him in 1991, which would put him at the ripe old age of almost one hundred. But this,' he said, thumping the files on the table, 'this is unbelievable.'

'I've heard the name, but I don't know much about him,' said Josh. 'Who the hell was this Kaganovich?'

Laco massaged the small of his back. 'Lazar Moiseyevich Kaganovich was a renegade Jew who did a couple of things which make him into one of the world's great humanitarians. He wiped out about seven million people – probably a third of the population of the Ukraine – by deliberately introducing policies which created one of the worst famines in human history. And many hundreds of thousands more, maybe even millions, died in his purges. That was on a national basis. But the thing that people most remember about him was his utter ruthlessness, even with his family. He was told by Stalin that his brother, Mikhail, was hobnobbing with Rightists, a favourite Stalin expression. Kaganovich had no hesitation in sending in the secret police to have him arrested. Mikhail killed himself. Some Mr Nice Guy, huh!'

'Those were only some of the better-known incidents in his life. I know quite a lot about him,' Felix told them.

'My Master's thesis was on the role of the commissar in Stalin's Russia. Kaganovich figured prominently.'

'I didn't realise you had a Master's degree,' said Sarah ingenuously, sitting up on the bed. The moment the words were out, she realised how patronising they sounded. Lately, she had been saying things which, without intent, were hurting people. Why, she didn't know, but if she wasn't going to end up alienating everyone, she had to watch the way she treated people.

'You sound surprised,' Felix said to her. 'There is a strong tradition of intellectual achievement in the Eastern Bloc, despite the heavy hand of Russia.'

'I'm sorry,' she said, 'I didn't mean to sound trite. I wasn't commenting on your intellect, just your profession.'

'James Bond is a figment of Western fiction. Real intelligence work is done by analysts and experts in numerous fields. I worked in the intelligence community after university, but was always fascinated by the work of field agents. Starting Executive Security after the fall of the communist system seemed a natural thing to do.'

'Kaganovich?' prompted Josh, eager to learn more.

Felix took on the persona of a teacher. 'As Laco told you, Kaganovich was born a Jew near Kiev in the Ukraine in 1893. Very poor. He worked as a shoemaker but fought against heavy odds to rise up from his poverty, and used the Party to do it. He quickly became one of the fastest growing stars in the empire because he was a brilliant administrator . . .'

'One man's administrative brilliance is another man's vicious dictatorship,' Laco intervened.

'At the age of thirty-seven he was a full member of the Politbureau. He had helped Stalin to defeat most of his serious rivals, so was very well-positioned for rapid advancement. It was he, more than anybody, who was the instrument of Stalin's policy of collectivisation. Suddenly everything was under the control of the Party Headquarters.'

This time it was Josh who interrupted: 'So what turned this guy into a monster?'

'In many ways he was the model commissar, the ideal product of the Soviet system. It was he, along with Khrushchev, who built the Moscow underground. He was the Commissar-in-Charge who organised transportation, heavy industry, fuel and petrol in the Soviet Union. But there was another side to him. It was Kaganovich who was merciless in carrying out Stalin's policies that killed millions of human beings. In the Ukraine, in the mid-1930s, one hundred thousand entire families were deported to Siberia and Kazakhastan. He collectivised the farms, despite fantastic resistance, revolts and destruction of farm machinery. He laughed at the efforts of the peasants to retain their independence and simply increased taxes and quotas and confiscated their foodstuffs to be sent to his bosses in Moscow. In one year alone, as Laco told you, seven million people died – the greatest man-made catastrophe in peacetime this century. One year,' he said pointedly to Sarah. 'That's more Jews than died in the six years of the Second World War. Odd how little the Western world knows about it, isn't it? You know, the Ukrainian countryside was so denuded of human beings that they had to bring in people from Russia to repopulate the farms and villages.'

'Shit!' said Josh.

'Shit indeed. But not content with being one of the greatest mass murderers in history, Kaganovich was also party to attempting to destroy Ukrainian culture. The repression of the Ukrainian Autocephalous Orthodox Church was so vicious that the entire church was liquidated in 1930. Four-fifths of the Ukraine's cultural elite was repressed, committed suicide or died in exile during the 1930s.' He looked at Josh and Sarah, who remained silent. 'And that is the man whose legacy we are dealing with. Like Laco said, Mr Nice Guy.'

Sarah got up off the bed with renewed anger, and returned to the desk around which the others were still congregated. 'Let's just review again what Kaganovich has got to do with the Syndicate.'

'We've only got the word of Alexander Hasek, of course,' said Laco, 'but according to these files, it was Kaganovich who was the founding father, the brains behind the creation of the organisation. After Stalin died, Nikita Khrushchev took control of the Soviet Union from Beria and Malenkov. Times were tough for Kaganovich, but he and Khrushchev had been close comrades when they worked together in the Ukraine. Perhaps because of that, Khrushchev allowed him to do minor administrative jobs, until Kaganovich actively opposed Khrushchev's de-Stalinisation program. He joined a group of rebels who tried to depose Khrushchev, failed and was never heard of again. According to Hasek's documentation, Kaganovich realised in about 1955 or '56 that the old-style Stalinists' days were numbered. It became even more obvious after Khrushchev's secret speech to the twentieth Party Congress on 25 February 1956 when he spoke about the excesses of Stalin's one-man rule.'

Laco flicked through the file to refresh his memory. 'He attacked Stalin's intolerance, his brutality and his abuse of power. That was it for Kaganovich. He hit the roof and secretly began to invite old Stalinists up to his dacha. The way he created the cabal that he formed around him was based on the the methods by which most of the Nazi SS guard managed to avoid being captured after the Second World War. Looks like my father was right.'

'And Hasek was invited to become a member,' said Felix.

'On 20 April 1956. Interesting, that's Adolf Hitler's birthday. I wonder if there's any significance,' said Laco.

'The list of Stalinists who have been protected by the Syndicate,' said Josh, 'what shall we do with it? There must be two hundred names. We don't have the resources to track down all those people. And how do we know they're still alive? Sure, he only typed it out recently for our benefit, but how do we know that this isn't just the original list from 1955 that's not been updated? Over the last forty years, most of these bastards could have died.'

'I think you're missing the point, if I might say so,' said Felix. 'We have in our possession one of the most closely guarded, secret documents in the world. God knows how many people have died over the years because of it. The Syndicate will fight like tigers to get it back and to prevent us ever making it public. Without this list, some of us were in grave danger. With this list . . .' He let the rest of the sentence hang ominously in the air.

Boris Maximovich Tranov enjoyed the warmth of the sunshine as he sipped his beer. The state of tension created by his enforced inactivity and the incompetence of those around him during the past week had suddenly evaporated. He had reached a state of composure, an understanding with himself. It was no longer a cat-and-mouse situation, of neurotically wondering how far this thing would develop and how he could limit the damage to the organisation he had taken over a quarter of a century earlier and had nurtured like a child. Twenty-five years of maintaining the secret. But now he had glimpsed the bottom of the barrel, now he knew the true quantum of danger to himself and his colleagues. No more insecurity, trying to determine what was in people's minds. Now he knew. He had stared into the abyss and now was the time for retribution.

His young lieutenant, Vladimir, sat glumly at the table, watching, looking at his mentor, the older man who used to have all the answers. He had failed Tranov. He had reported the total collapse of their security arrangements and now expected to be punished. After reporting the loss of the cars, and their sudden reappearance two hours later at the Hotel Ruze, he had expected Tranov to explode, to order his removal as head of security. That meant an assassin's bullet in the back of the head. He had done it himself a dozen times. It was the rule. And if you lived by the rule, you were expected to die by the rule; which meant that he would have to put his escape plans into action fairly soon.

But Tranov looked as though he had no intention of applying the rule. Instead he was smiling slightly, absorbing the details of the report, sipping his beer and glancing absent-mindedly at the tourists and passers-by in the square.

'I would assume that by now they have examined the list of our clients,' said Tranov quietly.

Vladimir had to lean forward to hear him above the clamour of voices. 'The list?' he asked.

'Hasek is not a fool. He is a bureaucrat. He was in touch with that civil servant in Kosice, the one you injected with adrenalin, then made it look as if he had gassed himself in his garage. He was our local coordinator in eastern Slovakia. His territory covered our clients in southern Russia, the Ukraine and Hungary. I thought I could trust him, but he was a coward. He went to pieces at the first sign of trouble. Typical bourgeois apparatchik – no balls, no stomach for trouble. Instead of following procedure, he dissolved like jelly. He must have given the list of our clients to Hasek just in case anything happened to him. So he could use it against me as some form of petty blackmail if the shit hit the fan.'

'But how do you know that Hasek has got the list? Nobody has a list except for regional coordinators, and they . . .' he stopped in mid-sentence.

Tranov smiled. 'Precisely. That idiot in Slovakia had one. It's obvious if you think about it. These Westerners are on the trail of Hasek because they discovered an incident involving him when they delved into the past. Who knows – a petty crime involving someone's family perhaps. But they managed to find out about Hasek. They searched and they found him. He realises that they aren't going to go away and also that he has been stupid enough to breach our security protocols. He realises that the Westerners are going to find him sooner or later ... and that we're going to realise that it was he who exposed us to danger. He knows that if we catch him he is a dead man, so he decides to do a deal with the enemy.'

He looked at his young colleague. 'Instead of going into hiding, he arranges a meeting. Now why would he do that unless he had information to trade? Us for him. Information about the Syndicate in return for his freedom.'

Vladimir looked at him in astonishment. He had come here to terminate either Hasek or the Westerners to prevent them uncovering the existence of the Syndicate. Now, suddenly, the very existence of the Syndicate itself was under threat.

'What shall we do?' he asked.

'We shall do nothing. Any precipitate action we take now will be extremely dangerous.'

'But if we don't stop them, they will inform the authorities. If they bring in the police, we are finished.'

Tranov picked up his beer and drained the glass. 'That's the one thing they won't do,' he said with total self-assurance.

'Why?'

'Think about it for a minute. What crimes have been committed by the people whose names appear on the list?'

Vladimir's brow creased. 'But ... we have committed crimes. We have assassinated people all over Slovakia and Prague. There's the old woman who used to work at the University and ...'

'I'm not talking about the Syndicate. I'm talking about the comrades whose names are on the list.'

Vladimir remained silent.

Tranov continued, 'We are dealing with men and women whose activities for Stalin ended half a century ago. The War Crimes Tribunals can't decide what to do with eighty-year-old Nazis, so why would they bother with a group of decaying apparatchiks who once worked for Stalin? Precisely what do you think the attitude of an overstretched and underpaid police force will be to that sort of complaint? Especially when you consider that President Vaclav Havel himself was against lustration.'

'Lustration?'

'Opening old KGB, St. B and other secret files created during the Cold War. Files on what citizens were doing. Most of them were useless, but people wanted to find out who had reported them. Havel said it was wrong to open up old wounds. He had a point. What happened was that husbands found that wives had informed on them, lovers on lovers, neighbours on neighbours. It was a shit fight. So the Czechs put a stop to it. That's why any report about old men and old files will come to nothing now.'

'Okay,' said Vladimir. 'But surely they will take the information somewhere else then? The War Crimes Tribunal, the United Nations, the International Court in the Hague – somewhere.'

Tranov shook his head. 'Perhaps they will find somebody to listen, but somehow I doubt it. We are dealing with an American film director and an archaeologist here. One wants to make this into an international, number one, smash hit movie. And the other only wants to dig and dig and dig until he has exposed the truth. He's the dangerous one, but right now he's probably coming to terms with reality, especially after our attempt on his father.'

'But there's also the girl lawyer, don't forget. And this Czech security man they've hired.'

Tranov waved his hand dismissively. 'Functionaries. Paid employees. They are not decision-makers. They will do whatever they are told.'

'But they know of the existence of the list. They know about the Syndicate. We are still exposed. Surely we have to deal with them? Terminate them?'

'Certainly. But not until we know exactly what they know and what they're going to do with it. If we go in now with guns blazing like in a western movie, the roof will cave in. What is needed now is circumspection, quiet contemplation. We don't want to frighten them into going underground. At the moment, they are feeling potent, powerful; they feel they are holding the fruit of the tree of knowledge. They are concerned about us, but they believe that possession of the list will protect them somehow, as though it were an amulet, a magical charm against which the forces of darkness become impotent. They will soon come to understand how naive they are.'

'So, right now, we're to sit on our asses and do nothing?'

'I didn't say that. There is one thing we have to do. Immediately. Terminate the incompetent Colonel-General Nikolai Alexandrovich Zamov.'

Vladimir nodded and left the table without another word.

For the past half hour, the silence in the room had been punctuated only by an occasional gratuitous comment, the odd phatic remark. All conversation had been exhausted, all options canvassed, all possibilities examined in the two hours since they returned from meeting with Alexander Hasek. And still no definition, no resolution.

The telephone rang. It was so jarring and so unexpected that it caused Sarah to jump. Josh walked over to the bedside table and picked it up.

'Yes?'

'Your quarry is sitting in the central square of Cesky Krumlov, drinking a beer. In case you haven't caught up with him yet, his name is Boris Maximovich Tranov. He is fat, unattractive and very dangerous. Despite his appearance, he has a sharp and treacherous mind. Treat him as you would treat a sleeping bear, with great respect and considerable caution. His colleague, Colonel–General Nikolai Alexandrovich Zamov is not with him. I have no idea where he is. They are your enemy. Not me. Have you examined the papers I gave you?'

'We've just started,' answered Josh.

'I have given you a gift.'

'A gift of evil.'

'Worth my old skin. But they are interesting, aren't they? They are worth giving me a passport and letting me live the remaining years of my life in the peace and quiet of Australia.'

'We've already made that agreement.'

'What are you going to do with them?' asked Hasek.

'We're discussing that right now.'

'Ha! You've got no idea, have you? You don't know which way to move. Should you inform the authorities, tell the police, track each one of them down yourselves? You haven't got a clue how to proceed. Not that it matters at all to me. I'm beyond all that now.'

Josh remained silent.

'Take my advice. Forget about people like me and the others on the list. We were only servants of the government. The men you want are Zamov and Tranov. They are the masterminds, the ones who have organised everything. Who have killed people to maintain the secrecy of the Syndicate. They are the enemy. I am only the victim.'

He laughed again and hung up.

The others looked at Josh, who still clutched the receiver to his ear. Slowly he replaced it in the cradle. He looked at their expectant faces; they were desperate for information. He smiled. 'That was Alexander Hasek. He thought he'd give us some advice.'

Felix lost the argument. He tried to convince them that since he was the only one who was both a native speaker and had a knowledge of espionage he should go alone, but in the end he had to give way to Sarah's insistence that she and Josh should be there. And Laco.

'This is turning into a circus,' Felix argued.

They disagreed. They were the clients. But, as there was no real danger – his men would be there to guard against anything happening – he conceded the point. Better to give in on minor matters now and save his energy for an important victory when there were real problems.

They left the hotel and within minutes emerged into the central square. It was a brilliantly sunny, hot day. Tourists swarmed around the streets, milling around cafés, or looking up at the medieval buildings in awe of their age and marvellous preservation.

Sarah wondered how they would ever find one man sitting in a sidewalk café within this mass of people. But find him they did.

'Over there,' said Felix, nodding to a café with tables and chairs protruding into the square. 'I'll bet that's him.'

The others looked in the direction he had indicated.

A large gathering of people were sitting enjoying their food and drink under the ubiquitous umbrellas. In their midst, alone, was a portly, elderly man wearing a white short-sleeved shirt. He was staring at them intently. Beneath his knitted eyebrows he had the eyes of a fox.

'Why does he allow himself to be so exposed?' Sarah asked in an undertone as she and Felix walked towards him, ahead of Josh and Laco.

'Because he's totally confident,' replied the security man. Sarah looked at the old man more closely as they neared the café. The more clearly she could see his old face and flabby body, the less menacing a figure he became. She said so to Felix.

'Sarah, look into his eyes. There is a man whom I find very frightening. Don't underestimate him. Do so and you could die.'

As they crossed the square the elderly man's eyes flashed over to his left before returning to stare at them. Felix followed the direction of his eyes and saw three sturdy young men stand from their table in another café and rapidly walk towards them. The old man shook his head. The movement was almost imperceptible. But the three young men stopped immediately and waited at a distance, ready to pounce at a moment's notice.

Felix, Josh, Sarah and Laco chose a table on the café's verandah. A waiter came over and gave them menus. Without looking, they ordered drinks, then sat in silence for five minutes. Tranov was immobile, like an Easter Island statue. Sarah knew that, at this moment, they were in control. Then Felix stood slowly, deliberately, and walked over to Tranov's table. The old man shifted uncomfortably.

'Would you like to join us, Boris Maximovich?'

Tranov nodded, picked up his glass of beer and followed Felix back to where the others were sitting.

'I assume that introductions are unnecessary,' Felix said.

'Of course.'

His voice was much gruffer than Sarah had assumed, his English, overladen with a heavy Russian accent, straight out of Central Casting. Josh thought that he was far less lean and hungry than a spymaster was supposed to look. Laco judged him with utter contempt as the man responsible for destroying his father's career, his prospects and for the attempt on his life.

'So,' said Tranov, 'we meet at last. I must congratulate you for surprising me. I hadn't expected you to do this. I thought you would use an attacking manoeuvre or diversionary tactics. Yet I can see the purpose of your approach. Discussion of mutual problems is the most sensible objective.'

'Then let's begin,' said Laco, 'with why you tried to kill my father.'

'We begin, Professor Plastov, where I want to begin. I don't want to sound arrogant, but I believe that I hold all of the cards – or is that,' he said looking at Josh, 'too similar to what a character in one of your movies might say?'

Everyone remained silent. They had agreed beforehand to allow Sarah, the most experienced at cross-examination, to lead the assault. But Laco, tempestuous as ever, hadn't been able to restrain himself. Now he glanced at Sarah, handing the interrogation over to her.

'Why precisely do you think that you have any cards in your hand?' she asked Tranov.

'So, they have instructed the lawyer to do the questioning. Good! I was hoping you weren't just some hack brought over here to say yes and no to the great Hollywood director. You know, when I was a diplomat in Washington I had a lot to do with American lawyers. I never found one I would trust. Not one. Pity. You, Miss Kaplan, are to be trusted, I assume?'

'If we can trust you, Mr Tranov, I'm certain that you can trust us.'

He burst out laughing, a roaring bellowing laugh. People at other tables turned around to look. He ignored them. 'Touché, Well, to answer your question, I think I really do hold all of the cards. I have armed men who can kill you at the drop of a hat. I have backup from a small army stationed in the outskirts of the town . . .'

Sarah interrupted, 'We have enough men with us to counter any threat you might make, and if you have got a small army, how come we managed to give you the slip so easily this morning?'

'I didn't say they were competent, just many.' He looked at Sarah, then at the others. They remained straight-faced, not knowing how to respond. He found their reaction the most amusing thing of all and laughed again. They were so much like Kremlin functionaries. He was enjoying this.

'Why do you find this situation so amusing, Mr Tranov?' asked Josh.

'For reasons which you, as an American, couldn't possibly understand, Mr Krantz.' He turned back to Sarah. 'But, as I was saying, I hold all the cards. What do you have? A list of names of elderly people given to you by an idiotic old man making absurd, senile claims about a conspiracy. Take that to the police and they will laugh at you. Am I correct?'

Sarah smiled at him. She didn't respond.

'Very good, Miss Kaplan. Say nothing. Keep him guessing. Tell me, do you play chess? I am an excellent player. Russians are world champions, you know! That's because chess is an intellectual game played by people who don't wear their hearts on their sleeves. They keep their thoughts to themselves while they are planning and plotting their manoeuvres. So different from the Americans,' he said with a sneer.

'Maybe, but an American computer kicked a Russian's ass last time there was a chess game,' mumbled Josh. Tranov ignored him.

'Mr Tranov, my colleagues and I are in possession of information which could send you to prison for the rest of your life. Along with a couple of hundred others. I don't think this is a suitable time to discuss chess or other party games,' she told him.

'But you are so wrong, my dear. This is just the time to discuss chess. We are at the opening gambit; soon I hope we will move on to the middle game where we will establish our positions for the kill. Your opening gambit was to capture a pawn. Congratulations. But I am afraid that pawns don't count for much in the scheme of the game. An old rook, on the other hand, storming a castle, that might get you somewhere. But a pawn!'

Sarah bridled at his patronising attitude, but managed to calm herself. She knew what he was doing. 'You think we have a pawn, Mr Tranov,' she said. 'I prefer to think of him as a knight, riding into battle with us to assault the king.'

'Oh, I'm afraid the king died many years ago. All your pawn has left to do battle with are a couple of elderly bishops and one sad old queen, who, I hasten to add, is not me.' Again he laughed loudly at his own joke.

'Can we cease the chess metaphor for a bit?' said Josh, irritated at Tranov's attitude. 'We're dealing here with crimes against the human race, with murder – and murder not committed decades ago, but within the last couple of days.'

'And who do you think committed those murders?'

'You,' said Sarah, looking directly at him.

Tranov's avuncular jowly face slowly metamorphosed from openness to closure, from joviality to contempt.

'No doubt you have overwhelming proof of my involvement in these murders? Clear and direct evidence which a judge and jury will find incontrovertible?'

'Not direct proof,' said Sarah, 'but certainly enough circumstantial evidence to present a case.'

Tranov nodded and sipped his beer. 'And what ties me into your web of mystery, Miss Kaplan? The testimony of one old man who admits to having been one of Stalin's mass murderers. I am a retired diplomat, living out my twilight years in comfortable senescence in Bratislava. I have no criminal record and I am on excellent terms with ministers in the Slovakian, Czech, Soviet, Hungarian,

Polish and Romanian governments. And it is just possible that I still have friends in America. But your informant, Mr Hasek, is a self-confessed mass murderer who changed his identity to hide his crimes on three occasions, who has been hiding under an alias to avoid capture and punishment.'

Joviality crept back into his face as he studied the expressions of the Westerners. 'You see your difficulties, madam prosecuting counsellor? I don't believe any American Attorney General would give you permission to prosecute me. Your evidence isn't even flimsy, it is non-existent.'

Sarah remained cool and collected. 'I wasn't aware that the defendant was in a position to give advice to the prosecuting attorney.'

'But I am not a defendant.'

'On the contrary, Mr Tranov, we have a great deal more evidence against you than you are willing to admit . . . or maybe realise.'

He guffawed and waved his hand at her dismissively. 'A crude negotiating tactic.'

'We are not negotiating, Mr Tranov. We are informing you that we are in possession of documentation which will lead to your arrest.'

'Then have me arrested. Just stop these silly games. The man you want is Hasek, not me. Nowhere will you find a direct connection between Stalin and myself. I was one of a million functionaries; I was never a member of his staff, nor did I take orders directly from him.'

'I'm not talking about Stalin. My colleagues and I are dealing with the cover-up by Kaganovich after Stalin's death,' Sarah said softly.

For a second, Tranov's eyes narrowed. An expression of concern passed ephemerally across his face. She knew she had scored a direct hit. It had been a risk.

'The evidence we have against you is about your relationship with the butcher of the Ukraine. And it doesn't just come from Hasek.'

'Really?' he said gruffly. 'Would you mind telling me what that evidence is?'

'It will be delivered to you by the proper authorities after your arrest,' she said.

'And who are the proper authorities, Miss Kaplan? Are they in Prague or Moscow or at the United Nations headquarters? Where will you go with that information?'

'That's why we're here, Mr Tranov.'

Laco was stunned by what Sarah was saying. So far, the negotiating ploy had gone well. But this? What kind of a statement was she making?

Tranov was surprised also. 'I don't understand.'

'It's very simple, Mr Tranov,' she said, the confidence seeping back into her body. 'There are three distinct places we could take you for prosecution. One is to Moscow, where we could hand you over to the Kremlin for prosecution as a war criminal. The second is to Prague, where we could do a similar thing. And the third is to offer you the same deal we've offered Mr Hasek: immunity. Immunity from prosecution provided you give us full details of the Syndicate, its composition, its membership and its current status.'

Tranov's mind was reeling. He had deduced from the meeting that Hasek had organised with the Americans that he held in his possession a list of Syndicate members. But nobody knew about Kaganovich, nobody outside of the closely guarded inner circle. How the hell had this girl cracked the system? And how did Hasek know about Kaganovich? All he could do was play for time.

He smiled broadly, took out a handkerchief and mopped his brow. 'Such a hot day,' he said. He finished his beer and stood. 'Miss Kaplan, Professor Plastov, Mr Krantz and you, sir,' he said, bowing to Felix, 'I bid you all good day. Do enjoy your stay in Cesky Krumlov. Such an interesting place. I strongly recommend a visit to the castle if you haven't yet availed yourself.'

He pushed back his chair, bowed again to Sarah, smiling at her as if he was her grandfather, and walked slowly out of the café and across the square. Vladimir and the two other security men joined him. They had watched the interchange with consternation, but knew to remain silent. One look at Boris Maximovich's face was enough to discourage speech. When they were halfway into the square and far enough away from the Westerners, Tranov turned to Vladimir and hissed, 'Operation Ivan. How long from start to finish?'

Vladimir looked shocked. 'Two weeks. Maybe three.'

'Are our records up to date?'

'Of course.'

'How many on that Kosice idiot's list are still alive?'

'Out of the two hundred and twenty, perhaps sixty. I don't know. I'll have to check.'

'Put Operation Ivan into effect immediately. And fuck two or three weeks. I want it under way in one week. Not a day more.'

'Well,' said Sarah, 'that went about as well as I dared to hope. We scored at least two serious blows against him.' She leaned back in her chair, feeling as drained as if she had taken part in a courtroom drama.

Laco asked, 'How can you be so confident? It was he who walked away with a smile on his face.'

'Oh no,' said Sarah. 'He wouldn't have walked away unless he wanted to play for time. It was the mention of Kaganovich that did it. You see, he had no idea what Hasek had told us. He probably thought Hasek was just an old man raving on about people trying to kill him; that he had given us Tranov's name and maybe a couple of others. Information that would be easy to deny, just as he did at the beginning. But the moment I said the name

Kaganovich, it told him that we've got the inside running. It means that Hasek knows a hell of a lot more than Tranov realised. And so do we. It means we've got details on him and his organisation that he thought were top secret. Excuse the expression, gentlemen, but right now he's shitting bricks.'

Felix shook his head. 'You're too confident, Sarah, and too naive. You're not dealing with a petty criminal or a traffic violator. This man controls a force which is quite comfortable using deadly methods. He could wipe us out instantly by making one telephone call. This isn't somebody to be toyed with or somebody to be threatened. Put his back into a corner and he's likely to over-react. Your whole approach was wrong. Instead of going in like a negotiator, you went in like Nike the winged avenger. You've made him desperate.'

'Felix,' said Sarah, 'you're going to have to trust me on this one. Any other way and there would have been blood in the streets. Our blood, as well as his. But frighten him, undermine his composure, and he won't know how to act. He's a tactician, a chess player. Right now I've put him in check. He's withdrawn to study the battlefield and see how the pieces lie. He'll come back with a counter offer or a counter attack but we're not at the stage of guns yet. We *were* there this morning, when he was confident, but not any more. He won't lay a finger on us until he knows exactly what we hold in our possession. And who we've shown it to. Only when he's confident that he knows everything we know will he move against us.'

'So what's our next move?' asked Josh.

'We find a weakness in the barricade. We find somebody within the organisation who will give us the information we need. The surprise witness that every prosecuting attorney dreams about, the witness that comes from nowhere and spills the beans.'

The three men looked at her in surprise. She smiled at them. 'I wonder where Colonel-General Nikolai Alexandrovich Zamov is? He figured prominently in Hasek's files. He'd be an interesting man to talk to.'

She sipped the last of her beer. Josh noticed a glint in her eye. She was enjoying herself.

Later that day Josh was disturbed in his room by a knock on the door. His heart raced. While there were security guards downstairs and at each end of the corridor they occupied, being involved with men like Tranov and organisations like the Syndicate had made him unusually tense. He walked to the door.

'Who is it?'

'Sarah.'

He opened the door and let her in.

'Josh, I need to talk to you.' She sat down on a chair near the window, overlooking the courtyard. He sat opposite.

'Felix,' she said.

'Yeah?'

'What do you think about him?'

He hesitated. 'He's good. Very good. Methodical, thorough, capable. Why?'

'How honest do you think he is?'

'Where is this leading, Sarah?'

'Things are falling into place just a little too easily. I have an uneasy feeling about things and they seem to centre on Felix. He's . . . I don't know. It's hard to put it into words. He's too prescient. He seems to know what's going on in people's minds before things happen. Sometimes I find him just staring at me.'

'You're a very attractive woman', said Josh.

'No,' she said irritably. 'As if he's sizing me up. Josh, what I'm saying is that I don't think we should trust him nearly as much as we are.'

'I think you're being paranoid. He's saved our asses on too many occasions for him to have any hidden agenda.'

She stared out of the window, wondering if Josh was right or whether she should trust her instincts.

In his heyday, when things had been under his control, he had suffered anything between fifteen and twenty phone calls a day. Yet the silence in his apartment now was deafening. The telephone's silence was as good as a death penalty; he had been around long enough to understand that. But it was all so unfair. It wasn't as if he had been incompetent. How was he to know that this stupid fuckwit, this old nobody, Alexander Hasek, had been secretly corresponding with a former lover? There were over six hundred people in twelve countries for whom he was responsible. He kept tabs on them all and had done for decades without one single slip-up. Ever. Until this idiot Hasek had broken the rules, ignored the protocols. And because of him, Zamov knew he was going to die. He poured himself another brandy. It was supposed to have a warming and comforting effect but it tasted bitter. Of course there was no way he could avoid the assassin's bullet. Nowhere he could hide, nowhere he could go. Tranov would ensure that he was followed wherever he went and his death would be swift and merciless. It might even happen today. His front door might burst open and two or three burly security men – his own security men – would come in with pistols blazing and blast him out of existence. It was the way it was done in the old Stalin days. In the days of Kaganovich and Beria. And in the days of Tranov. Boris Maximovich Tranov. May the devil rot his miserable flabby body.

Maps and travel plans were spread out on the coffee table. Useless, all useless. America? Hong Kong? South Africa? He could go anywhere he wanted but Tranov would find him. He breathed deeply. His hands felt numb from the brandy. He clenched his fists, tensed his fingers, bit the inside of his cheek to try to get some feeling back. But why the hell did he want feeling? Who wanted to feel the bullet of an assassin?

When the telephone rang a moment later, he jumped so violently that the brandy flew out of the balloon and stained his trousers. His heart thumped wildly. He cleared his throat, flexed his fingers again and picked up the receiver.

'Yes?' he said, trying to sound authoritative.

'Am I speaking to Colonel-General Nikolai Alexandrovich Zamov?'

It was a young woman, an American, speaking in English. Zamov's befuddled brain couldn't understand a word she was saying.

'My name is Sarah Kaplan. I'm an American lawyer. Am I speaking to Colonel-General Zamov?'

'Yes,' he said slowly. He understood English well enough but wasn't comfortable speaking it.

'Do you speak English enough to understand me? I have somebody with me who can translate.'

'I understand,' he said.

'We have just spoken to Boris Maximovich Tranov and discussed certain matters with him which are enlightening. Do you understand me, General?'

If only he hadn't drunk so much. He couldn't fully comprehend. 'I don't know. I don't understand properly.'

'Sir,' she said, 'I'm speaking to you from Cesky Krumlov. You know who I am. You have attempted to stop our investigation of Alexander Hasek. We are at the stage now where we need to talk to you. There are three men outside your apartment at this very moment to prevent you from leaving. You can come to Cesky Krumlov or I can be in Prague within four hours. Which is it to be?'

'Who are you?' said Zamov.

Sarah realised that he was drunk. 'Please, don't try to leave your apartment.'

She put the phone down. Zamov looked at the receiver for several moments before replacing it. His clouded brain began to clear, things began to make sense. A smile spread across his face.

When Sarah opened the door to a gentle, almost apologetic knock she was surprised to find Josh standing there. She had only said goodbye to him an hour earlier. She invited him into her room. All the formalities had disappeared long ago: the thought of inviting a client into her hotel room in America would never have entered her mind, but they were way beyond sensibilities now. They had both seen the face of death. Formalities were an unnecessary contrivance.

Josh sat down on the bed. 'Sarah, there's something I have to say to you. It's going to come as a surprise.'

She looked at his olive-skinned, square face, deep-set eyes. Suddenly he was no longer Josh; he was her client, and his face was that of the man she had interviewed in her office all those weeks ago. Odd. Only an hour earlier it had been the face of a friend. He patted the bed and she sat beside him. He put his arm around her shoulder and pulled her body close to his. He kissed her gently on the cheek. She had been expecting this approach for days now. She had even rehearsed a polite apology, but it had been an apology to a friend . . . not to a client.

'Sarah, there's a part of me which is in love with you. I think we both know that.'

She remained silent.

'We're in very dangerous waters here. And I don't just mean between the two of us – I'm talking about our physical situation. I'd be much happier for you not to be around, not now, not at the moment. Not while things are so dangerous.'

It wasn't what she had been expecting. She felt so much a part of the team that the concept of her running to safety while the others were still in trouble simply hadn't occured to her. She was nonplussed 'Josh,' she began, stammering, 'I think it's . . .'

He put his finger to her lips and said gently, 'I'm your client. I'm paying for you to be here. Now I'm instructing you to go to Bratislava and deal with the lawyers there to get my house back. They've been going crazy sending messages to your office. They have to talk to you urgently. There are decisions that have to be made, instructions that have to be followed.'

'How do you know?' she asked, puzzled. 'I haven't been in touch with the office. We weren't allowed to make calls.'

'Felix said that now we've met with Tranov, it doesn't really matter what he overhears of our day-to-day conversations. We just have to make sure he hears nothing about what we're planning to do in relation to the Syndicate. From now on, I can phone Hollywood and you can phone your office, David, whoever you like.'

She nodded. She was shocked. One moment, he was talking about his love for her — something she had been dreading ever since their conversation in the castle in Slovakia — and the next he was telling her to leave. 'But what about Colonel-General Zamov? I've just arranged for us to drive to Prague to speak with him. He could be our most valuable source of information about Tranov.'

'Maybe, and then again, maybe not. Why should a man as senior as him suddenly spill the beans and risk his own neck? But I'll go and see him, with Felix. We'll go tomorrow morning, first thing.'

Now she was angry. 'Josh, what the hell's going on?'

'I told you. I think it's time for you to leave here . . .'

'Bullshit! I've lived through some of the worst nightmares of my life in the last couple of weeks and now, just when we're reaching some sort of a resolution, you give me my marching orders. No way! I'm here to the end.'

'No, you're not, Sarah. Look, I don't want to get heavy, but you have to go and do what I want you to do. My house was the reason we came over here. We can't just leave all that work hanging up in the air.'

'Your house! Dammit Josh, we both know that's all bullshit. You and I came over to skewer the Slovakian government for what they did to your family. Well, here's what it's all about. All the old ghosts and nightmares that we escaped from are right here, right now. This needs exposing. It's not about some half-assed way of getting back a shed in the back of beyond anymore.'

'Sarah, I'm the client and I make the decisions about when you work, how you work and whether you work.'

'Excuse me?'

Josh realised that he'd been too didactic, too stern. He'd meant to show his concern, to assure her that she'd done a wonderful job but now she could leave matters safely in the hands of the men. Wrong!

'What I meant to say was, I came here to get my house back. That's still a priority. All the other things, like Tranov and the crap going down here, can be left to Felix and me.'

Sarah felt her jaw drop. Instinctively she reached up and touched her amulet. Not since being dumped peremptorily by a young man who she'd been sure was going to ask her to marry him had she been so surprised. She was being excluded. She knew the feeling from childhood, remembered the rejection, the embarrassment of being isolated, of seeing people huddling in a group talking about her, laughing at her. But she hadn't felt like this since those times so long ago. Yet here she was, grown and sophisticated, sitting on a hotel bed in an ancient city with a famous and gorgeous Hollywood director, feeling like she had felt years earlier. Her face flushed with bewilderment.

Josh sensed her discomfort, but the task had to be done. He stood up to leave.

'And Laco. Is he being fired too?'

Josh's voice was soft, softer than usual. 'Sarah, nobody's being fired . . . especially not you. And not Laco. But I'm sure that he's been as useful as he can be and the time is right now for him to go back to his museum.'

He glanced over at her. She looked as she might if she were sitting in front of a partner in her law firm, being dressed down, or fired. He knew she was on the verge of tears.

'I know you feel excluded,' he said, 'but please don't. It's important that I get my house back. And that's why you're here. That's why I'm here.' He smiled and left the room.

Sarah stared at the closed door for a full five minutes. Then she stood. Her legs felt wobbly, but she was angry. Very angry. It was the end of the journey. She had come this far; she had met her fears, confronted them and seen how banal the demons were. From America they had always seemed overwhelming. She sat down on the bed again, lay back and stared at the ceiling. She felt desperately hurt that Josh was excluding her, just at the time when events were coming to a head. For her, the time had been enlightening. She had seen the enemy, and, at the same time, come to realise that the enemy lay deep within her. The fears she held of old Europe, of the nightmares perpetrated against her people, were no different from any other fears of any other evil. Because she had confronted evil and, face-to-face, it was so ordinary.

'We need to talk.'

Felix was discussing the security plans for the day with his employees when Josh walked into the room and spoke directly to him. He nodded and dismissed his men. He pointed Josh to a chair, but Josh said, 'No, outside, walking around the town. I need some fresh air.'

Without a word, Felix stood and followed Josh out of the hotel. They turned right instead of left, avoiding the route to the town square and a possible meeting with Tranov. That was the last thing Josh wanted. The silent shadows of two security men followed close behind them, while two others walked swiftly ahead, monitoring their progress.

'I'm sending Sarah away in order for her to deal with the job of getting back my house in Slovakia. The Bratislava lawyers need to deal with her urgently.'

Felix nodded, but remained silent. His face was impassive.

'You don't believe that's the real reason I'm sending her away, do you?'

'Does it matter what I believe?' asked Felix.

'Yes. Since we brought you into the scene, you've saved our asses, and made us all aware of dangers we had no idea we were facing. But, now that I do know, I'm not prepared to endanger the lives of others any longer.'

'Does that include me?'

'You're paid to be in danger.'

Felix nodded. He didn't believe Josh, but he wasn't being paid to determine his employer's motives, methods or state of mind – or whether the American's gonads were ruling his intellect. 'So, Joshua, where do we go from here? If you are sending Sarah away . . .'

'And Laco. I'm sending him back to Kosice.'

'Which will leave you, me and our guards.'

'Correct.'

'Why?' Felix's tone was deceptively casual.

Josh delayed his answer for a few moments while they passed a group of schoolchildren hurrying to play in the central square. It was a warm morning and already the sun was streaming between the buildings, lighting the street ahead in a chequerboard pattern. 'Why? Good question. As I said before, you don't believe I'm sending them away for the reasons I've given them.'

Felix shrugged.

'Tell me, Felix, how do you think all this is going to resolve itself? Is there going to be a shoot out? Are we going to hand over our information to the authorities, or is Tranov right and we would just be ridiculed?'

'I think Tranov's right: no one will believe us. The only direct proof we have is the files of Alexander Hasek, a tainted man, a confessed mass murderer. And this man is accusing a former senior Russian diplomat of being involved in a monumental plan to protect criminals and murderers from justice. I think they will laugh in our faces.'

'What about Zamov? Sarah's keen to interview him.'

'He may be willing to tell us something. My men have microphones in his apartment in Prague. They say he is wandering from room to room, mumbling. Occasionally he shouts out something in Russian. They think he's cursing. Certainly he's drunk. If that level of weakness continues, we may get something. It's worth a try.'

'But to spike these guys we need a grand slam. A king hit. Don't we?'

Felix nodded.

'Any ideas?'

'You don't have any yourself?' asked Felix.

'As a matter of fact, I do.'

'And does it have anything to do with sending away Sarah and Laco?'

Josh smiled. 'The less said, the better.'

They continued their walk through the pleasant byways of the town. After some quiet deliberation, Felix surprised Josh by saying, 'Joshua, I think it would be best if you go back to Prague and interview Zamov. I will send an interpreter with you. There are things he could tell us which would enable us to be more pro-active ... and there are things to be done here that I don't want you to be a part of. Please don't ask for an explanation.'

Josh thought for a time. Then he nodded his agreement.

Boris Maximovich Tranov sat in what was now his customary chair in the café in which he had spent most of his time over the past few days. It was an enjoyable way to while away the time and, under any other circumstances, he would have felt relaxed and comfortable. But not at the present moment. Not right now.

Sitting there, with the sun streaming between the buildings, his usually precise mind was in turmoil. Zamov had been locked in his apartment for days and was unapproachable. He had goons guarding him; to eliminate him would require a massive artillery battle, which Tranov would not permit. Then there were these damned Westerners. They knew where Hasek was, and he had given them information which could crucify Tranov and every other member of the Syndicate. Yet, despite their approach two days earlier, not a word since. The girl had been sent back to Bratislava. The archaeologist had returned to Kosice. The film director was heading for Prague, and the security team was still in Cesky Krumlov, shadowing Tranov's men in their efforts to find Hasek. The hotel was overrun with security guards, making searching the rooms for the documents an impossibility.

What the fuck was going on? He had either played a move which had sent the white knights packing, withdrawing into defence from their attacking position, or else they were planning a manoeuvre which would see him checkmated in a couple of moves, his game plan in ruins, his life at an end. He had been over every possible scenario, but still couldn't understand why the group had suddenly dissipated immediately after the threats. They were scattering in all directions. What was it all about?

While he was pondering the disposition of the major players, he noticed their head of security, the man called Felix, walking slowly towards him. His own security chief, Vladimir, stood as the man neared the café. A nod from Tranov instructed him to sit down again.

Felix reached his table and nodded curtly. 'May I join you?'

'Of course.'

The waitress arrived. Felix ordered a beer.

'A question, Boris Maximovich,' he began. 'I am interested in your assessment. What would you say differentiated the mind of the Westerner from that of men like us, men who live in the East of Europe?'

Tranov thought for a moment. 'Of the many differences, I would have to say that we in the East have a clear understanding of the nature of reason. We are rationalists, corporatists.'

Felix was surprised. He had expected the authorised Marxist line: capitalism versus communism; the weak and dissipated West versus the focused and determined East.

Tranov smiled and continued: 'Oh, I know that people in the West think they're corporatists and that all their businesses and decisions are based on feeding the beast called capitalism. Their unions, their companies, their social structures are corporations, but they are not corporatists. All the huge multinationals like IBM and General Motors, and even the Pentagon, are based on the principle of hierarchy and status. Utter nonsense, of course, because true corporatists – people like us – understand the real nature of being a member of a large and comforting corpus. We lose our identity to the needs of the group. We have transcended petty bourgeois individual preferences and needs. Westerners think that they have been endowed with the capacity for reason, but they are wrong. That is our privilege. We are the ones who understand the value of true reason. We have developed the ability to marry reason and ideology and closed the door on superstition, gods and the hysteria of belief. Our minds are centred in the ascendancy of our power to reason. That is what differentiates us from the West. That is why they are joining moronic groups like Heavenly Gate and Hare Krishna and the Ku Klux Klan. They are reverting to superstition, chanting its mantras. They created the Age of Reason, but they can't cope with its demands.'

Felix smiled. He raised his glass of beer, toasting Tranov before drinking from it.

'You have a purpose for asking questions like this?' the older man asked.

'It interests me,' said Felix. 'You have managed to successfully hide a large body of people from the scrutiny of authority and the vengeance of history. It occurs to me that such a feat could never have been achieved in the West. It is not just their open society; it is the way their minds work. They suffer from the desire to search out and seek, or the need to expiate their guilt. Yet you do not seem to be saddled with those same debilitating emotions.'

'True,' said Tranov. 'But where is this leading, Felix? Why am I enjoying the privilege of your company when our friend from Hollywood is in Prague, presumably talking to Zamov, your attractive Miss Kaplan is in Bratislava talking to lawyers and Professor Plastov has returned to minister to the needs of his museum?'

'I just thought,' Felix said, 'that the two of us should talk.'

'And what do we have to talk about?'

'Do you know much about the workings of prostitutes?'

'More questions?'

'Indulge me,' said Felix.

Tranov studied the younger man carefully before answering. 'I have used prostitutes from time to time. They serve a purpose.'

'Most people look at the relationship with prostitutes from the viewpoint of the client,' said Felix. 'Few consider the relationship from the perspective of the prostitute. My understanding — not that I've had more than cursory experience, you understand — is that prostitutes see themselves as *bona fide* business women. They are a marketable commodity. They know the value of their bodies and how high a fee the market can bear. They know how best to find willing customers and they limit their sales strictly by the hour. And if the customer fails to find satisfaction, there are no refunds. Product failure is the client's problem, not the prostitute's.'

Tranov beamed. Now he knew why Felix was sitting here . . . and why the others had been sent away. 'Are you equating yourself with a prostitute?' he asked.

'Anybody who has something to sell effectively treads along the same path.'

Tranov looked around the square, at the waiters taking orders from customers, and, inside the souvenir shops, counter staff taking money from tourists. They were all order-takers, not real sales people.

'Don't you find it interesting,' he said, 'that in the old days people used to go out of their way to buy things because the retailer had a reputation for honesty, or for selling the best products at the right price. But car, insurance or real estate salespeople no longer care about their products these days. They base all their selling on their personality. They sell trust and confidence in themselves, never mind about the product. A bit like the prostitutes. What is it that *you* are selling, Felix? I am too old and set in my ways to be interested in your body.'

'I am offering you the information that Hasek gave us.'

'And why do you think I would be interested in buying it?'

'Because you will never find him. And you have to stop the information he gave us from getting to the authorities.'

'Why are you turning against your previous master?'

'Because he is an American, a fool. He is emotionally insecure and makes irrational decisions. He will damage my reputation if I continue with him. He is like a Hollywood stunt man, always taking risks. And anyway, you have far more to lose. Your purse will be much deeper.'

'How do I know that I am not being set up, that this isn't a ploy to enable you to do something else – play for time maybe, or divert my attention?'

'You don't,' said Felix.

'So all you are offering to sell me are the documents? Well, I want more than that. I want Hasek.'

Felix shook his head. 'No! The documents or nothing.'

'Then it's nothing,' Tranov growled. He stood and walked out of the café towards where Vladimir was sitting. Vladimir and three of his colleagues joined the old man as he headed towards one of the exits from the old town square.

'Well?' asked Vladimir.

'We have been offered the lists. It is only a matter of time before he offers us Hasek. He has lost confidence in the American. I don't blame him. Joshua Krantz has no experience of this sort of game. He is playing it like a Western movie, all melodrama and image. But Felix is one of us. He can see through the American. He knows how dangerous he is.'

'So Felix is changing sides?'

'He knows whose bed is the warmest. He is no fool.'

'How do we know that he has not made copies of the list?'

'Of course he has made copies. But without Hasek, they are useless. One more negotiating session and he will cough up Hasek. We'll deal with him, and then we'll deal with Mr Felix. And the fucking archaeologists — both the father and the son. And from that time onwards the lists will become redundant. There will be no proof, and without proof who will listen to an American making absurd claims about the times of Stalin? Especially a Hollywood movie producer who is all wind and bullshit. Tell me, Vladimir, how long before Operation Ivan begins?'

'Next week at the earliest.'

'Good. Once that is complete, our problems will be over.'

The attic was stuffy and claustrophobic. The smell of their bodies in the heat of the tiny room quickly threatened to overwhelm them, that and the fetid stench of the pigeons that were nesting in the rooftops, scratching and cooing and stinking like rotten meat. Phil changed the lens and adjusted the camera's focal length while Jerry took the makeshift clapper and placed it in front of the camera, surreptitiously identifying the scene. Far below them a thousand pigeons flocked and wheeled above the heads of the crowds in the ancient central square of Cesky Krumlov. Phil peered beyond the central marker in the lens aperture, moving the camera so that its eyepiece roved slowly across the diners in one of the cafés. He stopped on an attractive young woman with large curvaceous breasts, whose skimpy blouse was not designed to pay heed to modesty. Her companion was a young, muscular, blond-haired Aryan — they were clearly a German backpacking couple. He moved quickly on to other people sitting in the café, trying to identify their nationality by their face and body type or even their clothes. He had been peering down at the same scene for what seemed like hours and was bored. So was Jerry, whose sound skills were useless for a silent and taciturn subject sitting so far away. Phil had taken to describing the breasts and bodies of the female diners for Jerry's vicarious pleasure.

He moved the camera back to where his target had been sitting for what felt like hours. A large man, bulbous and ponderous, yet, beneath the blubber and accretions of old age, with a firm and potent torso. A man who, in his youth, would have been described as powerfully built. Boris Maximovich Tranov. He pulled the focus until Tranov was again sitting four-square in the centre of the eyepiece, then pulled back and forward, changing the size of Tranov's image in the lens: thirty seconds of wide angle taking in much of the surrounding view, followed by an extreme close-up, detailed enough to see the liver spots on his neck and temple, the hairs in his nostril. Tranov was talking to a man who had his back to the camera. Suddenly he stood. He looked down contemptuously at the man sitting beside him and walked away from the open air café.

Phil pulled the camera back to cover him as a lone figure pushing through crowds of tourists then moved in to a medium close-up as he was joined by a tall, lean, young man. The two spoke to each other and the young man smiled. The men walked out of the square, out of frame and out of the picture.

# CHAPTER
# TWENTY-THREE

When Felix slowly walked for the second time to meet Boris Maximovich Tranov in the café the attic high above the square was empty. Phil and Jerry had decamped the previous evening and driven back to Prague to catch a flight to London, then New York, then Los Angeles. Tranov and his security staff were unaware that his movements over the past two days had been captured on film. Phil had shot him sitting in the café, walking through the square, strolling along the banks of the Vltava, entering shops and talking to school children on the road leading up to the old castle. But the pigeons, omnipresent and eternal, were still in their attic space, wheeling around the tiny room like water swirling in a bottle.

Of course, Tranov's men had pursued Josh, Laco and Sarah to their various destinations, and were now trying to understand their tactics. The woman lawyer was suddenly working to retrieve the Krantz house again; the archaeologist was back in his office in Kosice and the Hollywood film director was running around town, talking to studio and movie production people. It was as if their time in Cesky Krumlov had been merely a momentary diversion from the task they had come to Eastern Europe to undertake. It was all very odd. Tranov was uncertain as to the purpose behind the moves, but one thing was sure – it was nowhere near as innocent as they were trying to make out. Something was about to happen. Why else would they have allowed Felix to remain in Cesky Krumlov?

Tranov saw Felix walking towards him. It was precisely as he had predicted: two days of waiting before Felix ignominiously crawled back, begging for a deal. Tranov forced himself not to smile. You never smiled in a game of chess. You never telegraphed your emotions to your opponent. Felix sat down opposite the old man.

'And how is life treating you, Boris Maximovich?'

'Life is treating me well, thank you.'

A strained silence developed between the two men. Felix was hooked but not landed. It would be preemptive for Tranov to comment at this stage. Let the younger man negotiate.

'Why do you want Hasek so badly?' Felix asked eventually.

'I am a father with a prodigal son,' Tranov replied. 'There were certain protocols which had to be obeyed. Those protocols demanded absolute respect for the rules of an organisation which – as we both know – does not exist.' Tranov allowed himself a wry smile. 'Hasek broke those rules. I want to counsel him about his future behaviour. We want to bring him back into the fold to make him one of us again. He needs re-education.'

'And once I have handed Hasek over to you, how long will I stay alive?'

Tranov sounded surprised. 'Why on earth would I kill you?'

'Because I have seen the list. You must realise that I have photocopied it. You have no idea what I have already done with it – I may have circulated it to the authorities. I could cause you problems.'

'True,' said Tranov, 'but once Hasek is dealt with – or, should I say, is brought back into the fold – there will be no method of confirmation. A list is a list. I could show you two pages from the Moscow phone book and claim those people were child molesters. Proving it is a very different matter.'

'But I have spoken to Hasek. I have his evidence.'

'Yes,' said Tranov, 'but then so did the archaeologist and the two Americans. To be completely safe I would have to eliminate everybody. And that may just ring some warning bells. You see what I mean, my dear Felix? One has to be realistic. Hasek is the problem. Not you, not the Hollywood director, nor his lawyer.'

'And Dr Plastov, the archaeologist? What happens to him?'

Tranov shrugged his huge shoulders. 'He will continue to dig into the earth, hoping to establish how our ancestors lived. I wish him a long and peaceful life.'

'Why should I believe you?' asked Felix. 'Why should I believe that if I hand you Hasek you will leave me in peace?'

'That is a problem you will have to come to terms with yourself,' Tranov told him. 'In the meantime, I will continue to sit in this very pleasant café in this beautiful town passing the time of day. There are worse fates. Ultimately my men will find Hasek. It is a difficult task but not impossible. He can hide only for so long. All that is required is time. We are getting closer and closer as each day goes by, which means that your information is quickly becoming increasingly valueless. The choice is yours of course, Felix, but the decision could have a decided effect upon your future finances. If you are going to make me an offer, I suggest you make it very quickly. Tomorrow I will be willing to pay only half of what I will pay you today.'

Felix studied the old man's face. He was as close to emotionless a human being as anyone Felix had ever seen. His eyes were cold, hard and analytical; the muscles in his face were stony and solid. Not a momentary flicker, or frown, or the slightest facial movement betrayed what he was thinking. He was the ultimate negotiator.

'I am prepared to give you Hasek and the list.'

'Keep the list,' said Tranov. 'It is only a piece of paper. Just give me Hasek.'

Felix nodded.

The ringing of the phone surprised him. The house had been quiet for days. Alexander Hasek had almost come to believe, to hope, that everybody had gone away. His colleagues had reported that the frenzied questioning and movement of Tranov's security staff had come to an end and their tough, menacing faces had started to disappear from the streets. Tranov was still sitting in the café, hour after hour, day after day, but his minions no longer seemed to be as numerous. So the phone call in the middle of the morning took him by surprise. 'Hasek,' the voice said, 'this is Felix.'

'I haven't heard from you for a long time. I assumed you had forgotten me.'

'Of course not. Complex arrangements of the type you insisted upon take a long time. I warned you it could be a couple of weeks before we had things properly sorted out.'

'And are they sorted out?'

'We gave you a commitment. It has been met,' said Felix.

'My passport?'

'Your passport will be ready tonight. I will bring it to you tomorrow morning along with your tickets from Prague, to London, to Sydney, Australia. A hotel reservation has been made for you in Sydney in the name of Mr Smith. Your passport will carry a different name since we agreed that no one but the forger would know your new identity. When you get to the hotel in Sydney, you will have to explain the difference. But that is your problem.'

'Good,' said Hasek. 'And the information I gave you, have you passed it on to the authorities?'

'That is why I am calling you. I have with me a gentleman from the Commission for the Investigation of Czech War Crimes and Lustration.'

'You've brought a government man into this?' said Hasek. 'What does he want with me?'

'He wants to talk to you.'

'No!'

'You will talk to him. This is not negotiable.'

'No,' Hasek said firmly. 'I gave you the list. I gave you Tranov and everybody else. I made it clear that that was as far as I was prepared to go. I'm not willing to meet with anybody now or in the future.'

'But he just wants to talk to you for an hour or so.'

'No!' he shouted. 'I have made my conditions plain.'

'Do you want your passport?' Felix said softly.

'You bastard,' Hasek hissed. 'You made an agreement. I trusted you.'

'And you can still trust me. This is merely a matter of coming to terms with your responsibilities. This man will take a deposition from you and that's it. Can I bring him to the house now?'

'No. Why should I meet with him? You give him the details. I've nothing more to add.'

There were a few seconds' silence before Felix said, 'Hasek, I have given him all the details, but he must speak to the person who gave me the information. We are dealing here with a former Soviet diplomat and mass murder. This is not a joke. They will give you the same protection as I have given you, but they *must* speak to you.'

Hasek hesitated. 'What guarantees do I have of my anonymity after I have spoken to him? How do I know this isn't a trap? You could be setting me up.'

'Think about it logically. My life is in as much danger as yours. The only chance of safety I have is seeing Tranov arrested and in jail. If I am your escape route, then you are mine as well.'

Hasek agonised in the silence that followed. He wasn't as badly trapped as Felix thought. He had another passport in another name, but it had been made five years ago. He was reluctant to use it in case it set off alarm bells in an immigration computer somewhere. Damn! Why hadn't he updated his passport? He had been too confident, that's why. All those years without the slightest hint of trouble – he had become too certain of his invulnerability.

Softly, he spoke to Felix: 'Just off Hrbitovni there is a cemetery, a big one, close to the banks of the Vltava, to the east of the city. You can't miss it. There is a chapel. I will meet you inside in one hour. Not a minute later. If this is a trap, you will have no time to set it up. If you are not there in an hour, I will leave and you will never find me again. But after this, Felix, no more. This is as much as I'm willing to risk.'

'Agreed,' said Felix and hung up the phone.

Felix relayed the gist of the conversation to Tranov. 'You have exactly one hour,' he ended. 'Can you be ready in time?'

'Perhaps I have misjudged him,' said Tranov. 'He seems to be more prescient than I gave him credit for. An hour doesn't give us much time. Pity. I like to plan these things overnight.' He laughed.

Forty minutes later, three miles away from Tranov's hotel suite, Alexander Hasek checked his watch again. He would need to leave within ten minutes. He picked up his two-way radio and pressed the communication button. 'Quarry One to Quarry Two. Are you receiving me?'

The static hiss was interrupted by ghostly words from the speaker. 'Here, old friend. I am at the gates to the cemetery.'

'Is it clear?' asked Hasek.

'Completely. Two old ladies putting flowers on a grave, but that is all. You are safe to come.'

'Keep an eye out, for God's sake. I will have my radio with me. Let me know the moment you see them arrive. Don't forget, I want to know how many are in the car. There shouldn't be more than two. If there are, tell me.'

Hasek left the house and looked cautiously up and down the street. His army of old and retired people, who had been his eyes and ears for the past two weeks, had been of immense value in protecting him. They would be deeply disappointed when the job was over and he had disappeared to Australia. Not that anybody in Cesky Krumlov would know, of course, but it had been a marvellous break in their otherwise humdrum lives, and Hasek was even paying them for the privilege of doing something that gave them all such a thrill. If only he felt that same sense of excitement. But his life was at stake.

There were no cars driving along the street, no unidentified or unidentifiable people. He jumped quickly into the car parked in the driveway and drove off towards the cemetery. It was the first time he had been out of the house in days, except for the occasional stroll in the garden. He had been a prisoner of his environment, waiting for others to contact him and tell him the good or bad news. He had anticipated many scenarios, but not this one. He had always doubted that the Americans would go along with his plan and allow him to escape. It had been a negotiating gambit to get them off his back and onto Tranov's trail, but they had fallen for it, hook, line and sinker. He was within an inch of getting a new passport and new life, created for him by the Americans. Even if things fell through, he had a contingency plan – an escape route to Switzerland where most of his money was safely earning interest in a numbered account, and his safety deposit box held a couple of passports. The only mistake he had made was keeping only his real passport and an old forgery here; he should have kept the newer ones with him. A mistake he would never make again. Careless, downright careless. But, despite all that, he had managed to get everyone off his back: Tranov, the archaeologists and the Americans.

Driving to the cemetery, he began to regret agreeing to meet with the Czech official. He should have slammed the phone down, decamped and driven to his other house, where his bags were already packed, ready for him to assume yet another identity. The money was as safe as houses in Switzerland and he had tickets and other travel documents. Yet, when Felix had placed him on the spot, he had believed this was a cleaner way of doing things. Now he wasn't so sure. He drove in through the cemetery gates. Behind one of the large pillars holding up the wrought-iron gates was his old friend Jiri, with whom he played chess and drank beer. They exchanged waves.

Hasek parked his car outside the chapel and went inside. He looked at his watch – eight minutes until they were due. He examined the walls and the altar: the usual crucifixion scenes and icons. Obscene superstition. Why were Christians, Catholics especially, so concerned with death, fasting and penance? Why didn't they *celebrate* life more, he wondered. He paced up and down the aisle, looking at his watch frequently. He pressed the button on his radio – the static hiss sounded far louder in the chapel than it had done in the house half an hour earlier.

'Quarry One to Quarry Two. Any sign of them yet?'

He released his finger from the button. The loud hiss filled the church. He waited with increasing anxiety for his friend to answer. He pressed the button again: 'Jiri! Where are you? Answer me.' Again the static invaded the church. He stabbed the button. 'Jiri!' he shouted, panic in his voice.

He rushed down the aisle as quickly as his old legs could carry him and pulled the doors open to the blinding sunlight. But the rays were blocked by dark, spectral figures. Hasek felt himself go weak at the knees. He was dead. He knew it with an awful certainty. Filling his vision, and blocking his exit, was a man whom he knew only through photographs. A man whose reputation preceded him. A man whom he'd spied a week earlier, entering the town. Boris Maximovich Tranov. Hasek felt his legs begin to collapse beneath him. He grasped the brass handle of the door to hold himself upright. His back stiffened in fear.

'Hello, Alexander,' said Tranov softly, politely. 'You have been a very naughty boy. You have caused me a lot of difficulties. Now you know what happens to naughty boys, don't you?'

A younger man stepped around from behind Tranov's huge body before Hasek had a chance to speak. His throat went dry.

'I . . . I . . .' he mumbled.

The tall, young man pushed him with feather-light precision in the centre of his chest. The old man stumbled backwards and fell into the aisle. He lay spreadeagled in the shaft of sunlight, his arms outstretched in obscene mimicry of the crucified Christ hanging above the altar. He couldn't get up.

'Boris Maximovich, there has been a terrible mistake,' he stammered hoarsely. 'The Americans somehow found out about the Syndicate. I have tried to protect . . . but I . . . they found me. I did everything in my power . . .'

Tranov walked slowly forward and towered over the old man on the floor. A stain appeared at Hasek's crutch. Tranov sneered disdainfully. The weakling couldn't even hold his bladder together. Hasek mumbled again, 'I tried to stop them. They were too powerful.'

Tranov put a finger to his lips. 'Hush, Alexander. Be dignified. You have broken the rules; now you must pay. You have been living on borrowed time since you wrote those letters to your lover in Slovakia. You could have remained as one of our family; instead you chose to be other. And now you must pay the penalty.'

The young man took out a gun and shot Hasek cleanly above the bridge of his nose, between the eyes. The old man barely moved as the bullet entered his brain. The two men walked out of the chapel into the brilliant sunlight, got back into their car and drove out through the beautiful wrought-iron gate. The dead body of Jiri lay crumpled at the base of one of the gateposts, his head at a sickening angle to his body.

'Do you want me to kill Felix?' Vladimir asked.

'Immediately,' said Tranov. 'And order our men in Slovakia to terminate the archaeologist.'

'What about the Americans?'

'No. That would cause too many questions to be asked in all the wrong places. Western governments have a peculiar habit of caring for the welfare of their citizens.'

Laco Plastov had been feeling strange for days: disturbed, disassociated, as though he were in a trance from which he was incapable of awakening. When he had arrived back from Cesky Krumlov, his friends had been surprised and delighted. They had thrown their arms around his neck and kissed him on both cheeks, demanding he tell them where he had been for so many weeks. All he had told them was that because his old Volkswagen had been destroyed and his student killed, he was going away for an unspecified time. Since then nobody had heard a single word from him. Now his researchers, his curators, his colleagues, even the guards who worked in the museum, were overjoyed at his return, and hungry for news and information.

Over the last few days, whenever he had entered a room or passed somebody in the corridor, he had received a kindly word or a pat on the back, like a favourite dog. Yet even though he had settled back into work, catching up on what had been happening in the dig and on the recording of artefacts since he'd been away, he felt as if he wasn't really part of it. He could recall the desiccated feel of a skeletal limb, or the weight of the copper or bronze jewellery that had been discovered, but he found it hard to put himself back into the framework of what the others were doing, as though he were an observer rather than an integral part of the project. Every waking moment in his most recent past had been devoted to uncovering a vicious throwback to the days of Stalin, and escaping the consequences of the Syndicate. Even his father, whom he had telephoned at least once a day before his life had been blown apart, was no longer there to talk to. His world was different. It was frightening.

The telephone rang.

'It's Felix. I've got three security men approaching your office right now. They will identify themselves with a code word that only you will recognise, something to do with what has happened to you recently. That is how you will know they are genuine. The moment they arrive, be prepared to leave. Immediately. No baggage, no goodbyes, no questions. Your life is in immediate danger.'

'But . . .'

'I will explain everything when I see you.'

'Where am I going?'

'I can't discuss it over the phone. But believe me, it will all be over soon.'

'Wait!' Laco shouted. 'You can't do this. I've been here for nearly a week, but now suddenly you tell me my life is in danger. You've left me exposed, without protection, like a sacrificial lamb, and suddenly out of the blue . . .'

'Laco, nothing is happening out of the blue. And you were unprotected because you were not in danger.'

'But you just said that I was in immediate danger.'

'*Now* you are. Something has just happened in Cesky Krumlov which places you in grave and immediate danger. It was an eventuality which I had foreseen but of

which I could not warn you. But, please, believe me –
now that it has happened, you are a target and must be
protected by us again.'

Ten minutes later three brawny men were shown into
his office by his intimidated receptionist.

One of them smiled and said, 'Felix sent us to protect
you, to take you somewhere safe.'

Laco nodded. 'Your code word?'

The tall man leaned across the desk and whispered into
his ear, 'Kaganovich.'

Laco followed the men out of his office. For the second
time in a month, he failed to say goodbye to his staff
and friends.

Sarah quickly swallowed the remains of a meat and pickle
sandwich, laid the wad of papers on the floor and picked
up the telephone.

'Yes?'

'It's me, Josh. How are you?'

She was shocked. She had been expecting a call from the
Bratislava lawyer she had been working with for the past
six days about a final matter concerning Slovakian property
laws in 1955. It was the last detail that should wrap up the
appeal they would be making to the Slovak courts within
the next two weeks.

'Josh?'

'Good to talk to you, Sarah.'

'I thought you'd forgotten all about me. It's been a week
since we've spoken to each other. I've left messages, but . . .'

'Sarah, can you pack up your things and be in Prague
first thing tomorrow morning? There are three guys on
their way to your hotel to look after you.'

'Sure, but why?'

'Just because.'

'Josh, we're at a really delicate stage of the case here. We've found a tiny loophole in the property law which relates to the time two years after the death of Stalin. If we can convince a judge, it's possible that . . .'

'Sarah, never mind about the house. It's crap compared to what I'm doing. I'll see you in Prague tomorrow morning. Same hotel. I've made a reservation.' He rang off.

Sarah stared at the receiver, her face flushed hot with anger and humiliation. 'Crap!' she shouted, banging the receiver into its cradle. 'Crap! How dare he just dismiss my work like that!'

Sarah found a note under her door instructing her to be in Josh's suite of rooms in the Intercontinental Hotel in Prague at seven in the morning. Her mood was surly, uncertain. Felix was sitting in the corner of the room when Sarah walked in shortly before seven. He walked over and shook her hand formally. Josh emerged from the bedroom and beamed with pleasure when he saw her. He threw his arms around her and gave her a huge hug and a kiss on the cheek. Sarah was disdainfully cold. She felt in no mood to be touched by him, not after he had dismissed her work so contemptuously as crap. Not since he had marginalised her participation, since she had put her job on the line with Morrie and been booted back into place. She stared back at Josh. He was wearing an expression of child-like enthusiasm – or was it amusement? – on his face. She had prepared a speech on the flight from Bratislava and all through the previous night while she had been unable to sleep.

'Josh,' she said, 'I want to register my extreme disapproval of the way you've treated me this past week. You've dragged me away from important negotiations just at the most critical point. When we began our relationship in New York you . . .'

'Sarah, I wonder if we could hold this over until Laco arrives.'

'Laco? Is he : . . ?'

'Yeah, he phoned from his room a minute before you got here and said he was on his way up.'

Sarah looked over at Felix, barely able to control her anger. 'Would you mind telling me what the hell's going on here, Felix? I feel like a puppet being dragged one way and the other by people who don't know where they're going.'

'May I suggest, Sarah, that we follow Josh's proposal and wait until Laco gets here.'

As Felix finished speaking, the doorbell rang. Josh bounded over to the door like an enthusiastic schoolboy and pulled it open. Laco stood in the doorway, looking diminutive and reticent, a phalanx of three huge security men surrounding him like a suit of armour. Josh pulled him into the room and threw his arms around him, kissing him on both cheeks as he had done Sarah moments earlier. Laco's surprise at seeing Felix and Sarah in the room was evident. After his peremptory dismissal from Cesky Krumlov, discarded like a piece of useless cloth as he'd told his friends, he had never expected to see either of them again. His assistance no longer required, he had felt marginalised and downgraded.

'What's going on, Josh?' he asked. 'I don't understand. One minute . . .'

Josh held up his hand. 'I owe you both an explanation. You have my apologies, but it was necessary – it was a matter of life and death. In fact, it's best if Felix explains the details.'

Josh sat down. Felix drew a deep breath. It took him half an hour to cover the major events of the past six days, leaving out certain significant items – items that he knew he would have to deal with in the future, but not right now while Sarah and Laco were still absorbing information.

By the time Felix had finished, they both sat with jaws agape, stunned. The look of amusement on Josh's face transposed into one of unbridled joy.

Boris Maximovich Tranov rose late from his bed, his head heavy from drinking the previous night. Despite the dramatic upsets to his routine over the past month or so, matters had settled down very well. Except for the disappearance of Felix. Tranov could not think how he had managed it when he had been under such tight surveillance. But he was being hunted the length and breadth of the Czech Republic. That minor irritation aside, things were progressing smoothly. Operation Ivan would begin within the next day or two. A pity; so many comrades. Still, the Syndicate had to be protected and one thing was for sure – the Hollywood director and the American lawyer would never stop looking for another Hasek. For that reason alone, the comrades had to die.

Tranov took himself into the bathroom and ran a hot bath. He indulged himself by adding two cubes of bath salts and some lavender bath gel. The clear surface of the water was transmuted by alchemy into a steaming cloud of frothing white bubbles. He slipped off his bath robe and stepped into the hot water, but before he could lower himself into the soothing fragrances, the telephone rang.

'Damn, damn, damn,' he shouted. He got out of the bath and padded naked into the lounge room. 'Yes?' he demanded, snatching the receiver from its cradle.

'Boris Maximovich, how nice to talk to you again.'

Tranov froze. 'Zamov. Where are you?'

'What an original question. What a perceptive interrogator you are,' the voice dripped with sarcasm. 'Very safe from your goon squad, thank you. I imagine you are feeling frustrated at the moment at not being able to locate me, despite a week of trying. Well, I thought you might like to know where I am.'

Tranov thought quickly. 'I know where you are,' he lied. 'You are in bed with our enemy, like a smelly whore, a disgusting camp follower. You have gone over to the other side. I would congratulate you if I knew how much they were paying you, but your rewards will be short-lived. No, Zamov, I am not interested in where your old bones are at the moment. In fact, I have no interest in finding you at all any more. From now on, any information you give the Westerners will be sadly outdated. As outdated as Alexander Hasek, who is currently in a Czech morgue. Your turncoat actions will be no more than a thorn in my side, an irritation.'

'I am afraid you underestimate my knowledge,' said Zamov, 'and my usefulness to the Americans. For fifty years I have been amassing my own files, secret files which you know nothing about. Full of interesting information. These would have stayed under lock and key had you shown me the loyalty a lifelong friend deserves and expects. A small consideration. But you are more like Stalin than Stalin himself. You are another Beria or Kaganovich – a mindless automaton, a Party man, an apparatchik. Well, you have picked the wrong target this time. You have tried to terminate somebody with the balls to fight back. I have supplied the Americans with much from my files. You were a fool to underestimate me, Tranov. Now you will regret it. We could have resolved this situation, you and I. We are comrades whose relationship goes back nearly half a century. Yet the first sign of a problem with the Syndicate and you put on the mantle of Nemesis. Are you just saving your own old skin or do you really want to save our colleagues in the Syndicate?'

'You surprise me,' said Tranov. 'I wasn't aware that you were interested in our colleagues. It sounds to me as though you cannot wait to betray them.'

'Ah,' said Zamov, 'this should make a good topic of conversation. Why don't we discuss it this evening?'

'This evening?'

'Yes. I am inviting you to a movie.'

'What are you talking about?' demanded Tranov.

'Remember our American filmmaker? The one who started off trying to get his house back in some shithole of a place in Slovakia, right on the Ukraine border?'

'Yes, yes,' interrupted Tranov. 'Joshua Krantz. Of course I remember him. What's he got to do with this? The last time I heard of him he had completed his work in the Prague studios and was back in Hollywood. What movie are you talking about?'

'How little you know,' said Zamov. 'Our friend has returned and he has brought with him a film.'

'What do you mean?' Tranov was wary now.

'A film of his search for his home.'

'What has that to do with me?'

'Be my guest at the premiere of his documentary tonight. He has asked me to invite you, but to warn you that it is only a very rough cut, not the completed version. That will take another six months of work.'

'Stop playing games with me, you old fool,' growled Tranov. 'What am I, an ingenuous teenager? Somebody who is going to be frightened by a Hollywood movie director? Who the hell do you think you're talking to, Zamov?'

'But surely, old friend, you wouldn't want to miss out on a show like this.' His tone become clipped. 'Be at the Vladislav Hall in Hradcany Castle in Prague at eight o'clock tonight. And don't bother bringing your goon squad with you. They won't be admitted.'

Tranov felt the hairs at the back of his head prickling. He picked up the phone again and stabbed out a series of numbers. Without bothering to identify himself, he screamed a series of instructions to the voice that answered.

Vladimir reeled at Tranov's violence.

'Vladimir, you fool! Last night you told me Zamov had left the country. I've just heard from him. He's in Prague and so are Felix, and Joshua Krantz. Find them now, or I will have your balls.'

Tranov slammed down the phone. Somehow the relaxing bath was no longer as appealing.

Vladislav Hall, in the midst of Hradcany Castle, was traditionally used for art or jewellery exhibitions or matters of great national historical interest. Vaclav Havel, President of the Czech Republic, had ordered that the magnificent chandeliered room should be open to the public, given over for important public functions or available for use by cultural, scientific or artistic organisations. Josh's request to use the hall for the premiere of his latest movie had taken the entire public service body who worked within Hradcany Castle by complete surprise. The famous Hollywood director's request had filtered upwards from the desk of a senior civil servant incapable of making such on-the-spot decisions to his departmental head, then to the Minister for Domestic Affairs and finally to the Vice President of the Czech Republic. 'Of course Krantz can use it,' he said. 'Hopefully the film will be another *Star Wars* or *E.T.* Wouldn't that be something? A world premiere in Prague. We haven't hosted a premiere as important as this since Mozart's day.'

The following morning six hundred invitations to the premiere were sent out, written on Hotel Intercontinental letterheads. Invitations were delivered to the President of the Republic himself, the Vice President and senior members of the Ministry, the Cabinet and one hundred other worthies of Prague. They also went to CNN, ABC, NBC and all other American news media outlets, as well as the Prague offices of the European media, and found their way onto the desks of senior police officials and members of the British, American, Russian, Slovakian, Polish, Hungarian, German and French diplomatic services. Josh had hired a team of PR experts from a local Prague promotions agency to do the job, and they had performed with speed, efficiency and considerable style. Caterers who refused to undertake the evening's function because of the short notice were impressed into service with vast amounts of money. Wine, beer and spirits were purchased by the truckload. What would normally take a Hollywood PR agency three months of solid work on a fat monthly retainer was accomplished by the locals, along with Josh, Sarah and Laco, almost overnight. At five o'clock on the afternoon of the premiere, while chairs were being set out in rows in Vladislav Hall, Josh finally stood up from his desk in the Intercontinental's conference room and thanked everybody for their enormous effort. Of the six hundred invitations, over three hundred and fifty people had responded positively, despite being given only a day's notice.

Felix scrutinised the list of acceptances and nodded with satisfaction: 'All the ones we want are going to be there,' he said.'

'But is Tranov?' asked Josh.

Felix shrugged his shoulders. 'There was no other way of smoking the old bastard out of his lair. If he comes, all well and good. If not, all that's lost is the drama. But we've certainly got him worried. His goon squad's been all over Prague looking for us, dropping huge amounts of money to informants. Even if he doesn't come tonight, he's scared.'

'But he must come, Felix! It's the drama that's going to make or break this whole shit fight.'

It was a statement, not a question. Felix didn't reply.

At seven o'clock, they left the Hotel Intercontinental in a convoy of security cars. Former policemen, off-duty policemen, members of the armed services on leave, anybody who had ever applied to Felix for a full or part-time job had been pressed into service. There were twelve security men appointed just to guard Josh, Laco, Sarah and Zamov, who had been secreted in the hotel's penthouse suite, a floor normally reserved for visiting royalty or presidents.

Josh travelled with Felix; Sarah and Laco in a separate car just ahead of them. 'Do we have any idea what Tranov is up to?' he asked.

'I had word five minutes ago,' said Felix. 'He arrived on the five o'clock flight from Bratislava. He took a cab to the centre of the city, to the apartment used by his security staff. He hasn't emerged since.'

Josh smiled. 'That means he'll come to the Castle tonight.'

'I don't know. He's hard to read. He is here to find me and Zamov. That is his mission. Once we are dead, he will come looking for Laco. Then you. So far, we have successfully preempted his moves, but that was when he thought he was in charge. Our subterfuge gave us the extra time we needed for tonight, but now his back is to the wall. He could be capable of anything. To use one of your colourful expression, he could go ballistic.'

'You know,' said Josh, 'if it hadn't been for your stroke of genius, we could never have got this far.'

Felix stared indifferently ahead.

'I mean it,' said Josh. 'Selling out Hasek kept Tranov off our backs so that we could get this done. It was an outstanding bit of scheming, worthy of a thriller writer.'

'I wonder if Sarah will think so when we tell her everything we have done,' Felix said.

'That is going to be a problem,' admitted Josh. 'And so is the film. I hope she doesn't have a Western lawyer's attitude towards it.'

'She will,' Felix said.

In the foyer, the guests were enjoying champagne and canapés when the chandeliers began to slowly dim. They moved quickly and obediently to their seats inside the huge room. Phil, who was controlling the lights, dimmed them so slowly that even the stragglers at the bar and in the anteroom could find their way easily to their seats.

Felix whispered to Josh, 'Tranov is sitting in the fourth row from the back. He is definitely alone.'

Josh felt an enormous weight lift from his shoulders. This was exactly what he'd hoped for – and dreaded – ever since he and Felix had come up with the plan a week ago in Cesky Krumlov. And for now, things were going according to plan.

Josh squeezed Felix's arm; it was a gesture of friendship and admiration. 'Congratulations again. I owe you big for this.'

Felix smiled. 'Let's just get through tonight first.'

Jerry, wearing his headphones, whispered into Josh's ear: 'Ready for the big entrance?'

Josh took a few deep breaths. He wasn't used to presenting live in front of an audience. He just hoped that the words he'd been rehearsing all afternoon would flow as easily as they had flowed in his hotel room. Jerry handed him the cordless microphone and said, 'Go for it, boss. Give the bastards hell.'

Josh squared his shoulders and adjusted his tie. He repeated his opening sentences over and over again as he walked out onto the podium. Jerry whispered into the headphone microphones, 'Spotlights, Phil. He's coming out stage left now.'

Suddenly a brilliant cone of light illuminated the side door at the back of the hall. Joshua Krantz walked out into the centre of the auditorium, coming to a halt in front of the screen. At first only one or two people clapped. Most of the audience did not recognise the man whose name was a household word, but whose face was barely known to the millions of people who had seen his creative work. But as the whispers went around the hall that they were in the presence of one of the greatest film directors of the late twentieth century more people began to applaud. Before them was a man who had entertained more people with his creative imagination than any other human being alive.

Josh stood there, basking in the brilliant spotlight and the glory of the applause. He had been reassured by Felix that two snipers were peering down at the audience through vents above his head, ready to take out Tranov or anyone else in the audience who might pose a serious threat.

'Ladies and gentlemen,' began Josh, as the applause died down, 'my name is Joshua Krantz. May I thank you all so very much for coming at such incredibly short notice tonight to the premiere of the rough cuts of my latest movie. Let me start off by saying that this evening will not be like a normal Hollywood premiere, nor is this a normal Hollywood movie. In fact, as you will see from the rough cut which has been hastily assembled, much of the film comprises important, history-making footage, which will be seen in six months time on a major American television channel.'

The audience was breathless. He was saying things they hadn't expected, but they were concentrating hard, which was exactly what he wanted.

'This is a film of a personal odyssey, a journey which I have taken over the past three months in order to satisfy a promise I made to my late father when I was a much younger man. It was a promise that I was unable to keep, until the fall of Communism and the restitution of those people enslaved by a Communist regime to their rightful place as members of the family of the free world. Everyone gathered in this room has been carefully selected by me to witness the events which led up to my attempt to reclaim my father's property. Let me also reiterate that the film is incomplete: it doesn't have the usual titles, music, nor any of the other appurtenances that would make it the sort of Joshua Krantz production that audiences have come to expect. It may be rough, it may be unready, but it is vital that you see this movie and that you see it *today*, for reasons which will become obvious as you watch. I make no apologies for its crude appearance. When you have sat through the film and the final reel has come to an end, I hope you will understand why everybody has been gathered here for such a special performance.'

He could feel the audience shifting uncomfortably. They had expected to be part of a glamorous occasion, not this history-making drama. They settled back as the spotlight dimmed and the screen erupted into life. Loudspeakers around the hall carried forth the opening strains of Dvorak's *From the New World Symphony* as the titles rolled.

### *MY HOME*
*an Odyssey into the past and a return to the present,*
*produced and directed by Joshua Krantz*

The melodies, so familiar to everyone in the audience, swelled, surrounding each and every person in the room. Everyone watched in awe and anticipation as the titles rolled from the bottom to the top of the screen over an image of fields replete with vibrant flowers. Swathes of yellow, orange and gold filled the screen. A montage of a dark, early morning Prague slowly grew out of the rustic background, gradually transforming into a brilliant day. The Vltava ran swift and pure through the wakening city and the camera panned away from Hradcany Castle standing imperious and eternal in the hot summer sun across the rooftops of the many-spired cityscape. The scene changed again from the Hus Memorial in the Old Town Square, to the Tyn Cathedral, to children playing on boats in the Vltava. And then the narration, the voice of Joshua Krantz:

*A promise is a promise. An obligation is something to be revered. That's why I came to Prague. To fulfil a promise I made to my father and to his father before him, an obligation to my people . . . and to satisfy a need deep within myself.*

*My name is Joshua Krantz. I am a film director. This is the story of a small house in a distant part of Slovakia, close to the border with the Ukraine, a house where my grandparents and my father were born. Where my ancestors were born, going back many generations. A small and inconsequential house which was taken away from my family when the Nazis invaded at the beginning of the War. The remnants of my family, those who managed to escape death in the concentration camps, took back the house when they returned to try to put the past behind them and make a new life. This house once thrilled to the happiness of a large family, but now echoed with the thin voices of the few who had returned, having managed to escape Hitler's insanity. But even that tiny remnant of my family, struggling to rebuild their lives, managed only a few brief years of life there before the house was once again torn from them by the anti-Semites of Stalin's day.*

The image on the screen changed from Prague to Novosad. It was the scene Phil and Jerry had worked so hard to capture: the small, timeless village where men and women rode everywhere on bicycles, where cattle ambled down the central road at the behest of a farmer's boy with a stick. Josh's voiceover continued over Dvorak's music:

*That was why I returned to Europe. I came back in order to reclaim my modest home from those who had stolen my family's property. But what I found when I began the journey was something I could never have expected. Something which has implications for the tens of millions of faceless and nameless Eastern European people who were victims of the arch-criminal amongst all Communist dictators.*

*How often we are shocked when we lift a stone to discover what hideous subterranean creature lurks beneath it. When I was working to reclaim my home, I came across information which, at first, was totally beyond my comprehension. But as I examined the evidence more closely, I found compelling, indeed incontrovertible, proof of the existence of one of the most evil and malevolent secret forces since that which helped the infamous SS, the elite murderers of the Nazi regime, escape the retribution of their victims, setting up rat lines for them to South Africa, South America and other places happy to give a home to these wealthy butchers of humanity. You see, in looking for my home, I discovered the existence of the Syndicate.*

The music exploded into a tumultuous crescendo. The scene changed from today's Novosad, basking in the glorious and vibrant colours of summer, to the grainy black-and-white image of a column of Russian Red Army troops marching along a country road. Staring at them imperiously from a motor car was a young, powerful-looking man. The sound of tramping boots filled the auditorium.

*Boris Maximovich Tranov. Faithful servant and apparatchik of Josef Stalin. A man at whose behest thousands, perhaps even millions, would die. A man whose early career is shrouded in mystery and secrecy. A man who today controls the organisation called the Syndicate.*

Tranov's young face, bland and innocent on the black-and-white backdrop, slowly metamorphosed into the face of an old man, jowled and florid but still bearing the hallmarks of a past vitality. The grainy black and white transmuted to full colour. The camera panned back: Tranov was sitting in a café in an ancient town square, sipping beer.

*Boris Maximovich Tranov, former Russian diplomat and the man who controls the safety and continued existence of hundreds of the murderers and monsters who brutalised millions upon millions of people in the former Soviet Union in the days of Josef Stalin, men and women who, by any standard of human decency, should have been tried and convicted of crimes against humanity decades ago.*

Josh stood at the side of the room listening to the sound of his own voice. He peered through the dark at the figure of the old, heavyset man four rows from the back of the ballroom. He was immobile. Josh was desperate to know what was going through Tranov's mind. The next scene would be the clincher: it was one that Phil and Jerry had spent the past six sleepless nights working on in Hollywood. The colour changed back to faded black and white. Josh looked around at the rest of the audience. They were spellbound, riveted to their seats by the magic his film he was weaving.

A column of Russian soldiers stood in a forest, identifiable by their fur hats and greatcoats. It was winter, the cold, friendless European winter of bare trees and hard ground covered in grey snow. The film was so old that sometimes it was difficult to distinguish between the soldiers and the trees, but the grainy texture of the film gave the scene a mystic, menacing feel. The camera pulled back to reveal the panorama of the forest . . . and the nightmare truth of the scene. The line of soldiers, standing rigidly to attention, faced a deep gouge in the earth, a freshly dug trench, open and suppurating with moisture. Huddled together in a single mass were thousands of raggedly dressed civilians, unarmed, terrified, waiting for death.

In the background, a young officer raised his arm. In his hand was a pistol. The details of his face couldn't be seen, he was too far away from the camera. There was no sound, but a thin puff of white smoke emerged from his raised gun. The soldiers raised their weapons and aimed at the terrified mass of people. White smoke rose from their rifles. Silently, in the macabre ritual of death, the men, women and children huddling together at the front of the line peeled away from the others and dropped like rag dolls into the prepared grave. They fell where they were standing, the press of people behind them preventing escape. Heavily armed soldiers at the rear stopped those at the back from fleeing, forcing the mass of people to move robotically forward to their death. White smoke continued to puff upwards from the guns as volley after volley of rifle fire silently flew through time, felling people into the earth.

The auditorium was still, only the occasional gasp of horror breaking the silence. Even the music faded away. Josh allowed the horrific images of mass murder to speak for themselves. Volley after volley of silent rifle shots were fired; hundreds upon hundreds of people fell into the trench. All the while, the officer in charge stood emotionless, patient, watching the slaughter.

The camera had been stationary during the massacre, static, an observer rather than a participant. But now it began to pan across the line of soldiers, focusing in on their sweat-streaked faces. Some grimaced with the full knowledge of the crime they were committing; others appeared unmoved as though it were all in a day's work. One young man, a Slav by his looks, wept as he pulled the trigger to extinguish yet another human life.

The camera found the officer and closed in to where he was standing. Slowly the lone figure began to dominate the screen; the previously indistinct details of his size and shape were now clearly visible. The camera moved in on the officer's face. He wasn't looking into the camera; his eyes were fixed, like those of a snake, on his line of men to ensure that they were doing his bidding. As his face grew to fill the screen, the music again swelled to fill the auditorium and Josh's voice, even more powerful because of the silence which had preceded it, said simply: *'Boris Maximovich Tranov.'* For the second time the young man's features metamorphosed into the face of a florid old man with watery eyes and dull, wrinkled skin. The camera pulled back to reveal Boris Maximovich Tranov sitting in a café, contemptuously watching the world pass by.

From the back of the ballroom, a strangulated voice roared out, 'No!'

The audience gasped. Heads turned in shock. The spotlight, which had illuminated Josh's entrance minutes earlier, now pinpointed an elderly man four rows from the back, standing with his clenched fist raised, shouting defiantly. The film faded into the background as the attention of every man and woman in the room shifted to that one old man yelling at the screen. 'Lies! It is all lies! That is not me. It is a child's trick, a lie. I had nothing to do with that purge. I was never in the army. It's a Hollywood trick.'

Boris Maximovich Tranov stabbed his finger accusingly at his own gigantic face. 'It is a distortion, a pretence. That young man is not me. You have superimposed my face onto the face of someone else. I was never there. I wasn't that officer.' He began to splutter and stammer in his fury, choking on his words.

Slowly, the lights in the auditorium began to rise. The whispered queries grew to a hubbub of shock and disbelief. Josh picked up his microphone and walked to the back of the hall.

'Ladies and gentlemen, may I present Boris Maximovich Tranov: mass murderer, Stalinist henchman, close confidant and conspirator of some of the bloodiest and cruellest men of the twentieth century. The man responsible for running the Syndicate, an organisation dreamed up by the evil mind of Lazar Kaganovich just after the death of Stalin, an organisation devoted to hiding some of the most evil killers of the Soviet regime.'

Tranov looked at Josh with hatred. He spat his anger at him: 'You! You think you are so clever with your Hollywood tricks and your special effects. I will destroy you for this . . . this . . .' He pointed to the screen where his ghostly image was walking around Cesky Krumlov, stabbing at his own figure as though this would make it disappear. 'You have not one shred of proof. Not one bit of real evidence. This is all a lie. It is what Stalin would have done with photographs. It is using lies and trickery!' he shouted defiantly.

The audience turned to Josh, waiting breathlessly for his rebuttal. But Josh just smiled as the trap closed around Tranov.

'There's your evidence,' he said softly, pointing to the screen. 'There's your proof.'

# CHAPTER
# TWENTY-FOUR

The moment Josh walked into the antechamber, he knew he had a problem. Everyone crowded around to congratulate him on his theatrical brilliance. Everyone except Sarah. Once he had responded to all the congratulations, he sought her out. She was standing in the far corner of the room, leaning against a floor-to-ceiling window that looked out over the castle's courtyard.

'You have a problem?' he asked her.

'Yes, I have a problem. It's called falsifying evidence.'

'What do you mean?'

'Oh, come on, Josh. I wasn't born yesterday. You've used a computer to manipulate those pictures. You've taken real footage and superimposed Tranov's face onto it. It's as clear as day. That wasn't Tranov in the forest ordering the killing of those people. They weren't real images. Were they?!'

'Laco thinks so. And so does everybody else in the audience. They believe their eyes; why don't you?'

'Because I don't trust my eyes. I only trust my brain, my intellect. And those pictures were false.' Her tone was aggressive, condemnatory. 'You think you're so smart, but now any conviction will be tainted. It'll be unworthy of the effort we've all put in, the risks we've all taken.'

Josh laughed. 'You're talking like a Western lawyer, Sarah. That man is a mass murderer. So are the hundreds of people he's protecting. What does it matter what methods we use to bring them to justice?'

'The end justifies the means – is that what you're saying? Can you really be that naive? Hasn't that been the catchcry of every tinpot dictator and ideologue throughout history?'

'It does justify the means for people like us. And the millions of victims who died because of bastards like him and those others he's shielding. All I did was precisely what he, Stalin, Beria and all the other lying propagandists and manipulators have done through history. Yes, Sarah, the end *does* justify the means if the result is bringing a man like that to justice. Think of his victims, of how they'll be able to rest peacefully in their graves. Isn't that good enough for you? And anyway, how *do* you know that the evidence was falsified? How do you know it wasn't genuine?'

'Oh, come on! You can fool some of the people all of the time, but you can't fool me, Josh. That crock of shit on the screen was Hollywood magic. Pure fabrication. If you tried that on in an American court, they'd throw the key away. You don't seriously expect a prosecutor to use that in evidence, do you?' Her hand moved involuntarily to clutch her amulet.

'No. But it was never intended to be used as evidence in a court of law. All it was meant to do is precisely what we've achieved: bring him out into the open; make him defend himself. How else would we have publicly accused Tranov of all those crimes? Got him to stand up in front of all the heavyweights of Prague and identify himself so he could be arrested in full view of everyone? There's no more hiding under a rock for our Mr Tranov. Now he's exposed, out in the open. If we'd sent the police down to his home in Bratislava, his lawyer would have used all sorts of delaying tactics. We both know it.

'And anyway, Sarah. Think beyond the square for a goddamn minute, before you get on to your legal high horse and start moralising. This was the only way for you and me to be safe, and it's given the authorities the time they need to gather evidence to build a real case against him. And don't forget that his goon squad has been arrested as well, which puts an end to Operation Ivan. That means the Ministry of Justice and the police have fifty to a hundred other people to accuse. Some of them will turn State's evidence when they're offered immunity. That should cook his goose.'

Sarah was still angry. He was using sophism to contravene every principle upon which she ran her professional life.

'Don't you see, Sarah, if we'd relied only on Zamov's evidence alone, Tranov would have walked all over it. Discounted it, made him look a fool. But it's marvellous how convincing images on a screen are. You know what they say: the camera never lies.'

She shook her head in disagreement. 'But you didn't *need* to resort to lies and deception. We have Hasek. We could have forced him into open court and that would have been the basis of a prosecution. Once Tranov was locked up on Hasek's evidence, and once Hasek had genuine immunity, he could have been our star witness. We know all about him and his crimes. He's even admitted them to us.'

'Hasek's left the country, Sarah. It was the deal we came to.'

'What?! But . . . but I thought that we'd agreed not to give him his passport until he'd given us a deposition. It was what we said back in Cesky Krumlov. How could you have allowed him to leave without a sworn statement? Are you mad?!'

'It wasn't my choice. While I was in Prague talking to Zamov, Felix gave Hasek the documentation and arranged for his passage out of the Czech Republic to Australia.'

'How dare he?! What right did he have to go against our instructions?'

She marched over to Felix, Josh in tow. Felix smiled a greeting, but the look on Sarah's face was anything but pleasant.

'Did you give Alexander Hasek a passport and help him to leave the country?' she demanded.

Felix looked at her sympathetically. 'He's gone to a better place.'

'What's that supposed to mean?'

'Precisely what I told you. Mr Hasek is no longer with us. He is in a safer and better place.'

Furious, she snapped, 'Don't play word games with me, Felix. Where's Hasek? Is he in Australia? If so, I want to know where. He's going to give a deposition whether he likes it or not.'

Josh had remained silent during the brief and acrimonious exchange. Now his curiosity was aroused. 'Where is he, Felix?'

Felix gave him a bemused look. 'There are some things, Josh, it's better not to know.'

'Where is he?'

Felix remained silent.

Sarah studied his eyes carefully. There was a look of sadness in them which she'd never seen there before. A wave of cold reality swept over her body.

'He's dead, isn't he?' she said softly.

Felix still did not speak.

'Isn't he?!' she shouted. People in the room turned to stare at them.

Felix nodded slowly.

'What!' whispered Josh. 'You've killed him?'

Felix recoiled at the suggestion. 'How could you think that of me?'

'I don't know what to think of you any more. Was it you?'

'It was Tranov.'

'How did he find him? Who told him where he was hiding?' demanded Sarah.

Again Felix declined to speak. Eventually, in defence against her relentless glare and Josh's growing anger, he was forced to explain. 'I told him. It was a bargaining chip, a sacrifice. It was necessary to betray Hasek in order to gain time, to get the goons away from the two of you and Laco so that Josh could return to Hollywood and make his movie.'

Sarah nodded abruptly. The conversation was over. She wheeled around and headed for the door. Josh didn't follow her. He wanted to deal with Felix. There was much he had been intending to settle with Alexander Hasek once Tranov was no longer a threat. Much that he had silently promised his recently dead father, his grandfather and grandmother — decent men and women who had been terrorised and ousted from their home by the hideous little man. And for the other villagers of Novosad who had been slaughtered at Hasek's whim, and the other hundreds, thousands, of nameless, forgotten victims of his reign of horror. But now it was too late.

Felix tried to defend himself. 'I understand your anger, Josh, but you have to understand what happened from my point of view. Hasek was the only thing Tranov had to have. Nothing else was as important, not the lists, not you, not me. That's why I had to delay for time. But ultimately I had to hand him over, or else you, Sarah and all the rest of us would have been on his hit list.'

'Why?' demanded Josh. 'We've arrested Tranov and his gang. They're gone, out of the picture. We could have done it without killing Hasek. I wanted that bastard. I wanted him to suffer like my father suffered. I wanted him to know the humiliation, the fear, the loneliness my father and his parents felt because of him. But now he's dead . . .'

'Josh, we couldn't have done it without handing them Hasek. Put yourself in my position. Tranov was convinced that I'd gone over to him, sold you out. He held you and Sarah in contempt, but he would have killed you at the drop of a hat if he thought that Hasek was going to give evidence. The only way to guarantee your safety, now and in the future, was to eliminate Hasek. You are safe now. We all are. It was worth the sacrifice.'

'The end justifying the means?' said Josh, his voice replete with contemptuous indignation.

'It is only in places like America and Western Europe, where they have elevated human rights into a religion, that you can make that fine distinction. We in the East don't think along those lines. We are far too busy getting on with the business of survival.'

Josh sighed. It wasn't what he'd wanted. Not at all. He'd left the press conference hailed as an international hero; now he was an accomplice to a murder. 'I have to go, Felix. I have to think.'

'Think what you will, Josh. But at the end of your soul-searching, think about this: evil men who committed crimes which destroyed the lives of countless millions of people have at last been brought before the merciless scrutiny of their victims. That, surely, should be satisfaction enough for you.'

Josh looked into the eyes of the man who had saved his life many times during the past few weeks. He smiled weakly, turned, made his farewells to those in the room who still wanted to talk to him and left in search of Sarah.

He found her an hour later in her room in the Intercontinental Hotel. Her bag was packed; she was sitting at the desk in her suite, writing a letter. She opened the door to his knock.

'Do you think I had any knowledge of what Felix had done?' he asked.

'No. I don't think that for one minute. But I feel tainted by the whole exercise. I want out.'

'Is it so bad that Hasek's dead?'

'No, it's probably a good thing. He deserved it after what he did. But that doesn't mean that Felix, or you, or I should be taking the law into our own hands. He should have been tried and properly convicted. Carrying out that sort of execution makes us just as guilty as him.'

'So you were expecting that he'd happily turn up to some sort of Nuremberg trial? We'd given him an assurance of immunity, a guarantee of free passage.'

'My conscience would allow me to break that. Not happily, but I could have lived with it. But murder? Josh, can you live with yourself now, knowing that you've been party to a murder?'

'I'm not a party, Sarah. I didn't agree to it, nor was I a participant. Look, Hasek was scum. A mass murderer. The lowest of the low. He deserved what was coming to him. Felix was wrong, very wrong, but he assured me that there was no alternative. Not if Laco you and I were to remain safe for the rest of our lives. And frankly, after what we've all been through these past weeks, I'm inclined to trust his judgement.'

Sarah's body slumped back into the chair. Josh realised that she was fighting back tears. Suddenly her body convulsed into paroxysms of sobs. She buried her face in her hands and cried as she hadn't cried since she was a little girl. With each breath, she muttered the words, 'I'm sorry. I'm so sorry. I . . .'

He walked over and knelt down beside her, putting his arm around her shoulder. He held her closely, tightly, pulling her body into his. And he kissed her gently on her head, her neck and her hands. She buried her face in his shoulder.

'I don't know why this is happening,' she sobbed.

'I do. You've been living on the edge of a nightmare for weeks. You're strung out, exhausted. You've finally given in to the fact that you're a human being. Tonight's drama and finding out about Hasek finally did it for you.'

He felt her nod, a soft movement on his chest. Her face felt hot and moist against his shirt. He moved her face up and kissed her cheek. Her eyes were smeared with runny mascara, her cheeks damp with emotion. He kissed her on the lips. She responded fully, pulling his face down towards her, then buried her face in his body again.

'I love you, Sarah. And I admire and respect you more than any other person I've ever met. I've loved you since we first met in New York. I want you to marry me.'

She held him closely, her face still pressed tightly into his body. He felt her heavy gold amulet pressing into his flesh, and heard her mumble something into his chest. It sounded like, 'Oh shit.'

# EPILOGUE

The courtroom was crowded to capacity with news media. Vans sporting satellite dishes lined the pavement outside Prague's Hall of Justice while teams of cameramen, sound recordists and journalists from thirty countries waited in anticipation for the events about to unfold.

Like guests at a wedding, the participants drew up in cars, stepping out into a barrage of flashlights. Reporters stepped forward eagerly, thrusting microphones into the newcomers' faces, some firing questions at those they recognised as worthy of a sound bite. Others were mere functionaries, not worthy of consideration, and their microphones passed them by. One such functionary smiled wryly as the photographers and reporters turned away from her, failing to recognise her pivotal role in the whole event. Sarah Kaplan walked unimpeded up the steps to the courtroom.

It was a big day for her. Perhaps the biggest in the whole year. She had spent the past twelve months based in the Czech Republic, travelling to most capital cities in Europe, preparing the groundwork for the prosecution and coordinating the Prague government's liaison with other governments in gathering evidence to be used in the forthcoming trial. She had been asked to assist by the Minister for Justice the day after Josh showed his film – the false film – of Tranov that led to his arrest.

Odd how it had transpired. In a rage of fury, Sarah had informed the Minister that the evidence was corrupt and couldn't be used as the basis of a prosecution, but that she had reams of evidence which she would gladly make available to him. The Minister had told her that he already knew about the film, that Joshua had admitted to him that it was merely a device to get Tranov to identify his role in public. It had worked. Now the film and its tricks would be put aside and the long, painstaking job of gathering evidence from witnesses would begin. And the first place they would start would be with the residents of the tiny village of Novosad, formerly Ujlak, near Kosice, in eastern Slovakia.

The Minister had asked her whether she had to return immediately to America. He knew of her role in the trial of Frank Darman, the Holocaust denier, and was aware of her skills and abilities. Such skills would be needed by the team of prosecutors who would be gathering evidence, he told her, and wondered if she would be interested in joining the team as a researcher and liaison officer? Sarah had accepted his invitation on the spot without even considering her career in New York. Somehow righting the wrongs of history made everything else pale into insignificance.

Sarah had begun the day of the trial in the usual way: a quick shower, a brisk walk to a nearby bakery to buy freshly baked sugar rolls and croissants, then back to her apartment near the Old City for a strong black coffee and breakfast. Normally she would then head off to the Ministry of Justice where she would spend her day preparing the case, helping the prosecution team or researching aspects of war crimes legislation and lustration laws in other countries as well as the law under which the Nuremberg Trials had been conducted. She had never been as busy nor as happy in her work life. Her personal life was another matter. But on this particular morning, just as she was about to leave for the first day in court, the telephone rang.

'Sarah, it's David. I'm just ringing to wish you the very best of luck with the first day of the trial today.'

If only he had been able to see her face, he would have caught the first plane over. She beamed the widest smile imaginable. Trust David, dear, gentle David.

'Darling, how incredibly thoughtful. I know how busy you are. And to have thought of me after all I've put you through.'

'I think of you all the time, Sarah. And when this is over, maybe you'll think of me?'

'David, honey, I think of you often. But you know why I'm here . . .'

She looked across at his picture on her mantelpiece. It stood next to a photo of Josh. At the other end of the ledge was a picture of Laco looking cheeky and mischievous, his semi-naked body disappearing into a hole in the ground as he dug up another skeleton.

'David, I'm rushing out the door. Can we speak later in the week when I know which way the trial's going? I mean, how much time I'll have to devote to being in court.'

They said goodbye.

She continued to smile as she made her way to the Hall of Justice. It was wonderful to hear David's voice again. They hadn't spoken in a month because he had been on tour in the deep south. And since her letter to him a year earlier, putting their relationship on hold, he had been distant yet courteous. She had hurt him, but he was too generous and gentle to rail against her. Far more so than her mother and father, who had called her almost every day during her first month of working on the trial, haranguing her about her stupidity in endangering her relationship with David.

Sarah entered the chandeliered lobby of the Hall of Justice. A policeman, recognising her from her many previous visits to the Office of the Ministry, saluted politely. She greeted him in now-familiar Czech and he answered back clearly and distinctly in deference to her attempts to learn the difficult language. Twelve months had been long enough for her to learn French or German but she found Czech difficult to master. After the best part of a year in Prague she was able to chat to people in the streets and order food in restaurants but anything like the complexity of preparing a legal case was completely outside her abilities. That's why the Minister for Justice had given her a full-time assistant to act as translator, guide and friend.

He was waiting for her at the top of the stairs. She beamed when she saw him. 'Maxim,' she said. The elderly man opened his arms to her and she kissed him warmly, hugging his frail body.

'Well, my dear, so begins the journey.'

'Really?' she said. 'I thought the journey was at an end. Isn't this the reward that we all deserve? Seeing Tranov and twenty others on trial.'

'But proving it. Have we got enough proof?'

She smiled. She had been working with him for the past eight months since his return from Paris. His skill as a seeker after truth, an uncoverer of buried secrets, had been of immense value to the team, and her work as liaison officer with countries in Western Europe had meant that the two of them often worked in concert. It had been one of the most satisfying and delightful periods of her life. She had admired Maxim Plastov when Laco had first introduced them all that time ago, but in the last eight months of their close association she had grown to love him. He was the grandfather every child dreamed about: courteous, intelligent, considerate, a mentor to her when she became unsure of why she had left the security of her work in New York and a loving and generous man who wanted to marry her.

Sarah threaded her arm through his and they walked along the corridor and up a further flight of stairs into the area reserved for officers of the Ministry. Here the floors were covered with plush red carpet.

'Sarah,' said Maxim, 'I heard from Laco this morning. He will be here for the trial. He is in Prague.'

She smiled. 'It'll be so good to see him again. I spoke to him a couple of weeks ago. Apparently his dig's going very well.'

'He has a present for you,' said Maxim.

'A present?'

'Yes. An adornment. It will go very nicely with your amulet.'

Sarah instinctively touched the amulet suspended around her neck.

'I must not tell you what it is, but he is very excited.'

Sarah's mood changed from one of concern and consternation at the magnitude of the proceedings to one of joy at the prospect of seeing Laco again. They had met three times during the past year and holidayed together once in the Tatra Mountains. They had enjoyed each other's company to the full, but Laco was like an over-grown schoolboy, always full of humour and irreverence, never the serious man she hoped he would be.

They entered the hall which was serving as a courtroom. A judicial bench had been constructed for the three judges who would be overseeing the trial. Opposite them, in the middle of the hall, was a large dock, spacious enough to accommodate the twenty defendants; all elderly and frail men, yet all monsters in their days as Stalin's minions. Tranov was by far the most important, the pivot around whom all the others had gathered and then disappeared into obscurity, until Sarah, Josh and Laco shone a searchlight into the dark and distant past.

On one side of the makeshift courtroom was the witness box, where, one after another, two hundred and thirty-two elderly men and women would appear to testify to crimes committed by the defendants half a century earlier. Sarah looked at the box: memories of the survivors of the Nazi concentration camps who had testified against her client,

Frank Darman, a year earlier flooded her mind. To her everlasting pleasure and pride, she had said, 'No questions' every time their attorney, Professor Klein, had sat down. To her pleasure and to Frank Darman's everlasting anger.

On the opposite side of the courtroom was the huge box where the reporters would sit to take down every detail of the trial to send out to the world. The case had sparked everyone's imagination. Stalin had been known as a mass murderer, but had somehow maintained a perennial legitimacy in Western eyes as a hard, firm-handed dictator who had built the Soviet Union into a superpower. Until now, he had never been labelled as Hitler had been labelled. Only academics and those who had suffered at his hands really knew the truth. But now, at last, there would be proof, living glaring proof of his crimes as one of the most brutal mass murderers of any century. And his minions would finally be brought to justice. No doubt they would fall back on the anticipated defence that they had merely been carrying out Stalin's orders – a replica of the Nuremberg trials fifty years earlier. But by now the world had changed. The world had grown wiser and was no longer willing to tolerate such excuses.

Sarah sat down at the desk appointed to her, behind the prosecutors, Maxim wandered over to his place as an observer. People slowly began to fill the room: prosecutors, defenders, reporters, international observers, diplomats given special leave as friends of the court, members of the Commission of International Jurists, men and women from Amnesty International, observers from other commissions of human rights. It was an august gathering, one that the Chief Justice of the Czech Republic knew would focus attention on his country's capacity to administer the rule of law. As Sarah squared her papers neatly into order a voice startled and surprised her: 'Hello, Sarah.'

She looked up to see Josh Krantz standing next to her, looking as raffish, casual and handsome as ever. Her body tingled with delight. She beamed at him and threw her arms around him.

'Josh, why didn't you tell me? How wonderful to see you.'

'I've come here to wish you the best of luck. I know how much this case means to you.'

'Oh, my dear friend,' she said, kissing him again on the cheek and squeezing his hand. 'It's wonderful of you to come. I can't tell you how thrilled I am. How long are you staying?'

'I'm just passing through. I'm actually on my way to Turkey but I thought I'd stop off in Prague to tell you that I'm still missing you.'

She smiled. 'Josh . . .'

'I mean it, Sarah. It's been a year but I don't think I've stopped thinking of you for one day in all that time. Did you get my flowers?'

'You know I got them. I just stopped writing thank-you notes after the tenth bunch. Every week, Josh. Don't you think that's extravagant?'

'I didn't want you to forget me,' he said.

'How could I possibly forget you? I'm your number one fan. When's the premiere?'

'Tonight in New York.'

'Tonight?'

'We're beaming over the President of the Czech Republic on satellite. He's going to introduce the film.'

'But you'll be in Turkey. I don't understand. Why aren't you there? This is your moment of glory.'

He shook his head and perched on the edge of her desk. 'It's not my moment of glory, Sarah. This is for my dad, for my grandparents. And for everybody else's family who were kicked out by people like Tranov and Hasek and the rest of those bastards. I'm just the filmmaker; it's *their* story.'

She realised how right he was and wondered how many other high-profile Hollywood directors would feel the same way.

'I've given you a special mention in the film, Sarah.'

'I know,' she said. 'You sent me a video, remember?'

'But I sent you a video without titles. You're mentioned in the titles in a fairly substantial way.' He looked up at the ceiling as if reading the words from a screen: *'This film is dedicated to my parents and grandparents and couldn't have been made without the extraordinary bravery and skill of three people – Sarah Kaplan and Drs Maxim and Laco Plastov – to whom it is also dedicated.'*

'Oh, Josh,' she said, 'that's so sweet.'

'Well, it means you can double your fees when you get back to New York. You are coming back, aren't you?'

'Eventually.'

'What does that mean, Sarah?'

'It means eventually. This trial is going to last at least two years.'

'Two years! But I thought once it . . . I didn't realise . . .'

'Josh, I have to see it through. That's why I resigned from my firm. That's why I'm not marrying David.'

'Or me,' he said.

'Or you.'

'Sarah, you can't devote your life to a cause. Your life is your own.'

'I know that. But until I've got this out of my system, I really can't think of anything else.'

He looked disconsolate, as though he still hadn't accepted the umpire's decision. She felt so sorry for him, knowing deep down that she was being unfair to the two most special men in her life.

'Remember when I first came over here? I really hated the idea of coming to Europe. You forced me to do it, Josh. I would never have done this if it hadn't been for you. I was so deeply convinced that we should have nothing to do with the old country, that we should close the door behind us and get on with our lives. But I've come to understand that you can't close your eyes to evil, or it will just happen again. You can't close your eyes to men like Tranov or Hasek and all the others. If they go unpunished, if they don't suffer justice and retribution, then their children will repeat their crimes. You taught me that and for that I owe you. I'm so desperately sorry I feel like this because it means that any relationship which you or I, or David and I, could have enjoyed has got to be put on hold. When the time is ready I hope you'll still be there for me.'

'Or David,' said Josh.

She nodded slowly. 'Or David.'

'Isn't that a bit of an each-way bet?'

'It's something I'll keep my mind open to. You're both gorgeous, you're both desirable, you're both wonderful and I love you both. It's going to be a hard decision. In the meantime, Josh, carry on with your Hollywood lifestyle. If you're still there for me at the end of all this — well, that would be wonderful.'

'Will David still be there for you?' he asked.

'He says he will. But only time will tell.'

She threw her arms around his neck and kissed him passionately.

Laco Plastov stood at the door on the opposite side of the courtroom. He watched Josh and Sarah talking, saw her hold Josh's hand, touch his cheek and kiss him. He looked down at the tiny jeweller's box he had brought to show her. Inside was a ring made of pure gold, a ring he had found in a grave close to the one where her amulet had been found by her great-grandfather all those years ago. Its markings mirrored those on her amulet. He had taken it from the repository with the intention of giving it to her, but now he smiled sadly, closed the lid, turned and walked away. The decision to give her the ring had been difficult. Not because he was uncertain about marrying her — that had been the easy part. But giving her the ring was like giving her a part of history. It had belonged to the young woman whose bones now lay in his museum, the young woman that Sarah had seen that first night they met, when he took her into the museum late at night. There had been something about the way Sarah had looked at the skeleton. In Laco's experience, few people were able to look at a skeleton and see the human being who had once lived, breathed and loved. Sarah had done that with this young woman, and Laco had sensed an empathy there, an attachment that drew her back into the mysterious past. A past in which the young woman, whoever she was, had been born, had grown and had been cut down in the prime of her youth and beauty, a sacrifice to propitiate one of the gods of her time.

Laco hurried down the steps of the old building, moving against the tide of people making their way inside for the trial. He was desperately sorry that he had missed the opportunity of forming a lasting relationship with Sarah. He had had many lovers during his life, but of them all it would be Sarah whom he remembered with the greatest joy. But now he would return to his museum in Kosice, to the ancient young woman whose story he would create from the clues she had brought with her, knowing all the while that the story he was putting together could only be fantasy.

Maxim watched his son leave the courtroom, saw the drama being acted out between its three main players. If only Laco had been more mature, less . . . wild and passionate . . . they would have made a wonderful couple. Maxim sighed.

The courtroom filled and the noise level grew. Josh kissed Sarah again and promised that he would drop in to Prague on his way back from Turkey. He left.

The prosecutor walked in and shook hands with Sarah. The defendants' team also greeted her; they would be conducting a joint defence of all twenty-one defendants. Then the judges walked in and silence fell on the entire courtroom. Everyone stood, bowed, then sat again when the Chief Justice and his two colleagues sat. Finally, Tranov and the twenty other defendants were brought in. Surrounded by a phalanx of policemen, they stood behind a bulletproof screen in the specially constructed dock, visible to all. They looked like exhibits in a zoo. And the reporters and observers peered closely at them for the first time, like voyeurs staring at monsters. Sarah also stared in fascination. She'd had nothing to do with the arrest, interviewing or arraigning of the defendants so this was her first real chance to view in all its enormity the discovery she, Josh and Laco had made all those months ago. This was the reason she was still in Europe, despite the promise she had made to herself that she would have nothing to do with the dark continent, the root cause of all the ancient hatreds of her people.

The clerk of the court stood and picked up the arraignment paper. It was the first of twenty-one he would read out, one for each of the defendants: 'Boris Maximovich Tranov, you are charged with multiple counts of murder, of conspiracy to pervert the course of justice and of conspiracy to murder. You have seen the charges against you. On each of these charges, how do you plead?'

Tranov, looking older and haggard from the year that he had spent in prison, turned to Sarah and smiled coyly. It was a gentle, generous smile, the smile of an uncle who knows his niece has been silly and misguided, but who forgives her. It shocked Sarah to her very core. What could he mean by it? Where was the hatred? That, she could deal with, but this ... Would she ever understand the European mind?

Tranov turned back to the judge and said, in a clear, distinct voice, 'Your Honours, I and all my co-defendants are not guilty, nor should we be standing trial by reason of being dutiful patriots of our country and following the lawful orders that we were given in the service of our leader, Josef Stalin.'

Sarah breathed deeply and picked up her pen. With her other hand she touched the amulet around her neck. The new Nuremberg trials were about to begin.